The Golden Silence

C. N. Williamson and
A. M. Williamson

Illustrated by George Brehm

THE
GOLDEN
SILENCE

by C.N & A.M
WILLIAMSON

BOOKS BY C. N. and A. M. WILLIAMSON

"'Allah sends thee a man—a strong man, whose brain and heart and arm are at thy service'"

The
GOLDEN
SILENCE

by

C.N. & A.M.
WILLIAMSON

Illustrated by GEORGE BREHM

GARDEN CITY, NEW YORK
DOUBLEDAY, PAGE & COMPANY
1911

TO

Effendi

HIS BOOK

I

Stephen Knight was very angry, though he meant to be kind and patient with Margot. Perhaps, after all, she had not given the interview to the newspaper reporter. It might be what she herself would call a "fake." But as for her coming to stop at a big, fashionable hotel like the Carlton, in the circumstances she could hardly have done anything in worse taste.

He hated to think that she was capable of taking so false a step. He hated to think that it was exactly like her to take it. He hated to be obliged to call on her in the hotel; and he hated himself for hating it.

Knight was of the world that is inclined to regard servants as automata; but he was absurdly self-conscious as he saw his card on a silver tray, in the hand of an expressionless, liveried youth who probably had the famous interview in his pocket. If not there, it was only because the paper would not fit in. The footman had certainly read the interview, and followed the "Northmorland Case" with passionate interest, for months, from the time it began with melodrama, and turned violently to tragedy, up to the present moment when (as the journalists neatly crammed the news into a nutshell) "it bade fair to end with marriage-bells."

Many servants and small tradespeople in London had taken shares, Stephen had heard, as a speculative investment, in the scheme originated to provide capital for the "other side," which was to return a hundred per cent. in case of success. Probably the expressionless youth was inwardly reviling the Northmorland family because he had lost his money and would be obliged to carry silver trays all the rest of his life, instead of starting a green grocery business. Stephen hoped that his own face was as expressionless, as he waited to receive the unwelcome message that Miss Lorenzi was at home.

It came very quickly, and in a worse form than Stephen had expected. Miss Lorenzi was in the Palm Court, and would Mr. Knight please come to her there?

Of course he had to obey; but it was harder than ever to remain expressionless.

There were a good many people in the Palm Court, and they all looked at Stephen Knight as he threaded his intricate way among chairs and little tables and palms, toward a corner where a young woman in black crape sat on a pink sofa. Her hat was very large, and a palm with enormous fan-leaves drooped above it like a sympathetic weeping willow on a mourning brooch. But under the hat was a splendidly beautiful dark face.

"Looks as if he were on his way to be shot," a man who knew all about the great case said to a woman who had lunched with him.

"Looks more as if he were on his way to shoot," she laughed, as one does laugh at other people's troubles, which are apt to be ridiculous. "He's simply glaring."

"Poor beggar!" Her companion found pleasure in pitying Lord Northmorland's brother, whom he had never succeeded in getting to know. "Which is he, fool or hero?"

"Both. A fool to have proposed to the girl. A hero to stick to her, now he has proposed. He must be awfully sick about the interview. I do think it's excuse enough to throw her over."

"I don't know. It's the sort of business a man can't very well chuck, once he's let himself in for it. Every one blames him now for having anything to do with Miss Lorenzi. They'd blame him a lot more for throwing her over."

"Women wouldn't."

"No. Because he happens to be young and good-looking. But all his popularity won't make the women who like him receive his wife. She isn't a woman's woman."

"I should think not, indeed! We're too clever to be taken in by that sort, all eyes and melodrama. They say Lord Northmorland warned his brother against her, and prophesied she'd get hold of him, if he didn't let her alone. The Duchess of Amidon told Lady Peggy Lynch—whom I know a little—that immediately after Lorenzi committed suicide, this Margot girl wrote to Stephen Knight and implored him to help her. I can quite believe she would. Fancy the daughter of the unsuccessful claimant to his brother's title writing begging letters to a young man like Stephen Knight! It appeals to one's sense of humour."

"What a pity Knight didn't see it in that light—what?"

"Yet he has a sense of humour, I believe. It's supposed to be one of his charms. But the sense of humour often fails where one's own affairs are concerned. You know he's celebrated for his quaint ideas about life. They say he has socialistic views, or something rather like them. His brother and he are as different from one another as light is from darkness. Stephen gives away a lot of money, and Lady Peggy says that nobody ever asks him for anything in vain. He can't stand seeing people unhappy, if he can do anything to help. Probably, after he'd been kind to the Lorenzi girl, against his brother's advice, and gone to see her a few times, she grovelled at his feet and told him she was all alone in the world, and would die if he didn't love her. He's just young enough and romantic enough to be caught in that way!"

"He's no boy. He must be nearly thirty."

"All nice, normal men are boys until after thirty. Lady Peggy's new name for this poor child is the Martyr Knight."

"St. Stephen the Second is the last thing I heard. Stephen the First was a martyr too, wasn't he? Stoned to death or something."

"I believe so," hastily returned the lady, who was not learned in martyrology. "He will be stoned, too, if he tries to force Miss Lorenzi on his family, or even on his friends. He'll find that he'll have to take her abroad."

"That might be a good working plan. Foreigners wouldn't shudder at her accent. And she's certainly one of the most gorgeously beautiful creatures I ever saw."

"Yes, that's just the right expression. Gorgeous. And—a *creature*."

They both laughed, and fell to talking again of the interview.

Stephen Knight's ears were burning. He could not hear any of the things people were saying; but he had a lively imagination, and, always sensitive, he had grown morbidly so since the beginning of the Northmorland-Lorenzi case, when all the failings and eccentricities of the family had been reviewed before the public eye, like a succession of cinematograph pictures. It did not occur to Stephen that he was an object of pity, but he felt that through his own folly and that of another, he had become a kind of scarecrow, a figure of fun: and because until now the world had laughed with instead of at him, he would rather have faced a shower of bullets than a ripple of ridicule.

"How do you do?" he inquired stiffly, and shook Miss Lorenzi's hand as she gave it without rising from the pink sofa. She gazed up at him with immense, yellowish brown eyes, then fluttered her long black lashes in a way she had, which was thrilling—the first time you saw it. But Stephen had seen it often.

"I am glad you've come, my White Knight!" she said in her contralto voice, which would have been charming but for a crude accent. "I was so afraid you were cross."

"I'm not cross, only extremely ang—vexed if you really did talk to that journalist fellow," Stephen answered, trying not to speak sharply, and keeping his tone low. "Only, for Heaven's sake, Margot, don't call me—what you did call me—anywhere, but especially here, where we might as well be on the stage of a theatre."

"Nobody can hear us," she defended herself. "You ought to like that dear little name I made up because you came to my rescue, and saved me from following my father—came into my life as if you'd been a modern St. George. Calling you my 'White Knight' shows you how I feel—how I appreciate you and everything. If you just *would* realize that, you couldn't scold me."

"I'm not scolding you," he said desperately. "But couldn't you have stopped in your sitting-room—I suppose you have one—and let me see you there? It's loathsome making a show of ourselves——"

"I *haven't* a private sitting-room. It would have been too extravagant," returned Miss Lorenzi. "Please sit down—by me."

Stephen sat down, biting his lip. He must not begin to lecture her, or even to ask why she had exchanged her quiet lodgings for the Carlton Hotel, because if he once began, he knew that he would be carried on to unsafe depths. Besides, he was foolish enough to hate hurting a woman's feelings, even when she most deserved to have them hurt.

"Very well. It can't be helped now. Let us talk," said Stephen. "The first thing is, what to do with this newspaper chap, if you didn't give him the interview——"

"Oh, I did give it—in a way," she admitted, looking rather frightened, and very beautiful. "You mustn't do anything to him. But—of course it was only because I thought it would be better to tell him the truth. Surely it was?"

"Surely it wasn't. You oughtn't to have received him."

"Then do you mind so dreadfully having people know you've asked me to marry you, and that I've said 'yes'?"

Margot Lorenzi's expression of pathetic reproach was as effective as her eyelash play, when seen for the first time, as Stephen knew to his sorrow. But he had seen the one as often as the other.

"You must know I didn't mean anything of the sort. Oh, Margot, if you don't understand, I'm afraid you're hopeless."

"If you speak like that to me, I shall simply end everything as my father did," murmured the young woman, in a stifled, breaking voice. But her eyes were blazing.

It almost burst from Stephen to order her not to threaten him again, to tell her that he was sick of melodrama, sick to the soul; but he kept silence. She was a passionate woman, and perhaps in a moment of madness she might carry out her threat. He had done a great deal to save her life—or, as he thought, to save it. After going so far he must not fail now in forbearance. And worse than having to live with beautiful, dramatic Margot, would it be to live without her if she killed herself because of him.

"Forgive me. I didn't mean to hurt you," he said when he could control his voice.

She smiled. "No, of course you didn't. It was stupid of me to fly out. I ought to know that you're always good. But I *don't* see what harm the interview could do you, or me, or any one. It lets all the world know how gloriously you've made up to me for the loss of the case, and the loss of my father; and how you came into my life just in time to save me from killing myself, because I was utterly alone, defeated, without money or hope."

She spoke with the curiously thrilling emphasis she knew how to give her words sometimes, and Stephen could not help thinking she did credit to her training. She had been preparing for the stage in Canada, the country of the Lorenzis' adoption, before her father brought her to England, whither he came with a flourish of trumpets to contest Lord Northmorland's rights to the title.

"The world knew too much about our affairs already," Stephen said aloud. "And when you wished our engagement to be announced in *The Morning Post*, I had it put in at once. Wasn't that enough?"

"Every one in the world doesn't read *The Morning Post*. But I should think every one in the world has read that interview, or will soon," retorted Margot. "It appeared only yesterday morning, and was copied in all the evening papers; in this morning's ones too; and they say it's been cabled word for word to the big Canadian and American dailies."

Stephen had his gloves in his hand, and he tore a slit across the palm of one, without knowing it. But Margot saw. He was thinking of the heading in big black print at the top of the interview: "Romantic Climax to the Northmorland-Lorenzi Case. Only Brother of Lord Northmorland to Marry the Daughter of Dead Canadian Claimant. Wedding Bells Relieve Note of Tragedy."

"We've nothing to be ashamed of—everything to be proud of," Miss Lorenzi went on. "You, of your own noble behaviour to me, which, as I said to the reporter, must be making my poor father happy in another world. Me, because I have won You, *far* more than because some day I shall have gained all that father failed to win for me and himself. His heart was broken, and he took his own life. My heart would have been broken too, and but for you I——"

"Don't, please," Stephen broke in. "We won't talk any more about the interview. I'd like to forget it. I should have called here yesterday, as I wired in answer to your telegram saying you were at the Carlton, but being at my brother's place in Cumberland, I couldn't get back till——"

"Oh, I understand," Margot cut in. Then she laughed a sly little laugh. "I think I understand too why you went to Cumberland. Now tell me. Confession's good for the soul. Didn't your brother wire for you the minute he saw that announcement in *The Morning Post*, day before yesterday?"

"He did wire. Or rather the Duchess did, asking me to go at once to Cumberland, on important business. I found your telegram, forwarded from my flat, when I got to Northmorland Hall. If I'd known you were moving, I wouldn't have gone till to-day."

"You mean, dear, you wouldn't have let me move? Now, do you think there's any harm in a girl of my age being alone in a hotel? If you do, it's dreadfully old-fashioned of you. I'm twenty-four."

During the progress of the case, it had been mentioned in court that the claimant's daughter was twenty-nine (exactly Stephen Knight's age); but Margot ignored this unfortunate slip, and hoped that Stephen and others had forgotten.

"No actual harm. But in the circumstances, why be conspicuous? Weren't you comfortable with Mrs. Middleton? She seemed a miraculously nice old body for a lodging-house keeper, and fussed over you no end — —"

"It was for your sake that I wanted to be in a good hotel, now our engagement has been announced," explained Miss Lorenzi. "I didn't think it suitable for the Honourable Stephen Knight's future wife to go on living in stuffy lodgings. And as you've insisted on my accepting an income of eighty pounds a month till we're married, I'm able to afford a little luxury, dearest. I can tell you it's a pleasure, after all I've suffered! — and I felt I owed you something in return for your generosity. I wanted your *fiancée* to do you credit in the eyes of the world."

Stephen bit his lip. "I see," he said slowly.

Yet what he saw most clearly was a very different picture. Margot as she had seemed the day he met her first, in the despised South Kensington lodgings, whither he had been implored to come in haste, if he wished to save a wretched, starving girl from following her father out of a cruel world. Of course, he had seen her in court, and had reluctantly encountered her photograph several times before he had given up looking at illustrated papers for fear of what he might find in them. But Margot's tragic beauty, as presented by photographers, or as seen from a distance, loyally seated at the claimant's side, was as nothing to the dark splendour of her despair when the claimant was in his new-made grave. It was the day after the burial that she had sent for Stephen; and her letter had arrived, as it happened, when he was thinking of the girl, wondering whether she had friends who would stand by her, or whether a member of his family might, without being guilty of bad taste, dare offer help.

Her tear-blotted letter had settled that doubt, and it had been so despairing, so suggestive of frenzy in its wording, that Stephen had impulsively rushed off to South Kensington at once, without stopping to think whether it would not be better to send a representative combining the gentleness of the dove with the wisdom of the serpent, and armed for emergencies with a blank cheque.

Margot's hair, so charmingly dressed now, folding in soft dark waves on either side her face, almost hiding the pink-tipped ears, had been tumbled, that gloomy afternoon six weeks ago, with curls escaping here and there; and in the course of their talk a great coil had fallen down over her shoulders. It was the sort of thing that happens to the heroine of a melodrama, if she has plenty of hair; but Stephen did not think of that then. He thought of nothing except his sympathy for a beautiful girl brought, through no fault of her own, to the verge of starvation and despair, and of how he could best set about helping her.

She had not even money enough to buy mourning. Lorenzi had left debts which she could not pay. She had no friends. She did not know what was to become of her. She had not slept for many nights. She had made up her mind to die as her father had died, because it seemed the only thing to do, when suddenly the thought of Stephen had flashed into her mind, as if sent there by her guardian angel. She had heard that he was good and charitable to everybody, and once she had seen him looking at her kindly, in court, as if he were sorry for her, and could read something of what was in her heart. She had imagined it perhaps. But would he forgive her for writing to him? Would he help her, and save her life?

Any one who knew Stephen could have prophesied what his answer would be. He had hated it when she snatched his hand to kiss at the end of their interview; but he would scarcely have been a human young man if he had not felt a sudden tingle of the blood at the touch of such lips as Margot Lorenzi's. Never had she seemed so beautiful to him since that first day; but he had called again and again, against his brother's urgent advice (when he had confessed the first visit); and the story that the Duchess of Amidon was telling her friends, though founded entirely on her own imagination of the scene which had brought about Stephen's undoing, was not very far from the truth.

Now, he saw a picture of Margot as he had seen her in the lodgings she hated; and he wished to heaven that he might think of her as he had thought of her then.

"I've got something important to say to you," the girl went on, when she realized that Stephen intended to dismiss the subject of the hotel, as he had dismissed the subject of the interview. "That's the reason I wired. But I won't speak a word till you've told me what your brother and the Duchess of Amidon think about you and me."

"There's nothing to tell," Stephen answered almost sullenly. And indeed there was no news of his Cumberland visit which it would be pleasant or wise to retail.

Margot Lorenzi's complexion was not one of her greatest beauties. It was slightly sallow, so she made artistic use of a white cosmetic, which gave her skin the clearness of a camellia petal. But she had been putting on rather more than usual since her father's death, because it was suitable as well as becoming to be pale when one was in deep mourning. Consequently Margot could not turn perceptibly whiter, but she felt the blood go ebbing away from her face back upon her heart.

"Stephen! Don't they mean to receive me, when we're married?" she stammered.

"I don't think they've much use for either of us," Stephen hedged, to save her feelings. "Northmorland and I have never been great pals, you know. He's twenty years older than I am; and since he married the Duchess of Amidon——"

"And her money! Oh, it's no use beating about the bush. I hate them both. Lord Northmorland has a fiendish, vindictive nature."

"Come, you mustn't say that, Margot. He has nothing of the sort. He's a curious mixture. A man of the world, and a bit of a Puritan——"

"So are you a Puritan, at heart," she broke in.

Stephen laughed. "No one ever accused me of Puritanism before."

"Maybe you've never shown any one else that side of you, as you show it to me. You're always being shocked at what I do and say."

For that, it was hardly necessary to be a Puritan. But Stephen shrugged his shoulders instead of answering.

"Your brother is a cold-hearted tyrant, and his wife is a snob. If she weren't, she wouldn't hang on to her duchess-hood after marrying again. It would be good enough for *me* to call myself Lady Northmorland, and I hope I shall some day."

Stephen's sensitive nostrils quivered. He understood in that moment how a man might actually wish to strike a nagging virago of a woman, no matter how beautiful. And he wondered with a sickening heaviness of heart how he was to go on with the wretched business of his engagement. But he pushed the question out of his mind, fiercely. He was in for this thing now. He *must* go on.

"Let all that alone, won't you?" he said, in a well-controlled tone.

"I can't," Margot exclaimed. "I hate your brother. He killed my father."

"Because he defended the honour of our grandfather, and upheld his own rights, when Mr. Lorenzi came to England to dispute them?"

"Who knows if they *were* his rights, or my father's? My father believed they were his, or he wouldn't have crossed the ocean and spent all his money in the hope of stepping into your brother's shoes."

There were those—and Lord Northmorland and the Duchess of Amidon were among them—who did not admit that Lorenzi had believed in his "rights." And as for the money he had spent in trying to establish a legal claim to the Northmorland title and estates, it had not been his own, but lent him by people he had hypnotized with his plausible eloquence.

"That question was decided in court——"

"It would be harder for a foreigner to get an English nobleman's title away than for a camel to go through the eye of the tiniest needle in the world. But never mind. All that's buried in his grave, and you're giving me everything father wanted me to have. I wish I could keep my horrid temper better in hand, and I'd never make you look so cross. But I inherited my emotional nature from Margherita Lorenzi, I suppose. What can you expect of a girl who had an Italian prima donna for a grandmother? And I oughtn't to quarrel with the fair Margherita for leaving me her temper, since she left me her face too, and I'm fairly well satisfied with that. Everybody says I'm the image of my grandmother. And you ought to know, after seeing her picture in dozens of illustrated papers, as well as in that pamphlet poor father published."

"If you want me to tell you that you are one of the handsomest women who ever lived, I'll do so at once," said Stephen.

Margot smiled. "You really mean it?"

"There couldn't be two opinions on that subject."

"Then, if you think I'm so beautiful, don't let your brother and his snobbish Duchess spoil my life."

"They can't spoil it."

"Yes, they can. They can keep me from being a success in their set, your set—the *only* set."

"Perhaps they can do that. But England isn't the only country, anyhow. I've been thinking that when—by and by—we might take a long trip round the world ——"

"*Hang* the world! England's my world. I've always looked forward to England, ever since I was a little thing, before mamma died, and I used to hear father repeating the romantic family story—how, if he could only find his mother's letters that she'd tried to tell him about when she was dying, perhaps he might make a legal claim to a title and a fortune. He used to turn to me and say: 'Maybe you'll be a great lady when you grow up, Margot, and I shall be an English viscount.' Then, when he did find the letters, behind the secret partition in grandmother's big old-fashioned sandal-wood fan-box, of which you've heard so much——"

"Too much, please, Margot."

"I *beg* your pardon! But anyway, you see why I want to live in England. My life and soul are bound up in my success here. And I could have a success. You know I could. I am beautiful. I haven't seen any woman whose face I'd change for mine. I won't be cheated out of my happiness——"

"Very well, we'll live in England, then. That's settled," said Stephen, hastily. "And you shall have all the success, all the happiness, that I can possibly give you. But we shall have to get on without any help from my brother and sister-in-law, and perhaps without a good many other people you might like to have for friends. It may seem hard, but you must make up your mind to it, Margot. Luckily, there'll be enough money to do pleasant things with; and people don't matter so immensely, once you've got used to——"

"They do, they do! The right people. I *shall* know them."

"You must have patience. Everybody is rather tired of our names just now. Things may change some day. I'm ready to begin the experiment whenever you are."

"You are a dear," said Margot. And Stephen did not even shiver. "That brings me to what I had to tell you. It's this: after all, we can't be married quite as soon as we expected."

"Can't we?" he echoed the words blankly. Was this to be a reprieve? But he was not sure that he wanted a reprieve. He thought, the sooner the plunge was made, the better, maybe. Looking forward to it had become almost unbearable.

"No, I *must* run over to Canada first, Stephen. I've just begun to see that. You might say, I could go there with you after we were married, but it wouldn't be the same thing at all. I ought to stay with some of my old friends while I'm still Margot Lorenzi. A lot of people were awfully good to father, and I must show my gratitude. The sooner I sail the better, now the news of our engagement has got ahead of me. I needn't stop away very long. Seven or eight weeks— or nine at most, going and coming."

"Would you like to be married in Canada?" Stephen asked; perhaps partly to please her, but probably more to disguise the fact that he had no impatient objections to raise against her plan. "If you wished, I could go whenever——"

"Oh no, no!" she exclaimed quickly. "I wouldn't have you come there for anything in the world. That is. I mean——" she corrected herself with an anxious, almost frightened side glance at him—"I must fight it out alone. No, I don't mean that either. What a stupid way of putting it! But it would bore you dreadfully to take such a journey, and it would be nicer anyhow to be married in England— perhaps at St. George's. That used to be my dream, when I was a romantic little girl, and loved to stuff my head full of English novels. I should adore a wedding at St. George's. And oh, Stephen, you won't change your mind while I'm gone? It would kill me if you jilted me after all. I shouldn't live a single day, if you weren't true."

"Don't talk nonsense, my dear girl. Of course I'm not going to change my mind," said Stephen. "When do you want to sail?"

"The end of this week. You're sure you won't let your brother and that cruel Duchess talk you over? I— —"

"There's not the slightest chance of their talking to me at all," Stephen answered sharply. "We've definitely quarrelled."

II

When he had dutifully seen Miss Lorenzi off at the ship, leaving her with as many flowers, novels, and sweets as even she could wish, Stephen expected to feel a sense of relief. But somehow, in a subtle way, he was more feverishly wretched than when Margot was near, and while planning to hurry on the marriage. He had been buoyed up with a rather youthful sense of defiance of the world, a hot desire to "get everything over." The flatness of the reaction which he felt on finding himself free, at least of Margot's society, was a surprise; and yet Stephen vaguely understood its real meaning. To be free, yet not free, was an aggravation. And besides, he did not know what to do or where to go, now that old friends and old haunts had lost much of their attraction.

Since the announcement of his engagement to Miss Lorenzi, and especially since the famous interview, copied in all the papers, he disliked meeting people he knew well, lest they should offer good advice, or let him see that they were dying to do so.

If it had been weak to say, "Be my wife, if you think I can make you happy," one day when Margot Lorenzi had tearfully confessed her love for him, it would be doubly weak—worse than weak, Stephen thought—to throw her over now. It would look to the world as if he were a coward, and it would look to himself the same—which would be more painful in the end. So he could listen to no advice, and he wished to hear none. Fortunately he was not in love with any other woman. But then, if he had loved somebody else, he would not have made the foolish mistake of saying those unlucky, irrevocable words to Margot.

Stephen would have liked to get away from England for a while, but he hardly knew where to look for a haven. Since making a dash through France and Italy just after leaving Oxford, he had been too busy amusing himself in his own country to find time for any other, with the exception of an occasional run over to Paris. Now, if he stopped in England it would be difficult to evade officious friends, and soon everybody would be gossiping about his quarrel with Northmorland. The Duchess was not reticent.

Stephen had not yet made up his mind what to do, or whether to do anything at all in his brief interval of freedom, when a letter came, to the flat near Albert Gate, where he had shut himself up after the sailing of Margot. The letter was post-marked Algiers, and it was a long time since he had seen the writing on the envelope—but not so long that he had forgotten it.

"Nevill Caird!" he said to himself as he broke the neat seal which was characteristic of the writer. And he wondered, as he slowly, almost reluctantly, unfolded the letter, whether Nevill Caird had been reminded of him by reading the interview with Margot. Once, he and Caird had been very good friends, almost inseparable during one year at Oxford. Stephen had been twenty then, and Nevill Caird about twenty-three. That would make him thirty-two now—and Stephen could hardly imagine what "Wings" would have developed into at thirty-two. They had not met since Stephen's last year at Oxford, for Caird had gone to live abroad, and if he came back to England sometimes, he had never made any sign of wishing to pick up the old friendship where it had dropped. But here was this letter.

Stephen knew that Caird had inherited a good deal of money, and a house in Paris, from an uncle or some other near relative; and a common friend had told him that there was also an Arab palace, very ancient and very beautiful, in or near Algiers. Several years had passed since Nevill Caird's name had been mentioned in his hearing, and lately it had not even echoed in his mind; but now, the handwriting and the neat seal on this envelope brought vividly before him the image of his friend: small, slight, boyish in face and figure, with a bright, yet dreamy smile, and blue-grey eyes which had the look of seeing beautiful things that nobody else could see.

"DEAR LEGS,"

began the letter ("Legs" being the name which Stephen's skill as a runner, as well as the length of his limbs, had given him in undergraduate days).

"Dear Legs, I've often thought about you in the last nine years, and hope you've occasionally thought of me, though somehow or other we haven't written. I don't know whether you've travelled much, or whether England has absorbed all your interests. Anyhow, can't you come out here and make me a visit—the longer it is, the more I shall be pleased. This country is interesting if you don't know it, and fascinating if you do. My place is rather nice, and I should like you to see it. Still better, I should like to see you. Do come if you can, and come soon. I should enjoy showing you my garden at its best. It's

15

one of the things I care for most, but there are other things. Do let me introduce you to them all. You can be as quiet as you wish, if you wish. I'm a quiet sort myself, as you may remember, and North Africa suits me better than London or Paris. I haven't changed for the worse I hope, and I'm sure you haven't, in any way.

"You can hardly realize how much pleasure it will give me if you'll say 'yes' to my proposal.

"Yours as ever

"NEVILL CAIRD, alias 'Wings,'"

Not a word of "the case," though, of course, he must know all about it—even in Algiers. Stephen's gratitude went out to his old friend, and his heart felt warmer because of the letter and the invitation. Many people, even with the best intentions, would have contrived to say the wrong thing in these awkward circumstances. There would have been some veiled allusion to the engagement; either silly, well- meant congratulations and good wishes, or else a stupid hint of advice to get out of a bad business while there was time. But Caird wrote as he might have written if there had been no case, and no entanglement; and acting on his first impulse, Stephen telegraphed an acceptance, saying that he would start for Algiers in two or three days. Afterwards, when he had given himself time to think, he did not regret his decision. Indeed, he was glad of it, and glad that he had made it so soon.

A few weeks ago, a sudden break in his plans would have caused him a great deal of trouble. There would have been dozens of luncheons and dinners to escape from, and twice as many letters to write. But nowadays he had few invitations and scarcely any letters to write, except those of business, and an occasional line to Margot. People were willing to be neglected by him, willing to let him alone, for now that he had quarrelled with Northmorland and the Duchess, and had promised to marry an impossible woman, he must be gently but firmly taught to expect little of Society in future.

Stephen broke the news to his man that he was going away, alone, and though the accomplished Molton had regrets, they were not as poignant as they would have been some weeks earlier. Most valets, if not all, are human, and have a weakness for a master whose social popularity is as unbounded as his generosity.

Molton's services did not cease until after he had packed Stephen's luggage, and seen him off at Victoria. He flattered himself, as he left the station with three months' wages in his pocket, that he would be missed; but Stephen was surprised at the sense of relief which came as Molton turned a respectable back, and the boat-train began to slide out of the station. It was good to be alone, to have loosed his moorings, and to be drifting away where no eyes, once kind, would turn from him, or turn on him with pity. Out there in Algiers, a town of which he had the vaguest conception, there would be people who read the papers, of course, and people who loved to gossip; but Stephen felt a pleasant confidence that Nevill Caird would know how to protect him from such people. He would not have to meet many strangers. Nevill would arrange all that, and give him plenty to think about during his weeks of freedom.

Algiers seemed a remote place to Stephen, who had loved life at home too passionately to care for foreign travel. Besides, there was always a great deal to do in England at every season of the year, and it had been difficult to find a time convenient for getting away. Town engagements began early in the spring, and lasted till after Cowes, when he was keen for Scotland. Being a gregarious as well as an idle young man, he was pleased with his own popularity, and the number of his invitations for country-house visits. He could never accept more than half, but even so, he hardly saw London until January; and then, if he went abroad at all, there was only time for a few days in Paris, and a fortnight on the Riviera, perhaps, before he found that he must get back. Just after leaving Oxford, before his father's death, he had been to Rome, to Berlin, and Vienna, and returned better satisfied than ever with his own capital; but of course it was different now that the capital was dissatisfied with him.

He had chosen the night train and it was not crowded. All the way to Dover he had the compartment to himself, and there was no rush for the boat. It was a night of stars and balmy airs; but after the start the wind freshened, and Stephen walked briskly up and down the deck, shivering slightly at first, till his blood warmed. By and by it grew so cold that the deck emptied, save for half a dozen men with pipes that glowed between turned-up coat collars, and one girl in a blue serge dress, with no other cloak than the jacket that matched her frock. Stephen hardly noticed her at first, but as men buttoned their coats or went below, and she remained, his attention was attracted to the slim figure leaning on the rail. Her face was turned away, looking over the sea where the whirling stars dipped into dark waves that sprang to engulf them. Her elbows rested on the railing, and her chin lay in the cup of her two hands; but her hair, under a blue sailor-hat held down with a veil, hung low in a great looped-up plait, tied with a wide black ribbon, so that Stephen, without wasting much thought upon her, guessed that she must be very young. It was red hair, gleaming where the light touched it, and the wind thrashed curly tendrils out from the thick clump of the braid, tracing bright threads in intricate, lacy lines over her shoulders, like the network of sunlight that plays on the surface of water.

Stephen thought of that simile after he had passed the girl once or twice, and thinking of it made him think of the girl herself. He was sure she must be cold in her serge jacket, and wondered why she didn't go below to the ladies' cabin. Also he wondered, even more vaguely, why her people didn't take better care of the child: there must be some one belonging to her on board.

At last she turned, not to look at him, but to pace back and forth as others were pacing. She was in front of Stephen, and he saw only her back, which seemed more girlish than ever as she walked with a light, springing step, that might have kept time to some dainty dance-music which only she could hear. Her short dress, of hardly more than ankle length, flowed past her slender shape as the black, white-frothing waves flowed past the slim prow of the boat; and there was something individual, something distinguished in her gait and the bearing of her head on the young throat. Stephen noticed this rather interesting peculiarity, remarking it more definitely because of the almost mean simplicity of the blue serge dress. It was of provincial cut, and looked as if the wearer might have bought it ready made in some country town. Her hat, too, was of the sort that is turned out by the thousand and sold at a few shillings for young persons between the ages of twelve and twenty.

By and by, when she had walked as far forward as possible, the deck rising under her feet or plunging down, while thin spray-wreaths sailed by on the wind, the girl wheeled and had the breeze at her back. It was then Stephen caught his first glimpse of her face, in a full white blaze of electric light: and he had the picture to himself, for by this time nearly every one else had gone.

He had not expected anything wonderful, but it seemed to him in a flash of surprise that this was an amazing beauty. He had never seen such hair, or such a complexion. The large eyes gave him no more than a passing glance, but they were so vivid, so full of blue light as they met his, that he had a startled impression of being graciously accosted. It seemed as if the girl had some message to give him, for which he must stop and ask.

As soon as they had passed each other, however, that curious, exciting impression was gone, like the vanishing glint on a gull's wing as it dips from sun into shadow. Of course she had not spoken; of course she had no word to give him. He had seemed to hear her speak, because she was a very vital sort of creature, no doubt, and therefore physically, though unconsciously, magnetic.

At their next crossing under the light she did not look at him at all, and he realized that she was not so extraordinarily beautiful as he had at first thought. The glory of her was more an effect of colouring than anything else. The creamy complexion of a very young girl, whipped to rose and white by the sea wind; brilliant turquoise blue eyes under a glitter of wavy red hair; these were the only marvels, for the small, straight nose was exactly like most pretty girls' noses, and the mouth, though expressive and sweet, with a short upper lip, was not remarkable, unless for its firmness.

The next time they passed, Stephen granted the girl a certain charm of expression which heightened the effect of beauty. She looked singularly innocent and interested in life, which to Stephen's mood seemed pathetic. He was convinced that he had seen through life, and consequently ceased forever to be interested in it. But he admired beauty wherever he saw it, whether in the grace of a breaking wave, or the sheen on a girl's bright hair, and it amused him faintly to speculate about the young creature with the brilliant eyes and blowing red locks. He decided that she was a schoolgirl of sixteen, being taken over to Paris, probably to finish her education there. Her mother or guardian was no doubt prostrate with sea- sickness, careless for the moment whether the child paraded the deck insufficiently clad, or whether she fell unchaperoned into the sea. Judging by her clothes, her family was poor, and she was perhaps intended for a governess: that was why they were sending her to France. She was to be given "every advantage," in order to command "desirable situations" by and by. Stephen felt dimly sorry for the little thing, who looked so radiantly happy now. She was much too pretty to be a governess, or to be obliged to earn her own living in any way. Women were brutes to each other sometimes. He had been finding this out lately. Few would care to bring a flowerlike creature of that type into their houses. The girl had trouble before her. He was sure she was going to be a governess.

After she had walked for half an hour she looked round for a sheltered corner and sat down. But the place she had chosen was only comparatively sheltered, and presently Stephen fancied that he saw her shivering with cold. He could not bear this, knowing that he had a rug which Molton had forced upon him to use on board ship between Marseilles and Algiers. It was in a rolled-up thing which Molton called a "hold-all," along with some sticks and an umbrella, Stephen believed; and the rolled-up thing was on deck, with other hand-luggage.

"Will you let me lend you a rug?" he asked, in the tone of a benevolent uncle addressing a child. "I have one close by, and it's rather cold when you don't walk."

"Thank you very much," said the girl. "I should like it, if it won't be too much trouble to you."

She spoke simply, and had a pretty voice, but it was an American voice. Stephen was surprised, because to find that she was an American upset his theories. He had never heard of American girls coming over to Paris with the object of training to be governesses.

He went away and found the rug, returning with it in two or three minutes. The girl thanked him again, getting up and wrapping the dark soft thing round her shoulders and body, as if it had been a big shawl. Then she sat down once more, with a comfortable little sigh. "That does feel good!" she exclaimed. "I *was* cold."

"I think you would have been wiser to stop in the ladies' cabin," said Stephen, still with the somewhat patronizing air of the older person.

"I like lots of air," explained the girl. "And it doesn't do me any harm to be cold."

"How about getting a chill?" inquired Stephen.

"Oh, I never have such things. They don't exist. At least they don't unless one encourages them," she replied.

He smiled, rather interested, and pleased to linger, since she evidently understood that he was using no arts to scrape an acquaintance. "That sounds like Christian Science," he ventured.

"I don't know that it's any kind of science," said she. "Nobody ever talked to me about it. Only if you're not afraid of things, they can't hurt you, can they?"

"Perhaps not. I suppose you mean you needn't let yourself feel them. There's something in the idea: be callous as an alligator and nothing can hit you."

"I don't mean that at all. I'd hate to be callous," she objected. "We couldn't enjoy things if we were callous."

Stephen, on the point of saying something bitter, stopped in time, knowing that his words would have been not only stupid but obvious, which was worse. "It is good to be young," he remarked instead.

"Yes, but I'm glad to be grown up at last," said the girl; and Stephen would not let himself laugh.

"I know how you feel," he answered. "I used to feel like that too."

"Don't you now?"

"Not always. I've had plenty of time to get tired of being grown up."

"Maybe you've been a soldier, and have seen sad things," she suggested. "I was thinking when I first saw you, that you looked like a soldier."

"I wish I had been. Unfortunately I was too disgustingly young, when our only war of my day was on. I mean, the sort of war one could volunteer for."

"In South Africa?"

"Yes. You were a baby in that remote time."

"Oh no, I wasn't. I'm eighteen now, going on nineteen. I was in Paris then, with my stepmother and my sister. We used to hear talk about the war, though we knew hardly any English people."

"So Paris won't be a new experience to you?" said Stephen, disappointed that he had been mistaken in all his surmises.

"I went back to America before I was nine, and I've been there ever since, till a few weeks ago. Oh see, there are the lights of France! I can't help being excited."

"Yes, we'll be in very soon — in about ten minutes."

"I am glad! I'd better go below and make my hair tidy. Thank you ever so much for helping me to be comfortable."

She jumped up, unrolled herself, and began to fold the rug neatly. Stephen would have taken it from her and bundled it together anyhow, but she would not let him do that. "I like folded things," she said. "It's nice to see them come straight, and I enjoy it more because the wind doesn't want me to do it. To succeed in spite of something, is a kind of little triumph—and seems like a sign. Good- bye, and thank you once more."

"Good-bye," said Stephen, and added to himself that he would not soon again see so pretty a child; as fresh, as frank, or as innocent. He had known several delightful American girls, but never one like this. She was a new type to him, and more interesting, perhaps, because she was simple, and even provincial. He was in a state of mind to glorify women who were entirely unsophisticated.

He did not see the girl getting into the train at Calais, though he looked for her, feeling some curiosity as to the stepmother and the sister whom he had imagined prostrate in the ladies' cabin. By the time he had arrived at Paris he felt sleepy and dull after an aggravating doze or two on the way, and had almost forgotten the red-haired child with the vivid blue eyes, until, to his astonishment, he saw her alone parleying with a *douanier*, over two great boxes, for one of which there seemed to be no key.

"Those selfish people of hers have left her to do all the work," he said to himself indignantly, and as she appeared to be having some difficulty with the official, he went to ask if he could help.

"Thank you, it's all right now," she said. "The key of my biggest box is mislaid, but luckily I've got the man to believe me when I say there's nothing in it except clothes, just the same as in the other. Still it would be very, very kind if you wouldn't mind seeing me to a cab. That is, if it's no bother."

Stephen assured her that he would be delighted.

"Have your people engaged the cab already," he wanted to know, "or are they waiting in this room for you?"

"I haven't any people," she answered. "I'm all by myself."

This was another surprise, and it was as much as Stephen could do not to blame her family audibly for allowing the child to travel alone, at night too. The thing seemed monstrous.

He took her into the court-yard, where the cabs stood, and engaged two, one for the girl, and one for her large luggage.

"You have rooms already taken at an hotel, I hope?" he asked.

"I'm going to a boarding-house—a *pension*, I mean," explained the girl. "But it's all right. They know I'm coming. I do thank you for everything."

Seated in the cab, she held out her hand in a glove which had been cleaned, and showed mended fingers. Stephen shook the small hand gravely, and for the second time they bade each other good-bye.

In the cold grey light of a rainy dawn, which would have suited few women as a background, especially after a night journey, the girl's face looked pearly, and Stephen saw that her lashes, darker at the roots, were bright golden at the turned-up ends.

It seemed to him that this pretty child, alone in the greyness and rain of the big foreign city, was like a spring flower thrown carelessly into a river to float with the stream. He felt an impulse of protection, and it went against his instincts to let her drive about Paris unprotected, while night had hardly yielded to morning. But he could not offer to go with her. He was interested, as any man of flesh and blood must be interested, in the fate of an innocent and charming girl left to take care of herself, and entirely unfitted for the task; yet she seemed happy and self-confident, and he had no right, even if he wished, to disturb her mind. He was going away without another word after the good-bye, but on second thoughts felt that he might ask if she had friends in Paris.

"Not exactly friends, but people who will look after me, and be kind, I'm sure," she answered. "Thank you for taking an interest. Will you tell the man to go to 278A Rue Washington, and the other cab to follow?"

Stephen obeyed, and as she drove away the girl looked back, smiling at him her sweet and childlike smile.

III

Stephen had meant to stop only one day in Paris, and travel at night to Marseilles, where he would have twelve or fifteen hours to wait before the sailing of the ship on which he had engaged a cabin. But glancing over a French paper while he breakfasted at the Westminster, he saw that a slight accident had happened to the boat during a storm on her return voyage from Algiers, and that she would be delayed three days for repairs. This news made Stephen decide to remain in Paris for those days, rather than go on and wait at Marseilles, or take another ship. He did not want to see any one he knew, but he thought it would be pleasant to spend some hours picture-gazing at the Louvre, and doing a few other things which one ought to do in Paris, and seldom does.

That night he went to bed early and slept better than he had slept for weeks. The next day he almost enjoyed, and when evening came, felt desultory, even light-hearted.

Dining at his hotel, he overheard the people at the next table say they were going to the Folies Bergères to see Victoria Ray dance, and suddenly Stephen made up his mind that he would go there too: for if life had been running its usual course with him, he would certainly have gone to see Victoria Ray in London. She had danced lately at the Palace Theatre for a month or six weeks, and absorbed as he had been in his own affairs, he had heard enough talk about this new dancer to know that she had made what is called a "sensation."

The people at the next table were telling each other that Victoria Ray's Paris engagement was only for three nights, something special, with huge pay, and that there was a "regular scramble" for seats, as the girl had been such a success in New York and London. The speakers, who were English and provincial, had already taken places, but there did not appear to be much hope that Stephen could get anything at the last minute. The little spice of difficulty gave a fillip of interest, however; and he remembered how the charming child on the boat had said that she "liked doing difficult things." He wondered what she was doing now; and as he thought of her, white and ethereal in the night and in the dawn-light, she seemed to him like the foam-flowers that had blossomed for an instant on the crests of dark waves, through which their vessel forged. "For a moment white, then gone forever." The words glittered in his mind, and fascinated him, calling up the image of the girl, pale against the night and rainy sea. "For a moment white, then gone forever," he repeated, and asked himself whence came the line. From Burns, he fancied; and thought it quaintly appropriate to the fair child whose clear whiteness had thrown a gleam into his life before she vanished.

All the seats for this second night of Victoria Ray's short engagement were sold at the Folies Bergères, he found, from the dearest to the cheapest: but there was standing room still when Stephen arrived, and he squeezed himself in among a group of light-hearted, long- haired students from the Latin Quarter. He had an hour to wait before Victoria Ray would dance, but there was some clever conjuring to be seen, a famous singer of *chansons* to be heard, and other performances which made the time pass well enough. Then, at last, it was the new dancer's "turn."

The curtain remained down for several minutes, as some scenic preparation was necessary before her first dance. Gay French music was playing, and people chattered through it, or laughed in high Parisian voices. A blue haze of smoke hung suspended like a thin veil, and the air was close, scented with tobacco and perfume. Stephen looked at his programme, beginning to feel bored. His elbows were pressed against his sides by the crowd. Miss Ray was down for two dances, the Dance of the Statue and the Dance of the Shadow. The atmosphere of the place depressed him. He doubted after all, that he would care for the dancing. But as he began to wish he had not come the curtain went up, to show the studio of a sculptor, empty save for the artist's marble masterpieces. Through a large skylight, and a high window at the back of the stage, a red glow of sunset streamed into the bare room. In the shadowy corners marble forms were grouped, but in the centre, directly under the full flood of rose-coloured light, the just finished statue of a girl stood on a raised platform. She was looking up, and held a cup in one lifted hand, as if to catch the red wine of sunset. Her draperies, confined by a Greek ceinture under the young bust, fell from shoulder to foot in long clear lines that seemed cut in gleaming stone. The illusion was perfect. Even in that ruddy blaze the delicate, draped form appeared to be of carved marble. It was almost impossible to believe it that of a living woman, and its grace of outline and pose was so perfect that Stephen, in his love of beauty, dreaded the first movement which must change, if not break, the tableau. He said to himself that there was some faint resemblance between this chiselled loveliness and the vivid charm of the pretty child he had met on the boat. He could imagine that a statue for which she had stood as model might look like this, though the features seemed to his eye more regular than those of the girl.

As he gazed, the music, which had been rich and colourful, fell into softer notes; and the rose-sunset faded to an opal twilight, purple to blue, blue to the silver of moonlight, the music changing as the light changed, until at last it was low and slumberous as the drip-drip of a plashing fountain. Then, into the dream of the music broke a sound like the distant striking of a clock. It was midnight, and all the statues in the sculptor's bare, white studio began to wake at the magic stroke which granted them a few hours of life.

There was just a shimmer of movement in the dim corners. Marble limbs stirred, marble face turned slowly to gaze at marble face; yet, as if they could be only half awakened in the shadows where the life-giving draught of moonlight might not flow, there was but the faintest flicker of white forms and draperies. It was the just finished statue of the girl which felt the full thrill of moonshine and midnight. She woke rapturously, and drained the silver moon-wine in her cup (the music told the story of her first thought and living heart-beat): then down she stepped from the platform where the sculptor's tools still lay, and began to dance for the other statues who watched in the dusk, hushed back into stillness under the new spell of her enchantments.

Stephen had never seen anything like that dance. Many pretty *premières danseuses* he had admired and applauded, charming and clever young women of France, of Russia, of Italy, and Spain: and they had roused him and all London to enthusiasm over dances eccentric, original, exquisite, or wild. But never had there been anything like this. Stephen had not known that a dance could move him as this did. He was roused, even thrilled by its poetry, and the perfect beauty of its poses, its poises. It must, he supposed, have been practised patiently, perhaps for years, yet it produced the effect of being entirely unstudied. At all events, there was nothing in the ordinary sense "professional" about it. One would say—not knowing the supreme art of supreme grace—that a joyous child, born to the heritage of natural grace, might dance thus by sheer inspiration, in ecstasy of life and worship of the newly felt beauty of earth. Stephen did know something of art, and the need of devotion to its study; yet he found it hard to realize that this awakened marble loveliness had gone through the same performance week after week, month after month, in America and England. He preferred rather to let himself fancy that he was dreaming the whole thing; and he would gladly have dreamed on indefinitely, forgetting the smoky atmosphere, forgetting the long-haired students and all the incongruous surroundings. The gracious dream gave him peace and pleasure such as he had not known since the beginning of the Northmorland case.

Through the house there was a hush, unusual at the Folies Bergères. People hardly knew what to make of the dances, so different from any ever seen in a theatre of Paris. Stephen was not alone in feeling the curious dream-spell woven by music and perfection of beauty. But the light changed. The moonlight slowly faded. Dancer and music faltered, in the falling of the dark hour before dawn. The charm was waning. Soft notes died, and quavered in apprehension. The magic charm of the moon was breaking, had broken: a crash of cymbals and the studio was dark. Then light began to glimmer once more, but it was the chill light of dawn, and growing from purple to blue, from blue to rosy day, it showed the marble statues fast locked in marble sleep again. On the platform stood the girl with uplifted arm, holding her cup, now, to catch the wine of sunrise; and on the delicately chiselled face was a faint smile which seemed to hide a secret. When the first ray of yellow sunshine gilded the big skylight, a door up-stage opened and the sculptor came in, wearing his workman's blouse. He regarded his handiwork, as the curtain came down.

When the music of the dream had ceased and suddenly became ostentatiously puerile, the audience broke into a tumult of applause. Women clapped their hands furiously and many men shouted "brava, brava," hoping that the curtain might rise once more on the picture; but it did not rise, and Stephen was glad. The dream would have been vulgarized by repetition.

For fully five minutes the orchestra played some gay tune which every one there had heard a hundred times; but abruptly it stopped, as if on a signal. For an instant there was a silence of waiting and suspense, which roused interest and piqued curiosity. Then there began a delicate symphony which could mean nothing but spring in a forest, and on that the curtain went up. The prophecy of the music was fulfilled, for the scene was a woodland in April, with young leaves a-flicker and blossoms in birth, the light song of the flutes and violins being the song of birds in love. All the trees were brocaded with dainty, gold-green lace, and daffodils sprouted from the moss at their feet.

The birds sang more gaily, and out from behind a silver-trunked beech tree danced a figure in spring green. Her arms were full of flowers, which she scattered as she danced, curtseying, mocking, beckoning the shadow that followed her along the daisied grass. Her little feet were bare, and flitted through the green folding of her draperies like white night-moths fluttering among rose leaves. Her hair fell over her shoulders, and curled below her waist. It was red hair that glittered and waved, and she looked a radiant child of sixteen. Victoria Ray the dancer, and the girl on the Channel boat were one.

IV

The Shadow Dance was even more beautiful than the Dance of the Statue, but Stephen had lost pleasure in it. He was supersensitive in these days, and he felt as if the girl had deliberately made game of him, in order that he should make a fool of himself. Of course it was a pose of hers to travel without chaperon or maid, and dress like a school girl from a provincial town, in cheap serge, a sailor hat, and a plait of hair looped up with ribbon. She was no doubt five or six years older than she looked or admitted, and probably her manager shrewdly prescribed the "line" she had taken up. Young women on the stage—actresses, dancers, or singers, it didn't matter which— must do something unusual, in order to be talked about, and get a good free advertisement. Nowadays, when professionals vied with each other in the expensiveness of their jewels, the size of their hats, or the smallness of their waists, and the eccentricity of their costumes, it was perhaps rather a new note to wear no jewels at all, and appear in ready-made frocks bought in bargain-sales; while, as for the young woman's air of childlike innocence and inexperience, it might be a tribute to her cleverness as an actress, but it was not a tribute to his intelligence as a man, that he should have been taken in by it. Always, he told himself, he was being taken in by some woman. After the lesson he had had, he ought to have learned wisdom, but it seemed that he was as gullible as ever. And it was this romantic folly of his which vexed him now; not the fact that a simple child over whose fate he had sentimentalized, was a rich and popular stage-dancer. Miss Ray was probably a good enough young woman according to her lights, and it was not she who need be shamed by the success of the Channel boat comedy.

He had another day and night in Paris, where he did more sightseeing than he had ever accomplished before in a dozen visits, and then travelled on to Marseilles. The slight damage to the *Charles Quex* had been repaired, and at noon the ship was to sail. Stephen went on board early, as he could think of nothing else which he preferred to do, and he was repaid for his promptness. By the time he had seen his luggage deposited in the cabin he had secured for himself alone, engaged a deck chair, and taken a look over the ship— which was new, and as handsome as much oak, fragrant cedar- wood, gilding, and green brocade could make her—many other passengers were coming on board. Travelling first class were several slim French officers, and stout Frenchmen of the commercial class; a merry theatrical company going to act in Algiers and Tunis; an English clergyman of grave aspect; invalids with their nurses, and two or three dignified Arabs, evidently of good birth as well as fortune. Arab merchants were returning from the Riviera, and a party of German students were going second class.

Stephen was interested in the lively scene of embarkation, and glad to be a part of it, though still more glad that there seemed to be nobody on board whom he had ever met. He admired the harbour, and the shipping, and felt pleasantly exhilarated. "I feel very young, or very old, I'm not sure which," he said to himself as a faint thrill ran through his nerves at the grinding groan of the anchor, slowly hauled out of the deep green water.

It was as if he heard the creaking of a gate which opened into an unknown garden, a garden where life would be new and changed. Nevill Caird had once said that there was no sharp, dividing line between phases of existence, except one's own moods, and Stephen had thought this true; but now it seemed as if the sea which silvered the distance was the dividing line for him, while all that lay beyond the horizon was mysterious as a desert mirage.

He was not conscious of any joy at starting, yet he was excited, as if something tremendous were about to happen to him. England, that he knew so well, seemed suddenly less real than Africa, which he knew not at all, and his senses were keenly alert for the first time in many days. He saw Marseilles from a new point of view, and wondered why he had never read anything fine written in praise of the ancient Phoenician city. Though he had not been in the East, he imagined that the old part of the town, seen from the sea, looked Eastern, as if the traffic between east and west, going on for thousands of years, had imported an Eastern taste in architecture.

The huge, mosque-like cathedral bubbled with domes, where fierce gleams of gold were hammered out by strokes of the noonday sun. A background of wild mountain ranges, whose tortured peaks shone opaline through long rents in mist veils, lent an air of romance to the scene, and Notre Dame de la Garde loomed nobly on her bleached and arid height. "Have no fear: I keep watch and ward over land and sea," seemed to say the majestic figure of gold on the tall tower, and Stephen half wished he were of the Catholic faith, that he might take comfort from the assurance.

As the *Charles Quex* steamed farther and farther away, the church on the mountainous hill appeared to change in shape. Notre Dame de la Garde looked no longer like a building made by man, but like a great sacred swan crowned with gold, and nested on a mountain-top. There she sat, with shining head erect on a long neck, seated on her nest, protecting her young, and gazing far across the sea in search of danger. The sun touched her golden crown, and dusky cloud-shadows grouped far beneath her eyrie, like mourners kneeling below the height to pray. The rock-shapes and island rocks that cut the blue glitter of the sea, suggested splendid tales of Phoenician mariners and Saracenic pirates, tales lost forever in the dim mists of time; and so Stephen wandered on to thoughts of Dumas, wishing he had brought "Monte Cristo," dearly loved when he was twelve. Probably not a soul on board had the book; people were so stupid and prosaic nowadays. He turned from the rail on which he had leaned to watch the fading land, and as he did so, his eyes fell upon a bright red copy of the book for which he had been wishing. There was the name in large gold lettering on a scarlet cover, very conspicuous on the dark blue serge lap of a girl. It was the girl of the Channel boat, and she wore the same dress, the same sailor hat tied on with a blue veil, which she had worn that night crossing from England to France.

While Stephen had been absorbed in admiration of Marseilles harbour, she had come up on deck, and settled herself in a canvas chair. This time she had a rug of her own, a thin navy blue rug which, like her frock, might have been chosen for its cheapness. Although she held a volume of "Monte Cristo," she was not reading, and as Stephen turned towards her, their eyes met.

Hers lit up with a pleased smile, and the pink that sprang to her cheeks was the colour of surprise, not of self-consciousness.

"I *thought* your back looked like you, but I didn't suppose it would turn out to be you," she said.

Stephen's slight, unreasonable irritation could not stand against the azure of such eyes, and the youth in her friendly smile. Since the girl seemed glad to see him, why shouldn't he be glad to see her? At least she was not a link with England.

"I thought your statue looked like you," he retorted, standing near her chair, "but I didn't suppose it would turn out to be you until your shadow followed."

"Oh, you saw me dance! Did you like it?" She asked the question eagerly, like a child who hangs upon grown-up judgment of its work.

"I thought both dances extremely beautiful and artistic," replied Stephen, a little stiffly.

She looked at him questioningly, as if puzzled. "No, I don't think you did like them, really," she said. "I oughtn't to have asked in that blunt way, because of course you would hate to hurt my feelings by saying no!"

Her manner was so unlike that of a spoiled stage darling, that Stephen had to remind himself sharply of her "innocent pose," and his own soft-hearted lack of discrimination where pretty women were concerned. By doing this he kept himself armed against the clever little actress laughing at him behind the blue eyes of a child. "You must know that there can't be two opinions of your dancing," said he coolly. "You have had years and years of flattery, of course; enough to make you sick of it, if a woman ever — —" He stopped, smiling.

"Why, I've been dancing professionally for only a few months!" she exclaimed. "Didn't you know?"

"I'm ashamed to say I was ignorant," Stephen confessed. "But before the dancing, there must have been something else equally clever. Floating — or flying — or — —"

She laughed. "Why don't you suggest fainting in coils? I'm certain you would, if you'd ever read 'Alice.'"

"As a matter of fact, I was brought up on 'Alice,'" said Stephen. "Do children of the present day still go down the rabbit hole?"

"I'm not sure about children of the *present* day. Children of my day went down," she replied with dignity. "I loved Alice dearly. I don't know much about other children, though, for I never had a chance to make friends as a child. But then I had my sister when I was a little girl, so nothing else mattered."

"If you don't think me rude to say so," ventured Stephen, "you would seem to me a little girl now, if I hadn't found out that you're an accomplished star of the theatres, admired all over Europe."

"Now you're making fun of me," said the dancer. "Paris was only my third engagement; and it's going to be my last, anyway for ever so long, I hope."

This time Stephen was really surprised, and all his early interest in the young creature woke again; the personal sort of interest which he had partly lost on finding that she was of the theatrical world.

"Oh, I see!" he ejaculated, before stopping to reflect that he had no right to put into words the idea which jumped into his mind.

"You see?" she echoed. "But how can you see, unless you know something about me already?"

"I beg your pardon," he apologized. "It was only a thought. I— —"

"A thought about my dancing?"

"Not exactly that. About your not dancing again."

"Then please tell me the thought."

"You may be angry. I rather think you'd have a right to be angry— not at the thought, but the telling of it."

"I promise."

"Why," explained Stephen, "when a young and successful actress makes up her mind to leave the stage, what is the usual reason?"

"I'm not an actress, so I can't imagine what you mean—unless you suppose I've made a great fortune in a few months?"

"That too, perhaps—but I don't think a fortune would induce you to leave the stage yet a while. You'd want to go on, not for the money perhaps, but for the fun."

"I haven't been dancing for fun."

"Haven't you?"

"No. I began with a purpose. I'm leaving the stage for a purpose. And you say you can guess what that is. If you know, you must have been told."

"Since you insist, it occurred to me that you might be going to marry. I thought maybe you were travelling to Africa to— —"

She laughed. "Oh, you *are* wrong! I don't believe there ever was a girl who thinks less about marrying. I've never had time to think of such things. I've always—ever since I was nine years old—looked to the one goal, and aimed for it, studied for it, lived for it—at last, danced towards it."

"You excite my curiosity immensely," said Stephen. And it was true. The girl had begun to take him out of himself.

"There is lunch," she announced, as a bugle sounded.

Stephen longed to say, "Don't go yet. Stop and tell me all about the 'goal' you're working for." But he dared not. She was very frank, and evidently willing, for some reason, to talk of her aims, even to a comparative stranger; yet he knew that it would be impertinent to suggest her sitting out on deck to chat with him, while the other passengers lunched.

He asked if she were hungry, and she said she was. So was he, now that he came to think of it; nevertheless he let her go in alone, and waited deliberately for several minutes before following. He would have liked to sit by Miss Ray at the table, but wished her to see that he did not mean to presume upon any small right of acquaintanceship. As she was on the stage, and extremely attractive, no doubt men often tried to take such advantage, and he didn't intend to be one of them; therefore he supposed that he had lost the chance of placing himself near her in the dining-room. To his surprise, however, as he was about to slip into a far-away chair, she beckoned from her table. "I kept this seat for you," she said. "I hoped you wouldn't mind."

"Mind!" He was on the point of repaying her kindness with a conventional little compliment, but thought better of it, and expressed his meaning in a smile.

The oak-panelled saloon was provided with a number of small tables, and at the one where Victoria Ray sat, were places for four. Three were already occupied when Stephen came; one by Victoria, the others by a German bride and groom.

At the next table were two French officers of the Chasseurs d'Afrique, the English clergyman Stephen had noticed on deck, and a remarkably handsome Arab, elaborately dressed. He sat facing Victoria Ray and Stephen Knight, and Stephen found it difficult not to stare at the superb, pale brown person whose very high white turban, bound with light grey cord, gave him a dignity beyond his years, and whose pale grey burnous, over a gold-embroidered vest of dark rose-colour, added picturesqueness which appeared theatrical in eyes unaccustomed to the East.

Stephen had never seen an Arab of the aristocratic class until to-day; and before, only a few such specimens as parade the Galerie Charles Trois at Monte Carlo, selling prayer-rugs and draperies from Algeria. This man's high birth and breeding were clear at first glance. He was certainly a personage aware of his own attractions, though not offensively self-conscious, and was unmistakably interested in the beauty of the girl at the next table. He was too well- bred to make a show of his admiration, but talked in almost perfect, slightly guttural French, with the English clergyman, speaking occasionally also to the officers in answer to some question. He glanced seldom at Miss Ray, but when he did look across, in a guarded way, at her, there was a light of ardent pleasure in his eyes, such as no eyes save those of East or South ever betray. The look was respectful, despite its underlying passion. Nevertheless, because the handsome face was some shades darker than his own, it offended Stephen, who felt a sharp bite of dislike for the Arab. He was glad the man was not at the same table with Miss Ray, and knew that it would have vexed him intensely to see the girl drawn into conversation. He wondered that the French officers should talk with the Arab as with an equal, yet knew in his heart that such prejudice was narrow-minded, especially at the moment when he was travelling to the Arab's own country. He tried, though not very strenuously, to override his conviction of superiority to the Eastern man, but triumphed only far enough to admit that the fellow was handsome in a way. His skin was hardly darker than old ivory: the aquiline nose delicate as a woman's, with sensitive nostrils; and the black velvet eyes under arched brows, that met in a thin, pencilled line, were long, and either dreamy or calmly calculating. A prominent chin and a full mouth, so determined as to suggest cruelty, certainly selfishness, preserved the face from effeminacy at the sacrifice of artistic perfection. Stephen noticed with mingled curiosity and disapproval that the Arab appeared to be vain of his hands, on which he wore two or three rings that might have been bought in Paris, or even given him by European women — for they looked like a woman's rings. The brown fingers were slender, tapering to the ends, and their reddened nails glittered. They played, as the man talked, with a piece of bread, and often he glanced down at them, with the long eyes which had a blue shadow underneath, like a faint smear of kohl.

Stephen wondered what Victoria Ray thought of her *vis-à-vis*; but in the presence of the staring bride and groom he could ask no questions, and the expression of her face, as once she quietly regarded the Arab, told nothing. It was even puzzling, as an expression for a young girl's face to wear in looking at a handsome man so supremely conscious of sex and of his own attraction. She was evidently thinking about him with considerable interest, and it annoyed Stephen that she should look at him at all. An Arab might misunderstand, not realizing that he was a legitimate object of curiosity for eyes unused to Eastern men.

After luncheon Victoria went to her cabin. This was disappointing. Stephen, hoping that she might come on deck again soon, and resume their talk where it had broken off in the morning, paced up and down until he felt drowsy, not having slept in the train the night before. To his surprise and disgust, it was after five when he waked from a long nap, in his stateroom; and going on deck he found Miss Ray in her chair once more, this time apparently deep in "Monte Cristo."

V

He walked past, and she looked up with a smile, but did not ask him to draw his chair near hers, though there was a vacant space. It was an absurd and far-fetched idea, but he could not help asking himself if it were possible that she had picked up any acquaintance on board, who had told her he was a marked man, a foolish fellow who had spoiled his life for a low-born, unscrupulous woman's sake. It was a morbid fancy, he knew, but he was morbid now, and supposed that he should be for some time to come, if not for the rest of his life. He imagined a difference in the girl's manner. Maybe she had read that hateful interview in some paper, when she was in London, and now remembered having seen his photograph with Margot Lorenzi's. He hated the thought, not because he deliberately wished to keep his engagement secret, but because the newspaper interview had made him seem a fool, and somehow he did not want to be despised by this dancing girl whom he should never see again after to-morrow. Just why her opinion of his character need matter to him, it was difficult to say, but there was something extraordinary about the girl. She did not seem in the least like other dancers he had met. He had not that feeling of comfortable comradeship with her that a man may feel with most unchaperoned, travelling actresses, no matter how respectable. There was a sense of aloofness, as if she had been a young princess, in spite of her simple and friendly ways.

Since it appeared that she had no intention of picking up the dropped threads of their conversation, Stephen thought of the smoking-room; but his wish to know whether she really had changed towards him became so pressing that he was impelled to speak again. It was an impulse unlike himself, at any rate the old self with which he was familiar, as with a friend or an intimate enemy.

"I hoped you would tell me the rest," he blurted out.

"The rest?"

"That you were beginning to tell."

The girl blushed. "I was afraid afterwards, you might have been bored, or anyway surprised. You probably thought it 'very American' of me to talk about my own affairs to a stranger, and it *isn't*, you know. I shouldn't like you to think Americans are less well brought up than other girls, just because *I* may do things that seem queer. I have to do them. And I am quite different from others. You mustn't suppose I'm not."

Stephen was curiously relieved. Suddenly he felt young and happy, as he used to feel before knowing Margot Lorenzi. "I never met a brilliantly successful person who was as modest as you," he said, laughing with pleasure. "I was never less bored in my life. Will you talk to me again—and let me talk to you?"

"I should like to ask your advice," she replied.

That gave permission for Stephen to draw his chair near to hers. "Have you had tea?" he inquired, by way of a beginning.

"I'm too American to drink tea in the afternoon," she explained. "It's only fashionable Americans who take it, and I'm not that kind, as you can see. I come from the country—or almost the country."

"Weren't you drawn into any of our little ways in London?" He was working up to a certain point.

"I was too busy."

"I'm sure you weren't too busy for one thing: reading the papers for your notices."

Victoria shook her head, smiling. "There you're mistaken. The first morning after I danced at the Palace Theatre, I asked to see the papers they had in my boarding-house, because I hoped so much that English people would like me, and I wanted to be a success. But afterwards I didn't bother. I don't understand British politics, you see—how could I?—and I hardly know any English people, so I wasn't very interested in their papers."

Again Stephen was relieved. But he felt driven by one of his strange new impulses to tell her his name, and watch her face while he told it.

"'Curiouser and curiouser,' as our friend Alice would say," he laughed. "No newspaper paragraphs, and a boarding-house instead of a fashionable hotel. What was your manager thinking about?"

"I had no manager of my very own," said Victoria. "I 'exploited' myself. It costs less to do that. When people in America liked my dancing I got an offer from London, and I accepted it and made all the arrangements about going over. It was quite easy, you see, because there were only costumes to carry. My scenery is so simple, they either had it in the theatres or got something painted: and the statues in the studio scene, and the sculptor, needed very few rehearsals. In Paris they had only one. It was all I had time for, after I arrived. The lighting wasn't difficult either, and though people told me at first there would be trouble unless I had my own man, there never was any, really. In my letters to the managers I gave the dates when I could come to their theatres, how long I could stay, and all they must do to get things ready. The Paris engagement was made only a little while beforehand. I wanted to pass through there, so I was glad to accept the offer and earn extra money which I thought I might need by and by."

"What a mercenary star!" Stephen spoke teasingly; but in truth he could not make the girl out.

She took the accusation with a smile. "Yes, I am mercenary, I suppose," she confessed with unashamed frankness, "but not entirely for myself. I shouldn't like to be that! I told you how I've been looking forward always to one end. And now, just when that end may be near, how foolish I should be to spend a cent on unnecessary things! Why, I'd have felt *wicked* living in an expensive hotel, and keeping a maid, when I could be comfortable in a Bloomsbury boarding-house on ten dollars a week. And the dresser in the theater, who did everything very nicely, was delighted with a present of twenty dollars when my London engagement was over."

"No doubt she was," said Stephen. "But——"

"I suppose you're thinking that I must have made lots of money, and that I'm a sort of little miseress: and so I have—and so I am. I earned seven hundred and fifty dollars a week—isn't that a hundred and fifty pounds?—for the six weeks, and I spent as little as possible; for I didn't get as large a salary as that in America. I engaged to dance for three hundred dollars a week there, which seemed perfectly wonderful to me at first; so I had to keep my contract, though other managers would have given me more. I wanted dreadfully to take their offers, because I was in such a hurry to have enough money to begin my real work. But I knew I shouldn't be blessed in my undertaking if I acted dishonourably. Try as I might, I've only been able to save up ten thousand dollars, counting the salary in Paris and all. Would you say that was enough to *bribe* a person, if necessary? Two thousand of your pounds."

"It depends upon how rich the person is."

"I don't know how rich he is. Could an Arab be *very* rich?"

"I daresay there are still some rich ones. But maybe riches aren't the same with them as with us. That fellow at lunch to-day looks as if he'd plenty of money to spend on embroideries."

"Yes. And he looks important too—as if he might have travelled, and known a great many people of all sorts. I wish it were proper for me to talk to him."

"Good Heavens, why?" asked Stephen, startled. "It would be most improper."

"Yes, I'm afraid so, and I won't, of course, unless I get to know him in some way," went on Victoria. "Not that there's any chance of such a thing."

"I should hope not," exclaimed Stephen, who was privately of opinion that there was only too good a chance if the girl showed the Arab even the faintest sign of willingness to know and be known. "I've no right to ask it, of course, except that I'm much older than you and have seen more of the world—but do promise not to look at that nigger. I don't like his face."

"He isn't a nigger," objected Victoria. "But if he were, it wouldn't matter—nor whether one liked his face or not. He might be able to help me."

"To help you—in Algiers?"

"Yes, in the same way that you might be able to help me—or more, because he's an Arab, and must know Arabs."

Stephen forgot to press his request for her promise. "How can I help you?" he wanted to know.

"I'm not sure. Only, you're going to Algiers. I always ask everybody to help, if there's the slightest chance they can."

Stephen felt disappointed and chilled. But she went on. "I should hate you to think I *gush* to strangers, and tell them all my affairs, just because I'm silly enough to love talking. I must talk to strangers. I *must* get help where I can. And you were kind the other night.

Everybody is kind. Do you know many people in Algeria, or Tunisia?"

"Only one man. His name is Nevill Caird, and he lives in Algiers. My name is Stephen Knight. I've been wanting to tell you—I seemed to have an unfair advantage, knowing yours ever since Paris."

He watched her face almost furtively, but no change came over it, no cloud in the blueness of her candid eyes. The name meant nothing to her.

"I'm sorry. It's hardly worth while my bothering you then."

Stephen wished to be bothered. "But Nevill Caird has lived in Algiers for eight winters or so," he said. "He knows everybody, French and English—Arab too, very likely, if there are Arabs worth knowing."

A bright colour sprang to the girl's cheeks and turned her extreme prettiness into brilliant beauty. It seemed to Stephen that the name of Ray suited her: she was dazzling as sunshine. "Oh, then, I will tell you—if you'll listen," she said.

"If I had as many ears as a spear of wheat, they'd all want to listen." His voice sounded young and eager. "Please begin at the beginning, as the children say."

"Shall I really? But it's a long story. It begins when I was eight."

"All the better. It will be ten years long."

"I can skip lots of things. When I was eight, and my sister Saidee not quite eighteen, we were in Paris with my stepmother. My father had been dead just a year, but she was out of mourning. She wasn't old—only about thirty, and handsome. She was jealous of Saidee, though, because Saidee was so much younger and fresher, and because Saidee was beautiful—Oh, you can't imagine how beautiful!"

"Yes, I can," said Stephen.

"You mean me to take that for a compliment. I know I'm quite pretty, but I'm nothing to Saidee. She was a great beauty, though with the same colouring I have, except that her eyes were brown, and her hair a little more auburn. People turned to look after her in the street, and that made our stepmother angry. *She* wanted to be the one looked at. I knew, even then! She wouldn't have travelled with us, only father had left her his money, on condition that she gave Saidee and me the best of educations, and allowed us a thousand dollars a year each, from the time our schooling was finished until we married. She had a good deal of influence over him, for he was ill a long time, and she was his nurse—that was the way they got acquainted. And she persuaded him to leave practically everything to her; but she couldn't prevent his making some conditions. There was one which she hated. She was obliged to live in the same town with us; so when she wanted to go and enjoy herself in Paris after father died, she had to take us too. And she didn't care to shut Saidee up, because if Saidee couldn't be seen, she couldn't be married; and of course Mrs. Ray wanted her to be married. Then she would have no bother, and no money to pay. I often heard Saidee say these things, because she told me everything. She loved me a great deal, and I adored her. My middle name is Cecilia, and she was generally called Say; so she used to tell me that our secret names for each other must be 'Say and Seal.' It made me feel very grown-up to have her confide so much in me: and never being with children at all, gave me grown-up thoughts."

"Poor child!" said Stephen.

"Oh, I was very happy. It was only after—but that isn't the way to tell the story. Our stepmother—whom we always called 'Mrs. Ray,' never 'mother'—liked officers, and we got acquainted with a good many French ones. They used to come to the flat where we lived. Some of them were introduced by our French governess, whose brother was in the army, but they brought others, and Saidee and Mrs. Ray went to parties together, though Mrs. Ray hated being chaperon. If poor Saidee were admired at a dinner, or a dance, Mrs. Ray would be horrid all next day, and say everything disagreeable she could think of. Then Saidee would cry when we were alone, and tell me she was so miserable, she would have to marry in self- defence. That made me cry too—but she promised to take me with her if she went away.

"When we had been in Paris about two months, Saidee came to bed one night after a ball, and waked me up. We slept in the same room. She was excited and looked like an angel. I knew something had happened. She told me she'd met a wonderful man, and every one was fascinated with him. She had heard of him before, but this was the first time they'd seen each other. He was in the French army, she said, a captain, and older than most of the men she knew best, but very handsome, and rich as well as clever. It was only at the last, after she'd praised the man a great deal, that she mentioned his having Arab blood. Even then she hurried on to say his mother was a Spanish woman, and he had been partly educated in France, and spoke perfect French, and English too. They had danced together, and Saidee had never met so interesting a man. She thought he was like the hero of some romance; and she told me I would see him, because he'd begged Mrs. Ray to be allowed to call. He had asked Saidee lots of questions, and she'd told him even about me—so he sent me his love. She seemed to think I ought to be pleased, but I wasn't. I'd read the 'Arabian Nights', with pictures, and I knew Arabs were dark people. I didn't look down on them particularly, but I couldn't bear to have Say interested in an Arab. It didn't seem right for her, somehow."

The girl stopped, and apparently forgot to go on. She had been speaking with short pauses, as if she hardly realized that she was talking aloud. Her eyebrows drew together, and she sighed. Stephen knew that some memory pressed heavily upon her, but soon she began again.

"He came next day. He was handsome, as Saidee had said—as handsome as the Arab on board this ship, but in a different way. He looked noble and haughty—yet as if he might be very selfish and hard. Perhaps he was about thirty-three or four, and that seemed old to me then—old even to Saidee. But she was fascinated. He came often, and she saw him at other houses. Everywhere she was going, he would find out, and go too. That pleased her—for he was an important man somehow, and of good birth. Besides, he was desperately in love— even a child could see that. He never took his eyes off Saidee's face when she was with him. It was as if he could eat her up; and if she flirted a little with the real French officers, to amuse herself or tease him, it drove him half mad. She liked that—it was exciting, she used to say. And I forgot to tell you, he wore European dress, except for a fez—no turban, like this man's on the boat, or I'm sure she couldn't have cared for him in the way she did—he wouldn't have seemed *possible*, for a Christian girl. A man in a turban! You understand, don't you?"

"Yes, I understand," Stephen said. He understood, too, how violently such beauty as the girl described must have appealed to the dark man of the East. "The same colouring that I have," Victoria Ray had said. If he, an Englishman, accustomed to the fair loveliness of his countrywomen, were a little dazzled by the radiance of this girl, what compelling influence must not the more beautiful sister have exercised upon the Arab?

"He made love to Saidee in a fierce sort of way that carried her off her feet," went on Victoria. "She used to tell me things he said, and Mrs. Ray did all she could to throw them together, because he was rich, and lived a long way off—so she wouldn't have to do anything for Say if they were married, or even see her again. He was only on leave in Paris. He was a Spahi, stationed in Algiers, and he owned a house there."

"Ah, in Algiers!" Stephen began to see light—rather a lurid light.

"Yes. His name was Cassim ben Halim el Cheikh el Arab. Before he had known Saidee two weeks, he proposed. She took a little while to think it over, and I begged her to say 'no'—but one day when Mrs. Ray had been crosser and more horrid than usual, she said 'yes'. Cassim ben Halim was Mohammedan, of course, but he and Saidee were married according to French law. They didn't go to church, because he couldn't do that without showing disrespect to his own religion, but he promised he'd not try to change hers. Altogether it seemed to Saidee that there was no reason why they shouldn't be as happy as a Catholic girl marrying a Protestant—or *vice versa*; and she hadn't any very strong convictions. She was a Christian, but she wasn't fond of going to church."

"And her promise that she'd take you away with her?" Stephen reminded the girl.

"She would have kept it, if Mrs. Ray had consented—though I'm sure Cassim didn't want me, and only agreed to do what Saidee asked because he was so deep in love, and feared to lose my sister if he refused her anything. But Mrs. Ray was afraid to let me go, on account of the condition in father's will that she should keep me near her while I was being educated. There was an old friend of father's who'd threatened to try and upset the will, for Saidee's sake and mine, so I suppose she thought he might succeed if she disobeyed father's instructions. It ended in Saidee and her husband going to Algiers without me, and Saidee cried—but she couldn't help being happy, because she was in love, and very excited about the strange new life, which Cassim told her would be wonderful as some gorgeous dream of fairyland. He gave her quantities of jewellery, and said they were nothing to what she should have when she was in her own home with him. She should be covered from head to foot with diamonds and pearls, rubies and emeralds, if she liked; and of course she would like, for she loved jewels, poor darling."

"Why do you say 'poor?'" asked Stephen. "Are you going to tell me the marriage wasn't a success?"

"I don't know," answered the girl. "I don't know any more about her than if Cassim ben Halim had really carried my sister off to fairyland, and shut the door behind them. You see, I was only eight years old. I couldn't make my own life. After Saidee was married and taken to Algiers, my stepmother began to imagine herself in love with an American from Indiana, whom she met in Paris. He had an impressive sort of manner, and made her think him rich and important. He was in business, and had come over to rest, so he couldn't stay long abroad; and he urged Mrs. Ray to go back to America on the same ship with him. Of course she took me, and this Mr. Henry Potter told her about a boarding-school where they taught quite little girls, not far from the town where he lived. It had been a farmhouse once, and he said there were 'good teachers and good air.' I can hear him saying it now. It was easy to persuade her; and she engaged rooms at a hotel in the town near by, which was called Potterston, after Mr. Potter's grandfather. By and by they were married, but their marriage made no difference to me. It wasn't a bad little old-fashioned school, and I was as happy as I could be anywhere, parted from Saidee. There was an attic where I used to be allowed to sit on Saturdays, and think thoughts, and write letters to my sister; and there was one corner, where the sunlight came in through a tiny window shaped like a crescent, without any glass, which I named Algiers. I played that I went there to visit Saidee in the old Arab palace she wrote me about. It was a splendid play—but I felt lonely when I stopped playing it. I used to dance there, too, very softly in stockinged feet, so nobody could hear—dances she and I made up together out of stories she used to tell me. The Shadow Dance and the Statue Dance which you saw, came out of those stories, and there are more you didn't see, which I do sometimes—a butterfly dance, the dance of the wheat, and two of the East, which were in stories she told me after we knew Cassim ben Halim. They are the dance of the smoke wreath, and the dance of the jewel-and- the-rose. I could dance quite well even in those days, because I loved doing it. It came as natural to dance as to breathe, and Saidee had always encouraged me, so when I was left alone it made me think of her, to dance the dances of her stories."

"What about your teachers? Did they never find you out?" asked Stephen.

"Yes. One of the young teachers did at last. Not in the attic, but when I was dancing for the big girls in their dormitory, at night—they'd wake me up to get me to dance. But she wasn't much older than the biggest of the big girls, so she laughed—I suppose I must have looked quaint dancing in my nighty, with my long red hair. And though we were all scolded afterwards, I was made to dance sometimes at the entertainments we gave when school broke up in the summer. I was the youngest scholar, you see, and stayed through the vacations, so I was a kind of pet for the teachers. They were of one family, aunts and nieces—Southern people, and of course good- natured. But all this isn't really in the story I want to tell you. The interesting part's about Saidee. For months I got letters from her, written from Algiers. At first they were like fairy tales, but by and by—quite soon—they stopped telling much about herself. It seemed as if Saidee were growing more and more reserved, or else as if she were tired of writing to me, and bored by it—almost as if she could hardly think of anything to say. Then the letters stopped altogether. I wrote and wrote, but no answer came—no answer ever came."

"You've never heard from your sister since then?" The thing appeared incredible to Stephen.

"Never. Now you can guess what I've been growing up for, living for, all these years. To find her."

"But surely," Stephen argued, "there must have been some way to——"

"Not any way that was in my power, till now. You see I was helpless. I had no money, and I was a child. I'm not very old yet, but I'm older than my years, because I had this thing to do. There I was, at a farmhouse school in the country, two miles out of Potterston— and you would think Potterston itself not much better than the backwoods, I'm sure. When I was fourteen, my stepmother died suddenly— leaving all the money which came from my father to her husband, except several thousand dollars to finish my education and give me a start in life; but Mr. Potter lost everything of his own and of mine too, in some wild speculation about which the people in that part of Indiana went mad. The crash came a year ago, and the Misses Jennings, who kept the school, asked me to stay on as an under teacher—they were sorry for me, and so kind. But even if nothing had happened, I should have left then, for I felt old enough to set about my real work. Oh, I see you think I might have got at my sister before, somehow, but I couldn't, indeed. I tried everything. Not only did I write and write, but I begged the Misses Jennings to help, and the minister of the church where we went on Sundays. The Misses Jennings told the girls' parents and relations whenever they came to visit, and they all promised, if they ever went to Algiers, they would look for my sister's husband, Captain Cassim ben Halim, of the Spahis. But they weren't the sort of people who ever do go such journeys. And the minister wrote to the American Consul in Algiers for me, but the only answer was that Cassim ben Halim had disappeared. It seemed not even to be known that he had an American wife."

"Your stepmother ought to have gone herself," said Stephen.

"Oh—*ought*! I very seldom saw my stepmother after she married Mr. Potter. Though she lived so near, she never asked me to her house, and only came to call at the school once or twice a year, for form's sake. But I ran away one evening and begged her to go and find Saidee. She said it was nonsense; that if Saidee hadn't wanted to drop us, she would have kept on writing, or else she was dead. But don't you think I should have *known* if Saidee were dead?"

"By instinct, you mean—telepathy, or something of that sort?"

"I don't know what I mean, but *I should have known*. I should have felt her death, like a string snapping in my heart. Instead, I heard her calling to me—I hear her always. She wants me. She needs me. I know it, and nothing could make me believe otherwise. So now you understand how, if anything were to be done, I had to do it myself. When I was quite little, I thought by the time I should be sixteen or seventeen, and allowed to leave school—or old enough to run away if necessary—I'd have a little money of my own. But when my stepmother died I felt sure I should never, never get anything from Mr. Potter."

"But that old friend you spoke of, who wanted to upset the will? Couldn't he have done anything?" Stephen asked.

"If he had lived, everything might have been different; but he was a very old man, and he died of pneumonia soon after Saidee married Cassim ben Halim. There was no one else to help. So from the time I was fourteen, I knew that somehow I must make money. Without money I could never hope to get to Algiers and find Saidee. Even though she had disappeared from there, it seemed to me that Algiers would be the place to begin my search. Don't you think so?"

"Yes, Algiers is the place to begin," Stephen echoed. "There ought to be a way of tracking her. *Some one* must know what became of a more or less important man such as your brother-in-law seems to have been. It's incredible that he should have been able to vanish without leaving any trace."

"He must have left a trace, and though nobody else, so far, has found it, I shall find it," said the girl. "I did what I could before. I asked everybody to help; and when I got to New York last year, I used to go to Cook's office, to inquire for people travelling to Algiers. Then, if I met any, I would at once speak of my sister, and give them my address, to let me know if they should discover anything. They always seemed interested, and said they would really do their best, but they must have failed, or else they forgot. No news ever came back. It will be different with me now, though. I shall find Saidee, and if she isn't happy, I shall bring her away with me. If her husband is a bad man, and if the reason he left Algiers is because he lost his money, as I sometimes think, I may have to bribe him to let her go. But I have money enough for everything, I hope—unless he's very greedy, or there are difficulties I can't foresee. In that case, I shall dance again, and make more money, you know—that's all there is about it."

"One thing I do know, is that you are wonderful," said Stephen, his conscience pricking him because of certain unjust thoughts concerning this child which he had harboured since learning that she was a dancer. "You're the most wonderful girl I ever saw or heard of."

She laughed happily. "Oh no, I'm not wonderful at all. It's funny you should think so. Perhaps none of the girls you know have had a big work to do."

"I'm sure they never have," said Stephen, "and if they had, they wouldn't have done it."

"Yes, they would. Anybody would—that is, if they wanted to, *enough*. You can always do what you want to *enough*. I wanted to do this with all my heart and soul, so I knew I should find the way. I just followed my instinct, when people told me I was unreasonable, and of course it led me right. Reason is only to depend on in scientific sorts of things, isn't it? The other is higher, because instinct is your *You*."

"Isn't that what people say who preach New Thought, or whatever they call it?" asked Stephen. "A lot of women I know had rather a craze about that two or three years ago. They went to lectures given by an American man they raved over—said he was 'too fascinating.' And they used their 'science' to win at bridge. I don't know whether it worked or not."

"I never heard any one talk of New Thought," said Victoria. "I've just had my own thoughts about everything. The attic at school was a lovely place to think thoughts in. Wonderful ones always came to me, if I called to them—thoughts all glittering—like angels. They seemed to bring me new ideas about things I'd been born knowing— beautiful things, which I feel somehow have been handed down to me—in my blood."

"Why, that's the way my friends used to talk about 'waking their race-consciousness.' But it only led to bridge, with them."

"Well, it's led me from Potterston here," said Victoria, "and it will lead me on to the end, wherever that may be, I'm sure. Perhaps it will lead me far, far off, into that mysterious golden silence, where in dreams I often see Saidee watching for me: the strangest dream- place, and I've no idea where it is! But I shall find out, if she is really there."

"What supreme confidence you have in your star!" Stephen exclaimed, admiringly, and half enviously.

"Of course. Haven't you, in yours?"

"I have no star."

She turned her eyes to his, quickly, as if grieved. And in his eyes she saw the shadow of hopelessness which was there to see, and could not be hidden from a clear gaze.

"I'm sorry," she said simply. "I don't know how I could have lived without mine. I walk in its light, as if in a path. But yours must be somewhere in the sky, and you can find it if you want to very much."

He could have found two in her eyes just then, but such stars were not for him. "Perhaps I don't deserve a star," he said.

"I'm sure you do. You are the kind that does," the girl comforted him. "Do have a star!"

"It would only make me unhappy, because I mightn't be able to walk in its light, as you do."

"It would make you very happy, as mine does me. I'm always happy, because the light helps me to do things. It helped me to dance: it helped me to succeed."

"Tell me about your dancing," said Stephen, vaguely anxious to change the subject, and escape from thoughts of Margot, the only star of his future. "I should like to hear how you began, if you don't mind."

"That's kind of you," replied Victoria, gratefully.

He laughed. "Kind!"

"Why, it's nothing of a story. Luckily, I'd always danced. So when I was fourteen, and began to think I should never have any money of my own after all, I saw that dancing would be my best way of earning it, as that was the one thing I could do very well. Afterwards I worked in real earnest—always up in the attic, where I used to study the Arabic language too; study it very hard. And no one knew what I was doing or what was in my head, till last year when I told the oldest Miss Jennings that I couldn't be a teacher—that I must leave school and go to New York."

"What did she say?"

"She said I was crazy. So did they all. They got the minister to come and argue with me, and he was dreadfully opposed to my wishes at first. But after we'd talked a while, he came round to my way."

"How did you persuade him to that point of view?" Stephen catechized her, wondering always.

"I hardly know. I just told him how I felt about everything. Oh, and I danced."

"By Jove! What effect had that on him?"

"He clapped his hands and said it was a good dance, quite different from what he expected. He didn't think it would do any one harm to see. And he gave me a sort of lecture about how I ought to behave if

I became a dancer. It was easy to follow his advice, because none of the bad things he feared might happen to me ever did."

"Your star protected you?"

"Of course. There was a little trouble about money at first, because I hadn't any, but I had a few things—a watch that had been my mother's, and her engagement ring (they were Saidee's, but she left them both for me when she went away), and a queer kind of brooch Cassim ben Halim gave me one day, out of a lovely mother-o'-pearl box he brought full of jewels for Saidee, when they were engaged. See, I have the brooch on now—for I wouldn't *sell* the things. I went to a shop in Potterston and asked the man to lend me fifty dollars on them all, so he did. It was very good of him."

"You seem to consider everybody you meet kind and good," Stephen said.

"Yes, they almost always have been so to me. If you believe people are going to be good, it *makes* them good, unless they're very bad indeed."

"Perhaps." Stephen would not for a great deal have tried to undermine her confidence in her fellow beings, and such was the power of the girl's personality, that for the moment he was half inclined to feel she might be right. Who could tell? Maybe he had not "believed" enough—in Margot. He looked with interest at the brooch of which Miss Ray spoke, a curiously wrought, flattened ring of dull gold, with a pin in the middle which pierced and fastened her chiffon veil on her breast. Round the edge, irregularly shaped pearls alternated with roughly cut emeralds, and there was a barbaric beauty in both workmanship and colour.

"What happened when you got to your journey's end?" he went on, fearing to go astray on that subject of the world's goodness, which was a sore point with him lately. "Did you know anybody in New York?"

"Nobody. But I asked the driver of a cab if he could take me to a respectable theatrical boarding-house, and he said he could, so I told him to drive me there. I engaged a wee back room at the top of the house, and paid a week in advance. The boarders weren't very successful people, poor things, for it was a cheap boarding-house—it had to be, for me. But they all knew which were the best theatres and managers, and they were interested when they heard I'd come to try and get a chance to be a dancer. They were afraid it wasn't much use, but the same evening they changed their minds, and gave me lots of good advice."

"You danced for them?"

"Yes, in such a stuffy parlour, smelling of gas and dust and there were holes in the carpet it was difficult not to step into. A dear old man without any hair, who was on what he called the 'Variety Stage,' advised me to go and try to see Mr. Charles Norman, a fearfully important person—so important that even I had heard of him, away out in Indiana. I did try, day after day, but he was too important to be got at. I wouldn't be discouraged, though. I knew Mr. Norman must come to the theatre sometimes, so I bought a photograph in order to recognize him; and one day when he passed me, going in, I screwed up my courage and spoke. I said I'd been waiting for days and days. At first he scowled, and I think meant to be cross, but when he'd given me one long, terrifying glare, he grumbled out: "Come along with me, then. I'll soon see what you can do." I went in, and danced on an almost dark stage, with Mr. Norman and another man looking at me, in the empty theatre where all the chairs and boxes were covered up with sheets. They seemed rather pleased with my dancing, and Mr. Norman said he would give me a chance. Then, if I 'caught on'—he meant if people liked me—I should have a salary. But I told him I must have the salary at once, as my money would only last a few more days. I'd spent nearly all I had, getting to New York. Very well, said he, I should have thirty dollars a week to begin with, and after that, we'd see what we'd see. Well, people did like my dances, and by and by Mr. Norman gave me what seemed then a splendid salary. So now you know everything that's happened; and please don't think I'd have worried you by talking so much about myself, if you hadn't asked questions. I'm afraid I oughtn't to have done it, anyway."

Her tone changed, and became almost apologetic. She stirred uneasily in her deck chair, and looked about half dazedly, as people look about a room that is new to them, on waking there for the first time. "Why, it's grown dark!" she exclaimed.

This fact surprised Stephen equally. "So it has," he said. "By Jove, I was so interested in you—in what you were telling—I hadn't noticed. I'd forgotten where we were."

"I'd forgotten, too," said Victoria. "I always do forget outside things when I think about Saidee, and the golden dream-silence where I see her. All the people who were near us on deck have gone away. Did you see them go?"

"No," said Stephen, "I didn't."

"How odd!" exclaimed the girl.

"Do you think so? You had taken me to the golden silence with you."

"Where can everybody be?" She spoke anxiously. "Is it late? Maybe they've gone to get ready for dinner."

From a small bag she wore at her belt, American tourist-fashion, she pulled out an old-fashioned gold watch of the kind that winds up with a key—her mother's, perhaps, on which she had borrowed money to reach New York. "Something must be wrong with my watch," she said. "It can't be twenty minutes past eight."

The same thing was wrong with Stephen's expensive repeater, whose splendour he was ashamed to flaunt beside the modesty of the girl's poor little timepiece. There remained now no reasonable doubt that it was indeed twenty minutes past eight, since by the mouths of two witnesses a truth can be established.

"How dreadful!" exclaimed Victoria, mortified. "I've kept you here all this time, listening to me."

"Didn't I tell you I'd rather listen to you than anything else? Eating was certainly not excepted. I don't remember hearing the bugle."

"And I didn't hear it."

"I'd forgotten dinner. You had carried me so far away with you."

"And Saidee," added the girl. "Thank you for going with us."

"Thank you for taking me."

They both laughed, and as they laughed, people began streaming out on deck. Dinner was over. The handsome Arab passed, talking with the spare, loose-limbed English parson, whom he had fascinated. They were discussing affairs in Morocco, and as they passed Stephen and Victoria, the Arab did not appear to turn; yet

Stephen knew that he was thinking of them and not of what he was saying to the clergyman.

"What shall we do?" asked Victoria.

Stephen reflected for an instant. "Will you invite me to dine at your table?" he asked.

"Maybe they'll tell us it's too late now to have anything to eat. I don't mind for myself, but for you——"

"We'll have a better dinner than the others have had," Stephen prophesied. "I guarantee it, if you invite me."

"Oh, do please come," she implored, like a child. "I couldn't face the waiters alone. And you know, I feel as if you were a friend, now—though you may laugh at that."

"It's the best compliment I ever had," said Stephen. "And—it gives me faith in myself—which I need."

"And your star, which you're to find," the girl reminded him, as he unrolled her from her rug.

"I wish you'd lend me a little of the light from yours, to find mine by," he said half gaily, yet with a certain wistfulness which she detected under the laugh.

"I will," she said quickly. "Not a little, but half."

VI

Stephen's prophecy came true. They had a better dinner than any one else had, and enjoyed it as an adventure. Victoria thought their waiter a particularly good-natured man, because instead of sulking over his duties he beamed. Stephen might, if he had chosen, have thrown another light upon the waiter's smiles; but he didn't choose. And he was happy. He gave Victoria good advice, and promised help from Nevill Caird. "He's sure to meet me at the ship," he said, "and if you'll let me, I'll introduce him to you. He may be able to find out everything you want to know."

Stephen would have liked to go on talking after dinner, but the girl, ashamed of having taken up so much of his time, would not be tempted. She went to her cabin, and thought of him, as well as of her sister; and he thought of her while he walked on deck, under the stars.

"For a moment white, then gone forever."

Again the words came singing into his head. She was white — white as this lacelike foam that silvered the Mediterranean blue; but she had not gone forever, as he had thought when he likened her whiteness to the spindrift on the dark Channel waves. She had come into his life once more, unexpectedly; and she might brighten it again for a short time on land, in that unknown garden his thoughts pictured, behind the gate of the East. Yet she would not be of his life. There was no place in it for a girl. Still, he thought of her, and went on thinking, involuntarily planning things which he and Nevill Caird would do to help the child, in her romantic errand. Of course she must not be allowed to travel about Algeria alone. Once settled in Algiers she must stay there quietly till the authorities found her sister.

He used that powerful-sounding word "authorities" vaguely in his mind, but he was sure that the thing would be simple enough. The police could be applied to, if Nevill and his friends should be unable to discover Ben Halim and his American wife. Almost unconsciously, Stephen saw himself earning Victoria Ray's gratitude. It was a pleasant fancy, and he followed it as one wanders down a flowery path found in a dark forest.

Victoria's thoughts of him were as many, though different.

She had never filled her mind with nonsense about men, as many girls do. As she would have said to herself, she had been too busy. When girls at school had talked of being in love, and of marrying, she had been interested, as if in a story-book, but it had not seemed to her that she would ever fall in love or be married. It seemed so less than ever, now that she was at last actually on her way to look for Saidee. She was intensely excited, and there was room only for the one absorbing thought in mind and heart; yet she was not as anxious as most others would have been in her place. Now that Heaven had helped her so far, she was sure she would be helped to the end. It would be too bad to be true that anything dreadful should have happened to Saidee— anything from which she, Victoria, could not save her; and so now, very soon perhaps, everything would come right. It seemed to the girl that somehow Stephen was part of a great scheme, that he had been sent into her life for a purpose. Otherwise, why should he have been so kind since the first, and have appeared this second time, when she had almost forgotten him in the press of other thoughts? Why should he be going where she was going, and why should he have a friend who had known Algiers and Algeria since the time when Saidee's letters had ceased?

All these arguments were childlike; but Victoria Ray had not passed far beyond childhood; and though her ideas of religion were her own—unlearned and unconventional—such as they were they meant everything to her. Many things which she had heard in churches had seemed unreal to the girl; but she believed that the Great Power moving the Universe planned her affairs as well as the affairs of the stars, and with equal interest. She thought that her soul was a spark given out by that Power, and that what was God in her had only to call to the All of God to be answered. She had called, asking to find Saidee, and now she was going to find her, just how she did not yet know; but she hardly doubted that Stephen Knight was connected with the way. Otherwise, what was the good of him to her? And Victoria was far too humble in her opinion of herself, despite that buoyant confidence in her star, to imagine that she could be of any use to him. She could be useful to Saidee; that was all. She hoped for nothing more. And little as she knew of society, she understood that Stephen belonged to a different world from hers; the world where people were rich, and gay, and clever, and amused themselves; the high world, from a social point of view. She supposed, too, that Stephen looked upon her as a little girl, while she in her turn regarded him gratefully and admiringly, as from a distance. And she believed that he must be a very good man.

It would never have occurred to Victoria Ray to call him, even in thought, her "White Knight," as Margot Lorenzi persisted in calling him, and had called him in the famous interview. But it struck her, the moment she heard his name, that it somehow fitted him like a suit of armour. She was fond of finding an appropriateness in names, and sometimes, if she were tired or a little discouraged, she repeated her own aloud, several times over: "Victoria, Victoria. I am Victoria," until she felt strong again to conquer every difficulty which might rise against her, in living up to her name. Now she was of opinion that Stephen's face would do very well in the picture of a young knight of olden days, going out to fight for the True Cross. Indeed, he looked as if he had already passed through the preparation of a long vigil, for his face was worn, and his eyes seldom smiled even when he laughed and seemed amused. His features gave her an idea that the Creator had taken a great deal of pains in chiselling them, not slighting a single line. She had seen handsomer men—indeed, the splendid Arab on the ship was handsomer—but she thought, if she were a general who wanted a man to lead a forlorn hope which meant almost certain death, she would choose one of Stephen's type. She had the impression that he would not hesitate to sacrifice himself for a cause, or even for a person, in an emergency, although he had the air of one used to good fortune, who loved to take his own way in the small things of life.

And so she finally went to sleep thinking of Stephen.

It is seldom that even the *Charles Quex*, one of the fastest ships plying between Marseilles and Algiers, makes the trip in eighteen hours, as advertised. Generally she takes two half-days and a night, but this time people began to say that she would do it in twenty-two hours. Very early in the dawning she passed the Balearic Isles, mysterious purple in an opal sea, and it was not yet noon when the jagged line of the Atlas Mountains hovered in pale blue shadow along a paler horizon. Then, as the turbines whirred, the shadow materialized, taking a golden solidity and wildness of outline. At length the tower of a lighthouse started out clear white against blue, as a shaft of sunshine struck it. Next, the nearer mountains slowly turned to green, as a chameleon changes: the Admiralty Island came clearly into view; the ancient nest of those fierce pirates who for centuries scourged the Mediterranean; and last of all, the climbing town of Algiers, old Al-Djézair-el-Bahadja, took form like thick patterns of mother-o'-pearl set in bright green enamel, the patterns eventually separating themselves into individual buildings. The strange, bulbous domes of a Byzantine cathedral on a hill sprang up like a huge tropical plant of many flowers, unfolding fantastic buds of deep rose-colour, against a sky of violet flame.

"At last, Africa!" said Victoria, standing beside Stephen, and leaning on the rail. She spoke to herself, half whispering the words, hardly aware that she uttered them, but Stephen heard. The two had not been long together during the morning, for each had been shy of giving too much of himself or herself, although they had secretly wished for each other's society. As the voyage drew to a close, however, Stephen was no longer able to resist an attraction which he felt like a compelling magnetism. His excuse was that he wanted to know Miss Ray's first impressions of the place she had constantly seen in her thoughts during ten years.

"Is it like what you expected?" he asked.

"Yes," she said, "it's like, because I have photographs. And I've read every book I could get hold of, old and new, in French as well as English. I always kept up my French, you know, for the same reason that I studied Arabic. I think I could tell the names of some of the buildings, without making mistakes. Yet it looks different, as the living face of a person is different from a portrait in black and white. And I never imagined such a sky. I didn't know skies could be of such a colour. It's as if pale fire were burning behind a thin veil of blue."

It was as she said. Stephen had seen vivid skies on the Riviera, but there the blue was more opaque, like the blue of the turquoise. Here it was ethereal and quivering, like the violet fire that hovers over burning ship-logs. He was glad the sky of Africa was unlike any other sky he had known. It intensified the thrill of enchantment he had begun to feel. It seemed to him that it might be possible for a man to forget things in a country where even the sky was of another blue.

Sometimes, when Stephen had read in books of travel (at which he seldom even glanced), or in novels, about "the mystery of the East," he had smiled in a superior way. Why should the East be more mysterious than the West, or North, or South, except that women were shut up in harems and wore veils if they stirred out of doors? Such customs could scarcely make a whole country mysterious. But now, though he had not yet landed, he knew that he would be compelled to acknowledge the indefinable mystery at which he had sneered. Already he fancied an elusive influence, like the touch of a ghost. It was in the pulsing azure of the sky; in the wild forms of the Atlas and far Kabyle mountains stretching into vague, pale distances; in the ivory white of the low-domed roofs that gleamed against the vivid green hill of the Sahel, like pearls on a veiled woman's breast.

"Is it what you thought it would be?" Victoria inquired in her turn.

"I hadn't thought much about it," Stephen had to confess, fearing she would consider such indifference uninteresting. He did not add what remained of the truth, that he had thought of Algiers as a refuge from what had become disagreeable, rather than as a beautiful place which he wished to see for its own sake. "I'd made no picture in my mind. You know a lot more about it all than I do, though you've lived so far away, and I within a distance of forty- eight hours."

"That great copper-coloured church high on the hill is Notre Dame d'Afrique," said the girl. "She's like a dark sister of Notre Dame de la Garde, who watches over Marseilles, isn't she? I think I could love her, though she's ugly, really. And I've read in a book that if you walk up the hill to visit her and say a prayer, you may have a hundred days' indulgence."

Much good an "indulgence" would do him now, Stephen thought bitterly.

As the ship steamed closer inshore, the dreamlike beauty of the white town on the green hillside sharpened into a reality which might have seemed disappointingly modern and French, had it not been for the sprinkling of domes, the pointing fingers of minarets with glittering tiles of bronzy green, and the groups of old Arab houses crowded in among the crudities of a new, Western civilization. Down by the wharf for which the boat aimed like a homing bird, were huddled a few of these houses, ancient dwellings turned into commercial offices where shipping business was transacted. They looked forlorn, yet beautiful, like haggard slavewomen who remembered days of greatness in a far-off land.

The *Charles Quex* slackened speed as she neared the harbour, and every detail of the town leaped to the eyes, dazzling in the southern sunshine. The encircling arms of break-waters were flung out to sea in a vast embrace; the smoke of vessels threaded with dark, wavy lines the pure crystal of the air; the quays were heaped with merchandise, some of it in bales, as if it might have been brought by caravans across the desert. There was a clanking of cranes at work, a creaking of chains, a flapping of canvas, and many sounds which blend in the harsh poetry of sea-harbours. Then voices of men rose shrilly above all heavier noises, as the ship slowly turned and crept beside a floating pontoon. The journey together was over for Stephen Knight and Victoria Ray.

VII

A first glance, at such close quarters, would have told the least instructed stranger that he was in the presence of two clashing civilizations, both tenacious, one powerful.

In front, all along the shore, towered with confident effrontery a massive line of buildings many stories high, great cubes of brick and stone, having elaborate balconies that shadowed swarming offices with dark, gaping vaults below. Along the broad, stone-paved street clanged electric tramcars. There was a constant coming and going of men. Cloaked and hooded white forms, or half-clad apparitions wrapped in what looked like dirty bagging, mingled with commonplace figures in Western dress. But huddled in elbow-high with this busy town of modern France (which might have been Marseilles or Bordeaux) was something alien, something remote in spirit; a ghostly band of white buildings, silent and pale in the midst of colour and noise. Low houses with flat roofs or miniature domes, small, secret doorways, tiny windows like eyes narrowed for spying, and overhanging upper stories supported on close-set, projecting sticks of mellow brown which meant great age. Minarets sprang up in mute protest against the infidel, appealing to the sky. All that was left of old Algiers tried to boast, in forced dumbness, of past glories, of every charm the beautiful, fierce city of pirates must have possessed before the French came to push it slowly but with deadly sureness back from the sea. Now, silent and proud in the tragedy of failure, it stood masked behind pretentious French houses, blocklike in ugliness, or flauntingly ornate as many buildings in the Rue de Rivoli or Boulevard Haussmann.

In those low-browed dwellings which thickly enamelled the hill with a mosaic of pink and pearly whiteness, all the way up to the old fortress castle, the Kasbah, the true life of African Algiers hid and whispered. The modern French front along the fine street was but a gay veneer concealing realities, an incrusted civilization imposed upon one incredibly ancient, unspeakably different and ever unchanging.

Stephen remembered now that he had heard people decry Algiers, pronouncing it spoiled and "completely Frenchified." But it occurred to him that in this very process of spoiling, an impression of tragic romance had been created which less "spoiled" towns might lack.

Here were clashing contrasts which, even at a glance, made the strangest picture he had ever seen; and already he began to feel more and more keenly, though not yet to understand, something of the magic of the East. For this place, though not the East according to geographers, held all the spirit of the East—was in essence truly the East.

Before the ship lay fairly in harbour, brown men had climbed on board from little boats, demanding to be given charge of the passengers' small luggage, which the stewards had brought on deck, and while one of these was arguing in bad French with Stephen, a tall, dark youth beautifully dressed in crimson and white, wearing a fez jauntily on one side, stepped up with a smile. *"Pardon, monsieur,"* he ventured. *"Je suis le domestique de Monsieur Caird."* And then, in richly guttural accents, he offered the information that he was charged to look after monsieur's baggage; that it was best to avoid *tous ces Arabes là,* and that Monsieur Caird impatiently awaited his friend on the wharf.

"But you—aren't you Arab?" asked Stephen, who knew no subtle differences between those who wore the turban or fez. He saw that the good-looking, merry-faced boy was no browner than many a Frenchman of the south, and that his eyes were hazel; still, he did not know what he might be, if not Arab.

"Je suis Kabyle, monsieur; Kabyle des hauts plateaux," replied the youth with pride, and a look of contempt at the shouting porters, which was returned with interest. They darted glances of scorn at his gold-braided vest and jacket of crimson cloth, his light blue sash, and his enormously full white trousers, beneath which showed a strip of pale golden leg above the short white stockings, spurning the immaculate smartness of his livery, preferring, or pretending to prefer, their own soiled shabbiness and freedom. The Kabyle saw these glances, but, completely satisfied with himself, evidently attributed them to envy.

Stephen turned towards Victoria, of whom he had lost sight for a moment. He wished to offer the Kabyle boy's services, but already she had accepted those of a very old Arab who looked thin and ostentatiously pathetic. It was too late now. He saw by her face that she would refuse help, rather than hurt the man's feelings. But she had told him the name of the hotel where she had telegraphed to engage a room, and Stephen meant at the instant of greeting his host, to ask if it were suitable for a young girl travelling alone.

He caught sight of Caird, looking up and waiting for him, before he was able to land. It was the face he remembered; boyish, with beautiful bright eyes, a wide forehead, and curly light hair. The expression was more mature, but the same quaintly angelic look was there, which had earned for Nevill the nickname of "Choir Boy" and "Wings."

"Hullo, Legs!" called out Caird, waving his Panama.

"Hullo, Wings!" shouted Stephen, and was suddenly tremendously glad to see the friend he had thought of seldom during the last eight or nine years. In another moment he was introducing Nevill to Miss Ray and hastily asking questions concerning her hotel, while a fantastic crowd surged round all three. Brown, skurrying men in torn bagging, the muscles of whose bare, hairless legs seemed carved in dark oak; shining black men whose faces were ebony under the ivory white of their turbans; pale, patient Kabyles of the plains bent under great sacks of flour which drained through ill-sewn seams and floated on the air in white smoke, making every one sneeze as the crowd swarmed past. Large grey mules roared, miniature donkeys brayed, and half-naked children laughed or howled, and darted under the heads of the horses, or fell against the bright bonnets of waiting motor cars. There were smart victorias, shabby cabs, hotel omnibuses, and huge carts; and, mingling with the floating dust of the spilt flour was a heavy perfume of spices, of incense perhaps blown from some far-off mosque, and ambergris mixed with grains of musk in amulets which the Arabs wore round their necks, heated by their sweating flesh as they worked or stalked about shouting guttural orders. There was a salt tang of seaweed, too, like an undertone, a foundation for all the other smells; and the air was warm with a hint of summer, a softness that was not enervating.

As soon as the first greeting and the introduction to Miss Ray were confusedly over, Caird cleverly extricated the newcomers from the thick of the throng, sheltering them between his large yellow motor car and a hotel omnibus waiting for passengers and luggage.

"Now you're safe," he said, in the young-sounding voice which pleasantly matched his whole personality. He was several years older than Stephen, but looked younger, for Stephen was nearly if not quite six feet in height, and Nevill Caird was less in stature by at least four inches. He was very slightly built, too, and his hair was as yellow as a child's. His face was clean-shaven, like Stephen's, and though Stephen, living mostly in London, was brown as if tanned by the sun, Nevill, out of doors constantly and exposed to hot southern sunshine, had the complexion of a girl. Nevertheless, thought Victoria—sensitive and quick in forming impressions—he somehow contrived to look a thorough man, passionate and ready to be violently in earnest, like one who would love or hate in a fiery way. "He would make a splendid martyr," the girl said to herself, giving him straight look for straight look, as he began advising her against her chosen hotel. "But I think he would want his best friends to come and look on while he burned. Mr. Knight would chase everybody away."

"Don't go to any hotel," Nevill said. "Be my aunt's guest. It's a great deal more her house than mine. There's lots of room in it—ever so much more than we want. Just now there's no one staying with us, but often we have a dozen or so. Sometimes my aunt invites people. Sometimes I do: sometimes both together. Now I invite you, in her name. She's quite a nice old lady. You'll like her. And we've got all kinds of animals—everything, nearly, that will live in this climate, from tortoises of Carthage, to white mice from Japan, and a baby panther from Grand Kabylia. But they keep themselves to themselves. I promise you the panther won't try to sit on your lap. And you'll be just in time to christen him. We've been looking for a name."

"I should love to christen the panther, and you are more than kind to say your aunt would like me to visit her; but I can't possibly, thank you very much," answered Victoria in the old-fashioned, quaintly provincial way which somehow intensified the effect of her brilliant prettiness. "I have come to Algiers on—on business that's very important to me. Mr. Knight will tell you all about it. I've asked him to tell, and he's promised to beg for your help. When you know, you'll see that it will be better for me not to be visiting anybody. I—I would rather be in a hotel, in spite of your great kindness."

That settled the matter. Nevill Caird had too much tact to insist, though he was far from being convinced. He said that his aunt, Lady MacGregor, would write Miss Ray a note asking her to lunch next day, and then they would have the panther-christening. Also by that time he would know, from his friend, how his help might best be given. But in any case he hoped that Miss Ray would allow his car to drop her at the Hotel de la Kasbah, which had no omnibus and therefore did not send to meet the boat. Her luggage might go up with the rest, and be left at the hotel.

These offers Victoria accepted gratefully; and as Caird put her into the fine yellow car, the handsome Arab who had been on the boat looked at her with chastened curiosity as he passed. He must have seen that she was with the Englishman who had talked to her on board the *Charles Quex*, and that now there was another man, who seemed to be the owner of the large automobile. The Arab had a servant with him, who had travelled second class on the boat, a man much darker than himself, plainly dressed, with a smaller turban bound by cheaper cord; but he was very clean, and as dignified as his master. Stephen scarcely noticed the two figures. The fine- looking Arab had ceased to be of importance since he had left the ship, and would see no more of Victoria Ray.

The chauffeur who drove Nevill's car was an Algerian who looked as if he might have a dash of dark blood in his veins. Beside him sat the Kabyle servant, who, in his picturesque embroidered clothes, with his jaunty fez, appeared amusingly out of place in the smart automobile, which struck the last note of modernity. The chauffeur had a reckless, daring face, with the smile of a mischievous boy; but he steered with caution and skill through the crowded streets where open trams rushed by, filled to overflowing with white-veiled Arab women of the lower classes, and French girls in large hats, who sat crushed together on the same seats. Arabs walked in the middle of the street, and disdained to quicken their steps for motor cars and carriages. Tiny children with charming brown faces and eyes like wells of light, darted out from the pavement, almost in front of the motor, smiling and begging, absolutely, fearless and engagingly impudent. It was all intensely interesting to Stephen, who was, however, conscious enough of his past to be glad that he was able to take so keen an interest. He had the sensation of a man who has been partially paralyzed, and is delighted to find that he can feel a pinch.

The Hotel de la Kasbah, which Victoria frankly admitted she had chosen because of its low prices, was, as its name indicated, close to the mounting of the town, near the corner of a tortuous Arab street, narrow and shadowy despite its thick coat of whitewash. The house was kept by an extremely fat Algerian, married to a woman who called herself Spanish, but was more than half Moorish; and the proprietor himself being of mixed blood, all the servants except an Algerian maid or two, were Kabyles or Arabs. They were cheap and easy to manage, since master and mistress had no prejudices. Stephen did not like the look of the place, which might suit commercial travellers or parties of economical tourists who liked to rub shoulders with native life; but for a pretty young girl travelling alone, it seemed to him that, though it was clean enough, nothing could be less appropriate. Victoria had made up her mind and engaged her room, however; and so as no definite objection could be urged, he followed Caird's example, and held his tongue. As they bade the girl good-bye in the tiled hall (a fearful combination of all that was worst in Arab and European taste) Nevill begged her to let them know if she were not comfortable. "You're coming to lunch to-morrow at half-past one," he went on, "but if there's anything meanwhile, call us up on the telephone. We can easily find you another hotel, or a pension, if you're determined not to visit my aunt."

"If I need you, I promise that I will call," Victoria said. And though she answered Caird, she looked at Stephen Knight.

Then they left her; and Stephen became rather thoughtful. But he tried not to let Nevill see his preoccupation.

VIII

As they left the arcaded streets of commercial Algiers, and drove up the long hill towards Mustapha Supérieur, where most of the best and finest houses are, Stephen and Nevill Caird talked of what they saw, and of Victoria Ray; not at all of Stephen himself. Nevill had asked him what sort of trip he had had, and not another question of any sort. Stephen was glad of this, and understood very well that it was not because his friend was indifferent. Had he been so, he would not have invited Stephen to make this visit.

To speak of the past they had shared, long ago, would naturally have led farther, and though Stephen was not sure that he mightn't some day refer, of his own accord, to the distasteful subject of the Case and Margot Lorenzi, he could not have borne to mention either now.

As they passed gateways leading to handsome houses, mostly in the Arab style, Nevill told him who lived in each one: French, English, and American families; people connected with the government, who remained in Algiers all the year round, or foreigners who came out every winter for love of their beautiful villa gardens and the climate.

"We've rather an amusing society here," he said. "And we'd defend Algiers and each other to any outsider, though our greatest pleasure is quarrelling among ourselves, or patching up one another's rows and beginning again on our own account. It's great fun and keeps us from stagnating. We also give quantities of luncheons and teas, and are sick of going to each other's entertainments; yet we're so furious if there's anything we're not invited to, we nearly get jaundice. I do myself—though I hate running about promiscuously; and I spend hours thinking up ingenious lies to squeeze out of accepting invitations I'd have been ill with rage not to get. And there are factions which loathe each other worse than any mere Montagus and Capulets. We have rival parties, and vie with one another in getting hold of any royalties or such like, that may be knocking about; but we who hate each other most, meet at the Governor's Palace and smile sweetly if French people are looking; if not, we snort like war- horses—only in a whisper, for we're invariably polite."

Stephen laughed, as he was meant to do. "What about the Arabs?" he asked, with Victoria's errand in his mind. "Is there such a thing as Arab society?"

"Very little—of the kind we'd call 'society'—in Algiers. In Tunis there's more. Much of the old Arab aristocracy has died out here, or moved away; but there are a few left who are rich and well born. They have their palaces outside the town; but most of the best houses have been sold to Europeans, and their Arab owners have gone into the interior where the Roumis don't rub elbows with them quite as offensively as in a big French town like this. Naturally they prefer the country. And I know a few of the great Arab Chiefs— splendid-looking fellows who turn up gorgeously dressed for the Governor's ball every year, and condescend to dine with me once or twice while they're staying on to amuse themselves in Algiers."

"Condescend!" Stephen repeated.

"By Jove, yes. I'm sure they think it's a great condescension. And I'm not sure you won't think so too, when you see them—as of course you will. You must go to the Governor's ball with me, even if you can't be bothered going anywhere else. It's a magnificent spectacle. And I get on pretty well among the Arabs, as I've learned to speak their lingo a bit. Not that I've worried. But nearly nine years is a long time."

This was Stephen's chance to tell what he chose to tell of his brief acquaintance with Victoria Ray, and of the mission which had brought her to Algiers. Somehow, as he unfolded the story he had heard from the girl on board ship, the scent of orange blossoms, luscious-sweet in this region of gardens, connected itself in his mind with thoughts of the beautiful woman who had married Cassim ben Halim, and disappeared from the world she had known. He imagined her in an Arab garden where orange blossoms fell like snow, eating her heart out for the far country and friends she would never see again, rebelling against a monstrous tyranny which imprisoned her in this place of perfumes and high white walls. Or perhaps the scented petals were falling now upon her grave.

"Cassim ben Halim—Captain Cassim ben Halim," Nevill repeated. "Seems familiar somehow, as if I'd heard the name; but most of these Arab names have a kind of family likeness in our ears. Either he's a person of no particular importance, or else he must have left Algiers before my Uncle James Caird died—the man who willed me his house, you know—brother of Aunt Caroline MacGregor who lives with me now. If I've ever heard anything about Ben Halim, whatever it is has slipped my mind. But I'll do my best to find out something."

"Miss Ray believes he was of importance," said Stephen. "She oughtn't to have much trouble getting on to his trail, should you think?"

Nevill looked doubtful. "Well, if he'd wanted her on his trail, she'd never have been off it. If he didn't, and doesn't, care to be got at, finding him mayn't be as simple as it would be in Europe, where you can always resort to detectives if worst comes to worst."

"Can't you here?" asked Stephen.

"Well, there's the French police, of course, and the military in the south. But they don't care to interfere with the private affairs of Arabs, if no crime's been committed—and they wouldn't do anything in such a case, I should think, in the way of looking up Ben Halim, though they'd tell anything they might happen to know already, I suppose— unless they thought best to keep silence with foreigners."

"There must be people in Algiers who'd remember seeing such a beautiful creature as Ben Halim's wife, even if her husband whisked her away nine years ago," Stephen argued.

"I wonder?" murmured Caird, with an emphasis which struck his friend as odd.

"What do you mean?" asked Stephen.

"I mean, I wonder if any one in Algiers ever saw her at all? Ben Halim was in the French Army; but he was a Mussulman. Paris and Algiers are a long cry, one from the other—if you're an Arab."

"Jove! You don't think——"

"You've spotted it. That's what I do think."

"That he shut her up?"

"That he forced her to live the life of a Mussulman woman. Why, what else could you expect, when you come to look at it?"

"But an American girl——"

"A woman who marries gives herself to her husband's nation as well as to her husband, doesn't she—especially if he's an Arab? Only, thank God, it happens to very few European girls, except of the class that doesn't so much matter. Think of it. This Ben Halim, a Spahi officer, falls dead in love with a girl when he's on leave in Paris. He feels he must have her. He can get her only by marriage. They're as subtle as the devil, even the best of them, these Arabs. He'd have to promise the girl anything she wanted, or lose her. Naturally he wouldn't give it away that he meant to veil her and clap her into a harem the minute he got her home. If he'd even hinted anything of that sort she wouldn't have stirred a step. But for a Mussulman to let his wife walk the streets unveiled, like a Roumia, or some woman of easy virtue, would be a horrible disgrace to them both. His relations and friends would cut him, and hoot her at sight. The more he loved his wife, the less likely he'd be to keep a promise, made in a different world. It wouldn't be human nature—Arab human nature—to keep it. Besides, they have the jealousy of the tiger, these Eastern fellows. It's a madness."

"Then perhaps no one ever knew, out here, that the man had brought home a foreign wife?"

"Almost surely not. No European, that is. Arabs might know— through their women. There's nothing that passes which they can't find out. How they do it, who can tell? Their ways are as mysterious as everything else here, except the lives of us *hiverneurs*, who don't even try very hard to hide our own scandals when we have any. But no Arab could be persuaded or forced to betray another Arab to a European, unless for motives of revenge. For love or hate, they stand together. In virtues and vices they're absolutely different from Europeans. And if Ben Halim doesn't want anybody, not excepting his wife's sister, to get news of his wife, why, it may be difficult to get it, that's all I say. Going to Miss Ray's hotel, you could see something of that Arab street close by, on the fringe of the Kasbah— which is what they call, not the old fort alone, but the whole Arab town."

"Yes. I saw the queer white houses, huddled together, that looked like blank walls only broken by a door, with here and there a barred window."

"Well, what I mean is that it's almost impossible for any European to learn what goes on behind those blank walls and those little square holes, in respectable houses. But we'll hope for the best. And here we are at my place. I'm rather proud of it."

They had come to the arched gateway of a white-walled garden. The sun had set fire to the gold of some sunken Arab lettering over the central arch, so that each broken line darted forth its separate flame. "Djenan el Djouad; House of the Nobleman," Nevill translated. "It was built for the great confidant of a particularly wicked old Dey of Algiers, in sixteen hundred and something, and the place had been allowed to fall into ruin when my uncle bought it, about twenty or thirty years ago. There was a romance in his life, I believe. He came to Algiers for his health, as a young man, meaning to stay only a few months, but fell in love with a face which he happened to catch a glimpse of, under a veil that disarranged itself—on purpose or by accident—in a carriage belonging to a rich Arab. Because of that face he remained in Algiers, bought this house, spent years in restoring it, exactly in Arab style, and making a beautiful garden out of his fifteen or sixteen acres. Whether he ever got to know the owner of the face, history doesn't state: my uncle was as secretive as he was romantic. But odd things have been said. I expect they're still said, behind my back. And they're borne out, I'm bound to confess, by the beauty of the decorations in that part of the house intended for the ladies. Whether it was ever occupied in Uncle James's day, nobody can tell; but Aunt Caroline, his sister, who has the best rooms there now, vows she's seen the ghost of a lovely being, all spangled gauze and jewels, with silver khal-khal, or anklets, that tinkle as she moves. I assure my aunt it must be a dream, come to punish her for indulging in two goes of her favourite sweet at dinner; but in my heart I shouldn't wonder if it's true. The whole lot of us, in our family, are romantic and superstitious. We can't help it and don't want to help it, though we suffer for our foolishness often enough, goodness knows."

The scent of orange blossoms and acacias was poignantly sweet, as the car passed an Arab lodge, and wound slowly up an avenue cut through a grove of blossoming trees. The utmost pains had been taken in the laying out of the garden, but an effect of carelessness had been preserved. The place seemed a fairy tangle of white and purple lilacs, gold-dripping laburnums, acacias with festoons of pearl, roses looping from orange tree to mimosa, and a hundred gorgeous tropical flowers like painted birds and butterflies. In shadowed nooks under dark cypresses, glimmered arum lilies, sparkling with the diamond dew that sprayed from carved marble fountains, centuries old; and low seats of marble mosaiced with rare tiles stood under magnolia trees or arbours of wistaria. Giant cypresses, tall and dark as a band of Genii, marched in double line on either side the avenue as it straightened and turned towards the house.

White in the distance where that black procession halted, glittered the old Arab palace, built in one long façade, and other façades smaller, less regular, looking like so many huge blocks of marble grouped together. Over one of these blocks fell a crimson torrent of bougainvillæa; another was veiled with white roses and purple clematis; a third was showered with the gold of some strange tropical creeper that Stephen did not know.

On the roof of brown and dark-green tiles, the sunlight poured, making each tile lustrous as the scale of a serpent, and all along the edge grew tiny flowers and grasses, springing out of interstices to wave filmy threads of pink and gold.

The principal façade was blank as a wall, save for a few small, mysterious windows, barred with *grilles* of iron, green with age; but on the other façades were quaint recessed balconies, under projecting roofs supported with beams of cedar; and the door, presently opened by an Arab servant, was very old too, made of oak covered with an armour of greenish copper.

Even when it had closed behind Stephen and Nevill, they were not yet in the house, but in a large court with a ceiling of carved and painted cedar-wood supported by marble pillars of extreme lightness and grace. In front, this court was open, looking on to an inner garden with a fountain more delicate of design than those Stephen had seen outside. The three walls of the court were patterned all over with ancient tiles rare as some faded Spanish brocade in a cathedral, and along their length ran low seats where in old days sat slaves awaiting orders from their master.

Out from this court they walked through a kind of pillared cloister, and the façades of the house as they passed on, were beautiful in pure simplicity of line; so white, they seemed to turn the sun on them to moonlight; so jewelled with bands and plaques of lovely tiles, that they were like snowy shoulders of a woman hung with necklaces of precious stones.

By the time they had left this cloistered garden and threaded their way indoors, Stephen had lost his bearings completely. He was convinced that, once in, he should never find the clue which would guide him out again as he had come. There was another garden court, much larger than the first, and this, Nevill said, had been the garden of the palace-women in days of old. It had a fountain whose black marble basin was fringed with papyrus, and filled with pink, blue, and white water lilies, from under whose flat dark pads glimmered the backs of darting goldfish. Three walls of this garden had low doorways with cunningly carved doors of cedar-wood, and small, iron-barred windows festooned with the biggest roses Stephen had ever seen; but the fourth side was formed by an immense loggia with a dais at the back, and an open-fronted room at either end. Walls and floor of this loggia were tiled, and barred windows on either side the dais looked far down over a world which seemed all sky, sea, and garden. One of the little open rooms was hung with Persian prayer-rugs which Stephen thought were like fading rainbows seen through a mist; and there were queer old tinselled pictures such as good Moslems love: Borak, the steed of the prophet, half winged woman, half horse; the Prophet's uncle engaged in mighty battle; the Prophet's favourite daughter, Fatma-Zora, daintily eating her sacred breakfast. The other room at the opposite end of the tiled loggia was fitted up, Moorish fashion, for the making of coffee; walls and ceiling carved, gilded, and painted in brilliant colours; the floor tiled with the charming "windmill" pattern; many shelves adorned with countless little coffee cups in silver standards; with copper and brass utensils of all imaginable kinds; and in a gilded recess was a curious apparatus for boiling water.

Nevill Caird displayed his treasures and the beauties of his domain with an ingenuous pride, delighted at every word of appreciation, stopping Stephen here and there to point out something of which he was fond, explaining the value of certain old tiles from the point of view of an expert, and gladly lingering to answer every question. Some day, he said, he was going to write a book about tiles, a book which should have wonderful illustrations.

"Do you really like it all?" he asked, as Stephen looked out from a barred window of the loggia, over the wide view.

"I never even imagined anything so fantastically beautiful," Stephen returned warmly. "You ought to be happy, even if you could never go outside your own house and gardens. There's nothing to touch this on the Riviera. It's a palace of the 'Arabian Nights.'"

"There was a palace in the 'Arabian Nights,' if you remember," said Nevill, "where everything was perfect except one thing. Its master was miserable because he couldn't get that thing."

"The Roc's egg, of Aladdin's palace," Stephen recalled. "Do you lack a Roc's egg for yours?"

"The equivalent," said Nevill. "The one thing which I want, and don't seem likely to get, though I haven't quite given up hope. It's a woman. And she doesn't want me—or my palace. I'll tell you about her some day—soon, perhaps. And maybe you'll see her. But never mind my troubles for the moment. I can put them out of my mind with comparative ease, in the pleasure of welcoming you. Now we'll go indoors. You haven't an idea what the house is like yet. By the way, I nearly forgot this chap."

He put his hand into the pocket of his grey flannel coat, and pulled out a green frog, wrapped in a lettuce leaf which was inadequate as a garment, but a perfect match as to colour.

"I bought him on the way down to meet you," Nevill explained. "Saw an Arab kid trying to sell him in the street, poor little beast. Thought it would be a friendly act to bring him here to join my happy family, which is large and varied. I don't remember anybody living in this fountain who's likely to eat him, or be eaten by him."

Down went the frog on the wide rim of the marble fountain, and sat there, meditatively, with a dawning expression of contentment, so Stephen fancied, on his green face. He looked, Stephen thought, as if he were trying to forget a troubled past, and as if his new home with all its unexplored mysteries of reeds and lily pads were wondrously to his liking.

"I wish you'd name that person after me," said Stephen. "You're being very good to both of us,—taking us out of Hades into Paradise."

"Come along in," was Nevill Caird's only answer. But he walked into the house with his hand on Stephen's shoulder.

IX

Djenan El Djouad was a labyrinth. Stephen Knight abandoned all attempt at keeping a mental clue before he had reached the drawing-room. Nevill led him there by way of many tile-paved corridors, lit by hanging Arab lamps suspended from roofs of arabesqued cedar-wood. They went up or down marble steps, into quaint little alcoved rooms furnished with nothing but divans and low tables or dower chests crusted with Syrian mother-o'-pearl, on into rooms where brocade-hung walls were covered with Arab musical instruments of all kinds, or long-necked Moorish guns patterned with silver, ivory and coral. Here and there as they passed, were garden glimpses, between embroidered curtains, looking through windows always barred with greenish wrought iron, so old as to be rarely beautiful; and some small windows had no curtains, but were thickly frilled outside with the violent crimson of bougainvillæa, or fringed with tassels of wistaria, loop on loop of amethysts. High above these windows, which framed flowery pictures, were other windows, little and jewelled, mere plaques of filigree workmanship, fine as carved ivory or silver lace, and lined with coloured glass of delicate tints— gold, lilac, and pale rose.

"Here's the drawing-room at last," said Nevill, "and here's my aunt."

"If you can call it a drawing-room," objected a gently complaining voice. "A filled-in court, where ghosts of murdered slaves come and moan, while you have your tea. How do you do, Mr. Knight? I'm delighted you've taken pity on Nevill. He's never so happy as when he's showing a new friend the house—except when he's obtained an old tile, or a new monster of some sort, for his collection."

"In me, he kills two birds with one stone," said Stephen, smiling, as he shook the hand of a tiny lady who looked rather like an elderly fairy disguised in a cap, that could have been born nowhere except north of the Tweed.

She had delicate little features which had been made to fit a pretty child, and had never grown up. Her hair, of a reddish yellow, had faded to a yellowish white, which by a faint fillip of the imagination could be made to seem golden in some lights. Her eyes were large and round, and of a china-blue colour; her eyebrows so arched as to give her an expression of perpetual surprise, her forehead full, her cheekbones high and pink, her small, pursed mouth of the kind which prefers to hide a sense of humour, and then astonish people with it when they have ceased to believe in its existence. If her complexion had not been netted all over with a lacework of infinitesimal wrinkles, she would have looked like a little girl dressed up for an old lady. She had a ribbon of the MacGregor tartan on her cap, and an uncompromising cairngorm fastened her fichu of valuable point lace. A figure more out of place than hers in an ancient Arab palace of Algiers it would be impossible to conceive; yet it was a pleasant figure to see there, and Stephen knew that he was going to like Nevill's Aunt Caroline, Lady MacGregor.

"I wish you looked more of a monster than you do," said she, "because you might frighten the ghosts. We're eaten up with them, the way some folk in old houses are with rats. Nearly all of them slaves, too, so there's no variety, except that some are female. I've given you the room with the prettiest ghosts, but if you're not the seventh son of a seventh son, you may not see or even hear them."

"Does Nevill see or hear?" asked Stephen.

"As much as Aunt Caroline does, if the truth were known," answered her nephew. "Only she couldn't be happy unless she had a grievance. Here she wanted to choose an original and suitable one, so she hit upon ghosts—the ghosts of slaves murdered by a cruel master."

"Hit upon them, indeed!" she echoed indignantly, making her knitting needles click, a movement which displayed her pretty, miniature hands, half hidden in lace ruffles. "As if they hadn't gone through enough, in flesh and blood, poor creatures! Some of them may have been my countrymen, captured on the seas by those horrid pirates."

"Who was the cruel master?" Stephen wanted to know, still smiling, because it was almost impossible not to smile at Lady MacGregor.

"Not my brother James, I'm glad to say," she quickly replied. "It was about three hundred years before his time. And though he had some quite irritating tricks as a young man, murdering slaves wasn't one of them. To be sure, they tell strange tales of him here, as I make no doubt Nevill has already mentioned, because he's immoral enough to be proud of what he calls the romance. I mean the story of the beautiful Arab lady, whom James is supposed to have stolen from her rightful husband — that is, if an Arab can be rightful — and hidden in this house far many a year, till at last she died, after the search for her had long, long gone by."

"You're as proud of the romance as I am, or you wouldn't be at such pains to repeat it to everybody, pretending to think I've already told it," said Nevill. "But I'm going to show Knight his quarters. Pretty or plain, there are no ghosts here that will hurt him. And then we'll have lunch, for which he's starving."

Stephen's quarters consisted of a bedroom (furnished in Tunisian style, with an imposing four-poster of green and gold ornamented with a gilded, sacred cow under a crown) and a sitting room gay with colourful decorations imported from Morocco. These rooms opened upon a wide covered balcony screened by a carved wooden lattice and from the balcony Stephen could look over hills, near and far, dotted with white villas that lay like resting gulls on the green wave of verdure which cascaded down to join the blue waves of the sea. Up from that far blueness drifted on the wind a murmurous sound like Æolian harps, mingled with the tinkle of fairy mandolins in the fountain of the court below.

At luncheon, in a dining-room that opened on to a white-walled garden where only lilies of all kinds grew, to Stephen's amazement two Highlanders in kilts stood behind his hostess's chair. They were young, exactly alike, and of precisely the same height, six foot two at least. "No, you are not dreaming them, Mr. Knight," announced Lady MacGregor, evidently delighted with the admiring surprise in the look he bestowed upon these images. "And you're quite right. They *are* twins. I may as well break it to you now, as I had to do to Nevill when he invited me to come to Algiers and straighten out his housekeeping accounts: they play Ruth to my Naomi. Whither I go, they go also, even to the door of the bathroom, where they carry my towels, for I have no other maid than they."

Stephen could not help glancing at the two giants, expecting to see some involuntary quiver of eye or nostril answer electrically to this frank revelation of their office; but their countenances (impossible to think of as mere faces) remained expressionless as if carved in stone. Lady MacGregor took nothing from Mohammed and the other Kabyle servant who waited on Nevill and Stephen. Everything for her was handed to one of the Highlanders, who gravely passed on the dish to their mistress. If she refused a *plat* favoured by them, instead of carrying it away, the giants in kilts silently but firmly pressed it upon her acceptance, until in self-defence she seized some of the undesired food, and ate it under their watchful eyes.

During the meal a sudden thunderstorm boiled up out of the sea: the sky became a vast brazen bowl, and a strange, coppery twilight bleached the lilies in the white garden to a supernatural pallor. The room, with its embroidered Moorish hangings, darkened to a rich gloom; but Mohammed touched a button on the wall, and all the quaint old Arab lamps that stood in corners, or hung suspended from the cedar roof, flashed out cunningly concealed electric lights. At the same moment, there began a great howling outside the door. Mohammed sprang to open it, and in poured a wave of animals. Stephen hastily counted five dogs; a collie, a white deerhound, a Dandy Dinmont, and a mother and child of unknown race, which he afterwards learned was Kabyle, a breed beloved of mountain men and desert tent-dwellers. In front of the dogs bounded a small African monkey, who leaped to the back of Nevill's chair, and behind them toddled with awkward grace a baby panther, a mere ball of yellow silk.

"They don't like the thunder, poor dears," Nevill apologised. "That's why they howled, for they're wonderfully polite people really. They always come at the end of lunch. Aunt Caroline won't invite them to dinner, because then she sometimes wears fluffy things about which she has a foolish vanity. The collie is Angus's. The deerhound is Hamish's. The dandy is hers. The two Kabyles are Mohammed's, and the flotsam and jetsam is mine. There's a great deal more of it out of doors, but this is all that gets into the dining-room except by accident. And I expect you think we are a very queer family."

Stephen did think so, for never till now had he been a member of a household where each of the servants was allowed to possess any animals he chose, and flood the house with them. But the queerer he thought the family, the better he found himself liking it. He felt a boy let out of school after weeks of disgrace and punishment, and, strangely enough, this old Arab palace, in a city of North Africa seemed more like home to him than his London flat had seemed of late.

When Lady MacGregor rose and said she must write the note she had promised Nevill to send Miss Ray, Stephen longed to kiss her. This form of worship not being permitted, he tried to open the dining-room door for her to go out, but Angus and Hamish glared upon him so superciliously that he retired in their favour.

The luncheon hour, even when cloaked in the mysterious gloom of a thunderstorm, is no time for confidences; besides, it is not conducive to sustained conversation to find a cold nose in your palm, a baby claw up your sleeve, or a monkey hand, like a bit of leather, thrust down your collar or into your ear. But after dinner that night, when Lady MacGregor had trailed her maligned "fluffiness" away to the drawing-room, and Nevill and Stephen had strolled with their cigarettes out into the unearthly whiteness of the lily garden, Stephen felt that something was coming. He had known that Nevill had a story to tell, by and by, and though he knew also that he would be asked no questions in return, now or ever, it occurred to him that Nevill's offer of confidences was perhaps meant to open a door, if he chose to enter by it. He was not sure whether he would so choose or not, but the fact that he was not sure meant a change in him. A few days ago, even this morning, before meeting Nevill, he would have been certain that he had nothing intimate to tell Caird or any one else.

They strolled along the paths among the lilies. Moon and sky and flowers and white-gravelled paths were all silver. Stephen thought of Victoria Ray, and wished she could see this garden. He thought, too, that if she would only dance here among the lilies in the moonlight, it would be a vision of exquisite loveliness.

"For a moment white, then gone forever," he caught himself repeating again.

It was odd how, whenever he saw anything very white and of dazzling purity, he thought of this dancing girl. He wondered what sort of woman it was whose image came to Nevill's mind, in the garden of lilies that smelt so heavenly sweet under the moon. He supposed there must always be some woman whose image was suggested to every man by all that was fairest in nature. Margot Lorenzi was the woman whose image he must keep in his mind, if he wanted to know any faint imitation of happiness in future. She would like this moonlit garden, and in one way it would suit her as a background. Yet she did not seem quite in the picture, despite her beauty. The perfume she loved would not blend with the perfume of the lilies.

"Aunt Caroline's rather a dear, isn't she?" remarked Nevill, apropos of nothing.

"She's a jewel," said Stephen.

"Yet she isn't the immediate jewel of my soul. I'm hard hit, Stephen, and the girl won't have me. She's poorer than any church or other mouse I ever met, yet she turns up her little French nose at me and my palace, and all the cheese I should like to see her nibble — my cheese."

"Her French nose?" echoed Stephen.

"Yes. Her nose and the rest of her's French, especially her dimples. You never saw such dimples. Miss Ray's prettier than my girl, I suppose. But I think mine's beyond anything. Only she isn't and won't be mine that's the worst of it."

"Where is she?" Stephen asked. "In Algiers?"

"No such luck. But her sister is. I'll take you to see the sister to-morrow morning. She may be able to tell us something to help Miss Ray. She keeps a curiosity-shop, and is a connoisseur of Eastern antiquities, as well as a great character in Algiers, quite a sort of queen in her way — a quaint way. All the visiting Royalties of every nation drop in and spend hours in her place. She has a good many Arab acquaintances, too. Even rich chiefs come to sell, or buy things from her, and respect her immensely. But my girl — I like to call her that — is away off in the west, close to the border of Morocco, at Tlemcen. I wish you were interested in mosques, and I'd take you there. People who care for such things sometimes travel from London or Paris just to see the mosque of Sidi Bou-Medine and a certain Mirab. But I suppose you haven't any fad of that kind, eh?"

"I feel it coming on," said Stephen.

"Good chap! Do encourage the feeling. I'll lend you books, lots of books, on the subject. She's 'malema,' or mistress of an *école indigène* for embroideries and carpets, at Tlemcen. Heaven knows how few francs a month she earns by the job which takes all her time and life, yet she thinks herself lucky to get it. And she won't marry me."

"Surely she must love you, at least a little, if you care so much for her," Stephen tried to console his friend.

"Oh, she does, a lot," replied Nevill with infinite satisfaction. "But, you see — well, you see, her family wasn't up to much from a social point of view — such rot! The mother came out from Paris to be a nursery governess, when she was quite young, but she was too pretty for that position. She had various but virtuous adventures, and married a non-com. in the Chasseurs d'Afrique, who chucked the army for her. The two kept a little hotel. Then the husband died, while the girls were children. The mother gave up the hotel and took in sewing. Everybody was interested in the family, they were so clever and exceptional, and people helped in the girls' education. When their mother became an invalid, the two contrived to keep her and themselves, though Jeanne was only eighteen then, and Josette, my girl, fifteen. She's been dead now for some years—the mother. Josette is nearly twenty-four. Do you see why she won't marry me? I'm hanged if I do."

"I can see what her feeling is," Stephen said. "She must be a ripping girl."

"I should say she is!—though as obstinate as the devil. Sometimes I could shake her and box her ears. I haven't seen her for months now. She wouldn't like me to go to Tlemcen—unless I had a friend with me, and a good excuse. I didn't know it could hurt so much to be in love, though I was in once before, and it hurt too, rather. But that was nothing. For the woman had no soul or mind, only her beauty, and an unscrupulous sort of ambition which made her want to marry me when my uncle left me his money. She'd refused to do anything more serious than flirt and reduce me to misery, until she thought I could give her what she wanted. I'd imagined myself horribly in love, until her sudden willingness to take me showed me once for all what she was. Even so, I couldn't cure the habit of love at first; but I had just sense enough to keep out of England, where she was, for fear I should lose my head and marry her. My cure was rather slow, but it was sure; and now I know that what I thought was love then wasn't love at all. The real thing's as different as—as— a modern Algerian tile is from an old Moorish one. I can't say anything stronger! That's why I cut England, to begin with, and after a while my interests were more identified with France. Sometimes I go to Paris in the summer—or to a little place in Dauphiny. But I haven't been back to England for eight years. Algeria holds all my heart. In Tlemcen is my girl. Here are my garden and my beasts. Now you have my history since Oxford days."

"You know something of *my* history through the papers," Stephen blurted out with a desperate defiance of his own reserve.

"Not much of your real history, I think. Papers lie, and people misunderstand. Don't talk of yourself unless you really want to. But I say, look here, Stephen. That woman I thought I cared for—may I tell you what she was like? Somehow I want you to know. Don't think me a cad. I don't mean to be. But—may I tell?"

"Of course. Why not?"

"She was dark and awfully handsome, and though she wasn't an actress, she would have made a splendid one. She thought only of herself. I—there was a picture in a London paper lately which reminded me of her—the picture of a young lady you know—or think you know. They—those two—are of the same type. I don't believe either could make a man happy."

Stephen laughed—a short, embarrassed laugh. "Oh, happy!" he echoed. "After twenty-five we learn not to expect happiness. But— thank you for—everything, and especially for inviting me here." He knew now why it had occurred to Nevill to ask him to Algiers. Nevill had seen Margot's picture. In silence they walked towards the open door of the dining-room. Somewhere not far away the Kabyle dogs were barking shrilly. In the distance rose and fell muffled notes of strange passion and fierceness, an Arab tom-tom beating like the heart of the conquered East, away in the old town.

Stephen's short-lived gaiety was struck out of his soul.

"For a moment white, then gone forever."

He pushed the haunting words out of his mind. He did not want them to have any meaning. They had no meaning.

It seemed to him that the perfume of the lilies was too heavy on the air.

X

A white peacock, screaming in the garden under Stephen's balcony, waked him early, and dreamily his thoughts strayed towards the events planned for the day.

They were to make a morning call on Mademoiselle Soubise in her curiosity-shop, and ask about Ben Halim, the husband of Saidee Ray. Victoria was coming to luncheon, for she had accepted Lady MacGregor's invitation. Her note had been brought in last night, while he and Nevill walked in the garden. Afterwards Lady MacGregor had shown it to them both. The girl wrote an interesting hand, full of individuality, and expressive of decision. Perhaps on her arrival they might have something to tell her.

This hope shot Stephen out of bed, though it was only seven, and breakfast was not until nine. He had a cold bath in the private bathroom, which was one of Nevill's modern improvements in the old house, and by and by went for a walk, thinking to have the gardens to himself. But Nevill was there, cutting flowers and whistling tunefully. It was to him that the jewelled white peacock had screamed a greeting.

"I like cutting the flowers myself," said he. "I don't think they care to have others touch them, any more than a cow likes to be milked by a stranger. Of course they feel the difference! Why, they know when I praise them, and preen themselves. They curl up when they're scolded, or not noticed, just as I do when people aren't nice to me. Every day I send off a box of my best roses to Tlemcen. *She* allows me to do that."

Lady MacGregor did not appear at breakfast, which was served on a marble loggia; and by half-past nine Stephen and Nevill were out in the wide, tree-shaded streets, where masses of bougainvillæa and clematis boiled over high garden-walls of old plaster, once white, now streaked with gold and rose, and green moss and lichen. After the thunderstorm of the day before, the white dust was laid, and the air was pure with a curious sparkling quality.

They passed the museum in its garden, and turned a corner.

"There's Mademoiselle Soubise's shop," said Nevill.

It was a low white building, and had evidently been a private house at one time. The only change made had been in the shape and size of the windows on the ground-floor; and these were protected by green *persiennes*, fanned out like awnings, although the house was shaded by magnolia trees. There was no name over the open door, but the word "*Antiquités*" was painted in large black letters on the house-wall.

Under the green blinds was a glitter of jewels displayed among brocades and a tangle of old lace, or on embossed silver trays; and walking in at the door, out of the shadowy dusk, a blaze of colour leaped to the eyes. Not a soul was there, unless some one hid and spied behind a carved and gilded Tunisian bed or a marqueterie screen from Bagdad. Yet there was a collection to tempt a thief, and apparently no precaution taken against invaders.

Delicate rugs, soft as clouds and tinted like opals, were heaped in piles on the tiled floor; rugs from Ispahan, rugs from Mecca; old rugs from the sacred city of Kairouan, such as are made no more there or anywhere. The walls were hung with Tunisian silks and embroidered stuffs from the homes of Jewish families, where they had served as screens for talismanic words too sacred to be seen by common eyes; and there was drapery of ancient banners, Tyrian- dyed, whose gold or silver fringes had been stained with blood, in battle. From the ceiling were suspended antique lamps, and chandeliers of rare rock crystal, whose prisms gave out rose and violet sparks as they caught the light.

On shelves and inlaid tables were beggars' bowls of strange dark woods, carried across deserts by wandering mendicants of centuries ago, the chains, which had hung from throats long since crumbled into dust, adorned with lucky rings and fetishes to preserve the wearer from evil spirits. There were other bowls, of crystal pure as full-blown bubbles, bowls which would ring at a tap like clear bells of silver. Some of these were guiltless of ornament, some were graven with gold flowers, but all seemed full of lights reflected from tilted, pearl-framed mirrors, and from the swinging prisms of chandeliers.

Chafing-dishes of bronze at which vanished hands had been warmed, stood beside chased brazen ewers made to pour rose-water over henna-stained fingers, after Arab dinners, eaten without knives or forks. In the depths of half-open drawers glimmered precious stones, strangely cut pink diamonds, big square turquoises and emeralds, strings of creamy pearls, and hands of Fatma, a different jewel dangling from each finger-tip.

The floor was encumbered, not only with rugs, but with heaps of priceless tiles, Persian and Moorish, of the best periods and patterns, taken from the walls of Arab palaces now destroyed; huge brass salvers; silver anklets, and chain armour, sabres captured from Crusaders, and old illuminated Korans. It was difficult to move without knocking something down, and one stepped delicately in narrow aisles, to avoid islands of piled, precious objects. Everywhere the eye was drawn to glittering points, or patches of splendid colour; so that at a glance the large, dusky room was like a temple decorated with mosaics. There was nothing that did not suggest the East, city or desert, or mountain village of the Kabyles; and the air was loaded with Eastern perfumes, ambergris and musk that blended with each other, and the scent of the black incense sticks brought by caravan from Tombouctou.

"Why doesn't some one come in and steal?" asked Stephen, in surprise at seeing the place deserted.

"Because there's hardly a thief in Algiers mean enough to steal from Jeanne Soubise, who gives half she has to the poor. And because, if there were one so mean, Haroun el Raschid would soon let her know what was going on," said Nevill. "His latest disguise is that of a parrot, but he may change it for something else at any moment."

Then Stephen saw, suspended among the crystal chandeliers and antique lamps, a brass cage, shaped like a domed palace. In this cage, in a coral ring, sat a grey parrot who regarded the two young men with jewel-eyes that seemed to know all good and evil.

"He yells if any stranger comes into the shop when his mistress is out," Nevill explained. "I am an humble friend of His Majesty's, so he says nothing. I gave him to Mademoiselle Jeanne."

Perhaps their voices had been heard. At all events, there was a light tapping of heels on unseen stairs, and from behind a red-curtained doorway appeared a tall young woman, dressed in black.

She was robust as well as tall, and Stephen thought she looked rather like a handsome Spanish boy; yet she was feminine enough in her outlines. It was the frank and daring expression of her face and great black eyes which gave the look of boyishness. She had thick, straight eyebrows, a large mouth that was beautiful when she smiled, to show perfect teeth between the red lips that had a faint, shadowy line of down above them.

"Ah, Monsieur Nevill Caird!" she exclaimed, in English, with a full voice, and a French accent that was pretty, though not Parisian. She smiled at Stephen, too, without waiting to be introduced. "Monsieur Caird is always kind in bringing his friends to me, and I am always glad to see them."

"I've brought Mr. Knight, not to buy, but to ask a favour," said Nevill.

"To buy, too," Stephen hastened to cut in. "I see things I can't live without. I must own them."

"Well, don't set your heart on anything Mademoiselle Soubise won't sell. She bought everything with the idea of selling it, she admits, but now she's got them here, there are some things she can't make up her mind to part with at any price."

"Oh, only a few tiles—and some Jewish embroideries—and bits of jewellery—and a rug or two or a piece of pottery—and maybe *one* copy of the Koran, and a beggar's bowl," Jeanne Soubise excused herself, hastily adding more and more to her list of exceptions, as her eyes roved wistfully among her treasures. "Oh, and an amphora just dug up near Timgad, with Roman oil still inside. It's a beauty. Will you come down to the cellar to look at it?"

Nevill thanked her, and reserved the pleasure for another time. Then he inquired what was the latest news from Mademoiselle Josette at Tlemcen; and when he heard that there was nothing new, he told the lady of the curiosity-shop what was the object of the early visit.

"But of course I have heard of Ben Halim, and I have seen him, too," she said; "only it was long ago—maybe ten years. Yes, I could not have been seventeen. It is already long that he went away from Algiers, no one knows where. Now he is said to be dead. Have you not heard of him, Monsieur Nevill? You must have. He lived at Djenan el Hadj; close to the Jardin d'Essai. You know the place well. The new rich Americans, Madame Jewett and her daughter, have it now. There was a scandal about Ben Halim, and then he went away—a scandal that was mysterious, because every one talked about it, yet no one knew what had happened—never surely at least."

"I told you Mademoiselle would be able to give you information!" exclaimed Nevill. "I felt sure the name was familiar, somehow, though I couldn't think how. One hears so many Arab names, and generally there's a 'Ben' or a 'Bou' something or other, if from the South."

"Flan-ben-Flan," laughed Jeanne Soubise. "That means," she explained, turning to Stephen, "So and So, son of So and So. It is strange, a young lady came inquiring about Ben Halim only yesterday afternoon; such a pretty young lady. I was surprised, but she said they had told her in her hotel I knew everything that had ever happened in Algiers. A nice compliment to my age. I am not so old as that! But," she added, with a frank smile, "all the hotels and guides expect commissions when they send people to me. I suppose they thought this pretty girl fair game, and that once in my place she would buy. So she did. She bought a string of amber beads. She liked the gold light in them, and said it seemed as if she might see a vision of something or some one she wanted to find, if she gazed through the beads. Many a good Mussulman has said his prayers with them, if that could bring her luck."

The two young men looked at one another.

"Did she tell you her name?" Stephen asked.

"But yes; she was Mees Ray, and named for the dead Queen Victoria of England, I suppose, though American. And she told me other things. Her sister, she said, married a Captain Ben Halim of the Spahis, and came with him to Algiers, nearly ten years ago. Now she is looking for the sister."

"We've met Miss Ray," said Nevill. "It's on her business we've come. We didn't know she'd already been to you, but we might have guessed some one would send her. She didn't lose much time."

"She wouldn't," said Stephen. "She isn't that kind."

"I knew nothing of the sister," went on Mademoiselle Soubise. "I could hardly believe at first that Ben Halim had an American wife. Then I remembered how these Mohammedan men can hide their women, so no one ever knows. Probably no one ever did know, otherwise gossip would have leaked out. The man may have been jealous of her. You see, I have Arab acquaintances. I go to visit ladies in the harems sometimes, and I hear stories when anything exciting is talked of. You can't think how word flies from one harem to another—like a carrier-pigeon! This could never have been a matter of gossip—though it is true I was young at the time."

"You think, then, he would have shut her up?" asked Nevill. "That's what I feared."

"But of course he would have shut her up—with another wife, perhaps."

"Good Heavens!" exclaimed Stephen. "The poor child has never thought of that possibility. She says he promised her sister he would never look at any other woman."

"Ah, the promise of an Arab in love! Perhaps she did not know the Arabs—that sister. It is only the men of princely families who take but one wife. And he would not tell her if he had already looked at another woman. He would be sure, no matter how much in love a Christian girl might be, she would not marry a man who already had a wife."

"We might find out that," suggested Stephen.

"It would be difficult," said the Frenchwoman. "I can try, among Arabs I know, but though they like to chat with Europeans, they will not answer questions. They resent that we should ask them, though they are polite. As for you, if you ask men, French or Arab, you will learn nothing. The French would not know. The Arabs, if they did, would not tell. They must not talk of each other's wives, even among themselves, much less to outsiders. You can ask an Arab about anything else in the world, but not his wife. That is the last insult."

"What a country!" Stephen ejaculated.

"I don't know that it has many more faults than others," said Nevill, defending it, "only they're different."

"But about the scandal that drove Ben Halim away?" Stephen ventured on.

"Strange things were whispered at the time, I remember, because Ben Halim was a handsome man and well known. One looked twice at him in his uniform when he went by on a splendid horse. I believe he had been to Paris before the scandal. What he did afterwards no one can say. But I could not tell Mees Ray what I had heard of that scandal any more than I would tell a young girl that almost all Europeans who become harem women are converted to the religion of Islam, and that very likely the sister wasn't Ben Halim's first wife."

"Can you tell us of the scandal, or—would you rather not talk of the subject?" Stephen hesitated.

"Oh, I can tell you, for it would not hurt your feelings. People said Ben Halim flirted too much with his Colonel's beautiful French wife, who died soon afterwards, and her husband killed himself. Ben Halim had not been considered a good officer before. He was too fond of pleasure, and a mad gambler; so at last it was made known to him he had better leave the army of his own accord if he did not wish to go against his will; at least, that was the story."

"Of course!" exclaimed Nevill. "It comes back to me now, though it all happened before I lived in Algiers. Ben Halim sold his house and everything in it to a Frenchman who went bankrupt soon after. It's passed through several hands since. I go occasionally to call on Mrs. Jewett and her daughter."

"It is said they wish you would call oftener, Monsieur Caird."

Nevill turned red. Stephen thought he could understand, and hid a smile. No doubt Nevill was a great "catch" in Algerian society. And he was in love with a teacher of Arab children far away in Tlemcen, a girl "poor as a church mouse," who wouldn't listen to him! It was a quaint world; as quaint in Africa as elsewhere.

"What did you tell Miss Ray?" Nevill hurried to ask.

"That Ben Halim had left Algiers nine years ago, and had never been heard of since. When I saw she did not love his memory, I told her people believed him to be dead; and this rumour might be true, as no news of him has ever come back. But she turned pale, and I was sorry I had been so frank. Yet what would you? Oh, and I thought of one more thing, when she had gone, which I might have mentioned. But perhaps there is nothing in it. All the rest of the day I was busy with many customers, so I was tired at night, otherwise I would have sent a note to her hotel. And this morning since six I have been hurrying to get off boxes and things ordered by some Americans for a ship which sails at noon. But you will tell the young lady when you see her, and that will be better than my writing, because sending a note would make it seem too important. She might build hopes, and it would be a pity if they did explode."

Both men laughed a little at this ending of the Frenchwoman's sentence, but Stephen was more impatient than Nevill to know what was to come next. He grudged the pause, and made her go on.

"It is only that I remember my sister telling me, when she was at home last year for a holiday, about a Kabyle servant girl who waits on her in Tlemcen. The girl is of a great intelligence, and my sister takes an interest in her. Josette teaches her many things, and they talk. Mouni — that is the Kabyle's name — tells of her home life to my sister. One thing she did was to serve a beautiful foreign lady in the house of a rich Arab. She was only a child then, not more than thirteen, for such girls grow up early; but she has always thought about that lady, who was good to her, and very sad. Mouni told Josette she had never seen any one so beautiful, and that her mistress had hair of a natural colour, redder than hair dyed with henna and powdered with gold dust. It was this describing of the hair which brought the story back to my head when Miss Ray had gone, because she has hair like that, and perhaps her sister had it too."

"By Jove, we'll run over to Tlemcen in the car, and see that Kabyle girl," Nevill eagerly proposed, carefully looking at his friend, and not at Jeanne Soubise. But she raised her eyebrows, then drew them together, and her frank manner changed. With that shadow of a frown, and smileless eyes and lips, there was something rather formidable about the handsome young woman.

"Mees Ray may like to manage all her own beesiness," she remarked. And it occurred to Stephen that it would be a propitious moment to choose such curios as he wished to buy. In a few moments Mademoiselle Soubise was her pleasant self again, indicating the best points of the things he admired, and giving him their history.

"There's apparently a conspiracy of silence to keep us from finding out anything about Miss Ray's sister as Ben Halim's wife," he said to Nevill when they had left the curiosity-shop. "Also, what has become of Ben Halim."

"You'll learn that there's always a conspiracy of silence in Africa, where Arabs are concerned," Nevill answered. There was a far-off, fatal look in his eyes as he spoke, those blue eyes which seemed at all times to see something that others could not see. And again the sense of an intangible, illusive, yet very real mystery of the East, which he had felt for a moment before landing, oppressed Stephen, as if he had inhaled too much smoke from the black incense of Tombouctou.

XI

Stephen and Nevill Caird were in the cypress avenue when Victoria Ray drove up in a ramshackle cab, guided by an Arab driver who squinted hideously. She wore a white frock which might have cost a sovereign, and had probably been made at home. Her wide brimmed hat was of cheap straw, wound with a scarf of thin white muslin; but her eyes looked out like blue stars from under its dove-coloured shadow, and a lily was tucked into her belt. To both young men she seemed very beautiful, and radiant as the spring morning.

"You aren't superstitious, engaging a man with a squint," said Nevill.

"Of course not," she laughed. "As if harm could come to me because the poor man's so homely! I engaged him because he was the worst looking, and nobody else seemed to want him."

They escorted her indoors to Lady MacGregor, and Stephen wondered if she would be afraid of the elderly fairy with the face of a child and the manner of an autocrat. But she was not in the least shy; and indeed Stephen could hardly picture the girl as being self-conscious in any circumstances. Lady MacGregor took her in with one look; white hat, red hair, blue eyes, lily at belt, simple frock and all, and—somewhat to Stephen's surprise, because she was to him a new type of old lady—decided to be charmed with Miss Ray.

Victoria's naïve admiration of the house and gardens delighted her host and hostess. She could not be too much astonished at its wonders to please them, and, both being thoroughbred, they liked her the better for saying frankly that she was unused to beautiful houses. "You can't think what this is like after school in Potterston and cheap boarding-houses in New York and London," she said, laughing when the others laughed.

Stephen was longing to see her in the lily-garden, which, to his mind, might have been made for her; and after luncheon he asked Lady MacGregor if he and Nevill might show it to Miss Ray.

The garden lay to the east, and as it was shadowed by the house in the afternoon, it would not be too hot.

"Perhaps you won't mind taking her yourself," said the elderly fairy. "Just for a few wee minutes I want Nevill. He is to tell me about accepting or refusing some invitations. I'll send him to you soon."

Stephen was ashamed of the gladness with which he could not help hearing this proposal. He had nothing to say to the girl which he might not say before Nevill, or even before Lady MacGregor, yet he had been feeling cheated because he could not be alone with Victoria, as on the boat.

"Gather Miss Ray as many lilies as she can carry away," were Nevill's parting instructions. And it was exactly what Stephen had wished for. He wanted to give her something beautiful and appropriate, something he could give with his own hands. And he longed to see her holding masses of white lilies to her breast, as she walked all white in the white lily-garden. Now, too, he could tell her what Mademoiselle Soubise had said about the Kabyle girl, Mouni. He was sure Nevill wouldn't grudge his having that pleasure all to himself. Anyway he could not resist the temptation to snatch it.

He began, as soon as they were alone together in the garden, by asking her what she had done, whether she had made progress; and it seemed that she retired from his questions with a vague suggestion of reserve she had not shown on the ship. It was not that she answered unwillingly, but he could not define the difference in her manner, although he felt that a difference existed.

It was as if somebody might have been scolding her for a lack of reserve; yet when he inquired if she had met any one she knew, or made acquaintances, she said no to the first question, and named only Mademoiselle Soubise in reply to the second.

That was Stephen's opportunity, and he began to tell of his call at the curiosity-shop. He expected Victoria to cry out with excitement when he came to Mouni's description of the beautiful lady with "henna-coloured, gold-powdered hair"; but though she flushed and her breath came and went quickly as he talked, somehow the girl did not appear to be enraptured with a new hope, as he had expected.

"My friend Caird proposes that he and I should motor to Tlemcen, which it seems is near the Moroccan border, and interview Mouni," he said. "We may be able to make sure, when we question her, that it was your sister she served; and perhaps we can pick up some clue through what she lets drop, as to where Ben Halim took his wife when he left Algiers—though, of course, there are lots of other ways to find out, if this should prove a false clue."

"You are both more than good," Victoria answered, "but I mustn't let you go so far for me. Perhaps, as you say, I shall be able to find out in other ways, from some one here in Algiers. It does sound as if it might be my sister the maid spoke of to Mademoiselle Soubise. How I should love to hear Mouni talk!—but you must wait, and see what happens, before you think of going on a journey for my sake."

"If only there were some woman to take you, you might go with us," said Stephen, more eagerly than he was aware, and thinking wild thoughts about Lady MacGregor as a chaperon, or perhaps Mademoiselle Soubise—if only she could be persuaded to leave her beloved shop, and wouldn't draw those black brows of hers together as though tabooing a forbidden idea.

"Let's wait—and see," Victoria repeated. And this patience, in the face of such hope, struck Stephen as being strange in her, unlike his conception of the brave, impulsive nature, ready for any adventure if only there were a faint flicker of light at the end. Then, as if she did not wish to talk longer of a possible visit to Tlemcen, Victoria said: "I've something to show you: a picture of my sister."

The white dress was made without a collar, and was wrapped across her breast like a fichu which left the slender white stem of her throat uncovered. Now she drew out from under the muslin folds a thin gold chain, from which dangled a flat, open-faced locket. When she had unfastened a clasp, she handed the trinket to Stephen. "Saidee had the photograph made specially for me, just before she was married," the girl explained, "and I painted it myself. I couldn't trust any one else, because no one knew her colouring. Of course, she was a hundred times more beautiful than this, but it gives you some idea of her, as she looked when I saw her last."

The face in the photograph was small, not much larger than Stephen's thumb-nail, but every feature was distinct, not unlike Victoria's, though more pronounced; and the nose, seen almost in profile, was perfect in its delicate straightness. The lips were fuller than Victoria's, and red as coral. The eyes were brown, with a suggestion of coquetry absent in the younger girl's, and the hair, parted in the middle and worn in a loose, wavy coil, appeared to be of a darker red, less golden, more auburn.

"That's exactly Saidee's colouring," repeated Victoria. "Her lips were the reddest I ever saw, and I used to say diamonds had got caught behind her eyes. Do you wonder I worshipped her—that I just *couldn't* let her go out of my life forever?"

"No, I don't wonder. She's very lovely," Stephen agreed. The coquetry in the eyes was pathetic to him, knowing the beautiful Saidee's history.

"She was eighteen then. She's twenty-eight now. Saidee twenty-eight! I can hardly realize it. But I'm sure she hasn't changed, unless to grow prettier. I used always to think she would." Victoria took back the portrait, and gazed at it. Stephen was sorry for the child. He thought it more than likely that Saidee had changed for the worse, physically and spiritually, even mentally, if Mademoiselle Soubise were right in her surmises. He was glad she had not said to Victoria what she had said to him, about Saidee having to live the life of other harem women.

"I bought a string of amber beads at that curiosity-shop yesterday," the girl went on, "because there's a light in them like what used to be in Saidee's eyes. Every night, when I've said my prayers and am ready to go to sleep, I see her in that golden silence I told you about, looking towards the west—that is, towards me, too, you know; with the sun setting and streaming right into her eyes, making that jewelled kind of light gleam in them, which comes and goes in those amber beads. When I find her, I shall hold up the beads to her eyes in the sunlight and compare them."

"What is the golden silence like?" asked Stephen. "Do you see more clearly, now that at last you've come to Africa?"

"I couldn't see more clearly than I did before," the girl answered slowly, looking away from him, through the green lace of the trees that veiled the distance. "Yet it's just as mysterious as ever. I can't guess yet what it can be, unless it's in the desert. I just see Saidee, standing on a large, flat expanse which looks white. And she's dressed in white. All round her is a quivering golden haze, wave after wave of it, endless as the sea when you're on a ship. And there's silence—not one sound, except the beating which must be my own heart, or the blood that sings in my ears when I listen for a long time—the kind of singing you hear in a shell. That's all. And the level sun shining in her eyes, and on her hair."

"It is a picture," said Stephen.

"Wherever Say was, there would always be a picture," Victoria said with the unselfish, unashamed pride she had in her sister.

"How I hope Saidee knows I'm near her," she went on, half to herself. "She'd know that I'd come to her as soon as I could—and she may have heard things about me that would tell her I was trying to make money enough for the journey and everything. If I hadn't hoped she *might* see the magazines and papers, I could never have let my photograph be published. I should have hated that, if it hadn't been for the thought of the portraits coming to her eyes, with my name under them; 'Victoria Ray, who is dancing in such and such a place.' *She* would know why I was doing it; dancing nearer and nearer to her."

"You darling!" Stephen would have liked to say. But only as he might have spoken caressingly to a lovely child whose sweet soul had won him. She seemed younger than ever to-day, in the big, drooping hat, with the light behind her weaving a gold halo round her hair and the slim white figure, as she talked of Saidee in the golden silence. When she looked up at him, he thought that she was like a girl-saint, painted on a background of gold. He felt very tender over her, very much older than she, and it did not occur to him that he might fall in love with this young creature who had no thought for anything in life except the finding of her sister.

A tiny streak of lily-pollen had made a little yellow stain on the white satin of her cheek, and under her blue eyes were a few faint freckles, golden as the lily-pollen. He had seen them come yesterday, on the ship, in a bright glare of sunlight, and they were not quite gone yet. He had a foolish wish to touch them with his finger, to see if they would rub off, and to brush away the lily-pollen, though it made her skin look pure as pearl.

"You are an inspiration!" was all he said.

"I? But how do you mean?" she asked.

He hardly knew that he had spoken aloud; yet challenged, he tried to explain. "Inspiration to new life and faith in things," he answered almost at random. But hearing the words pronounced by his own voice, made him realize that they were true. This child, of whose existence he had not known a week ago, could give him—perhaps was already giving him—new faith and new interests. He felt thankful for her, somehow, though she did not belong to him, and never would— unless a gleam of sunshine can belong to one on whom it shines. And he would always associate her with the golden sunshine and the magic charm of Algeria.

"I told you I'd given you half my star," she said, laughing and blushing a little.

"Which star is it?" he wanted to know. "When I don't see you any more, I can look up and hitch my thought-wagon to Mars or Venus."

"Oh, it's even grander than any planet you can see, with your real eyes. But you can look at the evening star if you like. It's so thrilling in the sunset sky, I sometimes call it my star."

"All right," said Stephen, with his elder-brother air. "And when I look I'll think of you."

"You can think of me as being with Saidee at last."

"You have the strongest presentiment that you'll find her without difficulty."

"When *I* say 'presentiment,' I mean creating a thing I want, making a picture of it happening, so it *has* to happen by and by, as God made pictures of this world, and all the worlds, and they came true."

"By Jove, I wish I could go to school to you!" Stephen said this laughing; but he meant every word. She had just given him two new ideas. He wondered if he could do anything with them. Yet no; his life was cut out on a certain plan. It must now follow that plan.

"If you should have any trouble—not that you *will*—but just 'if,' you know," he went on, "and if I could help you, I want you to remember this, wherever you are and whatever the trouble may be; there's nothing I wouldn't do for you—nothing. There's no distance I wouldn't travel."

"Why, you're the kindest man I ever met!" Victoria exclaimed, gratefully. "And I think you must be one of the best."

"Good heavens, what a character to live up to!" laughed Stephen. Nevertheless he suddenly lost his sense of exaltation, and felt sad and tired, thinking of life with Margot, and how difficult it would be not to degenerate in her society.

"Yes. It's a good character. And I'll promise to let you know, if I'm in any trouble and need help. If I can't write, I'll *call*, as I said yesterday."

"Good. I shall hear you over the wireless telephone." They both laughed; and Nevill Caird, coming out of the house was pleased that Stephen should be happy.

It had occurred to him while helping his aunt with the invitations, that something of interest to Miss Ray might be learned at the Governor's house. He knew the Governor more or less, in a social way. Now he asked Victoria if she would like him to make inquiries about Ben Halim's past as a Spahi?

"I've already been to the Governor," replied Victoria. "I got a letter to him from the American Consul, and had a little audience with him — is that what I ought to call it?—this morning. He was kind, but could tell me nothing I didn't know—any way, he would tell nothing more. He wasn't in Algiers when Saidee came. It was in the day of his predecessor."

Nevill admired her promptness and energy, and said so. He shared Stephen's chivalrous wish to do something for the girl, so alone, so courageous, working against difficulties she had not begun to understand. He was sorry that he had had no hand in helping Victoria to see the most important Frenchman in Algiers, a man of generous sympathy for Arabs; but as he had been forestalled, he hastened to think of something else which he might do. He knew the house Ben Halim had owned in Algiers, the place which must have been her sister's home. The people who lived there now were acquaintances of his. Would she like to see Djenan el Hadj?

The suggestion pleased her so much that Stephen found himself envying Nevill her gratitude. And it was arranged that Mrs. Jewett should be asked to appoint an hour for a visit next day.

XII

While Victoria was still in the lily-garden with her host and his friend, the cab which she had ordered to return came back to fetch her. It was early, and Lady MacGregor had expected her to stop for tea, as most people did stop, who visited Djenan el Djouad for the first time, because every one wished to see the house; and to see the house took hours. But the dancing-girl, appearing slightly embarrassed as she expressed her regrets, said that she must go; she had to keep an engagement. She did not explain what the engagement was, and as she betrayed constraint in speaking of it, both Stephen and Nevill guessed that she did not wish to explain. They took it for granted that it was something to do with her sister's affairs, something which she considered of importance; otherwise, as she had no friends in Algiers, and Lady MacGregor was putting herself out to be kind, the girl would have been pleased to spend an afternoon with those to whom she could talk freely. No questions could be asked, though, as Lady MacGregor remarked when Victoria had gone (after christening the baby panther), it did seem ridiculous that a child should be allowed to make its own plans and carry them out alone in a place like Algiers, without having any advice from its elders.

"I've been, and expect to go on being, what you might call a perpetual chaperon," said she resignedly; "and chaperoning is so ingrained in my nature that I hate to see a baby running about unprotected, doing what it chooses, as if it were a married woman, not to say a widow. But I suppose it can't be stopped."

"She's been on the stage," said Nevill reassuringly, Miss Ray having already broken this hard fact to the Scotch lady at luncheon.

"I tell you it's a baby! Even John Knox would see that," sharply replied Aunt Caroline.

There was nothing better to do with the rest of the afternoon, Nevill thought, than to take a spin in the motor, which they did, the chauffeur at the wheel, as Nevill confessed himself of too lazy a turn of mind to care for driving his own car. While Stephen waited outside, he called at Djenan el Hadj (an old Arab house at a little distance from the town, buried deep in a beautiful garden), but the ladies were out. Nevill wrote a note on his card, explaining that his aunt would like to bring a friend, whose relatives had once lived in the house; and this done, they had a swift run about the beautiful country in the neighbourhood of Algiers.

It was dinner-time when they returned, and meanwhile an answer had come from Mrs. Jewett. She would be delighted to see any friend of Lady MacGregor's, and hoped Miss Ray might be brought to tea the following afternoon.

"Shall we send a note to her hotel, or shall we stroll down after dinner?" asked Nevill.

"Suppose we stroll down," Stephen decided, trying to appear indifferent, though he was ridiculously pleased at the idea of having a few unexpected words with Victoria.

"Good. We might take a look at the Kasbah afterward," said Nevill. "Night's the time when it's most mysterious, and we shall be close to the old town when we leave Miss Ray's hotel."

Dinner seemed long to Stephen. He could have spared several courses. Nevertheless, though they sat down at eight, it was only nine when they started out. Up on the hill of Mustapha Supérieur, all was peaceful under the moonlight; but below, in the streets of French shops and cafés, the light-hearted people of the South were ready to begin enjoying themselves after a day of work. Streams of electric light poured from restaurant windows, and good smells of French cooking filtered out, as doors opened and shut. The native cafés were crowded with dark men smoking chibouques, eating kous-kous, playing dominoes, or sipping absinthe and golden liqueurs which, fortunately not having been invented in the Prophet's time, had not been forbidden by him. Curio shops and bazaars for native jewellery and brasswork were still open, lit up with pink and yellow lamps. The brilliant uniforms of young Spahis and Zouaves made spots of vivid colour among the dark clothes of Europeans, tourists, or employés in commercial houses out for amusement. Sailors of different nations swung along arm in arm, laughing and ogling the handsome Jewesses and painted ladies from the Levant or Marseilles. American girls just arrived on big ships took care of their chaperons and gazed with interest at the passing show, especially at the magnificent Arabs who appeared to float rather than walk, looking neither to right nor left, their white burnouses blowing behind them. The girls stared eagerly, too, at the few veiled and swathed figures of native women who mingled with the crowd, padding timidly with bare feet thrust into slippers. The foreigners mistook them no doubt for Arab ladies, not knowing that ladies never walk; and were but little interested in the old, unveiled women with chocolate-coloured faces, who begged, or tried to sell picture-postcards. The arcaded streets were full of light and laughter, noise of voices, clatter of horses' hoofs, carriage-wheels, and tramcars, bells of bicycles and horns of motors. The scene was as gay as any Paris boulevard, and far more picturesque because of the older, Eastern civilization in the midst of, though never part of, an imported European life—the flitting white and brown figures, like thronging ghosts outnumbering the guests at a banquet.

Stephen and Nevill Caird went up the Rue Bab-el-Oued, leading to the old town, and so came to the Hotel de la Kasbah, where Victoria Ray was staying. It looked more attractive at night, with its blaze of electricity that threw out the Oriental colouring of some crude decorations in the entrance-hall, yet the place appeared less than ever suited to Victoria.

An Arab porter stood at the door, smoking a cigarette. His fingers were stained with henna, and he wore an embroidered jacket which showed grease-spots and untidy creases. It was with the calmest indifference he eyed the Englishmen, as Nevill inquired in French for Miss Ray.

The question whether she were "at home" was conventionally put, for it seemed practically certain that she must be in the hotel. Where could she, who had no other friends than they, and no chaperon, go at night? It was with blank surprise, therefore, that he and Stephen heard the man's answer. Mademoiselle was out.

"I don't believe it," Stephen muttered in English, to Nevill.

The porter understood, and looked sulky. "I tell ze troot," he persisted. "Ze gentlemens no believe, zay ask some ozzer."

They took him at his word, and walked past the Arab into the hotel. A few Frenchmen and Spaniards of inferior type were in the hall, and at the back, near a stairway made of the cheapest marble, was a window labelled "Bureau." Behind this window, in a cagelike room, sat the proprietor at a desk, adding up figures in a large book. He was very fat, and his chins went all the way round his neck in grooves, as if his thick throat might pull out like an accordion. There was something curiously exotic about him, as there is in persons of mixed races; an olive pallor of skin, an oiliness of black hair, and a jetty brightness of eye under heavy lids.

This time it was Stephen who asked for Miss Ray; but he was given the same answer. She had gone out.

"You are sure?"

"Mais, oui, monsieur."

"Has she been gone long?" Stephen persisted, feeling perplexed and irritated, as if something underhand were going on.

"Of that I cannot tell," returned the hotel proprietor, still in guttural French. "She left word she would not be at the dinner."

"Did she say when she would be back?"

"No, monsieur. She did not say."

"Perhaps the American Consul's family took pity on her, and invited her to dine with them," suggested Nevill.

"Yes," Stephen said, relieved. "That's the most likely thing, and would explain her engagement this afternoon."

"We might explore the Kasbah for an hour, and call again, to inquire."

"Let us," returned Stephen. "I should like to know that she's got in all right."

Five minutes later they had left the noisy Twentieth Century behind them, and plunged into the shadowy silence of a thousand years ago.

The change could not have been more sudden and complete if, from a gaily lighted modern street, full of hum and bustle, they had fallen down an oubliette into a dark, deserted fairyland. Just outside was the imported life of Paris, but this old town was Turkish, Arab, Moorish, Jewish and Spanish; and in Algeria old things do not change.

After all, the alley was not deserted, though it was soundless as a tomb save for a dull drumming somewhere behind thick walls. They were in a narrow tunnel, rather than a street, between houses that bent towards each other, their upper stories supported by beams. There was no electric light, scarcely any light at all save a strip of moonshine, fine as a line of silver inlaid in ebony, along the cobbled way which ascended in steps, and a faint glimmer of a lamp here and there in the distance, a lamp small and greenish as the pale spark of a glow-worm. As they went up, treading carefully, forms white as spirits came down the street in heelless babouches that made no more noise than the wings of a bat. These forms loomed vague in the shadow, then took shape as Arab men, whose eyes gleamed under turbans or out from hoods.

Moving aside to let a cloaked figure go by, Stephen brushed against the blank wall of a house, which was cold, sweating dampness like an underground vault. No sun, except a streak at midday, could ever penetrate this tunnel-street.

So they went on from one alley into another, as if lost in a catacomb, or the troubling mazes of a nightmare. Always the walls were blank, save for a deep-set, nail-studded door, or a small window like a square dark hole. Yet in reality, Nevill Caird was not lost. He knew his way very well in the Kasbah, which he never tired of exploring, though he had spent eight winters in Algiers. By and by he guided his friend into a street not so narrow as the others they had climbed, though it was rather like the bed of a mountain torrent, underfoot. Because the moon could pour down a silver flood it was not dark, but the lamps were so dull that the moonlight seemed to put them out.

Here the beating was as loud as a frightened heart. The walls resounded with it, and sent out an echo. More than one nailed door stood open, revealing a long straight passage, with painted walls faintly lighted from above, and a curtain like a shadow, hiding the end. In these passages hung the smoky perfume of incense; and from over tile-topped walls came the fragrance of roses and lemon blossoms, half choked with the melancholy scent of things old, musty and decayed. Beautiful pillars, brought perhaps from ruined Carthage, were set deeply in the whitewashed walls, looking sad and lumpy now that centuries of chalk-coats had thickened their graceful contours. But to compensate for loss of shape, they were dazzling white, marvellous as columns of carved pearl in the moonlight, they and their surrounding walls seeming to send out an eerie, bleached light of their own which struck at the eye. The uneven path ran floods of moonlight; and from tiny windows in the leaning snow- palaces— windows like little golden frames—looked out the faces of women, as if painted on backgrounds of dull yellow, emerald-green, or rose-coloured light.

They were unveiled women, jewelled like idols, white and pink as wax-dolls, their brows drawn in black lines with herkous, their eyes glittering between bluish lines of kohl, their lips poppy-red with the tint of mesouak, their heads bound in sequined nets of silvered gauze, and crowned with tiaras of gold coins. The windows were so small that the women were hidden below their shoulders, but their huge hoop-earrings flashed, and their many necklaces sent out sparks as they nodded, smiling, at the passers; and one who seemed young and beautiful as a wicked fairy, against a purple light, threw a spray of orange blossoms at Stephen's feet.

Then, out of that street of muffled music, open doors, and sequined idols, the two men passed to another where, in small open-air cafés, bright with flaring torches or electric light squatting men smoked, listening to story-tellers; and where, further on, Moorish baths belched out steam mingled with smells of perfume and heated humanity. So, back again to black tunnels, where the blind walls heard secrets they would never tell. The houses had no eyes, and the street doors drew back into shadow.

"Do you wonder now," Nevill asked, "that it's difficult to find out what goes on in an Arab's household?"

"No," said Stephen. "I feel half stifled. It's wonderful, but somehow terrible. Let's get out of this 'Arabian Nights' dream, into light and air, or something will happen to us, some such things as befell the Seven Calendars. We must have been here an hour. It's time to inquire for Miss Ray again. She's sure to have come in by now."

Back they walked into the Twentieth Century. Some of the lights in the hotel had been put out. There was nobody in the hall but the porter, who had smoked his last cigarette, and as no one had given him another, he was trying to sleep in a chair by the door.

Mademoiselle might have come in. He did not know. Yes, he could ask, if there were any one to ask, but the woman who looked after the bedrooms had an evening out. There was only one *femme de chambre*, but what would you? The high season was over. As for the key of Mademoiselle, very few of the clients ever left their keys in the bureau when they promenaded themselves. It was too much trouble. But certainly, he could knock at the door of Mademoiselle, if the gentlemen insisted, though it was now on the way to eleven o'clock, and it would be a pity to wake the young lady if she were sleeping.

"Knock softly. If she's awake, she'll hear you," Stephen directed. "If she's asleep, she won't."

The porter went lazily upstairs, appearing again in a few minutes to announce that he had obeyed instructions and the lady had not answered. "But," he added, "one would say that an all little light came through the keyhole."

"Brute, to look!" mumbled Stephen. There was, however, nothing more to be done. It was late, and they must take it for granted that Miss Ray had come home and gone to bed.

XIII

That night Stephen dreamed troubled dreams about Victoria. All sorts of strange things were happening behind a locked door, he never quite knew what, though he seemed forever trying to find out. In the morning, before he was dressed, Mahommed brought a letter to his door; only one, on a small tray. It was the first letter he had received since leaving London—he, who had been used to sighing over the pile that heaped up with every new post, and must presently be answered.

He recognized the handwriting at a glance, though he had seen it only once, in a note written to Lady MacGregor. The letter was from Victoria, and was addressed to "Mr. Stephen Knight," in American fashion—a fashion unattractive to English eyes. But because it was Victoria's way, it seemed to Stephen simple and unaffected, like herself. Besides, she was not aware that he had any kind of handle to his name.

"Now I shall know where she was last night," he said to himself, and was about to tear open the envelope, when suddenly the thought that she had touched the paper made him tender in his usage of it. He found a paper-knife and with careful precision cut the envelope along the top. The slight delay whetted his eagerness to read what Victoria had to tell. She had probably heard of the visit which she had missed, and had written this letter before going to bed. It was a sweet thought of the girl's to be so prompt in explaining her absence, guessing that he must have suffered some anxiety.

"DEAR MR. KNIGHT,"

he read, the blood slowly mounting to his face as his eyes travelled from line to line,

"I don't know what you will think of me when I have told you about the thing I am going to do. But whatever you may think, don't think me ungrateful. Indeed, indeed I am not that. I hate to go away without seeing you again, yet I must; and I can't even tell you why, or where I am going—that is the worst. But if you could know why, I'm almost sure you would feel that I am doing the right thing, and the only thing possible. Before all and above all with me, must be my sister's good. Everything else has to be sacrificed to that, even things that I value very, very much.

"Don't imagine though, from what I say, that I'm making a great sacrifice, so far as any danger to myself is concerned. The sacrifice is, to risk being thought unkind, ungrateful, by you, and of losing your friendship. This is the *only* danger I am running, really; so don't fear for me, and please forgive me if you can. Just at the moment I must seem (as well as ungracious) a little mysterious, not because I want to be mysterious, but because it is forced on me by circumstances. I hate it, and soon I hope I shall be able to be as frank and open with you as I was at first, when I saw how good you were about taking an interest in my sister Saidee. I think, as far as I can see ahead, I may write to you in a fortnight. Then, I shall have news to tell, the *best of news*, I hope; and I won't need to keep anything back. By that time I may tell you all that has happened, since bidding you and Mr. Caird good-bye, at the door of his beautiful house, and all that will have happened by the time I can begin the letter. How I wish it were now!

"There's just one more word I want to say, that I really can say without doing harm to anybody or to any plan. It's this. I did feel so guilty when you talked about your motoring with Mr. Caird to Tlemcen. It was splendid of you both to be willing to go, and you must have thought me cold and half-hearted about it. But I couldn't tell you what was in my mind, even then. I didn't know what was before me; but there was already a thing which I had to keep from you. It was only a small thing. But now it has grown to be a very big one.

"Good-bye, my dear friend Mr. Knight. I like to call you my friend, and I shall always remember how good you were to me, if, for any reason, we should never see each other again. It is very likely we may not meet, for I don't know how long you are going to stay in Africa, or how long I shall stay, so it may be that you will go back to England soon. I don't suppose I shall go there. When I can leave this country it will be to sail for America with my sister — *never without her*. But I shall write, as I said, in a fortnight, if all is well — indeed, I shall write whatever happens. I shall be able to give you an address, too, I hope very much, because I should like to hear from you. And I shall pray that you may always be happy.

"I meant this to be quite a short letter, but after all it is a long one! Good-bye again, and give my best remembrances to Lady

MacGregor and Mr. Caird, if they are not disgusted with me for the way I am behaving. Gratefully your friend,

"VICTORIA RAY."

There was no room for any anger against the girl in Stephen's heart. He was furious, but not with her. And he did not know with whom to be angry. There was some one—there must be some one—who had persuaded her to take this step in the dark, and this secret person deserved all his anger and more. To persuade a young girl to turn from the only friends she had who could protect her, was a crime. Stephen could imagine no good purpose to be served by mystery, and he could imagine many bad ones. The very thought of the best among them made him physically sick. There was a throat somewhere in the world which his fingers were tingling to choke; and he did not know where, or whose it was. It made his head ache with a rush of beating blood not to know. And realizing suddenly, with a shock like a blow in the face, the violence of his desire to punish some person unknown, he saw how intimate a place the girl had in his heart. The longing to protect her, to save her from harm or treachery, was so intense as to give pain. He felt as if a lasso had been thrown round his body, pressing his lungs, roping his arms to his sides, holding him helpless; and for a moment the sensation was so powerful that he was conscious of a severe effort, as if to break away from the spell of a hypnotist.

It was only for a moment that he stood still, though a thousand thoughts ran through his head, as in a dream—as in the dreams of last night, which had seemed so interminable.

The thing to do was to find out at once what had become of Victoria, whom she had seen, who had enticed her to leave the hotel. It would not take long to find out these things. At most she could not have been gone more than thirteen or fourteen hours.

At first, in his impatience, he forgot Nevill. In two or three minutes he had finished dressing, and was ready to start out alone when the thought of his friend flashed into his mind. He knew that Nevill Caird, acquainted as he was with Algiers, would be able to suggest things that he might not think of unaided. It would be better that they two should set to work together, even though it might mean a delay of a few minutes in the beginning.

He put Victoria's letter in his pocket, meaning to show it to Nevill as the quickest way of explaining what had happened and what he wanted to do; but before he had got to his friend's door, he knew that he could not bear to show the letter. There was nothing in it which Nevill might not see, nothing which Victoria might not have wished him to see. Nevertheless it was now *his* letter, and he could not have it read by any one.

He knocked at the door, but Nevill did not answer. Then Stephen guessed that his friend must be in the garden. One of the under-gardeners, working near the house, had seen the master, and told the guest where to go. Monsieur Caird was giving medicine to the white peacock, who was not well, and in the stable-yard Nevill was found, in the act of pouring something down the peacock's throat with a spoon.

When he heard what Stephen had to say, he looked very grave.

"I wish Miss Ray hadn't stopped at that hotel," he said.

"Why?" Stephen asked sharply. "You don't think the people there——"

"I don't know what to think. But I have a sort of idea the brutes knew something last night and wouldn't tell."

"They'll have to tell!" exclaimed Stephen.

Nevill did not answer.

"I shall go down at once," Stephen went on.

"Of course I'll go with you," said his friend.

They had forgotten about breakfast. Stopping only to get their hats, they started for the town.

XIV

"Don't begin by accusing the landlord of anything," Nevill advised, at the hotel door. "He's got too much Arab blood in him to stand that. You'd only make him tell you lies. We must seem to know things, and ask questions as if we expected him to confirm our knowledge. That may confuse him if he wants to lie. He won't be sure what ground to take."

The Arab porter was not in his place, but the proprietor sat in his den behind the window. He was drinking a cup of thick, syrupy coffee, and soaking a rusk in it. Stephen thought this a disgusting sight, and could hardly bear to let his eyes rest on the thick rolls of fat that bulged over the man's low collar, all the way round his neck like a yellow ruff. Not trusting himself to speak just then, Stephen let Caird begin the conversation.

The landlord bowed over his coffee and some letters he was reading, but did not trouble to do more than half rise from his chair and sink back again, solidly. These fine gentlemen would never be clients of his, would never be instrumental in sending any one to him. Why should he put himself out?

"We've had a letter from Miss Ray this morning," Nevill announced, after a perfunctory exchange of "good days" in French.

The two young men both looked steadily at the proprietor of the hotel, as Nevill said these words. The fat man did not show any sign of embarrassment, however, unless his expectant gaze became somewhat fixed, in an effort to prevent a blink. If this were so, the change was practically imperceptible. "She had left here before six o'clock last evening, hadn't she?"

"I cannot tell you, Monsieur. It is as I answered yesterday. I do not know the time when she went out."

"You must know what she said when she went."

"On the contrary, Monsieur. The young lady did not speak with me herself. She sent a message."

"And the message was that she was leaving your hotel?"

"First of all, that she had the intention of dining out. With a lady."

Stephen and Nevill looked at each other. With a lady? Could it be possible that Mademoiselle Soubise, interested in the story, had called and taken the girl away?

"What then?" went on Caird. "She let you know eventually that she'd made up her mind to go altogether?"

"The message was that she might come back in some days. But yes, Monsieur, she let me know that for the present she was leaving."

"Yet you didn't tell us this when we called!" exclaimed Stephen. "You let us think she would be back later in the evening."

"Pardon me, Monsieur, if you remember, you asked *when* Mademoiselle would be back. I replied that I did not know. It was perfectly true. And desolated as I was to inconvenience you, I could not be as frank as my heart prompted. My regrettable reserve was the result of Mademoiselle's expressed wish. She did not desire to have it known that she was leaving the hotel, until she herself chose to inform her friends. As it seems you have had a letter, Monsieur, I can now speak freely. Yesterday evening I could not."

He looked like the last man whose heart would naturally prompt him to frankness, but it seemed impossible to prove, at the moment, that he was lying. It was on the cards that Miss Ray might have requested silence as to her movements.

Stephen bit his lip to keep back an angry reproach, nevertheless, and Caird reflected a moment before answering. Then he said slowly; "Look here: we are both friends of Miss Ray, the only ones she has in Algiers, except of course my aunt, Lady MacGregor, with whom she lunched yesterday. We are afraid she has been imprudently advised by some one, as she is young and inexperienced in travelling. Now, if you will find out from your servants, and also let us know from your own observation, exactly what she did yesterday, after returning from her visit to my aunt—what callers she had, if any; to whose house she went, and so on—we will make it worth your while. Lady MacGregor" (he made great play with his relative's name, as if he wished the landlord to understand that two young men were not the girl's only friends in Algiers) "is very anxious to see Miss Ray. To spare her anxiety, we offer a reward of a thousand francs for reliable information. But we must hear to-day, or to- morrow at latest."

As he evolved this proposal, Nevill and Stephen kept their eyes upon the man's fat face. He looked politely interested, but not excited, though the offer of a thousand francs was large enough to rouse his cupidity, it would seem, if he saw his way to earning it.

He shrugged his shoulders with a discouraged air when Nevill finished.

"I can tell you now, Monsieur, all that I know of Mademoiselle's movements—all that anybody in the hotel knows, I think. No one came to see her, except yourselves. She was out all the morning of yesterday, and did not return here till sometime after the *déjeuner*. After that, she remained in her room until towards evening. It was the head-waiter who brought me the message of which I have told you, and requested the bill. At what hour the young lady actually went out, I do not know. The porter can probably tell you."

"But her luggage," Stephen cut in quickly. "Where did it go? You can at least tell that?"

"Mademoiselle's luggage is still in the hotel. She asked permission to store it, all but a dressing-bag of some sort, which, I believe she carried with her."

"In a cab?"

"That I do not know. It will be another question for the porter. But were I in the place of Monsieur and his friend, I should have no uneasiness about the young lady. She is certain to have found trustworthy acquaintances, for she appeared to be very sensible."

"We shall be glad if you will let us have a short talk with several of your servants," said Nevill—"the *femme de chambre* who took care of Miss Ray's room, and the waiter who served her, as well as the porter."

"Certainly, Monsieur. They shall be brought here," the landlord assented. "I will help you by questioning them myself."

"I think we'll do that without your help, thank you," replied Stephen drily.

The fat man looked slightly less agreeable, but touched a bell in the wall by his desk. A boy answered and was sent to command Angéle and Ahmed to report at once. Also he was to summon the porter, whether that man had finished his breakfast or not. These orders given, Monsieur Constant looked at the two Englishmen as if to say, "You see! I put my whole staff at your disposition. Does not this prove my good faith? What would you have more?"

Angéle was Algerian French, evidently of mixed parentage, like all those in the Hotel de la Kasbah who were not Arabs. She was middle-aged, with a weary, hatchet face, and eyes from which looked a crushed spirit. If Stephen and Nevill could have seen Madame Constant, they would hardly have wondered at that expression.

Ahmed had negro blood in his veins, and tried to smooth out the frizziness of the thick black hair under his fez, with much pomatum, which smelled of cheap bergamot.

These two, with the porter who soon appeared, brushing breadcrumbs from his jacket, stood in front of the bureau window, waiting to learn the purpose for which they had been torn from their various occupations. "It is these gentlemen who have something to ask you. They do not wish me to interfere," announced the master to his servants, with a gesture. He then turned ostentatiously to the sipping of his neglected coffee.

Nevill undertook the cross-questionings, with occasional help from Stephen, but they learned no detail of importance. Angéle said that she had been out when the demoiselle Americaine had left the hotel; but that the luggage of Mademoiselle was still in her room. Ahmed had taken a message to Monsieur le Patron, about the bill, and had brought back Mademoiselle's change, when the note was paid. The porter had carried down a large dressing-bag, at what time he could not be sure, but it was long before dark. He had asked if Mademoiselle wished him to call a *voiture*, but she had said no. She was going out on foot, and would presently return in a carriage. This she did. The porter believed it was an ordinary cab in which Mademoiselle had driven back, but he had not thought much about it, being in a hurry as he took the bag. He was at least certain that Mademoiselle had been alone. She had received no callers while she was in the hotel, and had not been seen speaking to any one: but she had gone out a great deal. Why had he not mentioned in the evening that the young lady had driven away with luggage? For the sufficient reason that Mademoiselle had particularly requested him to say nothing of her movements, should any one come to inquire. It was for the same reason that he had been obliged to deceive Monsieur in the matter of knocking at her door. And as the porter made this answer, he looked far more impudent than he had looked last night, though he was smiling blandly.

How much of this was lies and how much truth? Stephen wondered, when, having given up hope of learning more from landlord or servants, they left the hotel.

Nevill had to confess that he was puzzled. "Their stories hold together well enough," he said, "but if they have anything to hide (mind, I don't say they have) they're the sort to get up their tale beforehand, so as to make it water-tight. We called last night, and that man Constant must have known we'd come again, whether we heard from Miss Ray or whether we didn't—still more, if we *didn't*. Easy as falling off a log to put the servants up to what he wanted them to say, and prepare them for questions, without giving them tips under our noses."

"If they know anything that fat old swine doesn't want them to give away, we can bribe it out of them," said Stephen, savagely. "Surely these Arabs and half-breeds love money."

"Yes, but there's something else they hold higher, most of them, I will say in their favour—loyalty to their own people. If this affair has to do with Arabs, like as not we might offer all we've got without inducing them to speak—except to tell plausible lies and send us farther along the wrong track. It's a point of pride with these brown faces. Their own above the Roumis, and I'm hanged if I can help respecting them for that, lies and all."

"But why should they lie?" broke out Stephen. "What can it be to them?"

"Nothing, in all probability," Nevill tried to soothe him. "The chances are, they've told us everything they know, in good faith, and that they're just as much in the dark about Miss Ray's movements as we are—without the clue we have, knowing as we do why she came to Algiers. It's mysterious enough anyhow, what's become of her; but it's more likely than not that she kept her own secret. You say she admitted in her letter having heard something which she didn't mention to us when she was at my house; so she must have got a clue, or what she thought was a clue, between the time when we took her from the boat to the Hotel de la Kasbah, and the time when she came to us for lunch."

"It's simply hideous!" Stephen exclaimed. "The only way I can see now is to call in the police. They must find out where that cab came from and where it took Miss Ray. That's the important thing."

"Yes, to get hold of the cabman is the principal thing," said Nevill, without any ring of confidence in his voice. "But till we learn the contrary, we may as well presume she's safe. As for the police, for her sake they must be a last resort."

"Let's go at once and interview somebody. But there's one hope. She may have gone to Tlemcen to see that Kabyle maid of Mademoiselle Soubise, for herself. Perhaps that's why she didn't encourage us to motor there. She's jolly independent."

Nevill's face brightened. "When we've done what we can in Algiers, we might run there ourselves in the car, just as I proposed before," he said eagerly. "If nothing came of it, we wouldn't be wasting time, you know. She warned you not to expect news for a fortnight, so there's no use hanging about here in hopes of a letter or telegram. We can go to Tlemcen and get back inside five days. What do you say?"

What Stephen might have said was, that they could save the journey by telegraphing to Mademoiselle Soubise to ask whether Miss Ray had arrived in Tlemcen. But the brightness in Nevill's eyes and the hopefulness in his voice kept back the prosaic suggestion.

"I say, by all means let's go to Tlemcen," he answered. "To-morrow, after we've found out what we can here about the cab, inquired at the railway stations and so on. Besides, we can at least apply to the police for information about Ben Halim. If we learn he's alive, and where he is living, it may be almost the same as knowing where Miss Ray has gone."

XV

Nothing could be heard of Victoria at any place of departure for ships, nor at the railway stations. Stephen agreed with Nevill that it would not be fair to lay the matter in the hands of the police, lest in some way the girl's mysterious "plan" should be defeated. But he could not put out of his head an insistent idea that the Arab on board the *Charles Quex* might stand for something in this underhand business. Stephen could not rest until he had found out the name of this man, and what had become of him after arriving at Algiers. As for the name, having appeared on the passenger list, it was easily obtained without expert help. The Arab was a certain Sidi Maïeddine ben el Hadj Messaoud; and when Jeanne Soubise was applied to for information concerning him, she was able to learn from her Arab friends that he was a young man of good family, the son of an Agha or desert chief, whose douar lay far south, in the neighbourhood of El-Aghouat. He was respected by the French authorities and esteemed by the Governor of Algiers. Known to be ambitious, he was anxious to stand well with the ruling power, and among the dissipated, sensuous young Arabs of his class and generation, he was looked upon as an example and a shining light. The only fault found in him by his own people was that he inclined to be too modern, too French in his political opinions; and his French friends found no fault with him at all.

It seemed impossible that a person so highly placed would dare risk his future by kidnapping a European girl, and Jeanne Soubise advised Stephen to turn his suspicions in another direction. Still he would not be satisfied, until he had found and engaged a private detective, said to be clever, who had lately seceded from a Paris agency and set up for himself in Algiers. Through him, Stephen hoped to learn how Sidi Maïeddine ben el Hadj Messaoud had occupied himself after landing from the *Charles Quex*; but all he did learn was that the Arab, accompanied by his servant and no one else, had, after calling on the Governor, left Algiers immediately for El- Aghouat. At least, he had taken train for Bogharie, and was known to have affairs of importance to settle between his father the Agha, and the French authorities. Secret inquiries at the Hotel de la Kasbah elicited answers, unvaryingly the same. Sidi Maïeddine ben el Hadj Messaoud was not a patron of the house, and had never been seen there. No one answering at all to his description had stopped in, or even called at, the hotel.

Of course, the value of such assurances was negatived by the fact that Arabs hold together against foreigners, and that if Si Maïeddine wished to be incognito among his own people, his wish would probably be respected, in spite of bribery. Besides, he was rich enough to offer bribes on his own part. Circumstantial evidence, however, being against the supposition that the man had followed Victoria after landing, Stephen abandoned it for the time, and urged the detective, Adolphe Roslin, to trace the cabman who had driven Miss Ray away from her hotel. Roslin was told nothing about Victoria's private interests, but she was accurately described to him, and he was instructed to begin his search by finding the squint-eyed cab-driver who had brought the girl to lunch at Djenan el Djouad.

Only in the affair of Cassim ben Halim did Stephen and Nevill decide to act openly, Nevill using such influence as he had at the Governor's palace. They both hoped to learn something which in compassion or prudence had been kept from the girl; but they failed, as Victoria had failed. If a scandal had driven the Arab captain of Spahis from the army and from Algiers, the authorities were not ready to unearth it now in order to satisfy the curiosity, legitimate or illegitimate, of two Englishmen.

Captain Cassim ben Halim el Cheik el Arab, had resigned from the army on account of ill-health, rather more than nine years ago, and having sold his house in Algiers had soon after left Algeria to travel abroad. He had never returned, and there was evidence that he had been burned to death in a great fire at Constantinople a year or two later. The few living relatives he had in Algeria believed him to be dead; and a house which Ben Halim had owned not far from Bou Saada, had passed into the hands of his uncle, Caïd of a desert- village in the district. As to Ben Halim's marriage with an American girl, nobody knew anything. The present Governor and his staff had come to Algiers after his supposed death; and if Nevill suspected a deliberate reticence behind certain answers to his questions, perhaps he was mistaken. Cassim ben Halim and his affairs could now be of little importance to French officials.

It did not take Roslin an hour to produce the squinting cabman; but the old Arab was able to prove that he had been otherwise engaged than in driving Miss Ray on the evening when she left the Hotel de la Kasbah. His son had been ill, and the father had given up work in order to play nurse. A doctor corroborated this story, and nothing was to be gained in that direction.

Then it was that Nevill almost timidly renewed his suggestion of a visit to Tlemcen. They could find out by telegraphing Josette, he admitted, whether or no Victoria Ray had arrived, but if she were not already in Tlemcen, she might come later, to see Mouni. And even if not, they might find out how to reach Saidee, by catechizing the Kabyle girl. Once they knew the way to Victoria's sister, it was next best to knowing the way to find Victoria herself. This last argument was not to be despised. It impressed Stephen, and he consented at once to "try their luck" at Tlemcen.

Early in the morning of the second day after the coming of Victoria's letter, the two men started in Nevill's yellow car, the merry-eyed chauffeur charmed at the prospect of a journey worth doing. He was tired, he remarked to Stephen, "de tous ces petits voyages d'une demi-heure, comme les tristes promenades des enfants, sans une seule aventure."

They had bidden good-bye to Lady MacGregor, and most of the family animals, overnight, and it was hardly eight o'clock when they left Djenan el Djouad, for the day's journey would be long. A magical light, like the light in a dream, gilded the hills of the Sahel; and beyond lay the vast plain of the Metidja, a golden bowl, heaped to its swelling rim of mountains with the fairest fruits of Algeria.

The car rushed through a world of blossoms, fragrant open country full of flowers, and past towns that did their small utmost to bring France into the land which France had conquered. Boufarik, with its tall monument to a brave French soldier who fought against tremendous odds: Blidah, a walled and fortified mixture of garrison and orange-grove, with a market-place like a scene in the "Arabian Nights": Orleansville, modern and ostentatiously French, built upon ruins of vast antiquity, and hotter than all other towns in the dry cup of the Chelif Valley: Relizane, Perrégaux, and finally Oran (famed still for its old Spanish forts), which they reached by moonlight.

Always there were fields embroidered round the edges with wild flowers of blue and gold, and rose. Always there were white, dusty roads, along which other motors sometimes raced, but oftener there were farm-carts, wagons pulled by strings of mules, and horses with horned harness like the harness in Provence or on the Spanish border. There were huge, two-storied diligences, too, drawn by six or eight black mules, crammed under their canvas roofs with white- or brown-robed Arabs, and going very fast.

From Oran they might have gone on the same night, reaching the end of their journey after a few hours' spin, but Nevill explained that haste would be vain. They could not see Mademoiselle Soubise until past nine, so better sleep at Oran, start at dawn, and see something of the road,—a road more picturesque than any they had travelled.

It was not for Stephen to offer objections, though he was in a mood which made him long to push on without stopping, even though there were no motive for haste. He was ashamed of the mood, however, and hardly understood what it meant, since he had come to Algeria in search of peace. When first he landed, and until the day of Victoria's letter, he had been enormously interested in the panorama of the East which passed before his eyes. He had eagerly noticed each detail of colour and strangeness, but now, though the London lethargy was gone, in its place had been born a disturbing restlessness which would not let him look impersonally at life as at a picture.

Questioning himself as he lay awake in the Oran hotel, with windows open to the moonlight, Stephen was forced to admit that the picture was blurred because Victoria had gone out of it. Her figure had been in the foreground when first he had seen the moving panorama, and all the rest had been only a magical frame for her. The charm of her radiant youth, and the romance of the errand which had brought her knocking, when he knocked, at the door of the East, had turned the glamour into glory. Now she had vanished; and as her letter said, it might be that she would never come back. The centre of interest was transferred to the unknown place where she had gone, and Stephen began to see that his impatience to be moving was born of the wish not only to know that she was safe, but to see her again.

He was angry with himself at this discovery, and almost he was angry with Victoria. If he had not her affairs to worry over, Africa would be giving him the rest cure he had expected. He would be calmly enjoying this run through beautiful country, instead of chafing to rush on to the end. Since, in all probability, he could do the girl no good, and certainly she could do him none, he half wished that one or the other had crossed from Marseilles to Algiers on a different ship. What he needed was peace, not any new and feverish personal interest in life. Yes, decidedly he wished that he had never known Victoria Ray.

But the wish did not live long. Suddenly her face, her eyes, came before him in the night. He heard her say that she would give him "half her star," and his heart grew sick with longing.

"I hope to Heaven I'm not going to love that girl," he said aloud to the darkness. If no other woman came into his life, he might be able to get through it well enough with Margot. He could hunt and shoot, and do other things that consoled men for lack of something better. But if— he knew he must not let there be an "if." He must go on thinking of Victoria Ray as a child, a charming little friend whom he wished to help. Any other thought of her would mean ruin.

Before dawn they were called, and started as the sun showed over the horizon.

So they ran into the western country, near to the Morocco border. Dull at first, save for its flooding flowers, soon the way wound among dark mountains, from whose helmeted heads trailed the long plumes of white cascades, and whose feet—like the stone feet of Egyptian kings in ruined temples—were bathed by lakes that glimmered in the depths of gorges.

It was a land of legends and dreams round about Tlemcen, the "Key of the West," city of beautiful mosques. The mountains were honeycombed with onyx mines; and rising out of wide plains were crumbling brown fortresses, haunted by the ghosts of long-dead Arabs who had buried hoards of money in secret hiding-places, and died before they could unearth their treasure. Tombs of kings and princes, and koubbahs of renowned marabouts, Arab saints, gleamed white, or yellow as old gold, under the faded silver of ancient olive trees, in fields that ran red with blood of poppies. Minarets jewelled like peacocks' tails soared above the tops of blossoming chestnuts. On low trees or bushes, guarding the graves of saints, fluttered many-coloured rags, left there by faithful men and women who had prayed at the shrine for health or fortune; and for every foot of ground there was some wild tale of war or love, an echo from days so long ago that history had mingled inextricably with lore of fairies.

Nevill was excited and talkative as they drove into the old town, once the light of western Algeria. They passed in by the gateway of Oran, and through streets that tried to be French, but contrived somehow to be Arab. Nevill told stories of the days when Tlemcen had queened it over the west, and coined her own money; of the marabouts after whom the most famous mosques were named: Sidi-el-Haloui, the confectioner-saint from Seville, who preached to the children and made them sweetmeats; of the lawyer-saint, Sidi Aboul Hassan from Arabia, and others. But he did not speak of Josette Soubise, until suddenly he touched Stephen's arm as they passed the high wall of a garden.

"There, that's where *she* teaches," he said; and it was not necessary to add a name.

Stephen glanced at him quickly. Nevill looked very young. His eyes no longer seemed to gaze at far-away things which no one else could see. All his interests were centred near at hand.

"Don't you mean to stop?" Stephen asked, surprised that the car went on.

"No; school's begun. We'll have to wait till the noon interval, and even then we shan't be allowed indoors, for a good many of the girls are over twelve, the age for veiling—*hadjabah*, they call it—when they're shut up, and no man, except near relations, can see their faces. Several of the girls are already engaged. I believe there's one, not fourteen, who's been divorced twice, though she's still interested in dolls. Weird, isn't it? Josette will talk with us in the garden. But we'll have time now to take rooms at the hotel and wash off the dust. To eat something too, if you're hungry."

But Stephen was no hungrier than Nevill, whose excitement, perhaps, was contagious.

The hotel was in a wide *place*, so thickly planted with acacias and chestnut trees as to resemble a shabby park. An Arab servant showed them to adjoining rooms, plain but clean, and a half-breed girl brought tins of hot water and vases of syringas. As for roses, she said in hybrid French, no one troubled about them—there were too many in Tlemcen. Ah! but it was a land of plenty! The gentlemen would be happy, and wish to stay a long time. There was meat and good wine for almost nothing, and beggars need not ask twice for bread—fine, white bread, baked as the Moors baked, across the border.

As they bathed and dressed more carefully than they had dressed for the early-morning start, strange sounds came up from the square below, which was full of people, laughing, quarrelling, playing games, striking bargains, singing songs. Arab bootblacks clamoured for custom at the hotel-door, pushing one another aside, fiercely. Little boys in embroidered green or crimson jackets sat on the hard, yellow earth, playing an intricate game like "jack stones," and disputed so violently that men and even women stopped to remonstrate, and separate them; now a grave, prosperous Jew dressed in red (Jewish mourning in the province of Oran); then an old Kabyle woman of the plains, in a short skirt of fiery orange scarcely hiding the thin sticks of legs that were stained with henna half-way up the calves, like painted stockings. Moors from across the frontier—fierce men with eagle faces and striped cloaks—grouped together, whispering and gesticulating, stared at with suspicion by the milder Arabs, who attributed all the crimes of Tlemcen to the wild men from over the border. Black giants from the Negro quarter kept together, somewhat humble, yet laughing and happy. Slender, coffee-coloured youths drove miniature cows from Morocco, or tiny black donkeys, heavily laden and raw with sores, colliding with well-dressed Turks, who had the air of merchants, and looked as if they could not forget that Tlemcen had long been theirs before the French dominion. Bored but handsome officers rode through the square on Arab horses graceful as deer, and did not even glance at passing women, closely veiled in long white haïcks.

It was lively and amusing in the sunlight; but just as the two friends were ready to go out, the sky was swept with violet clouds. A storm threatened fiercely, but they started out despite its warning, turning deaf ears to the importunities of a Koulougli guide who wished to show them the mosques, "ver' cheap." He followed them, but they hurried on, pushing so sturdily through a flock of pink-headed sheep, which poured in a wave over the pavement, that they might have out-run the rain had they not been brought to a sudden standstill by a funeral procession.

It was the strangest sight Stephen had seen yet, and he hardly noticed that, in a burst of sunlight, rain had begun to pelt down through the canopy of trees.

The band of figures in brown burnouses marched quickly, with a sharp rustling of many slippered feet moving in unison, and golden spears of rain seemed to pierce the white turbans of the men who carried the bier. As they marched, fifty voices rose and fell wildly in a stirring chant, exciting and terrible as the beat-beat of a tom-tom, sometimes a shout of barbaric triumph, sometimes a mourning wail.

Then, abruptly, a halt was made in the glittering rain, and the bearers were changed, because of the luck it brings Arab men to carry the corpse of a friend.

Just in front of the two Englishmen the body rested for an instant, stretched out long and piteously flat, showing its thin shape through the mat of woven straw which wrapped it, only the head and feet being wound with linen. So, by and by, it would be laid, without a coffin, in its shallow grave in the Arab cemetery, out on the road to Sidi Bou-Medine.

There were but a few seconds of delay. Then the new bearers lifted the bier by its long poles, and the procession moved swiftly, feverishly, on again, the wild chant trailing behind as it passed, like a torn war-banner. The thrill of the wailing crept through Stephen's veins, and roused an old, childish superstition which an Irish nurse had implanted in him when he was a little boy. According to Peggy Brian it was "a cruel bad omen" to meet a funeral, especially after coming into a new town. "Wait for a corpse," said she, "an' ye'll wait while yer luck goes by."

"They're singing a song in praise of the dead man's good deeds, and of triumph for the joys he'll know in Paradise," explained Nevill. "It's only the women who weep and scratch their faces when those they love have died. The men rejoice, or try to. Soon, they are saying, this one who has gone will be in gardens fair as the gardens of Allah Himself, where sit beautiful houris, in robes woven of diamonds, sapphires, and rubies, each gem of which has an eye of its own that glitters through a vapour of smouldering ambergris, while fountains send up pearly spray in the shade of fragrant cedars."

"No wonder the Mohammedan poor don't fear death, if they expect to exchange their hovels for such quarters," said Stephen. "I wish I understood Arabic."

"It's a difficult language to keep in your mind, and I don't know it well," Nevill answered. "But Jeanne and Josette Soubise speak it like natives; and the other day when Miss Ray lunched with us, I thought her knowledge of Arabic wonderful for a person who'd picked it up from books."

Stephen did not answer. He wished that Nevill had not brought the thought of Victoria into his mind at the moment when he was recalling his old nurse's silly superstition. Victoria laughed at superstitions, but he was not sure that he could laugh, in this barbaric land where it seemed that anything might happen.

XVI

Nevill had not sent word to Josette Soubise that he was coming to see her. He wished to make the experiment of a surprise, although he insisted that Stephen should be with him. At the door in the high white wall of the school-garden, he asked an unveiled crone of a porteress to say merely that two gentlemen had called.

"She'll suspect, I'm afraid," he muttered to Stephen as they waited, "even if her sister hasn't written that I thought of turning up. But she won't have time to invent a valid excuse, if she disapproves of the visit."

In three or four minutes the old woman hobbled back, shuffling slippered feet along the tiled path between the gate and the low whitewashed house. Mademoiselle requested that ces Messieurs would give themselves the pain of walking into the garden. She would descend almost at once.

They obeyed, Nevill stricken dumb by the thought of his coming happiness. Stephen would have liked to ask a question or two about the school, but he refrained, sure that if Nevill were forced into speech he would give random answers.

This was being in love—the real thing! And Stephen dimly envied his friend, even though Caird seemed to have small hope of winning the girl. It was far better to love a woman you could never marry, than to be obliged to marry one you could never love.

He imagined himself waiting to welcome Margot, beautiful Margot, returning from Canada to him. He would have to go to Liverpool, of course. She would be handsomer than ever, probably, and he could picture their meeting, seven or eight weeks from now. Would his face wear such an expression as Nevill's wore at this moment? He knew well that it would not.

"She is coming!" said Nevill, under his breath.

The door of the schoolhouse was opening, and Nevill moved forward as a tall and charming young woman appeared, like a picture in a dark frame.

She was slender, with a tiny waist, though her bust was full, and her figure had the intensely feminine curves which artists have caused to be associated with women of the Latin races; her eyes were like those of her elder sister, but larger and more brilliant. So big and splendid they were that they made the smooth oval of her olive face seem small. Quantities of heavy black hair rippled away from a forehead which would have been square if the hair had not grown down in a point like a Marie Stuart cap. Her chin was pointed, with a deep cleft in the middle, and the dimples Nevill had praised flashed suddenly into being, as if a ray of sunshine had touched her pale cheeks.

"Mon bon ami!" she exclaimed, holding out both hands in token of comradeship, and putting emphasis on her last word.

"She's determined the poor chap shan't forget they're only friends," thought Stephen, wishing that Caird had not insisted upon his presence at this first meeting. And in a moment he was being introduced to Mademoiselle Josette Soubise.

"Did I surprise you?" asked Nevill, looking at her as if he could never tear his eyes away, though he spoke in an ordinary tone.

"Ah, I know you want me to say 'yes'," she laughed. "I'd like to tell a white fib, to please you. But no, I am not quite surprised, for my sister wrote that you might come, and why. What a pity you had this long journey for nothing. My Kabyle maid, Mouni, has just gone to her home, far away in a little village near Michélet, in la Grande Kabylia. She is to be married to her cousin, the chief's son, whom she has always loved—but there were obstacles till now."

"Obstacles can always be overcome," broke in Nevill.

Josette would not understand any hidden meaning. "It is a great pity about Mouni," she went on. "Only four days ago she left. I gave her the price of the journey, for a wedding present. She is a good girl, and I shall miss her. But of course you can write to ask her questions. She reads a little French."

"Perhaps we shall go ourselves," Nevill answered, glancing at Stephen's disappointed face. "For I know Miss Ray can't be here, or you would have said so."

"No, she is not here," echoed Josette, looking astonished. "Jeanne wrote about the American young lady searching for her sister, but she did not say she might visit Tlemcen."

"We hoped she would, that's all," explained Nevill. "She's left her hotel in Algiers in a mysterious way, not telling where she meant to go, although she assured us she'd be safe, and we needn't worry. However, naturally we do worry."

"But of course. I see how it is." The dimples were gone, and the brightness of Josette's eyes was overcast. She looked at Nevill wistfully, and a flash of sympathetic understanding enlightened Stephen. No doubt she was generously solicitous for the fate of Victoria Ray, but there was something different from solicitude in her darkening eyes.

"Good! she's jealous. She thinks Nevill's heart's been caught in the rebound," he told himself. But Nevill remained modestly unconscious.

"Miss Ray may arrive yet," he suggested. "We'd better stop to-day, anyhow, on the chance; don't you think so, Stephen? and then, if there's no news of her when we get back to Algiers, go on to interview the bride in Grand Kabylia?"

Stephen had not the heart to dispute the wisdom of this decision, though he was sure that, since Victoria was not in Tlemcen now, she would never come.

"So you think we've made a long journey for nothing, Mademoiselle Josette?" said Nevill.

"But yes. So it turns out."

"Seeing an old friend doesn't count, then?"

"Oh, well, that can seem but little—in comparison to what you hoped. Still, you can show Monsieur Knight the sights. He may not guess how beautiful they are. Have you told him there are things here as wonderful as in the Alhambra itself, things made by the Moors who were in Granada?"

"I've told him about all I care most for in Tlemcen," returned Nevill, with that boyish demureness he affected sometimes. "But I'm not a competent cicerone. If you want Knight to do justice to the wonders of this place, you'll have to be our guide. We've got room for several large-sized chaperons in the car. Do come. Don't say you won't! I feel as if I couldn't stand it."

His tone was so desperate that Josette laughed some of her brightness back again. "Then I suppose I mustn't refuse. And I should like going—after school hours. Madame de Vaux, who is the bride of a French officer, will join us, I think, for she and I are friends, and besides, she has had no chance to see things yet. She has been busy settling in her quarters—and I have helped her a little."

"When can you start?" asked Nevill, enraptured at the prospect of a few happy hours snatched from fate.

"Not till five."

His face fell. "But that's cruel!"

"It would be cruel to my children to desert them sooner. Don't forget I am malema—malema before all. And there will be time for seeing nearly everything. We can go to Sidi Bou-Medine, afterwards to the ruins of Mansourah by sunset. Meanwhile, show your friend the things near by, without me; the old town, with its different quarters for the Jews, the Arabs, and the Negroes. He will like the leather-workers and the bakers, and the weavers of haïcks. And you will not need me for the Grande Mosquée, or for the Mosquée of Aboul Hassan, where Monsieur Knight will see the most beautiful mihrab in all the world. When he has looked at that, he cannot be sorry he has come to Tlemcen; and if he has regrets, Sidi Bou-Medine will take them away."

"Has Sidi Bou-Medine the power to cure all sorrows?" Stephen asked, smiling.

"Indeed, yes. Why, Sidi Bou-Medine himself is one of the greatest marabouts. You have but to take a pinch of earth from his tomb, and make a wish upon it. Only one wish, but it is sure to be granted, whatever it may be, if you keep the packet of earth afterwards, and wear it near your heart."

"What a shame you never told me that before. The time I've wasted!" exclaimed Nevill. "But I'll make up for it now. Thank Heaven I'm superstitious."

They had forgotten Stephen, and laughing into each other's eyes, were perfectly happy for the moment. Stephen was glad, yet he felt vaguely resentful that they could forget the girl for whose sake the journey to Tlemcen had ostensibly been undertaken. They were ready to squander hours in a pretence of sightseeing, hours which might have been spent in getting back to Algiers and so hastening on the expedition to Grand Kabylia. How selfish people in love could be! And charming as Josette Soubise was, it seemed strange to Stephen that she should stand for perfection to a man who had seen Victoria Ray.

Nevill was imploring Josette to lunch with them, chaperoned by Madame de Vaux, and Josette was firmly refusing. Then he begged that they might leave money as a gift for the malema's scholars, and this offer she accepted, only regretting that the young men could not be permitted to give the *cadeau* with their own hands. "My girls are so pretty," she said, "and it is a picture to see them at their embroidery frames, or the carpet making, their fingers flying, their eyes always on the coloured designs, which are the same as their ancestresses used a century ago, before the industry declined. I love them all, the dear creatures, and they love me, though I am a Roumia and an unbeliever. I ought to be happy in their affection, helping them to success. And now I must run back to my flock, or the lambs will be getting into mischief. Au revoir—five o'clock. You will find me waiting with Madame de Vaux."

At luncheon, in the bare, cool dining-room of the hotel, Nevill was like a man in a dream. He sat half smiling, not knowing what he ate, hardly conscious of the talk and laughter of the French officers at another table. Just at the last, however, he roused himself. "I can't help being happy. I see her so seldom. And I keep turning over in my mind what new arguments in favour of myself I can bring forward when I propose this afternoon—for of course I shall propose, if you and the bride will kindly give me the chance. I know she won't have me—but I always do propose, on the principle that much dropping may wear away a stone."

"Suppose you break the habit just for once," ventured Stephen. Nevill

looked anxious. "Why, do you think the case is hopeless?"

"On the contrary. But—well, I can't help feeling it would do you more good to show an absorbing interest in Miss Ray's affairs, this time."

"So I have an absorbing interest," Nevill protested, remorsefully. "I don't want you to suppose I mean to neglect them. I assure you ——"

Stephen laughed, though a little constrainedly. "Don't apologise, my dear fellow. Miss Ray's no more to me than to you, except that I happened to make her acquaintance a few days sooner."

"I know," Nevill agreed, mildly. Then, after a pause, which he earnestly occupied in crumbling bread. "Only I'm head over ears in love with another woman, while you're free to think of her, or any other girl, every minute of the day."

Stephen's face reddened. "I am not free," he said in a low voice.

"I beg your pardon. I hoped you were. I still think—you ought to be." Nevill spoke quickly, and without giving Stephen time to reply, he hurried on; "Miss Ray may arrive here yet. Or she may have found out about Mouni in some other way, and have gone to see her in Grand Kabylia—who knows?"

"If she were merely going there to inquire about her sister, why should she have to make a mystery of her movements?"

"Well, it's on the cards that whatever she wanted to do, she didn't care to be bothered with our troublesome advice and offers of help. Our interest was, perhaps, too pressing."

"Mademoiselle Soubise is of that opinion, anyhow—in regard to you," remarked Stephen.

"What—that angel *jealous*? It's too good to be true! But I'll relieve her mind of any such idea."

"If you'll take one more tip from me, I'd leave her mind alone for the present."

"Why, you flinty-hearted reprobate?"

"Well, I'm no authority. But all's fair in love and war. And sometimes an outsider sees features of the game which the players don't see."

"That's true, anyhow," Nevill agreed. "Let's *both* remember that—eh?" and he got up from the table abruptly, as if to keep Stephen from answering, or asking what he meant.

They had several empty hours, between the time of finishing luncheon, and five o'clock, when they were to meet Mademoiselle

Soubise and her chaperon, so they took Josette's advice and went sightseeing.

Preoccupied as he was, Stephen could not be indifferent to the excursion, for Tlemcen is the shrine of gems in Arab architecture, only equalled at Granada itself. Though he was so ignorant still of eastern lore, that he hardly knew the meaning of the word mihrab, the arched recess looking towards Mecca, in the Mosque of the lawyer-saint Aboul Hassan, held him captive for many moments with its beauty. Its ornamentation was like the spread tail of Nevill's white peacock, or the spokes of a silver wheel incrusted with an intricate pattern in jewels. Not a mosque in town, or outside the gates, did they leave unvisited, lest, as Nevill said, Josette Soubise should ask embarrassing questions; and the last hour of probation they gave to the old town. There, as they stopped to look in at the workshops of the weavers, and the bakers, or stared at the hands of Fatma-Zora painted in henna on the doors of Jews and True Believers, crowds of ragged boys and girls followed them, laughing and begging as gaily as if begging were a game. Only this band of children, and heavily jewelled girls of Morocco or Spain, with unveiled, ivory faces and eyes like suns, looked at the Englishmen, as Stephen and Nevill passed the isolated blue and green houses, in front of which the women sat in a bath of sunshine. Arabs and Jews walked by proudly, and did not seem to see that there were strangers in their midst.

When at last it was time to go back to the hotel, and motor to the École Indigène, Josette was ready, plainly dressed in black. She introduced her friends to the bride, Madame de Vaux, a merry young woman, blonde by nature and art, who laughed always, like the children in the Arab town. She admired Knight far more than Caird, because she liked tall, dark men, her own husband being red and stout. Therefore, she would have been delighted to play the tactful chaperon, if Josette had not continually broken in upon her duet with Stephen, ordering them both to look at this or that.

The country through which they drove after passing out of the gate in the modern French wall, might have been the south of England in midsummer, had it not been peopled by the dignified Arab figures which never lost their strangeness and novelty for Stephen. Here, in the west country, they glittered in finery like gorgeous birds: sky-blue jacket, scarlet fez and sash glowing behind a lacework of green branches netted with flowers, where a man hoed his fields or planted his garden.

Hung with a tapestry of roses, immense brown walls lay crumbling—ruined gateways, and shattered traces of the triple fortifications which defended Tlemcen when the Almohades were in power. By a clear rill of water gushing along the roadside, a group of delicate broken arches marked the tomb of the "flying saint," Sidi Abou Ishad el Taïyer, an early Wright or Blériot who could swim through the air; and though in his grave a chest of gold was said to be buried, no one—not even the lawless men from over the border— had ever dared dig for the treasure. Close by, under the running water, a Moor had found a huge lump of silver which must have lain for no one could tell how many years, looking like a grey stone under a sheet of glass; nevertheless, the neighbouring tomb had still remained inviolate, for Sidi Abou Ishad el Taïyer was a much respected saint, even more loved than the marabout who sent rain for the gift of a sacrificed fowl, or he who cured sore eyes in answer to prayer. Only Sidi Bou-Medine himself was more important; and presently (because the distance was short, though the car had travelled slowly) they came to the footpath in the hills which must be ascended on foot, to reach the shrine of the powerful saint, friend of great Sidi Abd el Kader.

Already they could see the minaret of the mosque, high above the mean village which clustered round it, rising as a flame rises against a windless sky, while beneath this shining Giralda lay half-ruined houses rejuvenated with whitewash or coats of vivid blue. They passed up a narrow street redeemed from sordidness by a domed koubbah or two; and from the roofed balconies of cafés maures, Arabs looked down on them with large, dreamy eyes like clouded stars. All the glory and pride of the village was concentrated in the tomb and beautiful mosque of the saint whose name falls sweet on the ear as the music of a summer storm, the tinkle and boom of rain and thunder coming together: Sidi Bou-Medine.

Toddling girls with henna-dyed hair, and miniature brown men, like blowing flower-petals in scarlet, yellow, and blue, who had swarmed up the street after the Roumis, stopped at the portals of the mosque and the sacred tomb. But there was a humming in the air like the song of bees, which floated rhythmically out from the zaouïa, the school in the mosque where many boys squatted cross-legged before the aged Taleb who taught the Koran; bowing, swaying towards him, droning out the words of the Prophet, some half asleep, nodding against the onyx pillars.

In the shadow of the mosque it was cool, though the crown of the minaret, gemmed with priceless tiles from Fez, blazed in the sun's rays as if it were on fire. Into this coolness the four strangers passed, involuntarily hushing their voices in the portico of decorated walls and hanging honeycombs of stucco whence, through great doors of ancient, greenish bronze (doors said to have arrived miraculously from across the sea), they found their way into a courtyard open to the sky, where a fountain waved silver plumes over a marble basin. Two or three dignified Arab men bathed their feet in preparation for the afternoon prayer, and tired travellers from a distance slept upon mats of woven straw, spread on tiles like a pavement of precious stones, or dozed in the little cells made for the students who came in the grand old days. The sons of Islam were reverent, yet happy and at home on the threshold of Allah's house, and Stephen began to understand, as Nevill and Josette already understood, something of the vast influence of the Mohammedan religion. Only Madame de Vaux remained flippant. In the car, she had laughed at the women muffled in their haïcks, saying that as the men of Tlemcen were so tyrannical about hiding female faces, it was strange they did not veil the hens and cows. In the shadowy mosque, with its five naves, she giggled at the yellow babouches out of which her little high-heeled shoes slipped, and threatened to recite a French verse under the delicate arch of the pale blue mihrab.

But Stephen was impressed with the serene beauty of the Moslem temple, where, between labyrinths of glimmering pillars like young ash trees in moonlight, across vistas of rainbow-coloured rugs like flower-beds, the worshippers looked out at God's blue sky instead of peering through thick, stained-glass windows; where the music was the murmur of running water, instead of sounding organ-pipes; and where the winds of heaven bore away the odours of incense before they staled. He wondered whether a place of prayer like this—white-walled, severely simple despite the veil-like adornment of arabesques—did not more tend to religious contemplation than a cathedral of Italy or Spain, with its bloodstained Christs, its Virgins, and its saints. Did this Arab art perhaps more truly express the fervour of faith which needs no extraneous elaborations, because it has no doubts? But presently calling up a vision of the high, dim aisles, the strong yet soaring columns, all the mysterious purity of gothic cathedrals, he convinced himself that, after all, the old monkish architects had the real secret of mystic aspirations in the human heart.

When Josette and Nevill led the way out of the mosque, Stephen was in the right mood for the tomb of that ineffable saint of Islam, Shaoib ibn Husain el Andalousi, Sidi Bou-Medine. He was almost ready to believe in the extraordinary virtue of the earth which had the honour of covering the marabout's remains. It annoyed him that Madame de Vaux should laugh at the lowness of the doorway under which they had to stoop, and that she should make fun of the suspended ostrich eggs, the tinselled pictures and mirrors, the glass lustres and ancient lanterns, the spilt candle-wax of many colours, or the old, old flags which covered the walls and the high structure of carved wood which was the saint's last resting-place.

A grave Arab who approved their air of respect, gave a pinch of earth each to Stephen and Nevill, wrapped in paper, repeating Josette's assurance that their wishes would be granted. It would be necessary, he added, to reflect long before selecting the one desire of the soul which was to be put above all others. But Nevill had no hesitation. He wished instantly, and tucked the tiny parcel away in the pocket nearest his heart.

"And you, Monsieur?" asked Madame de Vaux, smiling at Stephen. "It does not appear easy to choose. Ah, now you have decided! Will you tell me what you wished?"

"I think I mustn't do that. Saints favour those who can keep secrets," said Stephen, teasingly. Yet he made his wish in earnest, after turning over several in his mind. To ask for his own future happiness, in spite of obstacles which would prove the marabout's power, was the most intelligent thing to do; but somehow the desire clamouring loudest at the moment was for Victoria, and the rest might go ungranted.

"I wish that I may find her safe and happy," he said over the pinch of earth before putting it into what Josette named his "poche du cœur."

"As for me," remarked Madame de Vaux, "I will not derange any of their Moslem saints, thank you. I have more influential ones of my own, who might be annoyed. And it is stuffy in this tomb. I am sure it is full of microbes. Let us go and see the ruined palace of the Black Sultan who, Josette says, founded everything here that was worth founding. That there should be a Black Sultan sounds like a fairy tale. And I like fairy tales next to bon-bons and new hats."

So they made their pilgrimage to the third treasure of the hill-village; and then away to where the crumbling walls of Mansourah, and that great tower, which is one of the noblest Moorish relics in all Algeria, rise out of a flowering plain.

Cherry blossoms fell in scented snow over their heads as the car ran back to Tlemcen, and out once more, through the Moorish Porte de Fez, past the reservoir built by a king for an Arab beauty to sail her boats upon. Sunset was near, and the sky blazed red as if Mansourah burned with ten thousand torches.

The way led through vast blue lakes which were fields of periwinkles, and along the road trotted pink-robed children, whose heads were wrapped in kerchiefs of royal purple. They led sheep with golden-gleaming fleece, and at the tombs of marabouts they paused to pray, among groups of kneeling figures in long white cloaks and turbans. All the atmosphere swam with changing colours, such as come and go in the heart of a fire-opal.

Very beautiful must have been the city of Mansourah, named after murdered Sultan el Mansour, the Victorious, who built its vast fortifications, its mosques and vanished palaces, its caravanserais and baths, in the seven years when he was besieging Tlemcen. And still are its ruins beautiful, after more than five centuries of pillage and destruction. Josette Soubise loved the place, and often came to it when her day's work was done, therefore she was happy showing it to Nevill and—incidentally—to the others.

The great brown wall pricked with holes like an enormous wasp's nest, the ruined watch-towers, and the soaring, honey-coloured minaret with its intricate carvings, its marble pillars, its tiles and inset enamels iridescent as a Brazilian beetle's wing, all gleamed with a splendour that was an enchantment, in the fire of sunset. The scent of aromatic herbs, such as Arabs love and use to cure their fevers, was bitter-sweet in the fall of the dew, and birds cried to each other from hidden nests among the ruins.

"Mussulmans think that the spirits of their dead fly back to visit their own graves, or places they have loved, in the form of birds," said Josette, looking up at the minaret, large marguerites with orange centres embroidering her black dress, as she stood knee-deep in their waving gold. "I half believe that these birds among the lovely carvings of the tower are the priests who used to read the Koran in the mosque, and could not bear to leave it. The birds in the walls are the soldiers who defended the city."

As she spoke there was a flight of wings, black against the rose and mauve of the sunset. "There!" she exclaimed. "Arabs would call that an omen! To see birds flying at sundown has a special meaning for them. If a man wanted something, he would know that he could get it only by going in the direction the birds take."

"Which way are they flying?" asked Stephen.

All four followed the flight of wings with their eyes.

"They are going south-east," said Nevill.

XVII

If Victoria Ray had accepted Nevill Caird's invitation to be Lady MacGregor's guest and his, at Djenan el Djouad, many things might have been different. But she had wished to be independent, and had chosen to go to the Hotel de la Kasbah.

When she went down to dinner in the *salle à manger*, shortly after seven o'clock on the evening of her arrival, only two other tables were occupied, for it was late in the season, and tourists were leaving Algiers.

No one who had been on board the *Charles Quex* was there, and Victoria saw that she was the only woman in the room. At one table sat a happy party of Germans, apparently dressed from head to foot by Dr. Jaeger, and at another were two middle-aged men who had the appearance of commercial travellers. By and by an elderly Jew came in, and dinner had reached the stage of peppery mutton ragout, when the door opened again. Victoria's place was almost opposite, and involuntarily, she glanced up. The handsome Arab who had crossed from Marseilles on the boat saluted her with grave courtesy as he met her look, and passed on, casting down his eyes. He was shown to a table at some distance, the manner of the Arab waiter who conducted him being so impressive, that Victoria was sure the newcomer must be a person of importance.

He was beautifully dressed, as before, and the Germans stared at him frankly, but he did not seem to be aware of their existence. Special dishes arrived for him, and evidently he had been expected.

There was but one waiter to serve the meal, and not only did he somewhat neglect the other diners for the sake of the latest arrival, but the landlord appeared, and stood talking with the Arab while he ate, with an air of respect and consideration.

The Germans, who had nearly finished their dinner when Victoria came in, now left the table, using their toothpicks and staring with the open-eyed interest of children at the picturesque figure near the door. The commercial travellers and the Jew followed. Victoria also was ready to go, when the landlord came to her table, bowing.

"Mademoiselle," he said, in French, "I am charged with a message from an Arab gentleman of distinction, who honours my house by his presence. Sidi Maïeddine ben el Hadj Messaoud is the son of an Agha, and therefore he is a lord, and Mademoiselle need have no uneasiness that he would condescend to an indiscretion. He instructs me to present his respectful compliments to Mademoiselle, whom he saw on the ship which brought him home, after carrying through a mission in France. Seeing that Mademoiselle travelled alone, and intends perhaps to continue doing so, according to the custom of her courageous and intelligent countrywomen, Sidi Maïeddine wishes to say that, as a person who has influence in his own land, he would be pleased to serve Mademoiselle, if she would honour him by accepting his offer in the spirit in which it is made: that is, as the chivalrous service of a gentleman to a lady. He will not dream of addressing Mademoiselle, unless she graciously permits."

As the landlord talked on, Victoria glanced across the room at the Arab, and though his eyes were bent upon his plate, he seemed to feel the girl's look, as if by a kind of telepathy, instantly meeting it with what seemed to her questioning eyes a sincere and disarming gaze.

"Tell Sidi Maïeddine ben el Hadj Messaoud that I thank him," she answered, rewarded for her industry in keeping up French, which she spoke fluently, with the Parisian accent she had caught as a child in Paris. "It is possible that he can help me, and I should be glad to talk with him."

"In that case Si Maïeddine would suggest that Mademoiselle grant him a short interview in the private sitting-room of my wife, Madame Constant, who will be honoured," the fat man replied promptly. "It would not be wise for Mademoiselle to be seen by strangers talking with the distinguished gentleman, whose acquaintance she is to make. This, largely for her own sake; but also for his, or rather, for the sake of certain diplomatic interests which he is appointed to carry out. Officially, he is supposed to have left Algiers to-day. And it is by his permission that I mention the matter to Mademoiselle."

"I will do whatever you think best," said Victoria, who was too glad of the opportunity to worry about conventionalities. She was so young, and inexperienced in the ways of society, that a small transgression against social laws appeared of little importance to a girl situated as she was.

"Would the time immediately after dinner suit Mademoiselle, for Si Maïeddine to pay his respects?"

Victoria answered that she would be pleased to talk with Si Maïeddine as soon as convenient to him, and Monsieur Constant hurried away to prepare his wife. While he was absent the Arab did not again look at Victoria, and she understood that this reserve arose from delicacy. Her heart began to beat, and she felt that the way to her sister might be opening at last. The fact that she did feel this, made her tell herself that it must be true. Instinct was not given for nothing!

She thought, too, of Stephen Knight. He would be glad to-morrow, when meeting her at luncheon in his friend's house, to hear good news. Already she had been to see Jeanne Soubise, in the curiosity-shop, and had bought a string of amber prayer-beads. She had got an introduction to the Governor from the American Consul, whom she had visited before unpacking, lest the consular office should be closed for the day; and she had obtained an appointment at the palace for the next morning; but all that was not much to tell Mr. Knight. It seemed to her that even in a few hours she ought to have accomplished more. Now, however, the key of the door which opened into the golden silence might be waiting for her hand.

In three or four minutes the landlord came back, and begged to show her his wife's *petit salon*. This time as she passed the Arab she bowed, and gave him a grateful smile. He rose, and stood with his head slightly bent until she had gone out, remaining in the dining-room until the landlord returned to say that he was expected by Mademoiselle.

"Remember," Si Maïeddine said in Arabic to the fat man, "everybody is to be discreet, now and later. I shall see that all are rewarded for obedience."

"Thou art considerate, even of the humblest," replied the half-breed, using the word "thou," as all Arabs use it. "Thy presence is an honour for my house, and all in it is thine."

Si Maïeddine—who had never been in the Hotel de la Kasbah before, and would not have considered it worthy of his patronage if he had not had an object in coming—allowed himself to be shown the door of Madame Constant's salon. On the threshold, the landlord retired, and the young man was hardly surprised to find, on entering, that Madame was not in the room.

Victoria was there alone; but free from self-consciousness as she always was, she received Si Maïeddine without embarrassment. She saw no reason to distrust him, just because he was an Arab.

Now, how glad she was that she had learned Arabic! She began to speak diffidently at first, stammering and halting a little, because, though she could read the language well after nine years of constant study, only once had she spoken with an Arab;—a man in New York from whom she had had a few lessons. Having learned what she could of the accent from phrase-books, her way had been to talk to herself aloud. But the flash of surprised delight which lit up the dark face told her that Si Maïeddine understood.

"Wonderful!" he exclaimed. "My best hope was that French might come easily to thy lips, as I have little English."

"I have a sister married to one of thy countrymen," Victoria explained at once. "I do not know where she is living, and it is in finding out, that I need help. Even on the ship I wished to ask thee if thou hadst knowledge of her husband, but to speak then seemed impossible. It is a fortunate chance that thou shouldst have come to this hotel, for I think thou wilt do what thou canst for me." Then she went on and told him that her sister was the wife of Captain Cassim ben Halim, who had once lived in Algiers.

Si Maïeddine who had dropped his eyes as she spoke of the fortunate chance which had brought him to the hotel, listened thoughtfully and with keen attention to her story, asking no questions, yet showing his interest so plainly that Victoria was encouraged to go on.

"Didst thou ever hear the name of Cassim ben Halim?" she asked.

"Yes, I have heard it," the Arab replied. "I have friends who knew him. And I myself have seen Cassim ben Halim."

"Thou hast seen him!" Victoria cried, clasping her hands tightly together. She longed to press them over her heart, which was like a bird beating its wings against the bars of a cage.

"Long ago. I am much younger than he."

"Yes, I see that," Victoria answered. "But thou knewest him! That is something. And my sister. Didst thou ever hear of her?"

"We of the Mussulman faith do not speak of the wives of our friends, even when our friends are absent. Yet—I have a relative in Algiers who might know something, a lady who is no longer young. I will go to her to-night, and all that is in her heart she will tell me. She has lived long in Algiers; and always when I come, I pay her my respects. But, there is a favour I would beg in return for any help I can give, and will give gladly. I am supposed to be already on my way south, to finish a diplomatic mission, and, for reasons connected with the French government, I have had to make it appear that I started to-day with my servant. There is also a reason, connected with Si Cassim, which makes it important that nothing I may do should be known to thy European friends. It is for his sake especially that I ask thy silence; and whatsoever might bring harm to him—if he be still upon the earth—would also harm thy sister. Wilt thou give me thy word, O White Rose of another land, that thou wilt keep thine own counsel?"

"I give thee my word—and with it my trust," said the girl.

"Then I swear that I will not fail thee. And though until I have seen my cousin I cannot speak positively, yet I think what I can do will be more than any other could. Wilt thou hold thyself free of engagements with thy European friends, until I bring news?"

"I have promised to lunch to-morrow with people who have been kind, but rather than risk a delay in hearing from thee, I will send word that I am prevented from going."

"Thou hast the right spirit, and I thank thee for thy good faith. But it may be well not to send that message. Thy friends might think it strange, and suspect thee of hiding something. It is better to give no cause for questionings. Go then, to their house, but say nothing of having met me, or of any new hope in thine heart. Yet let the hope remain, and be to thee like the young moon that riseth over the desert, to show the weary traveller a rill of sweet water in an oasis of date palms. And now I will bid thee farewell, with a night of dreams in which thy dearest desires shall be fulfilled before thine eyes. I go to my cousin, on thy business."

"Good night, Sidi. Henceforth my hope is in thee." Victoria held out her hand, and Si Maïeddine clasped it, bowing with the courtesy of his race. He was nearer to her than he had been before, and she noticed a perfume which hung about his clothing, a perfume that seemed to her like the East, heavy and rich, suggestive of mystery and secret things. It brought to her mind what she had read about harems, and beautiful, languid women, yet it suited Si Maïeddine's personality, and somehow did not make him seem effeminate.

"See," he said, in the poetic language which became him as his embroidered clothes and the haunting perfume became him; "see, how thine hand lies in mine like a pearl that has dropped into the hollow of an autumn leaf. But praise be to Allah, autumn and I are yet far apart. I am in my summer, as thou, lady, art in thine early spring. And I vow that thou shalt never regret confiding thy hand to my hand, thy trust to my loyalty."

As he spoke, he released her fingers gently, and turning, went out of the room without another word or glance.

When he had gone, Victoria stood still, looking at the door which Si Maïeddine had shut noiselessly.

If she had not lived during all the years since Saidee's last letter, in the hope of some such moment as this, she would have felt that she had come into a world of romance, as she listened to the man of the East, speaking the language of the East. But she had read too many Arabic tales and poems to find his speech strange. At school, her studies of her sister's adopted tongue had been confined to dry lesson-books, but when she had been free to choose her own literature, in New York and London, she had read more widely. People whom she had told of her sister's marriage, and her own mission, had sent her several rare volumes,—among others a valuable old copy of the Koran, and she had devoured them all, delighting in the facility which grew with practice. Now, it seemed quite simple to be talking with Sidi Maïeddine ben el Hadj Messaoud as she had talked. It was no more romantic or strange than all of life was romantic and strange. Rather did she feel that at last she was face to face with reality.

"He *does* know something about Cassim," she said, half aloud, and searching her instinct, she still thought that she could trust him to keep faith with her. He was not playing. She believed that there was sincerity in his eyes.

The next morning, when Victoria called at the Governor's palace, and heard that Captain Cassim ben Halim was supposed to have died in Constantinople, years ago, she was not cast down. "I know Si Maïeddine doesn't think he's dead," she told herself.

There was a note for her at the hotel, and though the writer had addressed the envelope to "Mademoiselle Ray," in an educated French handwriting, the letter inside was written in beautiful Arab lettering, an intentionally flattering tribute to her accomplishment.

Si Maïeddine informed her that his hope had been justified, and that in conversation with his cousin his own surmises had been confirmed. A certain plan was suggested, which he wished to propose to Mademoiselle Ray, but as it would need some discussion, there was not time to bring it forward before the hour when she must go out to keep her engagement. On her return, however, he begged that she would see him, in the salon of Madame Constant, where she would find him waiting. Meanwhile, he ventured to remind her that for the present, secrecy was even more necessary than he had at first supposed; he would be able to explain why, fully and satisfactorily, when they met in the afternoon.

With this appointment to look forward to, it was natural that Victoria should excuse herself to Lady MacGregor earlier than most people cared to leave Djenan el Djouad. The girl was more excited than she had ever been in her life, and it was only by the greatest self-control that she kept—or believed that she kept—her manner as usual, while with Stephen in the white garden of lilies. She was happy, because she saw her feet already upon the path which would lead through the golden silence to her sister; but there was a drawback to her happiness—a fly in the amber, as in one of the prayer-beads she had bought of Jeanne Soubise: her secret had to be kept from the man of whom she thought as a very staunch friend. She felt guilty in talking with Stephen Knight, and accepting his sympathy as if she were hiding nothing from him; but she must be true to her promise, and Si Maïeddine had the right to exact it, though of course Mr. Knight might have been excepted, if only Si Maïeddine knew how loyal he was. But Si Maïeddine did not know, and she could not explain. It was consoling to think of the time when Stephen might be told everything; and she wished almost unconsciously that it was his help which she had to rely upon now.

XVIII

True to his word, Si Maïeddine was waiting in Madame Constant's hideous sitting-room, when Victoria returned to the hotel from Djenan el Djouad.

To-day he had changed his grey bournous for a white one, and all his clothing was white, embroidered with silver.

"It is written," he began in Arabic, as he rose to welcome the girl, "that the messenger who brings good tidings shall come in white. Now thou art prepared for happiness. Thou also hast chosen white; but even in black, thy presence would bring a blessing, O Rose of the West."

The colour of the rose stained Victoria's cheeks, and Si Maïeddine's eyes were warm as he looked at her. When she had given him her hand, he kissed his own, after touching it. "Be not alarmed, or think that I take a liberty, for it is but a custom of my people, in showing respect to man or woman," he explained. "Thou hast not forgotten thy promise of silence?"

"No, I spoke not a word of thee, nor of the hope thou gavest me last night," Victoria answered.

"It is well," he said. "Then I will keep nothing back from thee."

They sat down, Victoria on a repulsive sofa of scarlet plush, the Arab on a chair equally offensive in design and colour.

"Into the life of thy brother-in-law, there came a great trouble," he said. "It befell after the days when he was known by thee and thy sister in Paris. Do not ask what it was, for it would grieve me to refuse a request of thine. Shouldst thou ever hear this thing, it will not be from my lips. But this I will say—though I have friends among the French, and am loyal to their salt which I have eaten, and I think their country great—France was cruel to Ben Halim. Were not Allah above all, his life might have been broken, but it was written that, after a time of humiliation, a chance to win honour and glory such as he had never known, should be put in his way. In order to take this blessing and use it for his own profit and that of others, it was necessary that Ben Halim—son of a warrior of the old fighting days, when nomads of high birth were as kings in the Sahara, himself lately a captain of the Spahis, admired by women, envied of men—it was necessary that he should die to the world."

"Then he is not really dead!" cried Victoria.

The face of Si Maïeddine changed, and wore that look which already the girl had remarked in Arab men she had passed among French crowds: a look as if a door had shut behind the bright, open eyes; as if the soul were suddenly closed.

"Thy brother-in-law was living when last I heard of him," Maïeddine answered, slowly.

"And my sister?"

"My cousin told me last night that Lella Saïda was in good health some months ago when news came of her from a friend."

"They call her Saïda!" murmured the girl, half sadly; for that Saidee should tolerate such a change of name, seemed to signify some subtle alteration in her spirit. But she knew that "Lella" meant "Madame" in Arab society.

"It is my cousin who spoke of the lady by that name. As for me, it is impossible that I should know anything of her. Thou wishest above all things to see thy sister?"

"Above all things. For more than nine years it has been the one great wish of my life to go to her."

"It is a long journey. Thou wouldst have to go far—very far."

"What would it matter, if it were to the end of the world?"

"As well try to reach the place where she is, as though it were beyond where the world ends, unless thou wert guided by one who knew the way."

Victoria looked the Arab full in the face. "I have always been sure that God would lead me there, one day, soon or late," she said.

"Thy God is my God, and Mohammed is his Prophet, as thy Christ was also among his Prophets. It is as thou sayest; Allah wills that thou shouldst make this journey, for He has sent me into thy life at the moment of thy need. I can take thee to thy sister's house, if thou wilt trust thyself to me. Not alone—I would not ask that. My cousin will take care of thee. She has her own reason for going on this great journey, a reason which in its way is as strong as thine, for it concerns her life or death. She is a noble lady of my race, who should be a Princess of Touggourt, for her grandfather was Sultan before the French conquered those warlike men of the desert, far south where Touggourt lies. Lella M'Barka Bent Djellab hears the voice of the Angel Azraïl in her ears, yet her spirit is strong, and she believes it is written in the Book that she shall reach the end of her journey. This is the plan she and I have made; that thou leave the hotel to-day, towards evening, and drive (in a carriage which she will send)—to her house, where thou wilt spend the night. Early in the morning of to-morrow she can be ready to go, taking thee with her. I shall guard thee, and we shall have an escort which she and I will provide. Dost thou consent? Because if the idea pleases thee, there are many arrangements which must be made quickly. And I myself will take all trouble from thy shoulders in the matter of leaving the hotel. I am known and well thought of in Algiers and even the landlord here, as thou hast seen, has me in consideration, because my name is not strange to him. Thou needst not fear misconstruction of thine actions, by any one who is here."

Si Maïeddine added these arguments, seeing perhaps that Victoria hesitated before answering his question.

"Thou art generous, and I have no fear," she said at last, with a faint emphasis which he could read as he chose. "But, since thou hast my word to be silent, surely thou wilt tell me where lies the end of the journey we must take?"

"Even so, I cannot tell thee," Si Maïeddine replied with decision which Victoria felt to be unalterable. "It is not for lack of trust in thee, O Rose, but for a reason which is not mine to explain. All I can do is to pledge my honour, and the honour of a princess, to conduct thee loyally to the house of thy sister's husband. If thou goest, it must be in the dress of an Arab lady, veiled from eyes which might spy upon thee; and so thou wilt be safe under the protection of my cousin."

"My thanks to thee and to her—I will go," Victoria said, after a moment's pause.

She was sure that Stephen Knight and his friend would prevent her from leaving Algiers with strangers, above all, in the company of Arabs, if they could know what was in her mind. But they were

146

unjustly prejudiced, she thought. Her brother-in-law was of Arab blood, therefore she could not afford to have such prejudices, even if she were so inclined; and she must not hesitate before such a chance as Si Maïeddine offered.

The great difficulty she had experienced in learning anything about Ben Halim made it easy for her to believe that she could reach her sister's husband only through people of his own race, who knew his secrets. She was ready to agree with Si Maïeddine that his God and her God had sent him at the right moment, and she would not let that moment pass her by.

Others might say that she was wildly imprudent, that she was deliberately walking into danger; but she was not afraid. Always she trusted to her star, and now it had brought her to Algiers, she would not weaken in that trust. Common sense, in which one side of the girl's nature was not lacking, told her that this Arab might be deceiving her, that he might know no more of Ben Halim than she herself had told him yesterday; but she felt that he had spoken the truth, and feelings were more to her than common sense. She would go to the house which Si Maïeddine said was the house of his cousin, and if there she found reason to doubt him, she had faith that even then no evil would be allowed to touch her.

At seven o'clock, Si Maïeddine said, Lella M'Barka would send a carriage. It would then be twilight, and as most people were in their homes by that hour, nobody would be likely to see her leave the hotel. The shutters of the carriage would be closed, according to the custom of Arab ladies, and on entering the vehicle Victoria would find a negress, a servant of Lella M'Barka Bent Djellab. This woman would dress her in a gandourah and a haïck, while they were on their way to the house of Victoria's hostess, and on stepping out she would have the appearance of a lady of Algiers. Thus all trace of her would be lost, as one Arab carriage was exactly like another.

Meanwhile, there would be time to pack, and write a letter which Victoria was determined to write. To satisfy Si Maïeddine that she would not be indiscreet in any admission or allusion, she suggested translating for him every word she wrote into French or Arabic; but he refused this offer with dignity. She trusted him. He trusted her also. But he himself would post the letter at an hour too late for it to be delivered while she was still in Algiers.

It was arranged that she should carry only hand-bags, as it would be too conspicuous to load and unload boxes. Her large luggage could be stored at the hotel until she returned or sent, and as Lella M'Barka intended to offer her an outfit suitable to a young Arab girl of noble birth, she need take from the hotel only her toilet things.

So it was that Victoria wrote to Stephen Knight, and was ready for the second stage of what seemed the one great adventure to which her whole life had been leading up.

XIX

Victoria did not wait in her room to be told that the carriage had come to take her away. It was better, Si Maïeddine had said, that only a few people should know the exact manner of her going. A few minutes before seven, therefore, she went down to the entrance-hall of the hotel, which was not yet lighted. Her appearance was a signal for the Arab porter, who was waiting, to run softly upstairs and return with her hand luggage.

For some moments Victoria stood near the door, interesting herself in a map of Algeria which hung on the wall. A clock began to strike as her eyes wandered over the desert, and was on the last stroke of seven, when a carriage drove up. It was drawn by two handsome brown mules with leather and copper harness which matched the colour of their shining coats, and was driven by a heavy, smooth-faced Negro in a white turban and an embroidered cafetan of dark blue. The carriage windows were shuttered, and as the black coachman pulled up his mules, he looked neither to the right nor to the left. It was the hotel porter who opened the door, and as Victoria stepped in without delay, he thrust two hand-bags after her, snapping the door sharply.

It was almost dark inside the carriage, but she could see a white figure, which in the dimness had neither face nor definite shape; and there was a perfume as of aromatic amulets grown warm on a human body.

"Pardon, lady, I am Hsina, the servant of Lella M'Barka Bent Djellab, sent to wait upon thee," spoke a soft and guttural voice, in Arabic. "Blessings be upon thee!"

"And upon thee blessings," Victoria responded in the Arab fashion which she had learned while many miles of land and sea lay between her and the country of Islam. "I was told to expect thee."

"Eïhoua!" cried the woman, "The little pink rose has the gift of tongues!" As she grew accustomed to the twilight, Victoria made out a black face, and white teeth framed in a large smile. A pair of dark eyes glittered with delight as the Roumia answered in Arabic, although Arabic was not the language of the negress's own people. She chattered as she helped Victoria into a plain white gandourah.

The white hat and hat-pins amused her, and when she had arranged the voluminous haïck in spite of the joltings of the carriage, she examined these European curiosities with interest. Whenever she moved, the warm perfume of amulets grew stronger, overpowering the faint mustiness of the cushions and upholstery.

"Never have I held such things in my hands!" Hsina gurgled. "Yet often have I wished that I might touch them, when driving with my mistress and peeping at the passers by, and the strange finery of foreign women in the French bazaars."

Victoria listened politely, answering if necessary; yet her interest was concentrated in peering through the slits in the wooden shutter of the nearest window. She did not know Algiers well enough to recognize landmarks; but after driving for what seemed like fifteen or twenty minutes through streets where lights began to turn the twilight blue, she caught a glint of the sea. Almost immediately the trotting mules stopped, and the negress Hsina, hiding Victoria's hat in the folds of her haïck, turned the handle of the door.

Victoria looked out into azure dusk, and after the closeness of the shuttered carriage, thankfully drew in a breath of salt-laden air. One quick glance showed her a street near the sea, on a level not much above the gleaming water. There were high walls, evidently very old, hiding Arab mansions once important, and there were other ancient dwellings, which had been partly transformed for business or military uses by the French. The girl's hasty impression was of a melancholy neighbourhood which had been rich and stately long ago in old pirate days, perhaps.

There was only time for a glance to right and left before a nailed door opened in the flatness of a whitewashed wall which was the front of an Arab house. No light shone out, but the opening of the door proved that some one had been listening for the sound of carriage wheels.

"Descend, lady. I will follow with thy baggage," said Hsina.

The girl obeyed, but she was suddenly conscious of a qualm as she had to turn from the blue twilight, to pass behind that half-open door into darkness, and the mystery of unknown things.

Before she had time to put her foot to the ground the door was thrown wide open, and two stout Negroes dressed exactly alike in flowing white burnouses stepped out of the house to stand on either side the carriage door. Raising their arms as high as their heads they made two white walls of their long cloaks between which Victoria could pass, as if enclosed in a narrow aisle. Hsina came close upon her heels; and as they reached the threshold of the house the white-robed black servants dropped their arms, followed the two women, and shut the nailed door. Then, despite the dimness of the place, they bowed their heads turning aside as if humbly to make it evident that their unworthy eyes did not venture to rest upon the veiled form of their mistress's guest. As for Hsina, she, too, was veiled, though her age and ugliness would have permitted her face to be revealed without offence to Mussulman ideas of propriety. It was mere vanity on her part to preserve the mystery as dear to the heart of the Moslem woman as to the jealous prejudice of the man.

A faint glittering of the walls told Victoria that the corridor she had entered was lined with tiles; and she could dimly see seats let in like low shelves along its length, on either side. It was but a short passage, with a turn into a second still shorter. At the end of this hung a dark curtain, which Hsina lifted for Victoria to pass on, round another turn into a wider hall, lit by an Arab lamp with glass panes framed in delicately carved copper. The chain which suspended it from cedar beams swayed slightly, causing the light to move from colour to colour of the old tiles, and to strike out gleams from the marble floor and ivory-like pillars set into the walls. The end of this corridor also was masked by a curtain of wool, dyed and woven by the hands of nomad tribes, tent-dwellers in the desert; and when Hsina had lifted it, Victoria saw a small square court with a fountain in the centre.

It was not on a grand scale, like those in the palace owned by Nevill Caird; but the fountain was graceful and charming, ornamented with the carved, bursting pomegranates beloved by the Moors of Granada, and the marble columns which supported a projecting balcony were wreathed with red roses and honeysuckle.

On each of the four sides of the quadrangle, paved with black and white marble, there were little windows, and large glass doors draped on the inside with curtains thin enough to show faint pink and golden lights.

"O my mistress, Lella M'Barka, I have brought thy guest!" cried Hsina, in a loud, sing-song voice, as if she were chanting; whereupon one of the glass doors opened, letting out a rosy radiance, and a Bedouin woman-servant dressed in a striped foutah appeared on the threshold. She was old, with crinkled grey hair under a scarlet handkerchief, and a blue cross was tattooed between her eyes.

"In the name of Lella M'Barka be thou welcome," she said. "My mistress has been suffering all day, and fears to rise, lest her strength fail for to-morrow's journey, or she would come forth to meet thee, O Flower of the West! As it is, she begs that thou wilt come to her. But first suffer me to remove thy haïck, that the eyes of Lella M'Barka may be refreshed by thy beauty."

She would have unfastened the long drapery, but Hsina put down Victoria's luggage, and pushing away the two brown hands, tattooed with blue mittens, she herself unfastened the veil. "No, this is *my* lady, and my work, Fafann," she objected.

"But it is my duty to take her in," replied the Bedouin woman, jealously. "It is the wish of Lella M'Barka. Go thou and make ready the room of the guest."

Hsina flounced away across the court, and Fafann held open both the door and the curtains. Victoria obeyed her gesture and went into the room beyond. It was long and narrow, with a ceiling of carved wood painted in colours which had once been violent, but were now faded. The walls were partly covered with hangings like the curtains that shaded the glass door; but, on one side, between gold- embroidered crimson draperies, were windows, and in the white stucco above, showed lace-like openings, patterned to represent peacocks, the tails jewelled with glass of different colours. On the opposite side opened doors of dark wood inlaid with mother-o'- pearl; and these stood ajar, revealing rows of shelves littered with little gilded bottles, or piled with beautiful brocades that were shot with gold in the pink light of an Arab lamp.

There was little furniture; only a few low, round tables, or maidas, completely overlaid with the snow of mother-o'-pearl; two or three tabourets of the same material, and, at one end of the room a low divan, where something white and orange-yellow and purple lay half buried in cushions.

Though the light was dim, Victoria could see as she went nearer a thin face the colour of pale amber, and a pair of immense dark eyes that glittered in deep hollows. A thin woman of more than middle age, with black hair, silver-streaked, moved slightly and held out an emaciated hand heavy with rings. Her head was tied round with a silk handkerchief or takrita of pansy purple; she wore seroual, full trousers of soft white silk, and under a gold-threaded orange-coloured jacket or rlila, a blouse of lilac gauze, covered with sequins and open at the neck. On the bony arm which she held out to Victoria hung many bracelets, golden serpents of Djebbel Amour, and pearls braided with gold wire and coral beads. Her great eyes, ringed with kohl, had a tortured look, and there were hollows under the high cheek-bones. If she had ever been handsome, all beauty of flesh had now been drained away by suffering; yet stricken as she was there remained an almost indefinable distinction, an air of supreme pride befitting a princess of the Sahara.

Her scorching fingers pressed Victoria's hand, as she gazed up at the girl's face with hungry curiosity and interest such as the Spirit of Death might feel in looking at the Spirit of Life.

"Thou art fresh and fair, O daughter, as a lily bud opening in the spray of a fountain, and radiant as sunrise shining on a desert lake," she said in a weary voice, slightly hoarse, yet with some flutelike notes. "My cousin spoke but truth of thee. Thou art worthy of a reward at the end of that long journey we shall take together, thou, and he, and I. I have never seen thy sister whom thou seekest, but I have friends, who knew her in other days. For her sake and thine own, kiss me on my cheeks, for with women of my race, it is the seal of friendship."

Victoria bent and touched the faded face under each of the great burning eyes. The perfume of *ambre*, loved in the East, came up to her nostrils, and the invalid's breath was aflame.

"Art thou strong enough for a journey, Lella M'Barka?" the girl asked.

"Not in my own strength, but in that which Allah will give me, I shall be strong," the sick woman answered with controlled passion. "Ever since I knew that I could not hope to reach Mecca, and kiss the sacred black stone, or pray in the Mosque of the holy Lella Fatima, I have wished to visit a certain great marabout in the south. The pity of Allah for a daughter who is weak will permit the blessing of this marabout, who has inherited the inestimable gift of Baraka, to be the same to me, body and soul, as the pilgrimage to Mecca which is beyond the power of my flesh. Another must say for me the Fatakah there. I believe that I shall be healed, and have vowed to give a great feast if I return to Algiers, in celebration of the miracle. Had it not been for my cousin's wish that I should go with thee, I should not have felt that the hour had come when I might face the ordeal of such a journey to the far south. But the prayer of Si Maïeddine, who, after his father, is the last man left of his line, has kindled in my veins a fire which I thought had burnt out forever. Have no fear, daughter. I shall be ready to start at dawn to-morrow."

"Does the marabout who has the gift of Baraka live near the place where I must go to find my sister?" Victoria inquired, rather timidly; for she did not know how far she might venture to question Si Maïeddine's cousin.

Lella M'Barka looked at her suddenly and strangely. Then her face settled into a sphinx-like expression, as if she had been turned to stone. "I shall be thy companion to the end of thy journey," she answered in a dull, tired tone. "Wilt thou visit thy room now, or wilt thou remain with me until Fafann and Hsina bring thy evening meal? I hope that thou wilt sup here by my side: yet if it pains thee to take food near one in ill health, who does not eat, speak, and thou shalt be served in another place."

Victoria hastened to protest that she would prefer to eat in the company of her hostess, which seemed to please Lella M'Barka. She began to ask the girl questions about herself, complimenting her upon her knowledge of Arabic; and Victoria answered, though only half her brain seemed to be listening. She was glad that she had trusted Si Maïeddine, and she felt safe in the house of his cousin; but now that she was removed from European influences, she could not see why the mystery concerning Ben Halim and the journey which would lead to his house, should be kept up. She had read enough books about Arab customs and superstitions to know that there are few saints believed to possess the gift of Baraka, the power given by Allah for the curing of all fleshly ills. Only the very greatest of the marabouts are supposed to have this power, receiving it direct from Allah, or inheriting it from a pious saint—father or more distant relative—who handed down the maraboutship. Therefore, if she had time and inclination, she could probably learn from any devout Mussulman the abiding places of all such famous saints as remained upon the earth. In that way, by setting her wits to work, she might guess the secret if Si Maïeddine still tried to make a mystery of their destination. But, somehow, she felt that it would not be fair to seek information which he did not want her to have. She must go on trusting him, and by and by he would tell her all she wanted to know.

Lella M'Barka had invited her guest to sit on cushions beside the divan where she lay, and the interest in her feverish eyes, which seldom left Victoria's face, was so intense as to embarrass the girl.

"Thou hast wondrous hair," she said, "and when it is unbound it must be a fountain of living gold. Is it some kind of henna grown in thy country, which dyes it that beautiful colour?"

Victoria told her that Nature alone was the dyer.

"Thou art not yet affianced; that is well," murmured the invalid. "Our young girls have their hair tinted with henna when they are betrothed, that they may be more fair in the eyes of their husbands. But thou couldst scarcely be lovelier than thou art; for thy skin is of pearl, though there is no paint upon it, and thy lips are pink as rose petals. Yet a little messouak to make them scarlet, like coral, and kohl to give thine eyes lustre would add to thy brilliancy. Also the hand of woman reddened with henna is as a brazier of rosy flame to kindle the heart of a lover. When thou seest thy sister, thou wilt surely find that she has made herself mistress of these arts, and many more."

"Canst thou tell me nothing of her, Lella M'Barka?"

"Nothing, save that I have a friend who has said she was fair. And it is not many moons since I heard that she was blessed with health."

"Is she happy?" Victoria was tempted to persist.

"She should be happy. She is a fortunate woman. Would I could tell thee more, but I live the life of a mole in these days, and have little knowledge. Thou wilt see her with thine own eyes before long, I have no doubt. And now comes food which my women have prepared for thee. In my house, all are people of the desert, and we keep the desert customs, since my husband has been gathered to his fathers—my husband, to whose house in Algiers I came as a bride from the Sahara. Such a meal as thou wilt eat to-night, mayst thou eat often with a blessing, in the country of the sun."

Fafann, who had softly left the room when the guest had been introduced, now came back, with great tinkling of khal-khal, and mnaguach, the huge earrings which hung so low as to strike the silver beads twisted round her throat. She was smiling, and pleasantly excited at the presence of a visitor whose arrival broke the tiresome monotony of an invalid's household. When she had set one of the pearly maidas in front of Victoria's seat of cushions, she held back the curtains for Hsina to enter, carrying a copper tray. This the negress placed on the maida, and uncovered a china bowl balanced in a silver stand, like a giant coffee cup of Moorish fashion. It contained hot soup, called cheurba, in which Hsina had put so much fell-fell, the red pepper loved by Arabs, that Victoria's lips were burned. But it was good, and she would not wince though the tears stung her eyes as she drank, for Lella M'Barka and the two servants were watching her eagerly.

Afterwards came a kouskous of chicken and farina, which she ate with a large spoon whose bowl was of tortoiseshell, the handle of ivory tipped with coral. Then, when the girl hoped there might be nothing more, appeared tadjine, a ragout of mutton with artichokes and peas, followed by a rich preserve of melon, and many elaborate cakes iced with pink and purple sugar, and powdered with little gold sequins that had to be picked off as the cake was eaten. At last, there was thick, sweet coffee, in a cup like a little egg-shell supported in filigree gold (for no Mussulman may touch lip to metal), and at the end Fafann poured rosewater over Victoria's fingers, wiping them on a napkin of fine damask.

"Now thou hast eaten and drunk, thou must allow thyself to be dressed by my women in the garments of an Arab maiden of high birth, which I have ready for thee," said Lella M'Barka, brightening with the eagerness of a little child at the prospect of dressing a beautiful new doll. "Fafann shall bring everything here, and thou shalt be told how to robe thyself afterwards. I wish to see that all is right, for to-morrow morning thou must arise while it is still dark, that we may start with the first dawn."

Fafann and Hsina had forgotten their jealousies in the delight of the new play. They moved about, laughing and chattering, and were not chidden for the noise they made. From shelves behind the inlaid doors in the wall, they took down exquisite boxes of mother-o'-pearl and red tortoiseshell. Also there were small bundles wrapped in gold brocade, and tied round with bright green cord. These were all laid on a dim-coloured Kairouan rug, at the side of the divan, and the two women squatted on the floor to open them, while their mistress leaned on her thin elbow among cushions, and skins of golden jackal from the Sahara.

From one box came wide trousers of white silk, like Lella M'Barka's; from another, vests of satin and velvet of pale shades embroidered with gold or silver. A fat parcel contained delicately tinted stockings and high-heeled slippers of different sizes. A second bundle contained blouses of thin silk and gauze, and in a pearl box were pretty little chechias of sequined velvet, caps so small as to fit the head closely; and besides these, there were sashes and gandourahs, and haïcks white and fleecy, woven from the softest wool.

When everything was well displayed, the Bedouin and the negress sprang up, lithe as leopards, and to Victoria's surprise began to undress her.

"Please let me do it myself!" she protested, but they did not listen or understand, chattering her into silence, as if they had been lively though elderly monkeys. Giggling over the hooks and buttons which were comical to them, they turned and twisted her between their hands, fumbling at neck and waist with black fingers, and brown fingers tattooed blue, until she, too, began to laugh. She laughed herself into helplessness, and encouraged by her wild merriment, and Lella M'Barka's smiles and exclamations punctuated with fits of coughing, they set to work at pulling out hairpins, and the tortoise-shell combs that kept the Roumia's red gold waves in place. At last down tumbled the thick curly locks which Stephen Knight had thought so beautiful when they flowed round her shoulders in the Dance of the Shadow.

The invalid made her kneel, just as she was in her petticoat, in order to pass long, ringed fingers through the soft masses, and lift them up for the pleasure of letting them fall. When the golden veil, as Lella M'Barka called it, had been praised and admired over and over again, the order was given to braid it in two long plaits, leaving the ends to curl as they would. Then, the game of dressing the doll could begin, but first the embroidered petticoat of batiste with blue ribbons at the top of its flounce, and the simple pretty little stays had to be examined with keen interest. Nothing like these things had ever been seen by mistress or servants, except in occasional peeps through shuttered carriage windows when passing French shops: for Lella M'Barka Bent Djellab, daughter of Princes of Touggourt, was what young Arabs call "vieux turban." She was old-fashioned in her ideas, would have no European furniture or decorations, and until to-night had never consented to know a Roumia, much less receive one into her house. She had felt that she was making a great concession in granting her cousin's request, but she had forgotten her sense of condescension in entertaining an unveiled girl, a Christian, now that she saw what the girl was like. She was too old and lonely to be jealous of Victoria's beauty; and as Si Maïeddine, her favourite cousin, deigned to admire this young foreigner, Lella M'Barka took an unselfish pride in each of the American girl's charms.

When she was dressed to all outward appearances precisely like the daughter of a high-born Arab family, Fafann brought a mirror framed in mother-o'-pearl, and Victoria could not help admiring herself a little. She wished half unconsciously that Stephen Knight could see her, with hair looped in two great shining braids on either side her face, under the sequined chechia of sapphire velvet; and then she was ashamed of her own vanity.

Having been dressed, she was obliged to prove, before the three women would be satisfied, that she understood how each garment ought to be arranged; and later she had to try on a new gandourah, with a white burnouse such as women wear, and the haïck she had worn in coming to the house. Hsina would help her in the morning, she was told, but it would be better that she should know how to do things properly for herself, since only Fafann would be with them on the journey, and she might sometimes be busy with Lella M'Barka when Victoria was dressing.

The excitement of adorning the beautiful doll had tired the invalid. The dark lines under her eyes were very blue, and the flesh of her face seemed to hang loose, making her look piteously haggard. She offered but feeble objections when her guest proposed to say good night, and after a few more compliments and blessings, Victoria was able to slip away, escorted by the negress.

The room where she was to sleep was on another side of the court from that of Lella M'Barka, but Hsina took great pains to assure her that there was nothing to fear. No one could come into this court; and she—Hsina—slept near by with Fafann. To clap the hands once would be to bring one of them instantly. And Hsina would wake her before dawn.

Victoria's long, narrow sleeping room had the bed across one end, in Arab fashion. It was placed in an alcove and built into the wall, with pillars in front, of gilded wood, and yellow brocaded curtains of a curious, Oriental design. At the opposite end of the room stood a large cupboard, like a buffet, beautifully inlaid with mother-o'-pearl, and along the length of the room ran shelves neatly piled with bright-coloured bed-clothing, or ferrachiyas. Above these shelves texts from the Koran were exquisitely illuminated in red, blue and gold, like a frieze; and there were tinselled pictures of relatives of the Prophet, and of Mohammed's Angel-horse, Borak. The floor was covered with soft, dark-coloured rugs; and on a square of white linen was a huge copper basin full of water, with folded towels laid beside it.

The bed was not uncomfortable, but Victoria could not sleep. She did not even wish to sleep. It was too wonderful to think that to-morrow she would be on her way to Saidee.

XX

Before morning light, Si Maïeddine was in his cousin's house. Hsina had not yet called Victoria, but Lella M'Barka was up and dressed, ready to receive Maïeddine in the room where she had entertained the Roumia girl last night. Being a near relation, Si Maïeddine was allowed to see Lella M'Barka unveiled; and even in the pink and gold light of the hanging lamps, she was ghastly under her paint. The young man was struck with her martyred look, and pitied her; but stronger than his pity was the fear that she might fail him—if not to-day, before the journey's end. She would have to undergo a strain terrible for an invalid, and he could spare her much of this if he chose; but he would not choose, though he was fond of his cousin, and grateful in a way. To spare her would mean the risk of failure for him.

Each called down salutations and peace upon the head of the other, and Lella M'Barka asked Maïeddine if he would drink coffee. He thanked her, but had already taken coffee. And she? All her strength would be needed. She must not neglect to sustain herself now that everything depended upon her health.

"My health!" she echoed, with a sigh, and a gesture of something like despair. "O my cousin, if thou knewest how I suffer, how I dread what lies before me, thou wouldst in mercy change thy plans even now. Thou wouldst go the short way to the end of our journey. Think of the difference to me! A week or eight days of travel at most, instead of three weeks, or more if I falter by the way, and thou art forced to wait."

Maïeddine's face hardened under her imploring eyes, but he answered with gentleness, "Thou knowest, my kind friend and cousin, that I would give my blood to save thee suffering, but it is more than my blood that thou askest now. It is my heart, for my heart is in this journey and what I hope from it, as I told thee yesterday. We discussed it all, thou and I, between us. Thou hast loved, and I made thee understand something of what I feel for this girl, whose beauty, as thou hast seen, is that of the houris in Paradise. Never have I found her like; and it may be I care more because of the obstacles which stand high as a wall between me and her. Because of the man who is her sister's husband, I must not fail in respect, or even seem to fail. I cannot take her and ride away, as I might with a maiden humbly placed, trusting to make her happy after she was mine. My winning must be done first, as is the way of the Roumis, and she will be hard to win. Already she feels that one of my race has stolen and hidden her sister; for this, in her heart, she fears and half distrusts all Arabs. A week would give me no time to capture her love, and when the journey is over it will be too late. Then, at best, I can see little of her, even if she be allowed to keep something of her European freedom. It is from this journey together—the long, long journey—that I hope everything. No pains shall be spared. No luxury shall she lack even on the hardest stretches of the way. She shall know that she owes all to my thought and care. In three weeks I can pull down that high wall between us. She will have learned to depend on me, to need me, to long for me when I am out of her sight, as the gazelle longs for a fountain of sweet water."

"Poet and dreamer thou hast become, Maïeddine," said Lella M'Barka with a tired smile.

"I have become a lover. That means both and more. My heart is set on success with this girl: and yesterday thou didst promise to help. In return, I offered thee a present that is like the gift of new life to a woman, the amulet my father's dead brother rubbed on the sacred Black Stone at Mecca, touched by the foot of the Prophet. I assured thee that at the end of our journey I would persuade the marabout to make the amulet as potent for good to thee as the Black Stone itself, against which thou canst never cool the fever in thy forehead. Then, when he has used his power, and thou hast pressed the amulet on thy brows, thou mayst read the destiny of men and women written between their eyes, as a sand-diviner reads fate in the sands. Thou wilt become in thine own right a marabouta, and be sure of Heaven when thou diest. This blessing the marabout will give, not for thy sake, but for mine, because I will do for him certain things which he has long desired, and so far I have never consented to undertake. Thou wilt gain greatly through keeping thy word to me. Believing in thy courage and good faith, I have made all arrangements for the journey. Not once last night did I close my eyes in sleep. There was not a moment to rest, for I had many telegrams to send, and letters to write, asking my friends along the different stages of the way, after we have left the train, to lend me relays of mules or horses. I have had to collect supplies, to think of and plan out details for which most men would have needed a week's preparation, yet I have completed all in twelve hours. I believe nothing has been forgotten, nothing neglected. And can it be that my prop will fail me at the last moment?"

"No, I will not fail thee, unless soul and body part," Lella M'Barka answered. "I but hoped that thou mightest feel differently, that in pity—but I see I was wrong to ask. I will pray that the amulet, and the hope of the divine benediction of the baraka may support me to the end."

"I, too, will pray, dear cousin. Be brave, and remember, the journey is to be taken, in easy stages. All the comforts I am preparing are for thee, as well as for this white rose whose beauty has stolen the heart out of my breast."

"It is true. Thou art kind, or I would not love thee even as I should have loved a son, had one been given me," said the haggard woman, meekly. "Does *she* know that there will be three weeks or more of travelling?"

"No. I told her vaguely that she could hardly hope to see her sister in less than a fortnight. I feared that, at first hearing, the thought of such distances, separating her from what she has known of life, might cause her to hesitate. But she will be willing to sacrifice herself and travel less rapidly than she hoped, when she sees that thou art weak and ailing. She has a heart with room in it for the welfare of others."

"Most women have. It is expected of us." Lella M'Barka sighed again, faintly. "But she is all that thou describedst to me, of beauty and sweetness. When she has been converted to the True Faith, as thy wife, nothing will be lacking to make her perfect."

Hsina appeared at the door. "Thy guest, O Lella M'Barka, is having her coffee, and is eating bread with it," she announced. "In a few minutes she will be ready. Shall I fetch her down while the gracious lord honours the house with his presence, or — —"

"My guest is a Roumia, and it is not forbidden that she show her face to men," answered Hsina's mistress. "She will travel veiled, because, for reasons that do not concern thee, it is wiser. But she is free to appear before the Lord Maïeddine. Bring her; and remember this, when I am gone. If to a living soul outside this house thou speakest of the Roumia maiden, or even of my journey, worse things will happen to thee than tearing thy tongue out by the roots."

"So thou saidst last night to me, and to all the others," the negress answered, like a sulky child. "As we are faithful, it is not necessary to say it again." Without waiting to be scolded for her impudence, as she knew she deserved, she went out, to return five minutes later with Victoria.

Maïeddine's eyes lighted when he saw the girl in Arab dress. It seemed to him that she was far more beautiful, because, like all Arabs, he detested the severe cut of a European woman's gowns. He loved bright colours and voluptuous outlines.

It was only beginning to be daylight when they left the house and went out to the carriage in which Victoria had been driven the night before. She and Lella M'Barka were both veiled, though there was no eye to see them. Hsina and Fafann took out several bundles, wrapped in dark red woollen haïcks, and the Negro servants carried two curious trunks of wood painted bright green, with coloured flowers and scrolls of gold upon them, and shining, flat covers of brass. In these was contained the luggage from the house; Maïeddine's had already gone to the railway station. He wore a plain, dark blue burnous, with the hood up, and his chin and mouth were covered by the lower folds of the small veil which fell from his turban, as if he were riding in the desert against a wind storm. It would have been impossible even for a friend to recognize him, and the two women in their white veils were like all native women of wealth and breeding in Algiers. Hsina was crying, and Fafann, who expected to go with her mistress, was insufferably important. Victoria felt that she was living in a fairy story, and the wearing of the veil excited and amused her. She was happy, and looked forward to the journey itself as well as to the journey's end.

There were few people in the railway station, and Victoria saw no European travellers. Maïeddine had taken the tickets already, but he did not tell her the name of the place to which they were going by rail. She would have liked to ask, but as neither Si Maïeddine nor Lella M'Barka encouraged questions, she reminded herself that she could easily read the names of the stations as they passed.

Soon the train came in, and Maïeddine put them into a first-class compartment, which was labelled "reserved," though all other Arabs were going second or third. Fafann arranged cushions and haïcks for Lella M'Barka; and at six o'clock a feeble, sulky-sounding trumpet blew, signalling the train to move out of the station.

Victoria was not sleepy, though she had lain awake thinking excitedly all night; but Lella M'Barka bade her rest, as the day would be tiring. No one talked, and presently Fafann began to snore. The girl's eyes met Si Maïeddine's, and they smiled at each other. This made him seem to her more like an ordinary human being than he had seemed before.

After a while, she dropped into a doze, and was surprised when she waked up, to find that it was nearly nine o'clock. Fafann had roused her by moving about, collecting bundles. Soon they would be "there." And as the train slowed down, Victoria saw that "there" was Bouira.

This place was the destination of a number of Arab travellers, but the instant they were out of the train, these passengers appeared to melt away unobtrusively. Only one carriage was waiting, and that was for Si Maïeddine and his party.

It was a very different carriage from Lella M'Barka's, in Algiers; a vehicle for the country, Victoria thought it not unlike old-fashioned chaises in which farmers' families sometimes drove to Potterston, to church. It had side and back curtains of canvas, which were fastened down, and an Arab driver stood by the heads of two strong black mules.

"This carriage belongs to a friend of mine, a Caïd," Maïeddine explained to Victoria. "He has lent it to me, with his driver and mules, to use as long as I wish. But we shall have to change the mules often, before we begin at last to travel in a different way."

"How quickly thou hast arranged everything," exclaimed the girl.

This was a welcome sign of appreciation, and Maïeddine was pleased. "I sent the Caïd a telegram," he said. "And there were many more telegrams to other places, far ahead. That is one good thing which the French have brought to our country. The telegraph goes to the most remote places in the Sahara. By and by, thou wilt see the poles striding away over desert dunes."

"By and by! Dost thou mean to-day?" asked Victoria.

"No, it will be many days before thou seest the great dunes. But thou wilt see them in the end, and I think thou wilt love them as I do. Meanwhile, there will be other things of interest. I shall not let thee tire of the way, though it be long."

He helped them into the carriage, the invalid first, then Victoria, and got in after them; Fafann, muffled in her veil, sitting on the seat beside the driver.

"By this time Mr. Knight has my letter, and has read it," the girl said to herself. "Oh, I do hope he won't be disgusted, and think me ungrateful. How glad I shall be when the day comes for me to explain."

As it happened, the letter was in Maïeddine's thoughts at the same moment. It occurred to him, too, that it would have been read by now. He knew to whom it had been written, for he had got a friend of his to bring him a list of passengers on board the *Charles Quex* on her last trip from Marseilles to Algiers. Also, he had learned at whose house Stephen Knight was staying.

Maïeddine would gladly have forgotten to post the letter, and could have done so without hurting his conscience. But he had thought it might be better for Knight to know that Miss Ray was starting on a journey, and that there was no hope of hearing from her for a fortnight. Victoria had been ready to show him the letter, therefore she had not written any forbidden details; and Knight would probably feel that she must be left to manage her own affairs in her own way. No doubt he would be curious, and ask questions at the Hotel de la Kasbah, but Maïeddine believed that he had made it impossible for Europeans to find out anything there, or elsewhere. He knew that men of Western countries could be interested in a girl without being actually in love with her; and though it was almost impossible to imagine a man, even a European, so cold as not to fall in love with Victoria at first sight, he hoped that Knight was blind enough not to appreciate her, or that his affections were otherwise engaged. After all, the two had been strangers when they came on the boat, or had met only once before, therefore the Englishman had no right to take steps unauthorized by the girl. Altogether, Maïeddine thought he had reason to be satisfied with the present, and to hope in the future.

XXI

Stephen and Nevill Caird returned from Tlemcen to Algiers, hoping for news of Victoria, but there was none; and after two days they left for Grand Kabylia.

The prophetic birds at Mansourah had flown in a south-easterly direction, but when Stephen and Nevill started in search of Josette's maid Mouni, they turned full east, their faces looking towards the dark heights of Kabylia. It was not Victoria they hoped to find there, however, or Saidee her sister, but only a hint as to their next move. Nevertheless, Nevill was superstitious about the birds, and said to Stephen when the car had run them out of Algiers, past Maison Carré, into open country: "Isn't it queer how the birds follow us? I never saw so many before. They're always with us. It's just as if they'd passed on word, the way chupatties are passed on in India, eh? Or maybe Josette has told her protegées to look after us."

And Stephen smiled, for Nevill's superstitions were engaging, rather than repulsive; and his quaintnesses were endearing him more and more to the man who had just taken up the dropped thread of friendship after eight or nine years. What an odd fellow Nevill was! Stephen thought, indulgently. No wonder he was worshipped by his servants, and even his chauffeur. No wonder Lady MacGregor adored her nephew, though treating him as if he were a little boy!

One of Nevill's idiosyncrasies, after arranging everything to fit a certain plan, was to rush off at the last minute and do something entirely different. Last night—the night before starting for Grand Kabylia—he had begged Stephen to be ready by eight, at which time the car was ordered. At nine—having sat up till three o'clock writing letters, and then having visited a lately imported gazelle in its quarters—Nevill was still in his bath. At length he arrived on the scene, beaming, with a sulky chameleon in his pocket, and flew about giving last directions, until he suddenly discovered that there was a violent hurry, whereupon he began to be boyishly peevish with the chauffeur for not getting off an hour ago. No sooner had the car started, however, than he fell into a serious mood, telling Stephen of many things which he had thought out in the night—things which might be helpful in finding Victoria. He had been lying awake, it seemed, brooding on this subject, and it had occurred to him that, if Mouni should prove a disappointment, they might later discover something really useful by going to the annual ball at the Governor's palace. This festivity had been put off, on account of illness in the chief official's family; but it would take place in a fortnight or so now. All the great Aghas and Caïds of the south would be there, and as Nevill knew many of them, he might be able to get definite information concerning Ben Halim. As for Saidee—to hear of Ben Halim was to hear of her. And then it was, in the midst of describing the ball, and the important men who would attend, that Nevill suddenly broke off to be superstitious about birds.

It was true that the birds were everywhere! little greenish birds flitting among the trees; larger grey-brown birds flying low; fairy- like blue and yellow birds that circled round the car as it ran east towards the far, looming mountains of the Djurdjura; larks that spouted music like a fountain of jewels as they soared into the quivering blue; and great, stately storks, sitting in their nests on tall trees or tops of poles, silhouetted against the sky as they gazed indifferently down at the automobile.

"Josette would tell us it's splendid luck to see storks on their nests," said Nevill. "Arabs think they bring good fortune to places. That's why people cut off the tops of the trees and make nests for them, so they can bless the neighbourhood and do good to the crops. Storks have no such menial work here as bringing babies. Arab babies have to come as best they can—sent into the world anyhow; for storks are men who didn't do their religious duties in the most approved style, so they have to revisit the world next time in the form of beneficent birds."

But Nevill did not want to answer questions about storks and their habits. He had tired of them in a moment, and was passionately interested in mules. "There ought to be an epic written about the mules of North Africa!" he exclaimed. "I tell you, it's a great subject. Look at those poor brave chaps struggling to pull carts piled up with casks of beastly Algerian wine, through that sea of mud, which probably goes all the way through to China. Aren't they splendid? Wait till you've been in this country as long as I have, and you'll respect mules as I do, from army mules down to the lowest dregs of the mule kingdom. I don't ask you to love them—and neither do they. But how they work here in Africa—and never a groan! They go on till they drop. And I don't believe half of them ever get anything to eat. Some day I'm going to start a Rest Farm for tired mules. I shall pay well for them. A man I know did write a pæan of praise for mules. I believe I'll have it translated into Arabic, and handed about as a leaflet. These natives are good to their horses, because they believe they have souls, but they treat their mules like the dirt under their feet." And Nevill began quoting here and there a verse or a line he remembered of the "mule music," chanting in time to the throbbing of the motor.

> "Key A minor, measure common,
> One and two and three and four and—
> Every hoof-beat half a second
> Every hoof-beat linked with heart-beat,
> Every heart-beat nearer bursting.
> Andantino sostenuto:
> In the downpour or the dryness,
> Hottest summer, coldest winter;
> Sick and sore and old and feeble,
> Hourly, hourly; daily, daily,
> From the sunrise to the setting;
> From the setting to the sunrise
> Scarce a break in all the circle
> For the rough and scanty eating,
> For the scant and muddy drinking,
> For the fitful, fearful resting,
> For the master haunted-sleeping.
> Dreams in dark of God's far heaven
> Tempo primo; tempo sempre."

And so, through pools of wild flowers and the blood of poppies, their road led to wild mountain scenery, then into the embrace of the Djurdjura mountains themselves—evil, snow-splashed, sterile-seeming mountains, until the car had passed the fortified town of Tizi Ouzou, an overgrown village, whose name Stephen thought like a drunken term of endearment. It was market-day there, and the long street was so full of Kabyles dressed apparently in low-necked woollen bags, of soldiers in uniform, of bold-eyed, scantily-clad children, and of dyed sheep and goats, that the car had to pass at a walk. Nevill bought a good deal of Kabyle jewellery, necklaces and long earrings, or boxes enamelled in crude greens and reds, blues and yellows. Not that he had not already more than he knew what to do with; but he could not resist the handsome unveiled girls, the wretched old women, or pretty, half-naked children who offered the work of the neighbouring hill villages, or family heirlooms. Sometimes he saw eyes which made him think of Josette's; but then, all beautiful things that he saw reminded him of her. She was an obsession. But, for a wonder, he had taken Stephen's advice in

Tlemcen and had not proposed again. He was still marvelling at his own strength of mind, and asking himself if, after all, he had been wise.

After Tizi Ouzou the mountains were no longer sterile-seeming. The road coiled up and up snakily, between rows of leering cactus; and far below the densely wooded heights lay lovely plains through which a great river wandered. There was a homely smell of mint, and the country did not look to Stephen like the Africa he had imagined. All the hill-slopes were green with the bright green of fig trees and almonds, even at heights so great that the car wallowed among clouds. This steep road was the road to Fort National—the "thorn in the eye of Kabylia," which pierces so deeply that Kabylia may writhe, but revolt no more. Already it was almost as if the car had brought them into another world. The men who occasionally emerged from the woolly white blankets of the clouds, were men of a very different type from the mild Kabyles of the plains they had met trooping along towards Algiers in search of work.

These were brave, upstanding men, worthy of their fathers who revolted against French rule and could not be conquered until that thorn, Fort National, was planted deeply in heart and eye. Some were fair, and even red-haired, which would have surprised Stephen if he had not heard from Nevill that in old days the Christian slaves used to escape from Algiers and seek refuge in Kabylia, where they were treated as free men, and no questions were asked.

Without Fort National, it seemed to Stephen that this strange Berber people would never have been forced to yield; for looking down from mountain heights as the motor sped on, it was as if he looked into a vast and intricate maze of valleys, and on each curiously pointed peak clung a Kabyle village that seemed to be inlaid in the rock like separate bits of scarlet enamel. It was the low house-roofs which gave this effect, for unlike the Arabs, whom the ancient Berber lords of the soil regard with scorn, the Kabyles build their dwellings of stone, roofed with red tiles.

This was a wild, tormented world, broken into a hundred sharp mountain ridges which seemed to cut the sky, because between the high peaks and the tangled skein of far-away villages surged foaming seas of cloud, which appeared to separate high, bright peaks from shadowed vales, by incredible distances. As far as the eye could travel with utmost straining, away to the dark, imposing background of the Djurdjura range, billowed ridges and ravines,

ravines and ridges, each pointing pinnacle or razor-shelf adorned with its coral-red hamlet, like a group of poisonous fungi, or the barnacles on a ship's steep side. Such an extraordinary landscape Stephen had never imagined, or seen except on a Japanese fan; and it struck him that the scene actually did resemble quaint prints picturing half-real, half-imaginary scenes in old Japan.

"What a country for war! What a country for defence!" he said to himself, as Nevill's yellow car sped along the levels of narrow ridges that gave, on either hand, vertical views far down to fertile valleys, rushed into clouds of weeping rain, or out into regions of sunlight and rainbows.

It was three o'clock when they reached Michélet, but they had not stopped for luncheon, as both were in haste to find Mouni: and Mouni's village was just beyond Michélet. Since Fort National, they had been in the heart of Grand Kabylia; and Michélet was even more characteristic of this strange mountain country, so different from transplanted Arabia below.

Not an Arab lived here, in the long, straggling town, built on the crest of a high ridge. Not a minaret tower pointed skyward. The Kabyle place of worship had a roof of little more height or importance than those that clustered round it. The men were in striped brown gandourahs of camel's hair; the lovely unveiled women were wrapped in woollen foutahs dyed red or yellow, blue or purple, and from their little ears heavy rings dangled. The blue tattoo marks on their brown cheeks and foreheads, which in forgotten times had been Christian crosses, gave great value to their enormous, kohl-encircled eyes; and their teeth were very white as they smiled boldly, yet proudly, at Stephen and Nevill.

There was a flight of steps to mount from the car to the hotel, and as the two men climbed the stairs they turned to look, across a profound chasm, to the immense mass of the Djurdjura opposite Michélet's thin ledge. From their point of view, it was like the Jungfrau, as Stephen had seen it from Mürren, on one of his few trips to Switzerland. Somehow, those little conventional potterings of his seemed pitiable now, they had been so easy to do, so exactly what other people did.

It was long past ordinary luncheon time, and hunger constrained the two men to eat before starting out to find the village where Mouni and her people lived. It was so small a hamlet, that Nevill, who knew

Kabylia well, had never heard of it until Josette Soubise wrote the name for him on one of her own cards. The landlord of the hotel at Michélet gave rapid and fluent directions how to go, saying that the distance was two miles, but as the way was a steep mountain path, les messieurs must go on foot.

Immediately after lunching they started, armed with a present for the bride; a watch encrusted with tiny brilliants, which, following Josette's advice, they had chosen as the one thing of all others calculated to win the Kabyle girl's heart. "It will be like a fairy dream to her to have a watch of her own," Josette had said. "Her friends will be dying of envy, and she will enjoy that. Oh, she will search her soul and tell you everything she knows, if you but give her a watch!"

For a little way the friends walked along the wild and beautiful road, which from Michélet plunges down the mountains toward Bougie and the sea; but soon they came to the narrow, ill-defined footpath described by the landlord. It led straight up a steep shoulder of rock which at its highest part became a ledge; and when they had climbed to the top, at a distance they could see a cluster of red roofs apparently falling down a precipice, at the far end.

Here and there were patches of snow, white as fallen lily-petals on the pansy-coloured earth. Looking down was like looking from a high wave upon a vast sea of other waves, each wave carrying on its apex a few bits of broken red mosaic, which were Kabyle roofs; and the pale sky was streaked with ragged violet clouds exactly like the sky and clouds painted on screens by Japanese artists.

They met not a soul as they walked, but while the village was still far away and unreal, the bark of guns, fired quickly one after the other, jarred their ears, and the mountain wind brought a crying of raïtas, African clarionettes, and the dull, yet fierce beat of tom-toms.

"Now I know why we've met no one," said Nevill. "The wedding feast's still on, and everybody who is anybody at Yacoua, is there. You know, if you're an Arab, or even a Kabyle, it takes you a week to be married properly, and you have high jinks every day: music and dancing and eating, and if you've money enough, above all you make the powder speak. Mouni's people are doing her well. What a good thing we've got the watch! Even with Josette's introduction we mightn't have been able to come near the bride, unless we had something to offer worth her having."

The mountain village of Yacoua had no suburbs, no outlying houses. The one-story mud huts with their pointed red roofs, utterly unlike Arab dwellings, were huddled together, with only enough distance between for a man and a mule or a donkey to pass. The best stood in pairs, with a walled yard between; and as Stephen and Nevill searched anxiously for some one to point out the home of Mouni, from over a wall which seemed to be running down the mountain- side, came a white puff of smoke and a strident bang, then more, one after the other. Again the wailing of the raïta began, and there was no longer any need to ask the way.

"That's where the party is—in that yard," said Nevill, beginning to be excited. "Now, what sort of reception will they give us? That's the next question."

"Can't we tell, the first thing, that we've come from Algiers with a present for the bride?" suggested Stephen.

"We can if they understand Arabic," Nevill answered. "But the Kabyle lingo's quite different—Berber, or something racy of the soil. I ought to have brought Mohammed to interpret."

So steeply did the yard between the low houses run downhill, that, standing at the top of a worn path like a seam in some old garment, the two Europeans could look over the mud wall. Squalid as were the mud huts and the cattle-yard connecting them, the picture framed in the square enclosure blazed with colour. It was barbaric, and beautiful in its savagery.

Squatting on the ground, with the last rank against the house wall, were several rows of women, all unveiled, their uncovered arms jewelled to the elbows, embracing their knees. The afternoon sunlight shone on their ceremonial finery, setting fire to the red, blue and green enamel of their necklaces, their huge hoop earrings and the jewelled silver chains pinned to their scarlet or yellow head- wrappings, struck out strange gleams from the flat, round brooches which fastened their gaily striped robes on their shoulders, and turned their great dark eyes into brown topazes. Twenty or thirty men, dressed in their best burnouses, draped over new gandourahs, their heads swathed in clean white muslin turbans, sat on the opposite side of the court, watching the "powder play" furnished by two tall, handsome boys, who handled with delicate grace and skill old-fashioned, long-muzzled guns inlaid with coral and silver, heirlooms perhaps, and of some value even to antiquaries.

While the powder spoke, nobody had a thought for anything else. All eyes were upon the boys with the guns, only travelling upward in ecstasy to watch the puffs of smoke that belched out round and white as fat snowballs. Then, when the music burst forth again, and a splendidly handsome young Kabyle woman ran forward to begin the wild dance of the body and of the hands—dear to the mountain men as to the nomads of the desert—every one was at first absorbed in admiration of her movements. But suddenly a child (one of a dozen in a row in front of all the women) tired of the show, less amusing to him than the powder play, and looking up, saw the two Roumis on the hill behind the wall. He nudged his neighbour, and the neighbour, who happened to be a little girl, followed with her eyes the upward nod of his head. So the news went round that strangers had come uninvited to the wedding-feast, and men began to frown and women to whisper, while the dancer lost interest in her own tinklings and genuflections.

It was time for the intruders to make it known that business of some sort, not idle curiosity, had brought them on the scene, and Nevill stepped forward, holding out the visiting card given him by Josette, and the crimson velvet case containing the watch which Stephen had bought in Algiers.

XXII

An elderly man, with a reddish beard, got up from the row of men grouped behind the musicians, and muttered to one of the youths who had been making the powder speak. They argued for a moment, and then the boy, handing his gun to the elder man, walked with dignity to a closed gate, large enough to let in the goats and donkeys pertaining to the two houses. This gate he opened half-way, standing in the aperture and looking up sullenly as the Roumis came down the narrow, slippery track which led to it.

"Cebah el-kheir, ia Sidi—Good day, sir," said Nevill, agreeably, in his best Arabic. "Ta' rafi el-a' riya?—Do you speak Arabic?"

The young man bowed, not yet conciliated. "Ach men sebba jit lhena, ia Sidi?—Why have you come here, sir?" he asked suspiciously, in very guttural Arabic.

Relieved to find that they would have no great difficulty in understanding each other, Nevill plunged into explanations, pointing to Josette's card. They had come recommended by the malema at Tlemcen. They brought good wishes and a present to the bride of the village, the virtuous and beautiful Mouni, from whom they would gladly receive information concerning a European lady. Was this the house of her father? Would they be permitted to speak with her, and give this little watch from Algiers?

Nevill made his climax by opening the velvet case, and the brown eyes of the Kabyle boy flashed with uncontrollable admiration, though his face remained immobile. He answered that this was indeed the house of Mouni's father, and he himself was the brother of Mouni. This was the last day of her wedding-feast, and in an hour she would go to the home of her husband. The consent of the latter, as well as of her father, must be asked before strangers could hope to speak with her. Nevertheless, the Roumis were welcome to enter the yard and watch the entertainment while Mouni's brother consulted with those most concerned in this business.

The boy stood aside, inviting them to pass through the gate, and the Englishmen availed themselves of his courtesy, waiting just inside until the red-bearded man came forward. He and his son consulted together, and then a dark young man in a white burnous was called

174

to join the conclave. He was a handsome fellow, with a haughtily intelligent face, and an air of breeding superior to the others.

"This is my sister's husband. He too speaks Arabic, but my father not so much." The boy introduced his brother-in-law. "Messaud- ben-Arzen is the son of our Caïd," (he spoke proudly). "Will you tell him and my father what your business is with Mouni?"

Nevill broke into more explanations, and evidently they were satisfactory, for, while the dancing and the powder play were stopped, and the squatting ranks of guests stared silently, the two Roumis were conducted into the house.

It was larger than most of the houses in the village, but apart from the stable of the animals through which the visitors passed, there was but one room, long and narrow, lighted by two small windows. The darkest corner was the bedroom, which had a platform of stone on which rugs were spread, and there was a lower mound of dried mud, roughly curtained off from the rest with two or three red and blue foutahs suspended on ropes made of twisted alfa, or dried grass. Toward the farther end, a hole in the floor was the family cooking-place, and behind it an elevation of beaten earth made a wide shelf for a long row of jars shaped like the Roman amphoræ of two thousand years ago. Pegs driven into one of the walls were hung with gandourahs and a foutah or two; and of furniture, worthy of that name in the eyes of Europeans, there was none.

At the bedroom end of the room, several women were gathered round a central object of interest, and though the light was dim after the vivid sunshine outside, the visitors guessed that the object of interest was the bride. Decorously they paused near the door, while a great deal of arguing went on, in which the shriller voices of women mingled with the guttural tones of the men. Nevill could catch no word, for they were talking their own Kabyle tongue which had come down from their forefathers the Berbers, lords of the land long years before the Arabs drove them into the high mountains. But at last the group opened, and a young woman stepped out with half- shy eagerness. She was loaded with jewels, and her foutah was barbarically splendid in colour, but she was almost as fair as her father; a slim creature with grey eyes, and brown curly hair that showed under her orange foulard.

Proud of her French, she began talking in that language, welcoming the guests, telling them how glad she was to see friends of her dear

Mademoiselle Soubise. But soon she must be gone to her husband's house, and already the dark young bridegroom, son of the Caïd, was growing impatient. There was no time to be lost, if they were to learn anything of Ben Halim's wife.

As a preface to what they wished to ask, Nevill made a presentation speech, placing the velvet watch-case in Mouni's hand, and she opened it with a kind of moan expressing intense rapture. Never had she seen anything so beautiful, and she would cheerfully have recalled every phase of her career from earliest babyhood, if by doing so she could have pleased the givers.

"But yes," she answered to Nevill's first questions, "the beautiful lady whom I served was the wife of Sidi Cassim ben Halim. At first it was in Algiers that I lived with her, but soon we left, and went to the country, far, oh, very far away, going towards the south. The house was like a large farmhouse, and to me as a child—for I was but a child—it seemed fine and grand. Yet my lady was not pleased. She found it rough, and different from any place to which she was used. Poor, beautiful lady! She was not happy there. She cried a great deal, and each day I thought she grew paler than the day before."

Mouni spoke in French, hesitating now and then for a word, or putting in two or three in Arabic, before she stopped to think, as she grew interested in her subject. Stephen understood almost all she said, and was too impatient to leave the catechizing to Nevill.

"Whereabouts was this farmhouse?" he asked. "Can't you tell us how to find it?"

Mouni searched her memory. "I was not yet thirteen," she said. "It is nine years since I left that place; and I travelled in a shut-up carriage, with a cousin, older than I, who had been already in the house of the lady when I came. She told her mistress of me, and I was sent for, because I was quick and lively in my ways, and white of face, almost as white as the beautiful lady herself. My work was to wait on the mistress, and help my cousin, who was her maid. Yamina—that was my cousin's name—could have told you more about the place in the country than I, for she was even then a woman. But she died a few months after we both left the beautiful lady. We left because the master thought my cousin carried a letter for her mistress, which he did not wish sent; and he gave orders that we should no longer live under his roof."

"Surely you can remember where you went, and how you went, on leaving the farmhouse?" Stephen persisted.

"Oh yes, we went back to Algiers. But it was a long distance, and took us many days, because we had only a little money, and Yamina would not spend it in buying tickets for the diligence, all the way. We walked many miles, and only took a diligence when I cried, and was too tired to move a step farther. At night we drove sometimes, I remember, and often we rested under the tents of nomads who were kind to us.

"While I was with the lady, I never went outside the great courtyard. It is not strange that now, after all these years, I cannot tell you more clearly where the house was. But it was a great white house, on a hill, and round it was a high wall, with towers that overlooked the country beneath. And in those towers, which were on either side the big, wide gate, were little windows through which men could spy, or even shoot if they chose."

"Did you never hear the name of any town that was near?" Stephen went on.

"I do not think there was a town near; yet there was a village not far off to the south. I saw it from the hill-top, both as I went in at the gate with my cousin, and when, months later, I was sent away with her. We did not pass through it, because our road was to and from the north; and I do not even know the name of the village. But there was a cemetery outside it, where some of the master's ancestors and relations were buried. I heard my lady speak of it one day, when she cried because she feared to die and be laid there without ever again seeing her own country and her own people. Oh, and once I heard Yamina talk with another servant about an oasis called Bou-Saada. It was not near, yet I think it could be reached by diligence in a long day."

"Good!" broke in Nevill. "There's our first real clue! Bou-Saada I know well. When people who come and visit me want a glimpse of the desert in a hurry, Bou-Saada is where I take them. One motors there from Algiers in seven or eight hours—through mountains at first, then on the fringe of the desert; but it's true, as Mouni says, going by diligence, and walking now and then, it would be a journey of days. Her description of the house on the hill, looking down over a village and cemetery, will be a big help. And Ben Halim's name is sure to be known in the country round, if he ever lived there."

"He may have been gone for years," said Stephen. "And if there's a conspiracy of silence in Algiers, why not elsewhere?"

"Well, at least we've got a clue, and will follow it up for all we know. By Jove, this is giving me a new interest in life!" And Nevill rubbed his hands in a boyish way he had. "Tell us what the beautiful lady was like," he went on to Mouni.

"Her skin was like the snow on our mountain-tops when the sunrise paints the white with rose," answered Mouni. "Her hair was redder than the red of henna, and when it was unfastened it hung down below her waist. Her eyes were dark as a night without moon, and her teeth were little, little pearls. Yet for all her beauty she was not happy. She wasted the flower of her youth in sadness, and though the master was noble, and splendid as the sun to look upon, I think she had no love to give him, perhaps because he was grave and seldom smiled, or because she was a Roumia and could not suit herself to the ways of true believers."

"Did she keep to her own religion?" asked Stephen.

"That I cannot tell. I was too young to understand. She never talked of such things before me, but she kept to none of our customs, that I know. In the three months I served her, never did she leave the house, not even to visit the cemetery on a Friday, as perhaps the master would have allowed her to do, if she had wished."

"Do you remember if she spoke of a sister?"

"She had a photograph of a little girl, whose picture looked like herself. Once she told me it was her sister, but the next day the photograph was gone from its place, and I never saw it again. Yamina thought the master was jealous, because our lady looked at it a great deal."

"Was there any other lady in that house," Nevill ventured, "or was yours the master's only wife?"

"There was no other lady at that time," Mouni replied promptly.

"So far, so good," said Nevill. "Well, Legs, I don't think there's any doubt we've got hold of the right end of the stick now. Mouni's beautiful lady and Miss Ray's sister Saidee are certainly one and the same. Ho for the white farmhouse on the hill!"

"Must we go back to Algiers, or can we get to Bou-Saada from here?" Stephen asked.

Nevill laughed. "You are in a hurry! Oh, we can get there from here all right. Would you like to start now?"

Stephen's face reddened. "Why not, if we've found out all we can from this girl?" He tried to speak indifferently.

Nevill laughed again. "Very well. There's nothing left then, except to say good-bye to the fair bride and her relations."

He had expected to get back to Algiers that night, slipping away from the high passes of Grand Kabylia before dusk, and reaching home late, by lamplight. But now the plan was changed. They were not to see Algiers again until Stephen had made acquaintance with the desert. By setting off at once, they might arrive at Bou-Saada some time in the dark hours; and Nevill upset his old arrangements with good grace. Why should he mind? he asked, when Stephen apologized shame-facedly for his impatience. Bou-Saada was as good a place as any, except Tlemcen, and this adventure would give him an excuse for a letter, even two letters, to Josette Soubise. She would want to hear about Mouni's wedding, and the stately Kabyle home which they had visited. Besides she would be curious to know whether they found the white farmhouse on the hill, and if so, what they learned there of the beautiful lady and her mysterious fate. Oh yes, it would certainly mean two letters at least: one from Bou-Saada, one after the search for the farmhouse; and Nevill thought himself in luck, for he was not allowed to write often to Josette.

After Michélet the road, a mere shelf projecting along a precipice, slants upward on its way to the Col de Tirouda, sharp as a knife aimed at the heart of the mountains. From far below clouds boil up as if the valleys smoked after a destroying fire, and through flying mists flush the ruddy earth, turning the white film to pinkish gauze. Crimson and purple stones shine like uncut jewels, and cascades of yellow gorse, under red-flowering trees, pour down over low- growing white flowers, which embroider the rose-coloured rocks.

Then, suddenly, gone is the green Kabyle mountain-world, gone like a dream the tangle of ridges and chasms, the bright tapestry of fig trees and silver olives, dark karoubias (the wild locusts of John the Baptist) and climbing roses. Rough, coarse grass has eaten up the flowers, or winds sweeping down from the Col have killed them. Only a few stunted trees bend grotesquely to peer over the sheer sides of shadowed gorges as the road strains up and up, twisting like a scar left by a whip-lash, on the naked brown shoulders of a slave. So at last it flings a loop over the Col de Tirouda. Then, round a corner the wand of an invisible magician waves: darkness and winter cold become summer warmth and light.

This light was the level golden glory of late afternoon when Stephen saw it from Nevill's car; and so green were the wide stretching meadows and shining rivers far below, that he seemed to be looking at them through an emerald, as Nero used to gaze at his gardens in Rome. Down the motor plunged towards the light, threading back and forth a network of zig-zags, until long before sunset they were in the warm lowlands, racing towards Bordj-bou Arreredj and Msila. Beyond Msila, they would follow the desert track which would bring them by and by to the oasis town of Bou-Saada.

If Stephen had been a tourist, guide-book in hand, he would have delighted in the stony road among the mountains between Bordj-bou Arreredj and Msila; but it was the future, not the past, which held his thoughts to-day, and he had no more than a passing glance for ruined mosques and palaces. It was only after nightfall, far beyond the town of Msila, far beyond the vast plain of the Hodna, that his first dim glimpse of the desert thrilled him out of self-absorption.

Even under the stars which crusted a moonless sky, the vast stretches of billowing sand glimmered faintly golden as a phosphorescent sea. And among the dimly gleaming waves of that endless waste the motor tossed, rocking on the rough track like a small boat in mid-ocean.

Nowhere was there any sound except the throbbing of their machinery, and a fairy fiddling of unseen crickets, which seemed to make the silence more intense, under the great sparkling dome that hung over the gold.

"Now I am in the place where she wished to be: the golden silence," Stephen said to himself. And he found himself listening, as if for the call Victoria had promised to give if she needed him.

XXIII

On the top of a pale golden hill, partly sand, partly rock, rises a white wall with square, squat towers which look north and south, east and west. The wall and the towers together are like an ivory crown set on the hill's brow, and from a distance the effect is very barbaric, very impressive, for all the country round about is wild and desolate. Along the southern horizon the desert goes billowing in waves of gold, and rose, and violet, that fade into the fainter violet of the sky; and nearer there are the strange little mountains which guard the oasis of Bou-Saada, like a wall reared to hide a treasure from some dreaded enemy; and even the sand is heaped in fantastic shapes, resembling a troop of tawny beasts crouched to drink from deep pools of purple shadow. Northward, the crumpled waste rolls away like prairie land or ocean, faint green over yellow brown, as if grass seed had been sprinkled sparsely on a stormy sea and by some miracle had sprouted. And in brown wastes, bright emerald patches gleam, vivid and fierce as serpents' eyes, ringed round with silver. Far away to the east floats the mirage of a lake, calm as a blue lagoon. Westward, where desert merges into sky, are high tablelands, and flat-topped mountains with carved sides, desert architecture, such as might have suggested Egyptian temples and colossal sphinxes.

Along the rough desert track beneath the hill, where bald stones break through sandy earth, camels come and go, passing from south to north, from north to south, marching slowly with rhythmic gait, as if to the sound of music which only they can hear, glancing from side to side with unutterable superciliousness, looking wistfully here and there at some miniature oasis thrown like a dark prayer-carpet on the yellow sand. Two or three in a band they go, led by desert men in blowing white, or again in a long train of twelve or twenty, their legs a moving lattice, their heart-shaped feet making a soft, swishing "pad-pad," on the hard road.

The little windows of the squat, domed towers on the hill are like eyes that spy upon this road,—small, dark and secret eyes, very weary of seeing nothing better than camels since old days when there were razzias, and wars, something worth shutting stout gates upon.

When, after three days of travelling, Victoria came southward along this road, and looked between the flapping carriage curtains at the white wall that crowned the dull gold hill, her heart beat fast, for the thought of the golden silence sprang to her mind. The gold did not burn with the fierce orange flames she had seen in her dreams—it was a bleached and faded gold, melancholy and almost sinister in colour; yet it would pass for gold; and a great silence brooded where prairie blended with desert. She asked no questions of Maïeddine, for that was a rule she had laid upon herself; but when the carriage turned out of the rough road it had followed so long, and the horses began to climb a stony track which wound up the yellow hill to the white towers, she could hardly breathe, for the throbbing in her breast. Always she had only had to shut her eyes to see Saidee, standing on a high white place, gazing westward through a haze of gold. What if this were the high white place? What if already Si Maïeddine was bringing her to Saidee?

They had been only three days on the way so far, it was true, and she had been told that the journey would be very, very long. Still, Arabs were subtle, and Si Maïeddine might have wanted to test her courage. Looking back upon those long hours, now, towards evening of the third day, it seemed to Victoria that she had been travelling for a week in the swaying, curtained carriage, with the slow-trotting mules.

Just at first, there had been some fine scenery to hold her interest; far-off mountains of grim shapes, dark as iron, and spotted with snow as a leper is spotted with scales. Then had come low hills, following the mountains (nameless to her, because Maïeddine had not cared to name them), and blue lakes of iris flowing over wide plains. But by and by the plains flattened to dullness; a hot wind ceaselessly flapped the canvas curtains, and Lella M'Barka sighed and moaned with the fatigue of constant motion. There was nothing but plain, endless plain, and Victoria had been glad, for her own sake as well as the invalid's, when night followed the first day. They had stopped on the outskirts of a large town, partly French, partly Arab, passing through and on to the house of a caïd who was a friend of Si Maïeddine's. It was a primitively simple house, even humble, it seemed to the girl, who had as yet no conception of the bareness and lack of comfort—according to Western ideas—of Arab country-houses. Nevertheless, when, after another tedious day, they rested under the roof of a village adel, an official below a caïd, the first house seemed luxurious in contrast. During this last, third day, Victoria had been eager and excited, because of the desert, through one gate of which they had entered. She felt that once in the desert she was so close to Saidee in spirit that they might almost hear the beating of each other's hearts, but she had not expected to be near her sister in body for many such days to come: and the wave of joy that surged over her soul as the horses turned up the golden hill towards the white towers, was suffocating in its force.

The nearer they came, the less impressive seemed the building. After all, it was not the great Arab stronghold it had looked from far away, but a fortified farmhouse a century old, at most. Climbing the hill, too, Victoria saw that the golden colour was partly due to a monstrous swarm of ochre-hued locusts, large as young canary birds, which had settled, thick as yellow snow, over the ground. They were resting after a long flight, and there were millions and millions of them, covering the earth in every direction as far as the eye could reach. Only a few were on the wing, but as the carriage stopped before the closed gates, fat yellow bodies came blundering against the canvas curtains, or fell plumply against the blinkers over the mules' eyes.

Si Maïeddine got down from the carriage, and shouted, with a peculiar call. There was no answering sound, but after a wait of two or three minutes the double gates of thick, greyish palm-wood were pulled open from inside, with a loud creak. For a moment the brown face of an old man, wrinkled as a monkey's, looked out between the gates, which he held ajar; then, with a guttural cry, he threw both as far back as he could, and rushing out, bent his white turban over Maïeddine's hand. He kissed the Sidi's shoulder, and a fold of his burnous, half kneeling, and chattering Arabic, only a word of which Victoria could catch here and there. As he chattered, other men came running out, some of them Negroes, all very dark, and they vied with one another in humble kissing of the master's person, at any spot convenient to their lips.

Politely, though not too eagerly, he made the gracious return of seeming to kiss the back of his own hand, or his fingers, where they had been touched by the welcoming mouths, but in reality he kissed air. With a gesture, he stopped the salutations at last, and asked for the Caïd, to whom, he said, he had written, sending his letter by the diligence.

Then there were passionate jabberings of regret. The Caïd, was away, had been away for days, fighting the locusts on his other farm, west of Aumale, where there was grain to save. But the letter had arrived, and had been sent after him, immediately, by a man on horseback. This evening he would certainly return to welcome his honoured guest. The word was "guest," not "guests," and Victoria understood that she and Lella M'Barka would not see the master of the house. So it had been at the other two houses: so in all probability it would be at every house along their way unless, as she still hoped, they had already come to the end of the journey.

The wide open gates showed a large, bare courtyard, the farmhouse, which was built round it, being itself the wall. On the outside, no windows were visible except those in the towers, and a few tiny square apertures for ventilation, but the yard was overlooked by a number of small glass eyes, all curtained.

As the carriage was driven in, large yellow dogs gathered round it, barking; but the men kicked them away, and busied themselves in chasing the animals off to a shed, their white-clad backs all religiously turned as Si Maïeddine helped the ladies to descend. Behind a closed window a curtain was shaking; and M'Barka had not yet touched her feet to the ground when a negress ran out of a door that opened in the same distant corner of the house. She was unveiled, like Lella M'Barka's servants in Algiers, and, with Fafann, she almost carried the tired invalid towards the open door. Victoria followed, quivering with suspense. What waited for her behind that door? Would she see Saidee, after all these years of separation?

"I think I'm dying," moaned Lella M'Barka. "They will never take me away from this house alive. White Rose, where art thou? I need thy hand under my arm."

Victoria tried to think only of M'Barka, and to wait with patience for the supreme moment—if it were to come. Even if she had wished it, she could not have asked questions now.

XXIV

It was midnight when Nevill's car ran into the beautiful oasis town, guarded by the most curious mountains of the Algerian desert, and they were at their strangest, cut out clear as the painted mountains of stage scenery, in the light of the great acetylene lamps. Stephen thought them like a vast, half-burned Moorish city of mosques and palaces, over which sand-storms had raged for centuries, leaving only traces here and there of a ruined tower, a domed roof, or an ornamental frieze.

Of the palms he could see nothing, except the long, dark shape of the oasis among the pale sand-billows; but early next morning he and Nevill were up and out on the roof of the little French hotel, while sunrise banners marched across the sky. Stephen had not known that desert dunes could be bright peach-pink, or that a river flowing over white stones could look like melted rubies, or that a few laughing Arab girls, ankle-deep in limpid water, could glitter in morning light like jewelled houris in celestial gardens. But now that he knew, he would never forget his first desert picture.

The two men stood on the roof among the bubbly domes for a long time, looking over the umber-coloured town and the flowing oasis which swept to Bou-Saada's brown feet like a tidal wave. It was not yet time to go and ask questions of the Caïd, whom Nevill knew.

Stephen was advised not to drink coffee in the hotel before starting on their quest. "We shall have to swallow at least three cups each of *café maure* at the Caïd's house, and perhaps a dash of tea flavoured with mint, on top of all, if we don't want to begin by hurting our host's feelings," Nevill said. So they fasted, and fed their minds by walking through Bou-Saada in its first morning glory. Already the old part of the town was alive, for Arabs love the day when it is young, even as they love a young girl for a bride.

The Englishmen strolled into the cool, dark mosque, where heavy Eastern scents of musk and benzoin had lain all night like fugitives in sanctuary, and where the roof was held up by cypress poles instead of marble pillars, as in the grand mosques of big cities. By the time they were ready to leave, dawn had become daylight, and coming out of the brown dusk, the town seemed flooded with golden wine, wonderful, bubbling, unbelievable gold, with scarlet and purple and green figures floating in it, brilliant as rainbow fish.

The Caïd lived near the old town, in an adobe house, with a garden which was a tangle of roses and pomegranate blossoms, under orange trees and palms. And there were narrow paths of hard sand, the colour of old gold, which rounded up to the centre, and had little runnels of water on either side. The sunshine dripped between the long fingers of the palm leaves, to trail in a lacy pattern along the yellow paths, and the sound of the running water was sweet.

It was in this garden that the Caïd gave his guests the three cups of coffee each, followed by the mint-flavoured tea which Nevill had prophesied. And when they had admired a tame gazelle which nibbled cakes of almond and honey from their hands, the Caïd insisted on presenting it to his good friend, Monsieur Caird.

Over the cups of *café maure*, they talked of Captain Cassim ben Halim, but their host could or would tell them nothing beyond the fact that Ben Halim had once lived for a little while not far from Bou- Saada. He had inherited from his father a country house, about fifty kilometres distant, but he had never stayed there until after retiring from the army, and selling his place in Algiers. Then he had spent a few months in the country. The Caïd had met him long ago in Algiers, but had not seen him since. Ben Halim had been ill, and had led a retired life in the country, receiving no one. Afterward he had gone away, out of Algeria. It was said that he had died abroad a little later. Of that, the Caïd was not certain; but in any case the house on the hill was now in the possession of the Caïd of Ain Dehdra, Sidi Elaïd ben Sliman, a distant cousin of Ben Halim, said to be his only living relative.

Then their host went on to describe the house with the white wall, which looked down upon a cemetery and a village. His description was almost precisely what Mouni's had been, and there was no doubt that the place where she had lived with the beautiful lady was the place of which he spoke. But of the lady herself they could learn nothing. The Caïd had no information to give concerning Ben Halim's family.

He pressed them to stay, and see all the beauties of the oasis. He would introduce them to the marabout at El Hamel, and in the evening they should see a special dance of the Ouled Naïls. But they made excuses that they must get on, and bade the Caïd good-bye after an hour's talk. As for the *gazelle approvoisée*, Nevill named her Josette, and hired an Arab to take her to Algiers by the diligence, with explicit instructions as to food and milk.

Swarms of locusts flew into their faces, and fell into the car, or were burned to death in the radiator, as they sped along the road towards the white house on the golden hill. They started from Bou-Saada at ten o'clock, and though the road was far from good, and they were not always sure of the way, the noon heat was scarcely at its height when Stephen said: "There it is! That must be the hill and the white wall with the towers."

"Yes, there's the cemetery too," answered Nevill. "We're seeing it on our left side, as we go, I hope that doesn't mean we're in for bad luck."

"Rot!" said Stephen, promptly. Yet for all his scorn of Nevill's grotesque superstitions, he was not in a confident mood. He did not expect much good from this visit to Ben Halim's old country house. And the worst was, that here seemed their last chance of finding out what had become of Saidee Ray, if not of her sister.

The sound of the motor made a brown face flash over the top of the tall gate, like a Jack popping out of his box.

"La Sidi, el Caïd?" asked Nevill. "Is he at home?"

The face pretended not to understand; and having taken in every detail of the strangers' appearance and belongings, including the motor-car, it disappeared.

"What's going to happen now?" Stephen wanted to know.

Nevill looked puzzled. "The creature isn't too polite. Probably it's afraid of Roumis, and has never been spoken to by one before. But I hope it will promptly scuttle indoors and fetch its master, or some one with brains and manners."

Several minutes passed, and the yellow motor-car continued to advertise its presence outside the Caïd's gate by panting strenuously. The face did not show itself again; and there was no evidence of life behind the white wall, except the peculiarly ominous yelping of Kabyle dogs.

"Let's pound on the gate, and show them we mean to get in," said Stephen, angry-eyed.

But Nevill counselled waiting. "Never be in a hurry when you have to do with Arabs. It's patience that pays."

"Here come two chaps on horseback," Stephen said, looking down at the desert track that trailed near the distant cluster of mud houses, which were like square blocks of gold in the fierce sunshine. "They seem to be staring up at the car. I wonder if they're on their way here!"

"It may be the Caïd, riding home with a friend, or a servant," Nevill suggested. "If so, I'll bet my hat there are other eyes than ours watching for him, peering out through some spy-hole in one of the gate-towers."

His guess was right. It was the Caïd coming home, and Maïeddine was with him; for Lella M'Barka had been obliged to rest for three days at the farmhouse on the hill, and the Caïd's guest had accompanied him before sunrise this morning to see a favourite white mehari, or racing camel, belonging to Sidi Elaïd ben Sliman, which was very ill, in care of a wise man of the village. Now the mehari was dead, and as Maïeddine seemed impatient to get back, they were riding home, in spite of the noon heat.

Maïeddine had left the house reluctantly this morning. Not that he could often see Victoria, who was nursing M'Barka, and looking so wistful that he guessed she had half hoped to find her sister waiting behind the white wall on the golden hill.

Though he could expect little of the girl's society, and there was little reason to fear that harm would come to her, or that she would steal away in his absence, still he had hated to ride out of the gate and leave her. If the Caïd had not made a point of his coming, he would gladly have stayed behind. Now, when he looked up and saw a yellow motor-car at the gate, he believed that his feeling had been a presentiment, a warning of evil, which he ought so have heeded.

He and the Caïd were a long way off when he caught sight of the car, and heard its pantings, carried by the clear desert air. He could not be certain of its identity, but he prided himself upon his keen sight and hearing, and where they failed, instinct stepped in. He was sure that it was the car which had waited for Stephen Knight when the *Charles Quex* came in, the car of Nevill Caird, about whom he had made inquiries before leaving Algiers. Maïeddine knew, of course, that Victoria had been to the Djenan el Djouad, and he was intensely suspicious as well as jealous of Knight, because of the letter Victoria had written. He knew also that the two Englishmen had been asking questions at the Hotel de la Kasbah; and he was not surprised to see the yellow car in front of the Caïd's gates. Now that he saw it, he felt dully that he had always known it would follow him.

If only he had been in the house, it would not have mattered. He would have been able to prevent Knight and Caird from seeing Victoria, or even from having the slightest suspicion that she was, or had been, there. It was the worst of luck that he should be outside the gates, for now he could not go back while the Englishmen were there. Knight would certainly recognize him, and guess everything that he did not know.

Maïeddine thought very quickly. He dared not ride on, lest the men in the car should have a field-glass. The only thing was to let Ben Sliman go alone, so that, if eyes up there on the hill were watching, it might seem that the Caïd was parting from some friend who lived in the village. He would have to trust Elaïd's discretion and tact, as he knew already he might trust his loyalty. Only—the situation was desperate. Tact, and an instinct for the right word, the frank look, were worth even more than loyalty at this moment. And one never quite knew how far to trust another man's judgment. Besides, the mischief might have been done before Ben Sliman could arrive on the scene; and at the thought of what might happen, Maïeddine's heart seemed to turn in his breast. He had never known a sensation so painful to body and mind, and it was hideous to feel helpless, to know that he could do only harm, and not good, by riding up the hill. Nevertheless, he said to himself, if he should see Victoria come out to speak with these men, he would go. He would perhaps kill them, and the chauffeur too. Anything rather than give up the girl now; for the sharp stab of the thought that he might lose her, that Stephen Knight might have her, made him ten times more in love than he had been before. He wished that Allah might strike the men in the yellow car dead; although, ardent Mussulman as he was, he had no hope that such a glorious miracle would happen.

"It is those men from Algiers of whom I told thee," he said to the Caïd. "I must stop below. They must not recognize me, or the dark one who was on the ship, will guess. Possibly he suspects already that I stand for something in this affair."

"Who can have sent them to my house?" Ben Sliman wondered. The two drew in their horses and put on the manner of men about to bid each other good-bye.

"I hope, I am almost sure, that they know nothing of *her*, or of me. Probably, when inquiring about Ben Halim, in order to hear of her sister, and so find out where she has gone, they learned only that Ben Halim once lived here. If thy servants are discreet, it may be that no harm will come from this visit."

"They will be discreet. Have no fear," the Caïd assured him. Yet it was on his tongue to say; "the lady herself, when she hears the sound of the car, may do some unwise thing." But he did not finish the sentence. Even though the young girl—whom he had not seen— was a Roumia, obsessed with horrible, modern ideas, which at present it would be dangerous to try and correct, he could not discuss her with Maïeddine. If she showed herself to the men, it could not be helped. What was to be, would be. Mektûb!

"Far be it from me to distrust my friend's servants," said Maïeddine; "but if in their zeal they go too far and give an impression of something to hide, it would be as bad as if they let drop a word too many."

"I will ride on and break any such impression if it has been made," Ben Sliman consoled him. "Trust me. I will be as gracious to these Roumis as if they were true believers."

"I do trust thee completely," answered the younger man. "While they are at thy gates, or within them, I must wait with patience. I cannot remain here in the open—yet I wish to be within sight, that I may see with my own eyes all that happens. What if I ride to one of the black tents, and ask for water to wash the mouth of my horse? If they have it not, it is no matter."

"Thine is a good thought," said Ben Sliman, and rode on, putting his slim white Arab horse to a trot.

To the left from the group of adobe houses, and at about the same distance from the rough track on which they had been riding, was a cluster of nomad tents, like giant bats with torpid wings spread out ink-black on the gold of the desert. A little farther off was another small encampment of a different tribe; and their tents were brown, striped with black and yellow. They looked like huge butterflies resting. But Maïeddine thought of no such similes. He was a child of the Sahara, and used to the tents and the tent-dwellers. His own father, the Agha, lived half the year in a great tent, when he was with his douar, and Maïeddine had been born under the roof of camel's hair. His own people and these people were not kin, and their lives lay far apart; yet a man of one nomad tribe understands all nomads, though he be a chief's son, and they as poor as their own ill-fed camels. His pride was his nomad blood, for all men of the Sahara, be they princes or camel-drivers, look with scorn upon the sedentary people, those of the great plain of the Tell, and fat eaters of ripe dates in the cities.

The eight or ten black tents were gathered round one, a little higher, a little less ragged than the others—the tent of the Kebir, or headman; but it was humble enough. There would have been room and to spare for a dozen such under the *tente sultane* of the Agha, at his douar south of El Aghouat.

As Maïeddine rode up, a buzz of excitement rose in the hive. Some one ran to tell the Kebir that a great Sidi was arriving, and the headman came out from his tent, where he had been meditating or dozing after the chanting of the midday prayer—the prayer of noon.

He was a thin, elderly man, with an eagle eye to awe his women- folk, and an old burnous of sheep's wool, which was of a deep cream colour because it had not been washed for many years. Yet he smelt good, with a smell that was like the desert, and there was no foul odour in the miniature douar, as in European dwellings of the very poor. There is never a smell of uncleanliness about Arabs, even those people who must perform most of the ablutions prescribed by their religion with sand instead of water. But the Saharian saying is that the desert purifies all things.

The Kebir was polite though not servile to Maïeddine, and while the horse borrowed from the Caïd was having its face economically sprinkled with water from a brown goat-skin, black coffee was being hospitably prepared for the guest by the women of the household, unveiled of course, as are all women of the nomad tribes, except those of highest birth.

Maïeddine did not want the coffee, but it would have been an insult to refuse, and he made laboured conversation with the Kebir, his eyes and thoughts fixed on the Caïd's gate and the yellow motor-car. He hardly saw the tents, beneath whose low-spread black wings eyes looked out at him, as the bright eyes of chickens look out from under the mother-hen's feathers. They were all much alike, though the Kebir's, as befitted his position, was the best, made of wide strips of black woollen material stitched together, spread tightly over stout poles, and pegged down into the hard sand. There was a partition dividing the tent in two, a partition made of one or two old haïcks, woven by hand, and if Maïeddine had been interested, he could have seen his host's bedding arranged for the day; a few coarse rugs and *frechias* piled up carelessly, out of the way. There was a bale of camels' hair, ready for weaving, and on top of it a little boy was curled up asleep. From the tent-poles hung an animal's skin, drying, and a cradle of netted cords in which swung and slept a swaddled baby no bigger than a doll. It was a girl, therefore its eyes were blackened with kohl, and its eyebrows neatly sketched on with paint, as they had been since the unfortunate day of its birth, when the father grumbled because it was not a "child," but only a worthless female.

The mother of the four weeks' old doll, a fine young woman tinkling with Arab silver, left her carpet-weaving to grind the coffee, while her withered mother-in-law brightened with brushwood the smouldering fire of camel-dung. The women worked silently, humbly, though they would have been chattering if the great Sidi stranger had not been there; but two or three little children in orange and scarlet rags played giggling among the rubbish outside the tent—a broken bassour-frame, or palanquin, waiting to be mended; date boxes, baskets, and wooden plates; old kous-kous bowls, bundles of alfa grass, chicken feathers, and an infant goat with its mother.

The sound of children's shrill laughter, which passed unnoticed by the parents, who had it always in their ears, rasped Maïeddine's nerves, and he would have liked to strike or kick the babies into silence. Most Arabs worship children, even girls, and are invariably kind to them, but to-day Maïeddine hated anything that ran about disturbingly and made a noise.

Now the Caïd had reached the gate, and was talking to the men in the motor-car. Would he send them away? No, the gate was being opened by a servant. Ben Sliman must have invited the Roumis in. Possibly it was a wise thing to do, yet how dangerous, how terribly dangerous, with Victoria perhaps peeping from one of the tiny windows at the women's corner of the house, which looked on the court! They could not see her there, but she could see them, and if she were tired of travelling and dancing attendance on a fidgety invalid—if she repented her promise to keep the secret of this journey?

Maïeddine's experience of women inclined him to think that they always did forget their promises to a man the moment his back was turned. Victoria was different from the women of his race, or those he had met in Paris, yet she was, after all, a woman; and there was no truer saying than that you might more easily prophesy the direction of the wind than say what a woman was likely to do. The coffee which the Kebir handed him made him feel sick, as if he had had a touch of the sun. What was happening up there on the hill, behind the gates which stood half open? What would she do—his Rose of the West?

XXV

It was a relief to Stephen and Nevill to see one of the horsemen coming up the rough hill-track to the gate, and to think that they need no longer wait upon the fears or inhospitable whims of the Arab servants on the other side of the wall.

As soon as the rider came near enough for his features to be sketched in clearly, Nevill remembered having noticed him at one or two of the Governor's balls, where all Arab dignitaries, even such lesser lights as caïds and adels show themselves. But they had never met. The man was not one of the southern chiefs whom Nevill Caird had entertained at his own house.

Stephen thought that he had never seen a more personable man as the Caïd rode up to the car, saluting courteously though with no great warmth.

His face was more tanned than very dark by nature, but it seemed brown in contrast to his light hazel eyes. His features were commanding, if not handsome, and he sat his horse well. Altogether he was a notable figure in his immensely tall white turban, wound with pale grey-brown camel's-hair rope, his grey cloth burnous, embroidered with gold, flung back over an inner white burnous, his high black boots, with wrinkled brown tops, and his wonderful Kairouan hat of light straw, embroidered with a leather appliqué of coloured flowers and silver leaves, steeple-crowned, and as big as a cart-wheel, hanging on his shoulders.

He and Nevill politely wished the blessings of Allah and Mohammed his Prophet upon each other, and Nevill then explained the errand which had brought him and his friend to the Caïd's house.

The Caïd's somewhat heavy though intelligent face did not easily show surprise. It changed not at all, though Stephen watched it closely.

"Thou art welcome to hear all I can tell of my dead relation, Ben Halim," he said. "But I know little that everybody does not know."

"It is certain, then, that Ben Halim is dead?" asked Nevill. "We had hoped that rumour lied."

"He died on his way home after a pilgrimage to Mecca," gravely replied the Caïd.

"Ah!" Nevill caught him up quickly. "We heard that it was in Constantinople."

Ben Sliman's expression was slightly strained. He glanced from Nevill's boyish face to Stephen's dark, keen one, and perhaps fancied suspicion in both. If he had intended to let the Englishmen drive away in their motor-car without seeing the other side of his white wall, he now changed his mind. "If thou and thy friend care to honour this poor farm of mine by entering the gates, and drinking coffee with me," he said, "We will afterwards go down below the hill to the cemetery where my cousin's body lies buried. His tombstone will show that he was El Hadj, and that he had reached Mecca. When he was in Constantinople, he had just returned from there."

Possibly, having given the invitation by way of proving that there was nothing to conceal, Ben Sliman hoped it would not be accepted; but he was disappointed. Before the Caïd had reached the top of the hill, Nevill had told his chauffeur to stop the motor, therefore the restless panting had long ago ceased, and when Ben Sliman looked doubtfully at the car, as if wondering how it was to be got in without doing damage to his wall, Nevill said that the automobile might stay where it was. Their visit would not be long.

"But the longer the better," replied the Caïd. "When I have guests, it pains me to see them go."

He shouted a word or two in Arabic, and instantly the gates were opened. The sketchily clad brown men inside had only been waiting for a signal.

"I regret that I cannot ask my visitors into the house itself, as I have illness there," Ben Sliman announced; "but we have guest rooms here in the gate-towers. They are not what I could wish for such distinguished personages, but thou canst see, Sidi, thou and thy friend, that this is a simple farmhouse. We make no pretension to the luxury of towns, but we do what we can."

As he spoke, the brown men were scuttling about, one unfastening the door of a little tower, which stuck as if it had not been opened for a long time, another darting into the house, which appeared silent and tenantless, a third and fourth running to a more distant part, and vanishing also through a dark doorway.

The Caïd quickly ushered his guests into the tower room, but not so quickly that the eyes of a girl, looking through a screened window, did not see and recognize both. The servant who had gone ahead unbarred a pair of wooden shutters high up in the whitewashed walls of the tower, which was stiflingly close, with a musty, animal odour. As the opening of the shutters gave light, enormous black- beetles which seemed to Stephen as large as pigeon's eggs, crawled out from cracks between wall and floor, stumbling awkwardly about, and falling over each other. It was a disgusting sight, and did not increase the visitors' desire to accept the Caïd's hospitality for any length of time. It may be that he had thought of this. But even if he had, the servants were genuinely enthusiastic in their efforts to make the Roumis at home. The two who had run farthest returned soonest. They staggered under a load of large rugs wrapped in unbleached sheeting, and a great sack stuffed full of cushions which bulged out at the top. The sheeting they unfastened, and, taking no notice of the beetles, hurriedly spread on the rough floor several beautifully woven rugs of bright colours. Then, having laid four or five on top of one another, they clawed the cushions out of the sack, and placed them as if on a bed.

Hardly had they finished, when the first servant who had disappeared came back, carrying over his arm a folding table, and dishes in his hands. The only furniture already in the tower consisted of two long, low wooden benches without backs; and as the servant from the house set up the folding table, he who had opened the windows placed the benches, one on either side. At the same moment, through the open door, a man could be seen running with a live lamb flung over his shoulder.

"Good heavens, what is he going to do with that?" Stephen asked, stricken with a presentiment.

"I'm afraid," Nevill answered quickly in English, "that it's going to be killed for our entertainment." His pink colour faded, and in Arabic he begged the Caïd to give orders that, if the lamb were for them, its life be spared, as they were under a vow never to touch meat. This was the first excuse he could think of; and when, to his joy, a message was sent after the slayer of innocence, he added that, very unfortunately, they had a pressing engagement which would tear them away from the Caïd's delightful house all too soon.

Perhaps the Caïd's face expressed no oppressive regret, yet he said kindly that he hoped to keep his guests at least until next morning.

In the cool of the day they would see the cemetery; they would return, and eat the evening meal. It would then be time to sleep. And with a gesture he indicated the rugs and cushions, under which the beetles were now buried like mountain-dwellers beneath an avalanche.

Nevill, still pale, thanked his host earnestly, complimented the rugs, and assured the Caïd that, of course, they would be extraordinarily comfortable, but even such inducements did not make it possible for them to neglect their duty elsewhere.

"In any case we shall now eat and drink together," said Ben Sliman, pointing to the table, and towards a servant now arriving from the house with a coffee-tray. The dishes had been set down on the bare board, and one contained the usual little almond cakes, the other, a conserve of some sort bathed in honey, where already many flies were revelling. The servant who had spread the table, quietly pulled the flies out by their wings, or killed them on the edge of the dish.

Nevill, whiter than before, accepted cordially, and giving Stephen a glance of despair, which said: "Noblesse oblige," he thrust his fingers into the honey, where there were fewest flies, and took out a sweetmeat. Stephen did the same. All three ate, and drank sweet black *café maure*. Once the Caïd turned to glance at something outside the door, and his secretive, light grey eyes were troubled. As they ate and drank, they talked, Nevill tactfully catechizing, the Caïd answering with pleasant frankness. He did not inquire why they wished to have news of Ben Halim, who had once lived in the house for a short time, and had now long been dead. Perhaps he wished to give the Roumis a lesson in discretion; but as their friendliness increased over the dripping sweets, Nevill ventured to ask a crucial question. What had become of Ben Halim's American wife?

Then, for the first time, the Caïd frowned, very slightly, but it was plain to see he thought a liberty had been taken which, as host, he was unable to resent.

"I know nothing of my dead cousin's family," he said. "No doubt its members went with him, if not to Mecca, at least a part of the way, and if any such persons wished to return to Europe after his death, it is certain they would have been at liberty to do so. This house my cousin wished me to have, and I took possession of it in due time, finding it empty and in good order. If you search for any one, I should advise searching in France or, perhaps, in America.

Unluckily, there I cannot help. But when it is cool, we will go to the cemetery. Let us go after the prayer, the prayer of *Moghreb*."

But Nevill was reluctant. So was Stephen, when the proposal was explained. They wished to go while it was still hot, or not at all. It may be that even this eccentric proposal did not surprise or grieve the Caïd, though as a rule he was not fond of being out of doors in the glare of the sun.

He agreed to the suggestion that the motor-car should take all three down the hill, but said that he would prefer to walk back.

The "teuf-teuf" of the engine began once more outside the white gates; and for the second time Victoria flew to the window, pressing her face against the thick green moucharabia which excluded flies and prevented any one outside from seeing what went on within.

"Calm thyself, O Rose," urged the feeble voice of Lella M'Barka. "Thou hast said these men are nothing to thee."

"One is my friend," the girl pleaded, with a glance at the high couch of rugs on which M'Barka lay.

"A young girl cannot have a man for a friend. He may be a lover or a husband, but never a friend. Thou knowest this in thy heart, O Rose, and thou hast sworn to me that never hast thou had a lover."

Victoria did not care to argue. "I am sure he has come here to try and find me. He is anxious. That is very good of him—all the more, because we are nothing to each other. How can I let him go away without a word? It is too hard-hearted. I do think, if Si Maïeddine were here, he would say so too. He would let me see Mr. Knight and just tell him that I'm perfectly safe and on the way to my sister. That once she lived in this house, and I hoped to find her here, but — —"

"Maïeddine would not wish thee to tell the young man these things, or any other things, or show thyself to him at all," M'Barka persisted, lifting herself on the bed in growing excitement. "Dost thou not guess, he runs many dangers in guiding thee to the wife of a man who is as one dead? Dost thou wish to ruin him who risks his whole future to content thee?"

"No, of course I would do nothing which could bring harm to Si Maïeddine," Victoria said, the eagerness dying out of her voice. "I have kept my word with him. I have let nobody know—nobody at all. But we could trust Mr. Knight and Mr. Caird. And to see them there, in the courtyard, and let them go—it is too much!"

"Why shouldst thou consider me, whom thou hast known but a few days, when thou wouldst be hurrying on towards thy sister Saïda? Yet it will surely be my death if thou makest any sign to those men. My heart would cease to beat. It beats but weakly now."

With a sigh, Victoria turned away from the moucharabia, and crossing the room to M'Barka, sat down on a rug by the side of her couch. "I do consider thee," she said. "If it were not for thee and Si Maïeddine, I might not be able to get to Saidee at all; so I must not mind being delayed a few days. It is worse for thee than for me, because thou art suffering."

"When a true believer lies ill for more than three days, his sins are all forgiven him," M'Barka consoled herself. She put out a hot hand, and laid it on Victoria's head. "Thou art a good child. Thou hast given up thine own will to do what is right."

"I'm not quite sure at this moment that I am doing what is right," murmured Victoria. "But I can't make thee more ill than thou art, so I must let Mr. Knight go. And probably I shall never see him, never hear of him again. He will look for me, and then he will grow tired, and perhaps go home to England before I can write to let him know I am safe with Saidee." Her voice broke a little. She bent down her head, and there were tears in her eyes.

She heard the creaking of the gate as it shut. The motor-car had gone panting away. For a moment it seemed as if her heart would break. Just one glimpse had she caught of Stephen's face, and it had looked to her more than ever like the face of a knight who would fight to the death for a good cause. She had not quite realized how noble a face it was, or how hard it would be to let it pass out of her life. He would always hate her if he guessed she had sat there, knowing he had come so far for her sake?—she was sure it was for her sake—and had made no sign. But he would not guess. And it was true, as Lella M'Barka said, he was nothing to her. Saidee was everything. And she was going to Saidee. She must think only of Saidee, and the day of their meeting.

Stephen had never seen an Arab cemetery; and it seemed to him that this Mussulman burial-place, scattered over two low hills, in the midst of desert wastes, was beautiful and pathetic. The afternoon sunshine beat upon the koubbahs of marabouts, and the plastered graves or headstones of less important folk; but so pearly pale were they all that the golden quality of the light was blanched as if by some strange, white magic, and became like moonlight shining on a field of snow.

There were no names on any of the tombs, even the grandest. Here and there on a woman's grave was a hand of Fatma, or a pair of the Prophet's slippers; and on those of a few men were turbans carved in marble, to tell that the dead had made pilgrimage to Mecca. All faces were turned towards the sacred city, as Mussulmans turn when they kneel to pray, in mosque or in desert; and the white slabs, narrow or broad, long or short, ornamental or plain, flat or roofed with fantastic maraboutic domes, were placed very close together. At one end of the cemetery, only bits of pottery marked the graves; yet each bit was a little different from the other, meaning as much to those who had placed them there as names and epitaphs in European burial grounds. On the snowy headstones and flat platforms, drops of rose-coloured wax from little candles, lay like tears of blood shed by the mourners, and there was a scattered spray of faded orange blossoms, brought by some loving hand from a far-away garden in an oasis.

"Here lies my cousin, Cassim ben Halim," said the Caïd, pointing to a grave comparatively new, surmounted at the head with a carved turban. Nearer to it than any other tomb was that of a woman, beautified with the Prophet's slippers.

"Is it possible that his wife lies beside him?" Stephen made Nevill ask.

"It is a lady of his house. I can say no more. When his body was brought here, hers was brought also, in a coffin, which is permitted to the women of Islam, with the request that it should be placed near my cousin's tomb. This was done; and it is all I can tell, because it is all I know."

The Arab looked the Englishman straight in the eyes as he answered; and Stephen felt that in this place, so simple, so peaceful, so near to nature's heart, it would be difficult for a man to lie to another, even though that man were a son of Islam, the other a "dog of a

Christian." For the first time he began to believe that Cassim ben Halim had in truth died, and that Victoria Ray's sister was perhaps dead also. Her death alone could satisfactorily explain her long silence. And against the circumstantial evidence of this little grave, adorned with the slippers of the Prophet, there was only a girl's impression—Victoria's feeling that, if Saidee were dead, she "must have known."

The two friends stood for a while by the white graves, where the sunshine lay like moonlight on snow; and then, because there was nothing more for them to do in that place, they thanked the Caïd, and made ready to go their way. Again he politely refused their offer to drive him up to his own gate, and bade them good-bye when they had got into the car. He stood and watched it go bumping away over the rough, desert road, pieces of which had been gnawed off by a late flood, as a cake is bitten round the edge by a greedy child.

They had had enough of motor-cars for that day, up there on the hill! The Caïd was glad when the sound died. The machine was no more suited to his country, he thought, than were the men of Europe who tore about the world in it, trying to interfere in other people's business.

"El hamdou-lillah! God be praised!" he whispered, as the yellow automobile vanished from sight and Maïeddine came out from the cluster of black tents in the yellow sand.

XXVI

Next day, Lella M'Barka was well enough to begin the march again. They started, in the same curtained carriage, at that moment before dawn while it is still dark, and a thin white cloth seems spread over the dead face of night. Then day came trembling along the horizon, and the shadows of horses and carriage grew long and grotesquely deformed. It was the time, M'Barka said, when Chitan the devil, and the evil Djenoun that possess people's minds and drive them insane, were most powerful; and she would hardly listen when Victoria answered that she did not believe in Djenoun.

In a long day, they came to Bou-Saada, reaching the hidden oasis after nightfall, and staying in the house of the Caïd with whom Stephen and Nevill had talked of Ben Halim. Lella M'Barka was related to the Caïd's wife, and was so happy in meeting a cousin after years of separation, that the fever in her blood was cooled; and in the morning she was able to go on.

Then came two days of driving to Djelfa, at first in a country strange enough to be Djinn-haunted, a country of gloomy mountains, and deep water-courses like badly healed wounds; passing through dry river-beds, and over broken roads with here and there a bordj where men brought water to the mules, in skins held together with ropes of straw. At last, after a night, not too comfortable, spent in a dismal bordj, they came to a wilderness which any fairytale-teller would have called the end of the world. The road had dwindled to a track across gloomy desert, all the more desolate, somehow, because of the dry asparto grass growing thinly among stones. Nothing seemed to live or move in this world, except a lizard that whisked its grey- green length across the road, a long-legged bird which hopped gloomily out of the way, or a few ragged black and white sheep with nobody to drive them. In the heat of the day nothing stirred, not even the air, though the distance shimmered and trembled with heat; but towards night jackals padded lithely from one rock shelter to another. The carriage drove through a vast plain, rimmed with far- away mountains, red as porphyry, but fading to purple at the horizon. Victoria felt that she would never come to the end of this plain, that it must finish only with eternity; and she wished in an occasional burst of impatience that she were travelling in Nevill Caird's motor-car. She could reach her sister in a third of the time!

She told herself that these thoughts were ungrateful to Maïeddine, who was doing so much for her sake, and she kept up her spirits whether they dragged on tediously, or stopped by the way to eat, or to let M'Barka rest. She tried to control her restlessness, but feared that Maïeddine saw it, for he took pains to explain, more than once, how necessary was the detour they were making. Along this route he had friends who were glad to entertain them at night, and give them mules or horses, and besides, it was an advantage that the way should be unfrequented by Europeans. He cheered her by describing the interest of the journey when, by and by, she would ride a mehari, sitting in a bassour, made of branches heated and bent into shape like a great cage, lined and draped with soft haoulis of beautiful colours, and comfortably cushioned. It would not be long now before they should come to the douar of his father the Agha, beyond El Aghouat. She would have a wonderful experience there; and according to Maïeddine, all the rest of the journey would be an enchantment. Never for a moment would he let her tire. Oh, he would promise that she should be half sorry when the last day came! As for Lella M'Barka, the Rose of the West need not fear, for the bassour was easy as a cradle to a woman of the desert; and M'Barka, rightfully a princess of Touggourt, was desert-born and bred.

Queer little patches of growing grain, or miniature orchards enlivened the dull plain round the ugly Saharian town of Djelfa, headquarters of the Ouled Naïls. The place looked unprepossessingly new and French, and obtrusively military; dismal, too, in the dusty sand which a wailing wind blew through the streets; but scarcely a Frenchman was to be seen, except the soldiers. Many Arabs worked with surprising briskness at the loading or unloading of great carts, men of the Ouled Naïls, with eyes more mysterious than the eyes of veiled women; tall fellows wearing high shoes of soft, pale brown leather made for walking long distances in heavy sand; and Maïeddine said that there was great traffic and commerce between Djelfa and the M'Zab country, where she and he and M'Barka would arrive presently, after passing his father's douar.

Maïeddine was uneasy until they were out of Djelfa, for, though few Europeans travelled that way, and the road is hideous for motors, still it was not impossible that a certain yellow car had slipped in before them, to lie in wait. The Caïd's house, where they spent that night, was outside the town, and behind its closed doors and little windows there was no fear of intruders. It was good to be sure of shelter and security under a friend's roof; and so far, in spite of the

adventure at Ben Sliman's, everything was going well enough. Only —
Maïeddine was a little disappointed in Victoria's manner towards
himself. She was sweet and friendly, and grateful for all he did, but
she did not seem interested in him as a man. He felt that she was eager
to get on, that she was counting the days, not because of any pleasure
they might bring in his society, but to make them pass more quickly.
Still, with the deep-rooted patience of the Arab, he went on hoping.
His father, Agha of the Ouled-Serrin, reigned in the desert like a petty
king. Maïeddine thought that the douar and the Agha's state must
impress her; and the journey on from there would be a splendid
experience, different indeed from this interminable jogging along,
cramped up in a carriage, with M'Barka sighing, or leaning a heavy
head on the girl's shoulder. Out in the open, Victoria in her bassour,
he on the horse which he would take from his father's goum,
travelling would be pure joy. And Maïeddine had been saving up
many surprises for that time, things he meant to do for the girl, which
must turn her heart towards him.

Beyond Djelfa, on the low mountains that alone broke the monotony
of the dismal plain, little watch-towers rose dark along the sky-line —
watch-towers old as Roman days. Sometimes the travellers met a
mounted man wearing a long, hooded cloak over his white burnous;
a cavalier of the Bureau Arabe, or native policeman on his beat, under
the authority of a civil organization more powerful in the Sahara than
the army. These men, riding alone, saluted Si Maïeddine almost with
reverence, and Lella M'Barka told Victoria, with pride, that her cousin
was immensely respected by the French Government. He had done
much for France in the far south, where his family influence was great,
and he had adjusted difficulties between the desert men and their
rulers. "He is more tolerant than I, to those through whom Allah has
punished us for our sins," said the woman of the Sahara. "I was
brought up in an older school; and though I may love one of the
Roumis, as I have learned to love thee, oh White Rose, I cannot love
whole Christian nations. Maïeddine is wiser than I, yet I would not
change my opinions for his; unless, as I often think, he really — —" she
stopped suddenly, frowning at herself. "This dreariness is not *our*
desert," she explained eagerly to the girl, as the horses dragged the
carriage over the sandy earth, through whose hard brown surface the
harsh, colourless blades of *drinn* pricked like a few sparse hairs on the
head of a shrivelled old man. "In the Sahara, there are four kinds of
desert, because Allah put four angels in charge, giving each his own
portion. The Angel of the Chebka was cold of nature, with no
kindness in his heart, and was jealous of the

others; so the Chebka is desolate, sown with sharp rocks which were upheaved from under the earth before man came, and its dark ravines are still haunted by evil spirits. The Angel of the Hameda was careless, and forgot to pray for cool valleys and good water, so the Hameda hardened into a great plateau of rock. The Angel of the Gaci was loved by a houri, who appeared to him and danced on the firm sand of his desert. Vanishing, she scattered many jewels, and fruits from the celestial gardens which turned into beautifully coloured stones as they fell, and there they have lain from that day to this. But best of all was the Angel of the Erg, our desert—desert of the shifting dunes, never twice the same, yet always more beautiful to-day than yesterday; treacherous to strangers, but kind as the bosom of a mother to her children. The first three angels were men, but the fourth and best is the angel woman who sows the heaven with stars, for lamps to light her own desert, and all the world beside, even the world of infidels."

M'Barka and Maïeddine both talked a great deal of El Aghouat, which M'Barka called the desert pearl, next in beauty to her own wild Touggourt, and Maïeddine laughingly likened the oasis-town to Paris. "It is the Paris of our Sahara," he said, "and all the desert men, from Caïds to camel-drivers, look forward to its pleasures."

He planned to let the girl see El Aghouat for the first time at sunset. That was to be one of his surprises. By nature he was dramatic; and the birth of the sun and the death of the sun are the great dramas of the desert. He wished to be the hero of such a drama for Victoria, with El Aghouat for his background; for there, he was leading her in at the gate of his own country.

When they had passed the strange rock-shape known as the Chapeau de Gendarme, and the line of mountains which is like the great wall of China, Maïeddine defied the danger he had never quite ceased to fear during the five long days since the adventure on the other side of Bou-Saada. He ordered the carriage curtains to be rolled up as tightly as they would go, and Victoria saw a place so beautiful that it was like the secret garden of some Eastern king. It was as if they had driven abruptly over the edge of a vast bowl half filled with gold dust, and ringed round its rim with quivering rosy flames. Perhaps the king of the garden had a dragon whose business it was to keep the fire always alight to prevent robbers from coming to steal the gold dust; and so ardently had it been blazing there for centuries, that all the sky up to the zenith had caught fire, burning with so dazzling an intensity of violet that Victoria thought she could warm her hands in its reflection on the sand. In the azure crucible diamonds were melting, boiling up in a radiant spray, but suddenly the violet splendour was cooled, and after a vague quivering of rainbow tints, the celestial rose tree of the Sahara sunset climbed blossoming over the whole blue dome, east, west, north and south.

In the bottom of the golden bowl, there was a river bed to cross, on a bridge of planks, but among the burning stones trickled a mere runnel of water, bright as spilt mercury. And Maïeddine chose the moment when the minarets of El Aghouat rose from a sea of palms, to point out the strange, pale hills crowned by old koubbahs of marabouts and the military hospital. He told the story of the Arab revolt of fifty odd years ago; and while he praised the gallantry of the French, Victoria saw in his eyes, heard in the thrill of his voice, that his admiration was for his own people. This made her thoughtful, for though it was natural enough to sympathize with the Arabs who had stood the siege and been reconquered after desperate fighting, until now his point of view had seemed to be the modern, progressive, French point of view. Quickly the question flashed through her mind —"Is he letting himself go, showing me his real self, because I'm in the desert with him, and he thinks I'll never go back among Europeans?"

She shivered a little at the thought, but she put it away with the doubt of Maïeddine that came with it. Never had he given her the least cause to fear him, and she would go on trusting in his good faith, as she had trusted from the first.

Still, there was that creeping chill, in contrast to the warm glory of the sunset, which seemed to shame it by giving a glimpse of the desert's heart, which was Maïeddine's heart. She hurried to say how beautiful was El Aghouat; and that night, in the house of the Caïd, (an uncle of Maïeddine's on his mother's side), as the women grouped round her, hospitable and admiring, she reproached herself again for her suspicion. The wife of the Caïd was dignified and gentle. There were daughters growing up, and though they knew nothing, or seemed to know nothing, of Saidee, they were sure that, if Maïeddine knew, all was well. Because they were his cousins they had seen and been seen by him, and the young girls poured out all the untaught romance of their little dim souls in praise of Maïeddine. Once they were on the point of saying something which their mother seemed to think indiscreet, and checked them quickly. Then they stopped, laughing; and their laughter, like the laughter of little children, was so contagious that Victoria laughed too.

There was some dreadful European furniture of sprawling, "nouveau art" design in the guest-room which she and Lella M'Barka shared; and as Victoria lay awake on the hard bed, of which the girls were proud, she said to herself that she had not been half grateful enough to Si Maïeddine. For ten years she had tried to find Saidee, and until the other day she had been little nearer her heart's desire than when she was a child, hoping and longing in the school garret. Now Maïeddine had made the way easy—almost too easy, for the road to the golden silence had become so wonderful that she was tempted to forget her haste to reach the end.

XXVII

"There is my father's douar," said Si Maïeddine; and Victoria's eyes followed his pointing finger.

Into a stony and desolate waste had billowed one golden wave of sand, and on the fringe of this wave, the girl saw a village of tents, black and brown, lying closely together, as a fleet of dark fishing-boats lie in the water. There were many little tents, very flat and low, crouched around one which even at a distance was conspicuous for its enormous size. It looked like a squatting giant among an army of pigmies; and the level light of late afternoon gave extraordinary value to its colours, which were brighter and newer than those of the lesser tents. As their swaying carriage brought the travellers nearer, Victoria could see deep red and brown stripes, separated by narrow bands of white. For background, there was a knot of trees; for they had come south of El Aghouat to the strange region of dayas, where the stony desolation is broken by little emerald hollows, running with water, like big round bowls stuck full of delicate greenery and blossoms.

Suddenly, as Victoria looked, figures began running about, and almost before she had time to speak, ten or a dozen men in white, mounted on horses, came speeding across the desert.

A stain of red showed in Maïeddine's cheeks, and his eyes lighted up. "They have been watching, expecting us," he said. "Now my father is sending men to bid us welcome."

"Perhaps he is coming himself," said Victoria, for there was one figure riding in the centre which seemed to her more splendidly dignified than the others, though all were magnificent horsemen.

"No. It would not be right that the Agha himself should come to meet his son," Maïeddine explained. "Besides he would be wearing a scarlet burnous, embroidered with gold. He does me enough honour in sending out the pick of his goum, which is among the finest of the Sahara."

Victoria had picked up a great deal of desert lore by this time, and knew that the "pick of the goum" would mean the best horses in the Agha's stables, the crack riders among his trained men—fighting men, such as he would give to the Government, if Arab soldiers were needed.

The dozen cavaliers swept over the desert, making the sand fly up under the horses' hoofs in a yellow spray; and nearing the carriage they spread themselves in a semi-circle, the man Victoria had mistaken for the Agha riding forward to speak to Maïeddine.

"It is my brother-in-law, Abderrhaman ben Douadi," exclaimed Maïeddine, waving his hand.

M'Barka pulled her veil closer, and because she did so, Victoria hid her face also, rather than shock the Arab woman's prejudices.

At a word from his master, the driver stopped his mules so quickly as to bring them on their haunches, and Maïeddine sprang out. He and his brother-in-law, a stately dark man with a short black beard under an eagle nose, exchanged courtesies which seemed elaborate to Victoria's European ideas, and Si Abderrhaman did not glance at the half-lowered curtains behind which the women sat.

The men talked for a few minutes; then Maïeddine got into the carriage again; and surrounded by the riders, it was driven rapidly towards the tents, rocking wildly in the sand, because now it had left the desert road and was making straight for the zmala.

The Arab men on their Arab horses shouted as they rode, as if giving a signal; and from the tents, reddened now by the declining sun, came suddenly a strange crying in women's voices, shrill yet sweet; a sound that was half a chant, half an eerie yodeling, note after note of "you-you!—you-you!" Out from behind the zeribas, rough hedges of dead boughs and brambles which protected each low tent, burst a tidal wave of children, some gay as little bright butterflies in gorgeous dresses, others wrapped in brilliant rags. From under the tents women appeared, unveiled, and beautiful in the sunset light, with their heavy looped braids and their dangling, clanking silver jewellery. "You-you! you-you!" they cried, dark eyes gleaming, white teeth flashing. It was to be a festival for the douar, this fortunate evening of the son and heir's arrival, with a great lady of his house, and her friend, a Roumia girl. There was joy for everyone, for the Agha's relatives, and for each man, woman and child in the zmala, mighty ones, or humble members of the tribe, the Ouled-Serrin. There would be feasting, and after dark, to give pleasure to the Roumia, the men would make the powder speak. It was like a wedding; and best of all, an exciting rumour had gone round the douar, concerning the foreign girl and the Agha's son, Si Maïeddine.

The romance in Victoria's nature was stirred by her reception; by the white-clad riders on their slender horses, and the wild "you-yous" of the women and little girls. Maïeddine saw her excitement and thrilled to it. This was his great hour. All that had gone before had been leading up to this day, and to the days to come, when they would be in the fiery heart of the desert together, lost to all her friends whom he hated with a jealous hatred. He helped M'Barka to descend from the carriage: then, as she was received at the tent door by the Agha himself, Maïeddine forgot his self-restraint, and swung the girl down, with tingling hands that clasped her waist, as if at last she belonged to him.

Half fearful of what he had done, lest she should take alarm at his sudden change of manner, he studied her face anxiously as he set her feet to the ground. But there was no cause for uneasiness. So far from resenting the liberty he had taken after so many days of almost ostentatious respect, Victoria was not even thinking of him, and her indifference would have been a blow, if he had not been too greatly relieved to be hurt by it. She was looking at his father, the Agha, who seemed to her the embodiment of some biblical patriarch. All through her long desert journey, she had felt as if she had wandered into a dream of the Old Testament. There was nothing there more modern than "Bible days," as she said to herself, simply, except the French quarters in the few Arab towns through which they had passed.

Not yet, however, had she seen any figure as venerable as the Agha's, and she thought at once of Abraham at his tent door. Just such a man as this Abraham must have been in his old age. She could even imagine him ready to sacrifice a son, if he believed it to be the will of Allah; and Maïeddine became of more importance in her eyes because of his relationship to this kingly patriarch of the Sahara.

Having greeted his niece, Lella M'Barka, and passed her hospitably into the tent where women were dimly visible, the Agha turned to Maïeddine and Victoria.

"The blessing of Allah be upon thee, O my son," he said, "and upon thee, little daughter. My son's messenger brought word of thy coming, and thou art welcome as a silver shower of rain after a long drought in the desert. Be thou as a child of my house, while thou art in my tent."

As she gave him her hand, her veil fell away from her face, and he saw its beauty with the benevolent admiration of an old man whose blood has cooled. He was so tall that the erect, thin figure reminded Victoria of a lonely desert palm. The young girl was no stern critic, and was more inclined to see good than evil in every one she met; therefore to her the long snowy beard, the large dreamy eyes under brows like Maïeddine's, and the slow, benevolent smile of the Agha meant nobility of character. Her heart was warm for the splendid old man, and he was not unaware of the impression he had made. As he bowed her into the tent where his wife and sister and daughter were crowding round M'Barka, he said in a low voice to Maïeddine: "It is well, my son. Being a man, and young, thou couldst not have withstood her. When the time is ripe, she will become a daughter of Islam, because for love of thee, she will wish to fulfil thine heart's desire."

"She does not yet know that she loves me," Maïeddine answered. "But when thou hast given me the white stallion El Biod, and I ride beside the girl in her bassour through the long days and the long distances, I shall teach her, in the way the Roumi men teach their women to love."

"But if thou shouldst not teach her?"

"My life is in it, and I shall teach her," said Maïeddine. "But if Chitan stands between, and I fail—which I will not do—why, even so, it will come to the same thing in the end, because——"

"Thou wouldst say——"

"It is well to know one's own meaning, and to speak of—date stones. Yet with one's father, one can open one's heart. He to whom I go has need of my services, and what he has for twelve months vainly asked me to do, I will promise to do, for the girl's sake, if I cannot win her without."

"Take care! Thou enterest a dangerous path," said the old man.

"Yet often I have thought of entering there, before I saw this girl's face."

"There might be a great reward in this life, and in the life beyond. Yet once the first step is taken, it is irrevocable. In any case, commit me to nothing with him to whom thou goest. He is eaten up with zeal. He is a devouring fire—and all is fuel for that fire."

"I will commit thee to nothing without thy full permission, O my father."

"And for thyself, think twice before thou killest the sheep. Remember our desert saying. 'Who kills a sheep, kills a bee. Who kills a bee, kills a palm, and who kills a palm, kills seventy prophets.'"

"I would give my sword to the prophets to aid them in killing those who are not prophets."

"Thou art faithful. Yet let the rain of reason fall on thy head and on thine heart, before thou givest thy sword into the hand of him who waits thine answer."

"Thine advice is of the value of many dates, even of the *deglet nour*, the jewel date, which only the rich can eat."

The old man laid his hand, still strong and firm, on his son's shoulder, and together they went into the great tent, that part of it where the women were, for all were closely related to them, excepting the Roumia, who had been received as a daughter of the house.

When it was evening, the douar feasted, in honour of the guests who had come to the *tente sultane*. The Agha had given orders that two sheep should be killed. One was for his own household; his relatives, his servants, many of whom lived under the one vast roof of red, and white, and brown. His daughter, and her husband who assisted him in many ways, and was his scribe, or secretary, had a tent of their own close by, next in size to the Agha's; but they were bidden to supper in the great tent that night, for the family reunion. And because there was a European girl present, the women ate with the men, which was not usual.

The second sheep was for the humbler folk of the zmala, and they roasted it whole in an open space, over a fire of small, dry wood, and of dead palm branches brought on donkey back twenty miles across the desert, from the nearest oasis town, also under dominion of the Agha. He had a house and garden there; but he liked best to be in his douar, with only his tent roof between him and the sky. Also it made him popular with the tribe of which he was the head, to spend most of his time with them in the desert. And for some reasons of which he never spoke, the old man greatly valued this popularity, though he treasured also the respect of the French, who assured his position and revenues.

The desert men had made a ring round the fire, far from the green *daya*, so that the blowing sparks might not reach the trees. They sat in a circle, on the sand, with a row of women on one side, who held the smallest children by their short skirts; and larger children, wild and dark, as the red light of the flames played over their faces, fed the fire with pale palm branches. There was no moon, but a fountain of sparks spouted towards the stars; and though it was night, the sky was blue with the fierce blue of steel. Some of the Agha's black Soudanese servants had made kous-kous of semolina with a little mutton and a great many red peppers. This they gave to the crowd, in huge wooden bowls; and the richer people boiled coffee which they drank themselves, and offered to those sitting nearest them.

When everybody had eaten, the powder play began round the fire, and at each explosion the women shrilled out their "you-you, you-you!" But this was all for the entertainment of outsiders. Inside the Agha's tent, the family took their pleasure more quietly.

Though a house of canvas, there were many divisions into rooms. The Agha's wife had hers, separated completely from her sister's, and there was space for guests, besides the Agha's own quarters, his reception room, his dining-room (invaded to-night by all his family) the kitchen, and sleeping place for a number of servants.

There were many dishes besides the inevitable cheurba, or Arab soup, the kous-kous, the mechoui, lamb roasted over the fire. Victoria was almost sickened by the succession of sweet things, cakes and sugared preserves, made by the hands of the Agha's wife, Alonda, who in the Roumia's eyes was as like Sarah as the Agha was like Abraham. Yet everything was delicious; and after the meal, when the coffee came, lagmi the desert wine distilled from the heart of a palm tree, was pressed upon Victoria. All drank a little, for, said

Lella Alonda, though strong drink was forbidden by the Prophet, the palms were dear to him, and besides, in the throats of good men and women, wine was turned to milk, as Sidi Aissa of the Christians turned water to wine at the marriage feast.

When they had finished at last, a Soudanese woman poured rose-water over their hands, from a copper jug, and wiped them with a large damask napkin, embroidered by Aichouch, the pretty, somewhat coquettish married daughter of the house, Maïeddine's only sister. The rose-water had been distilled by Lella Fatma, the widowed sister of Alonda, who shared the hospitality of the Agha's roof, in village or douar. Every one questioned Victoria, and made much of her, even the Agha; but, though they asked her opinions of Africa, and talked of her journey across the sea, they did not speak of her past life or of her future. Not a word was said concerning her mission, or Ben Halim's wife, the sister for whom she searched.

While they were still at supper, the black servants who had waited upon them went quietly away, but slightly raised the heavy red drapery which formed the partition between that room and another. They looped up the thick curtain only a little way, but there was a light on the other side, and Victoria, curious as to what would happen next, spied the servants' black legs moving about, watched a rough wooden bench placed on the blue and crimson rugs of Djebel Amour, and presently saw other black legs under a white burnous coil themselves upon the low seat.

Then began strange music, the first sound of which made Victoria's heart leap. It was the first time she had heard the music of Africa, except a distant beating of tobols coming from a black tent across desert spaces, while she had lain at night in the house of Maïeddine's friends; or the faint, pure note of a henna-dyed flute in the hand of some boy keeper of goats—a note pure as the monotonous purling of water, heard in the dark.

But this music was so close to her, that it was like the throbbing of her own heart. And it was no sweet, pure trickle of silver, but the cry of passion, passion as old and as burning as the desert sands outside the lighted tent. As she listened, struck into pulsing silence, she could see the colour of the music; a deep crimson, which flamed into scarlet as the tom-tom beat, or deepened to violent purple, wicked as belladonna flowers. The wailing of the raïta mingled with the heavy throbbing of the tom-tom, and filled the girl's heart with a vague foreboding, a yearning for something she had not known, and did not understand. Yet it seemed that she must have both known and understood long ago, before memory recorded anything—perhaps in some forgotten incarnation. For the music and what it said, monotonously yet fiercely, was old as the beginnings of the world, old and changeless as the patterns of the stars embroidered on the astrological scroll of the sky. The hoarse derbouka, and the languorous ghesbah joined in with the savage tobol and the strident raïta; and under all was the tired heart-beat of the bendir, dull yet resonant, and curiously exciting to the nerves.

Victoria's head swam. She wondered if it were wholly the effect of the African music, or if the lagmi she had sipped was mounting to her brain. She grew painfully conscious of every physical sense, and it was hard to sit and listen. She longed to spring up and dance in time to the droning, and throbbing, and crying of the primitive instruments which the Negroes played behind the red curtain. She felt that she must dance, a new, strange dance the idea of which was growing in her mind, and becoming an obsession. She could see it as if she were looking at a picture; yet it was only her nerves and her blood that bade her dance. Her reason told her to sit still. Striving to control herself she shut her eyes, and would have shut her ears too, if she could. But the music was loud in them. It made her see desert rivers rising after floods, and water pounding against the walls of underground caverns. It made her hear the wild, fierce love-call of a desert bird to its mate.

She could bear it no longer. She sprang up, her eyes shining, her cheeks red. "May I dance for you to that music, Lella Alonda?" she said to the Agha's wife. "I think I could. I long to try."

Lella Alonda, who was old, and accustomed only to the dancing of the Almehs, which she thought shameful, was scandalized at the thought that the young girl would willingly dance before men. She was dumb, not knowing what answer to give, that need not offend a guest, but which might save the Roumia from indiscretion.

The Agha, however, was enchanted. He was a man of the world still, though he was aged now, and he had been to Paris, as well as many times to Algiers. He knew that European ladies danced with men of their acquaintance, and he was curious to see what this beautiful child wished to do. He glanced at Maïeddine, and spoke to his wife: "Tell the little White Rose to dance; that it will give us pleasure."

"Dance then, in thine own way, O daughter," Lella Alonda was forced to say; for it did not even occur to her that she might disobey her husband.

Victoria smiled at them all; at M'Barka and Aichouch, and Aichouch's dignified husband, Si Abderrhaman: at Alonda and the Agha, and at Maïeddine, as, when a child, she would have smiled at her sister, when beginning a dance made up from one of Saidee's stories.

She had told Stephen of an Eastern dance she knew, but this was something different, more thrilling and wonderful, which the wild music put into her heart. At first, she hardly knew what was the meaning she felt impelled to express by gesture and pose. The spirit of the desert sang to her, a song of love, a song old as the love-story of Eve; and though the secret of that song was partly hidden from her as yet, she must try to find it out for herself, and picture it to others, by dancing.

Always before, when she danced, Victoria had called up the face of her sister, to keep before her eyes as an inspiration. But now, as she bent and swayed to catch the spirit's whispers, as wheat sways to the whisper of the wind, it was a man's face she saw. Stephen Knight seemed to stand in the tent, looking at her with a curiously wistful, longing look, over the heads of the Arab audience, who sat on their low divans and piled carpets.

She thrilled to the look, and the desert spirit made her screen her face from it, with a sequined gauze scarf which she wore. For a few measures she danced behind the glittering veil, then with a sudden impulse which the music gave, she tossed it back, holding out her arms, and smiling up to Stephen's eyes, above the brown faces, with a sweet smile very mysterious to the watchers. Consciously she called to Stephen then, as she had promised she would call, if she should ever need him, for somehow she did need and want him;— not for his help in finding Saidee: she was satisfied with all that Maïeddine was doing—but for herself. The secret of the music which she had been trying to find out, was in his eyes, and learning it slowly, made her more beautiful, more womanly, than she had ever been before. As she danced on, the two long plaits of her red hair loosened and shook out into curls which played round her white figure like flames. Her hands fluttered on the air as they rose and fell like the little white wings of a dove; and she was dazzling as a brandished torch, in the ill-lit tent with its dark hangings.

M'Barka had given her a necklace of black beads which the negresses had made of benzoin and rose leaves and spices, held in shape with pungent rezin. Worn on the warm flesh, the beads gave out a heady perfume, which was like the breath of the desert. It made the girl giddy, and it grew stronger and sweeter as she danced, seeming to mingle with the crying of the raïta and the sobbing of the ghesbah, so that she confused fragrance with music, music with fragrance.

Maïeddine stared at her, like a man who dreams with his eyes open. If he had been alone, he could have watched her dance on for hours, and wished that she would never stop; but there were other men in the tent, and he had a maddening desire to snatch the girl in his arms, smothering her in his burnous, and rushing away with her into the desert.

Her dancing astonished him. He did not know what to make of it, for she had told him nothing about herself, except what concerned her errand in Africa. Though he had been in Paris when she was there, he had been deeply absorbed in business vital to his career, and had not heard of Victoria Ray the dancer, or seen her name on the hoardings.

Like his father, he knew that European women who danced were not as the African dancers, the Ouled Naïls and the girls of Djebel Amour. But an Arab may have learned to know many things with his mind which he cannot feel with his heart; and with his heart Maïeddine felt a wish to blind Abderrhaman, because his eyes had seen the intoxicating beauty of Victoria as she danced. He was ferociously angry, but not with the girl. Perhaps with himself, because he was powerless to hide her from others, and to order her life as he chose. Yet there was a kind of delicious pain in knowing himself at her mercy, as no Arab man could be at the mercy of an Arab woman.

The sight of Victoria dancing, had shot new colours into his existence. He understood her less, and valued her more than before, a thousand times more, achingly, torturingly more. Since their first meeting on the boat, he had admired the American girl immensely. Her whiteness, the golden-red of her hair, the blueness of her eyes had meant perfection for him. He had wanted her because she was the most beautiful creature he had seen, because she was a Christian and difficult to win; also because the contrast between her childishness and brave independence was piquant. Apart from that contrast, he had not thought much about her nature. He had looked upon her simply as a beautiful girl, who could not be bought, but must be won. Now she had become a bewildering houri. Nothing which life could give him would make up for the loss of her. There was nothing he would not do to have her, or at least to put her beyond the reach of others.

If necessary, he would even break his promise to the Agha.

While she danced inside the great tent, outside in the open space round the fire, the dwellers in the little tents sat with their knees in their arms watching the dancing of two young Negroes from the Soudan. The blacks had torn their turbans from their shaven heads, and thrown aside their burnouses. Naked to their waists, with short, loose trousers, and sashes which other men seized, to swing the wearers round and round, their sweating skin had the gloss of ebony. It was a whirlwind of a dance, and an old wizard with a tom-tom, and a dark giant with metal castanets made music for the dancers, taking eccentric steps themselves as they played. The Soudanese fell into an ecstasy of giddiness, running about on their hands and feet like huge black tarantulas, or turning themselves into human wheels, to roll through the bed of the dying fire and out on the other side, sending up showers of sparks. All the while, they uttered a barking chant, in time to the wicked music, which seemed to shriek for war and bloodshed; and now and then they would dash after some toddling boy, catch him by the scalp-lock on his shaved head (left for the grasp of Azraïl the death-angel) and force him to join the dance.

Mean-faced Kabyle dogs, guarding deserted tents, howled their hatred of the music, while far away, across desert spaces, jackals cried to one another. And the scintillating network of stars was dimmed by a thin veil of sand which the wind lifted and let fall, as Victoria lifted and let fall the spangled scarf that made her beauty more mysterious, more desirable, in the eyes of Maïeddine.

XXVIII

"In the name of the All-Merciful and Pitiful! We seek refuge with the Lord of the Day, against the sinfulness of beings created by Him; against all evil, and against the night, lest they overcome us suddenly."

It was the Prayer of the Dawn, El Fejûr; and Victoria heard it cried in the voices of the old men of the zmala, early in the morning, as she dressed to continue her journey.

Every one was astir in the *tente sultane*, behind the different curtain partitions, and outside were the noises of the douar, waking to a new day. The girl could not wait for the coffee that Fafann would bring her, for she was eager to see the caravan that Si Maïeddine was assembling. As soon as she was ready she stole out into the dim dawn, more mystic in the desert than moon-rise or moon-setting. The air was crisp and tingling, and smelled of wild thyme, the herb that nomad women love, and wear crushed in their bosoms, or thrust up their nostrils. The camels had not come yet, for the men of the douar had not finished their prayer. In the wide open space where they had watched the dance last night, now they were praying, sons of Ishmael, a crowd of prostrate white figures, their faces against the sand.

Victoria stood waiting by the big tent, but she had not much need for patience. Soon the desert prayer was over, and the zmala was buzzing with excitement, as it had buzzed when the travellers arrived.

The Soudanese Negroes who had danced the wild dance appeared leading two white meharis, running camels, aristocrats of the camel world. On the back of each rose a cage-like bassour, draped with haoulis, striped rose-colour and purple. The desert beasts moved delicately, on legs longer and more slender than those of pack- camels, their necks swaying like the necks of swans who swim with the tide. Victoria thought them like magnificent, four-legged cousins of ostriches, and the superciliousness of their expressions amused her; the look they had of elderly ladies, dissatisfied with every one but themselves, and conscious of being supremely "well-connected." "A camel cannot see its own hump, but it can see those of others," she had heard M'Barka say.

As Victoria stood alone in the dawn, laughing at the ghostly meharis, and looking with interest at the heavily laden pack-camel and the mule piled up with tents and mattresses, Maïeddine came riding round from behind the great tent, all in white, on a white stallion. Seeing the girl, he tested her courage, and made a bid for her admiration by reining El Biod in suddenly, making him stand erect on his hind feet, pawing the air and dancing. But Roumia as she was, and unaccustomed to such manœuvres, she neither ran back nor screamed. She was not ashamed to show her admiration of man and horse, and Maïeddine did not know that her thoughts were more of El Biod the white, "drinker of air," the saddle of crimson velvet and tafilet leather embroidered in gold, and the bridle from Figuig, encrusted with silver, than of the rider.

"This is the horse of whom I told thee," Maïeddine said, letting El Biod come down again on all four feet. "He was blessed as a foal by having the magical words 'Bissem Allah' whispered over him as he drew the first draught of his mother's milk. But thou wilt endow him with new gifts if thou touchest his forehead with thy hand. Wilt thou do that, for his sake, and for mine?"

Victoria patted the flesh-coloured star on the stallion's white face, not knowing that, if a girl's fingers lie between the eyes of an Arab's horse, it is as much as to say that she is ready to ride with him to the world's end. But Maïeddine knew, and the thought warmed his blood. He was superstitious, like all Arabs, and he had wanted a sign of success. Now he had it. He longed to kiss the little fingers as they rested on El Biod's forehead, but he said to himself, "Patience; it will not be long before I kiss her lips."

"El Biod is my citadel," he smiled to her. "Thou knowest we have the same word for horse and citadel in Arabic? And that is because a brave stallion is a warrior's citadel, built on the wind, a rampart between him and the enemy. And we think the angels gave a horse the same heart as a man, that he might be our friend as well as servant, and carry us on his back to Paradise. Whether that is true or not, to-day El Biod and I are already on the threshold of Paradise, because we are thy guides, thy guardians through the desert which we love."

As he made this speech, Maïeddine watched the girl's face anxiously, to see whether she would resent the implication, but she only smiled in her frank way, knowing the Arab language to be largely the language of compliment; and he was encouraged. Perhaps he had been over-cautious with her, he thought; for, after all, he had no reason to believe that she cared for any man, and as he had a record of great successes with women, why be so timid with an unsophisticated girl? Each day, he told himself, he would take another and longer step forward; but for the moment he must be content. He began to talk about the meharis and the Negroes who would go with them and the beasts of burden.

When it was time for Victoria and M'Barka to be helped into their bassourahs, Maïeddine would not let the Soudanese touch the meharis. It was he who made the animals kneel, pulling gently on the bridle attached to a ring in the left nostril of each; and both subsided gracefully in haughty silence instead of uttering the hideous gobbling which common camels make when they get down and get up, or when they are loaded or unloaded. These beasts, Guelbi and Mansour, had been bought from Moors, across the border where Oran and Morocco run together, and had been trained since babyhood by smugglers for smuggling purposes. "If a man would have a silent camel," said Maïeddine, "he must get him from smugglers. For the best of reasons their animals are taught never to make a noise."

M'Barka was to have Fafann in the same bassour, but Victoria would have her rose and purple cage to herself. Maïeddine told her how, as the camel rose, she must first bow forward, then bend back; and, obeying carefully, she laughed like a child as the tall mehari straightened the knees of his forelegs, bearing his weight upon them as if on his feet, then got to his hind feet, while his "front knees," as she called them, were still on the ground, and last of all swung himself on to all four of his heart-shaped feet. Oh, how high in the air she felt when Guelbi was up, ready to start! She had had no idea that he was such a tall, moving tower, under the bassour.

"What a sky-scraping camel!" she exclaimed. And then had to explain to Maïeddine what she meant; for though he knew Paris, for him America might as well have been on another planet.

He rode beside Victoria's mehari, when good-byes had been said, blessings exchanged, and the little caravan had started. Looking out between the haoulis which protected her from sun and wind, the handsome Arab on his Arab horse seemed far below her, as Romeo must have seemed to Juliet on her balcony; and to him the fair face, framed with dazzling hair was like a guiding star.

"Thou canst rest in thy bassour?" he asked. "The motion of thy beast gives thee no discomfort?"

"No. Truly it is a cradle," she answered. "I had read that to ride on a camel was misery, but this is like being rocked on the bough of a tree when the wind blows."

"To sit in a bassour is very different from riding on a saddle, or even on a mattress, as the poor Bedouin women sometimes ride, or the dancers journeying from one place to another. I would not let thee travel with me unless I had been able to offer thee all the luxuries which a sultana might command. With nothing less would I have been content, because to me thou art a queen."

"At least thou hast given me a beautiful moving throne," laughed Victoria; "and because thou art taking me on it to my sister, I'm happy to-day as a queen."

"Then, if thou art happy, I also am happy," he said. "And when an Arab is happy, his lips would sing the song that is in his heart. Wilt thou be angry or pleased if I sing thee a love-song of the desert?"

"I cannot be angry, because the song will not really be for me," Victoria answered with the simplicity which had often disarmed and disconcerted Maïeddine. "And I shall be pleased, because in the desert it is good to hear desert songs."

This was not exactly the answer which he had wanted, but he made the best of it, telling himself that he had not much longer to wait.

"Leaders of camels sing," he said, "to make the beasts' burdens weigh less heavily. But thy mehari has no burden. Thou in thy bassour art lighter on his back than a feather on the wing of a dove. My song is for my own heart, and for thine heart, if thou wilt have it, not for Guelbi, though the meaning of Guelbi is 'heart of mine.'"

Then Maïeddine sang as he rode, his bridle lying loose, an old Arab song, wild and very sad, as all Arab music sounds, even when it is the cry of joy:

> "Truly, though I were to die, it would be naught,
> If I were near my love, for whom my bosom aches,
> For whom my heart is beating.
>
> "Yes, I am to die, but death is nothing

O ye who pass and see me dying,
For I have kissed the eyes, the mouth that I desired."

"But that is a sad song," said Victoria, when Maïeddine ceased his tragic chant, after many verses.

"Thou wouldst not say so, if thou hadst ever loved. Nothing is sad to a lover, except to lose his love, or not to have his love returned."

"But an Arab girl has no chance to love," Victoria argued. "Her father gives her to a man when she is a child, and they have never even spoken to each other until after the wedding."

"We of the younger generation do not like these child marriages," Maïeddine apologized, eagerly. "And, in any case, an Arab man, unless he be useless as a mule without an eye, knows how to make a girl love him in spite of herself. We are not like the men of Europe, bound down by a thousand conventions. Besides, we sometimes fall in love with women not of our own race. These we teach to love us before marriage."

Victoria laughed again, for she felt light-hearted in the beautiful morning. "Do Arab men always succeed as teachers?"

"What is written is written," he answered slowly. "Yet it is written that a strong man carves his own fate. And for thyself, wouldst thou know what awaits thee in the future?"

"I trust in God and my star."

"Thou wouldst not, then, that the desert speak to thee with its tongue of sand out of the wisdom of all ages?"

"What dost thou mean?"

"I mean that my cousin, Lella M'Barka, can divine the future from the sand of the Sahara, which gave her life, and life to her ancestors for a thousand years before her. It is a gift. Wilt thou that she exercise it for thee to-night, when we camp?"

"There is hardly any real sand in this part of the desert," said Victoria, seeking some excuse not to hear M'Barka's prophecies, yet not to hurt M'Barka's feelings, or Maïeddine's. "It is all far away, where we see the hills which look golden as ripe grain. And we cannot reach those hills by evening."

"My cousin always carries the sand for her divining. Every night she reads in the sand what will happen to her on the morrow, just as the women of Europe tell their fate by the cards. It is sand from the dunes round Touggourt; and mingled with it is a little from Mecca, which was brought to her by a holy man, a marabout. It would give her pleasure to read the sand for thee."

"Then I will ask her to do it," Victoria promised.

As the day grew, its first brightness faded. A wind blew up from the south, and slowly darkened the sky with a strange lilac haze, which seemed tangible as thin silk gauze. Behind it the sun glimmered like a great silver plate, and the desert turned pale, as in moonlight. Although the ground was hard under the camels' feet, the wind carried with it from far-away spaces a fine powder of sand which at last forced Victoria to let down the haoulis, and Maïeddine and the two Negroes to cover their faces with the veils of their turbans, up to the eyes.

"It will rain this afternoon," M'Barka prophesied from between her curtains.

"No," Maïeddine contradicted her. "There has been rain this month, and thou knowest better than I do that beyond El Aghouat it rains but once in five years. Else, why do the men of the M'Zab country break their hearts to dig deep wells? There will be no rain. It is but a sand-storm we have to fear."

"Yet I feel in the roots of my hair and behind my eyes that the rain is coming."

Maïeddine shrugged his shoulders, for an Arab does not twice contradict a woman, unless she be his wife. But the lilac haze became a pall of crape, and the noon meal was hurried. Maïeddine saved some of the surprises he had brought for a more favourable time. Hardly had they started on again, when rain began to fall, spreading over the desert in a quivering silver net whose threads broke and were constantly mended again. Then the rough road (to which the little caravan did not keep) and all the many diverging tracks became wide silver ribbons, lacing the plain broken with green dayas. A few minutes more—incredibly few, it seemed to Victoria — and the dayas were deep lakes, where the water swirled and bubbled round the trunks of young pistachio trees. A torrent poured from the mourning sky, and there was a wild sound of marching water, which Victoria could hear, under the haoulis which sheltered her. No water came through them, for the arching form of the bassour was like the roof of a tent, and the rain poured down on either side. She peeped out, enjoying her own comfort, while pitying Maïeddine and the Negroes; but all three had covered their thin burnouses with immensely thick, white, hooded cloaks, woven of sheep's wool, and they had no air of depression. By and by they came to an oued, which should have been a dry, stony bed without a trickle of water; but half an hour's downpour had created a river, as if by black magic; and Victoria could guess the force at which it was rushing, by the stout resistance she felt Guelbi had to make, as he waded through.

"A little more, and we could not have crossed," said Maïeddine, when they had mounted up safely on the other side of the oued.

"Art thou not very wet and miserable?" the girl asked sympathetically.

"I—miserable?" he echoed. "I—who am privileged to feast upon the deglet nour, in my desert?"

Victoria did not understand his metaphor, for the deglet nour is the finest of all dates, translucent as amber, sweet as honey, and so dear that only rich men or great marabouts ever taste it. "The deglet nour?" she repeated, puzzled.

"Dost thou not know the saying that the smile of a beautiful maiden is the deglet nour of Paradise, and nourishes a man's soul, so that he can bear any discomfort without being conscious that he suffers?"

"I did not know that Arab men set women so high," said Victoria, surprised; for now the rain had stopped, suddenly as it began, and she could look out again from between the curtains. Soon they would dry in the hot sun.

"Thou hast much to learn then, about Arab men," Maïeddine answered, "and fortunate is thy teacher. It is little to say that we would sacrifice our lives for the women we love, because for us life is not that great treasure it is to the Roumis, who cling to it desperately. We would do far more than give our lives for the beloved woman, we Arabs. We would give our heads, which is the greatest sacrifice a man of Islam could make."

"But is not that the same thing as giving life?"

"It is a thousandfold more. It is giving up the joy of eternity. For we are taught to believe that if a man's head is severed from his body, it alone goes to Paradise. His soul is maimed. It is but a bodiless head, and all celestial joys are for ever denied to it."

"How horrible!" the girl exclaimed. "Dost thou really believe such a thing?"

He feared that he had made a mistake, and that she would look upon him as an alien, a pagan, with whom she could have no sympathy. "If I am more modern in my ideas than my forefathers," he said tactfully, "I must not confess it to a Roumia, must I, oh Rose of the West?—for that would be disloyal to Islam. Yet if I did believe, still would I give my head for the love of the one woman, the star of my destiny, she whose sweet look deserves that the word 'aïn' should stand for bright fountain, and for the ineffable light in a virgin's eyes."

"I did not know until to-day, Si Maïeddine, that thou wert a poet," Victoria told him.

"All true Arabs are poets. Our language—the literary, not the common Arabic—is the language of poets, as thou must have read in thy books. But I have now such inspiration as perhaps no man ever had; and thou wilt learn other things about me, while we journey together in the desert."

As he said this he looked at her with a look which even her simplicity could not have mistaken if she had thought of it; but instantly the vision of Saidee came between her eyes and his. The current of her ideas was abruptly changed. "How many days now," she asked suddenly, "will the journey last?"

His face fell. "Art thou tired already of this new way of travelling, that thou askest me a question thou hast not once asked since we started?"

"Oh no, no," she reassured him. "I love it. I am not tired at all. But—I did not question thee at first because thou didst not desire me to know thy plans, while I was still within touch of Europeans. Thou didst not put this reason in such words, for thou wouldst not have let me feel I had not thy full trust. But it was natural thou shouldst not give it, when thou hadst so little acquaintance with me, and I did not complain. Now it is different. Even if I wished, I could neither speak nor write to any one I ever knew. Therefore I question thee."

"Art thou impatient for the end?" he wanted to know, jealously.

"Not impatient. I am happy. Yet I should like to count the days, and say each night, 'So many more times must the sun rise and set before I see my sister.'"

"Many suns must rise and set," Maïeddine confessed doggedly.

"But—when first thou planned the journey, thou saidst; 'In a fortnight thou canst send thy friends news, I hope.'"

"If I had told thee then, that it must be longer, wouldst thou have come with me? I think not. For thou sayest I did not wholly trust thee. How much less didst thou trust me?"

"Completely. Or I would not have put myself in thy charge."

"Perhaps thou art convinced of that now, when thou knowest me and Lella M'Barka, and thou hast slept in the tent of my father, and in the houses of my friends. But I saw in thine eyes at that time a doubt thou didst not wish to let thyself feel, because through me alone was there a way to reach thy sister. I wished to bring thee to her, for thy sake, and for her sake, though I have never looked upon her face and never shall——"

"Why dost thou say 'never shall'?" the girl broke in upon him suddenly.

The blood mounted to his face. He had made a second mistake, and she was very quick to catch him up.

"It was but a figure of speech," he corrected himself.

"Thou dost not mean that she's shut up, and no man allowed to see her?"

"I know nothing. Thou wilt find out all for thyself. But thou wert anxious to go to her, at no matter what cost, and I feared to dishearten thee, to break thy courage, while I was still a stranger, and could not justify myself in thine eyes. Now, wilt thou forgive me an evasion, which was to save thee anxiety, if I say frankly that, travel as we may, we cannot reach our journey's end for many days yet?"

"I must forgive thee," said Victoria, with a sigh. "Yet I do not like evasions. They are unworthy."

"I am sorry," Maïeddine returned, so humbly that he disarmed her. "It would be terrible to offend thee."

"There can be no question of offence," she consoled him. "I am very, very grateful for all thou hast done for me. I often lie awake in the night, wondering how I can repay thee everything."

"When we come to the end of the journey, I will tell thee of a thing thou canst do, for my happiness," Maïeddine said in a low voice, as if half to himself.

"Wilt thou tell me now to what place we are going? I should like to know, and I should like to hear thee describe it."

He did not speak for a moment. Then he said slowly; "It is a grief to deny thee anything, oh Rose, but the secret is not mine to tell, even to thee."

"The secret!" she echoed. "Thou hast never called it a secret."

"If I did not use that word, did I not give thee to understand the same thing?"

"Thou meanest, the secret about Cassim, my sister's husband?"

"Cassim ben Halim has ceased to live."

Victoria gave a little cry. "Dead! But thou hast made me believe, in spite of the rumours, that he lived."

"I cannot explain to thee," Maïeddine answered gloomily, as if hating to refuse her anything. "In the end, thou wilt know all, and why I had to be silent."

"But my sister?" the girl pleaded. "There is no mystery about her? Thou hast concealed nothing which concerns Saidee?"

"Thou hast my word that I will take thee to the place where she is. Thou gavest me thy trust. Give it me again."

"I have not taken it away. It is thine," said Victoria.

XXIX

That night they spent in a caravanserai, because, after the brief deluge of rain, the ground was too damp for camping, when an invalid was of the party. When they reached the place after sunset, the low square of the building was a block of marble set in the dull gold of the desert, carved in dazzling white against a deep-blue evening sky. Like Ben Halim's house, it was roughly fortified, with many loopholes in the walls, for it had been built to serve the uses of less peaceful days than these. Within the strong gates, on one side were rooms for guests, each with its own door and window opening into the huge court. On another side of the square were the kitchens and dining-room, as well as living-place for the Arab landlord and his hidden family; and opposite was a roofed, open-fronted shelter for camels and other animals, the ground yellow with sand and spilt fodder. Water overflowed from a small well, making a pool in the courtyard, in which ducks and geese waddled, quacking, turkey- cocks fought in quiet corners, barked at impotently by Kabyle puppies. Tall, lean hounds or sloughis, kept to chase the desert gazelles, wandered near the kitchens, in the hope of bones, and camels gobbled dismally as their tired drivers forced them to their knees, or thrust handfuls of date stones down their throats. There were sheep, too, and goats; and even a cow, the "perpetual mother" loved and valued by Arabs.

M'Barka refused to "read the sand" that night, when Maïeddine suggested it. The sand would yield up its secrets only under the stars, she said, and wished to wait until they should be in the tents.

All night, outside Victoria's open but shuttered window, there was a stealthy stirring of animals in the dark, a gliding of ghostly ducks, a breathing of sheep and camels. And sometimes the wild braying of a donkey or the yelp of a dog tore the silence to pieces.

The next day was hot; so that at noon, when they stopped to eat, the round blot of black shadow under one small tree was precious as a black pearl. And there were flies. Victoria could not understand how they lived in the desert, miles from any house, miles from the tents of nomads; where there was no vegetation, except an occasional scrubby tree, or a few of the desert gourds which the Arabs use to cure the bite of scorpions. But she had not seen the cages of bones, sometimes bleached like old ivory, sometimes of a dreadful red, which told of wayside tragedies. Always when they had come in sight of a skeleton, Maïeddine had found some excuse to make the girl look in another direction; for he wanted her to love the desert, not to feel horror of its relentlessness.

Now for the first time he had full credit for his cleverness as an organizer. Never before had they been so remote from civilization. When travelling in the carriage, stopping each night at the house of some well-to-do caïd or adel, it had been comparatively easy to provide supplies; but to-day, when jellied chicken and cream-cheese, almond cakes and oranges appeared at luncheon, and some popular French mineral water (almost cool because the bottles had been wrapped in wet blanket) fizzed in the glasses, Victoria said that Si Maïeddine must have a tame djinn for a slave.

"Wait till evening," he told her. "Then perhaps thou mayest see something to please thee." But he was delighted with her compliments, and made her drink water from the glass out of which he had drunk, that she might be sure of his good faith in all he had sworn to her yesterday. "They who drink water from the same cup have made an eternal pact together," he said. "I should not dare to be untrue, even if I would. And thou—I think that thou wilt be true to me."

"Why, certainly I will," answered Victoria, with the pretty American accent which Stephen Knight had admired and smiled at the night he heard it first. "Thou art one of my very best friends."

Maïeddine looked down into the glass and smiled, as if he were a crystal-gazer, and could see something under the bright surface, that no one else could see.

Night folded down over the desert, hot and velvety, like the wings of a mother-bird covering her children; but before darkness fell, the tents glimmered under the stars. There were two only, a large one for the women, and one very small for Maïeddine. The Negroes would roll themselves in their burnouses, and lie beside the animals. But sleeping-time had not come yet; and it was the Soudanese who prepared the evening meal.

One of them was a good cook, and for that reason Maïeddine had begged him from the Agha. He made desert bread, by mixing farina with salted water, and baking it on a flat tin supported by stones over a fire of dry twigs. When the thin loaf was crisply brown on top, the man took it off the fire, and covered it up, on the tin, because it was to be eaten hot.

While Victoria waited for all to be got ready, she strolled a little away from the tents and the group of resting animals, having promised Maïeddine to avoid the tufts of alfa grass, for fear of vipers which sometimes lurked among them. He would have liked to go with her, but the unfailing tact of the Arab told him that she wished to be alone with her thoughts, and he could only hope that they might be of him.

Here, it was no longer beautiful desert. They had passed the charming region of dayas, and were entering the grim world through which, long ago, the ever harried M'Zabites had fled to find a refuge beyond the reach of greedy pursuers. Nevertheless the enchantment of the Sahara, in all its phases, had taken hold of Victoria. She did not now feel that the desert was a place where a tired soul might find oblivion, though once she had imagined that it would be a land of forgetfulness. Arabs say, in talking idly to Europeans, that men forget their past in the desert, but she doubted if they really forgot, in these vast spaces where there was so much time to think. She herself began to feel that the illimitable skies, where flamed sunsets and sunrises whose miracles no eye saw, might teach her mysteries she had snatched at and lost, in dreams. The immensity of the desert sent her soul straining towards the immensity of the Beyond; and almost, in flashes elusive as the light on a bird's wing, she understood what eternity might mean. She felt that the last days of her childhood had been left behind, on the threshold of these mysterious spaces, this vastness into which she had plunged, as into an ocean. Yet she did not regret the loss, if it were a loss. Never, she thought, whatever might happen, would she wish not to have known this experience, not to have entered upon this great adventure, whose end Maïeddine still hid behind a veil of secrecy.

It was true, as she had told him, that she was not impatient, though she would have liked to count the days like the beads of a rosary. She looked forward to each one, as to the discovery of a beautiful thing new to the world and to her; for though the spaces surrounding her were wide beyond thinking, they were not empty. As ships, great and small, sail the sea, so sailed the caravans of the nomad tribes in the desert which surges on unchecked to Egypt: nomads who come and go, north and south, east and west, under the burning sun and the throbbing stars, as Allah has written their comings and goings in His book: men in white, journeying with their women, their children, and their trains of beasts, singing as they pass, and at night under the black tents resting to the music of the tom-tom and raïta.

Victoria's gaze waded through the shadows that flow over the desert at evening, deep and blue and transparent as water. She searched the distances for the lives that must be going on somewhere, perhaps not far away, though she would never meet them. They, and she, were floating spars in a great ocean; and it made the ocean more wonderful to know that the spars were there, each drifting according to its fate.

The girl drew into her lungs the strong air of the desert, born of the winds which bring life or death to its children.

The scent of the wild thyme, which she could never again disentangle from thoughts of the Sahara, was very sweet, even insistent. She knew that it was loved by nomad women; and she let pictures rise before her mind of gorgeous dark girls on camels, in plumed red bassourahs, going from one desert city to another, to dance—cities teeming with life, which she would never see among these spaces that seemed empty as the world before creation. She imagined the ghosts of these desert beauties crowding round her in the dusk, bringing their fragrance with them, the wild thyme they had loved in life, crushed in their bosoms; pathetic ghosts, who had not learned to rise beyond what they had once desired, therefore compelled to haunt the desert, the only world which they had known. In the wind that came sighing to her ears from the dark ravines of the terrible chebka, she seemed to hear battle-songs and groans of desert men who had fought and died ages ago, whose bones had crumbled under her feet, perhaps, and whose descendants had not changed one whit in religion, custom, or thought, or even in dress.

Victoria was glad that Maïeddine had let her have these desert thoughts alone, for they made her feel at home in the strange world her fancy peopled; but the touch of the thyme-scented ghosts was cold. It was good to turn back at last towards the tents, and see how the camp-fire crimsoned the star-dusk.

"Thou wert happy alone?" Maïeddine questioned her jealously.

"I was not alone."

He understood. "I know. The desert voices spoke to thee, of the desert mystery which they alone can tell; voices we can hear only by listening closely."

"That was the thought in my mind. How odd thou shouldst put it into words."

"Dost thou think it odd? But I am a man of the desert. I held back, for thee to go alone and hear the voices, knowing they would teach thee to understand me and my people. I knew, too, that the spirits would be kind, and say nothing to frighten thee. Besides, thou didst not go to them quite alone, for thine own white angel walked on thy right hand, as always."

"Thou makest poetical speeches, Si Maïeddine."

"It is no poetry to speak of thy white angel. We believe that each one of us has a white angel at his right hand, recording his good actions. But ordinary mortals have also their black angels, keeping to the left, writing down wicked thoughts and deeds. Hast thou not seen men spitting to the left, to show despite of their black angels? But because thy soul is never soiled by sinful thoughts, there was no need for a black angel, and whilst thou wert still a child, Allah discharged him of his mission."

"And thou, Si Maïeddine, dost thou think, truly, that a black angel walks ever at thy left side?"

"I fear so." Maïeddine glanced to the left, as if he could see a dark figure writing on a slate. Things concerning Victoria must have been written on that slate, plans he had made, of which neither his white angel nor hers would approve. But, he told himself, if they had to be carried out, she would be to blame, for driving him to extremes. "Whilst thou art near me," he said aloud, "my black angel lags behind, and if thou wert to be with me forever, I——"

"Since that cannot be, thou must find a better way to keep him in the background," Victoria broke in lightly. But Si Maïeddine's compliments were oppressive. She wished it were not the Arab way to pay so many. He had been different at first; and feeling the change in him with a faint stirring of uneasiness, she hurried her steps to join M'Barka.

The invalid reclined on a rug of golden jackal skins, and rested a thin elbow on cushions of dyed leather, braided in intricate strips by

Touareg women. Victoria sat beside her, Maïeddine opposite, and Fafann waited upon them as they ate.

After supper, while the Bedouin woman saw that everything was ready for her mistress and the Roumia, in their tent, M'Barka spread out her precious sand from Mecca and the dunes round her own Touggourt. She had it tied up in green silk, such as is used for the turbans of men who have visited Mecca, lined with a very old Arab brocade, purple and gold, like the banners that drape the tombs of marabouts. She opened the bag carefully, until it lay flat on the ground in front of her knees, the sand piled in the middle, as much perhaps as could have been heaped on a soup plate.

For a moment she sat gazing at the sand, her lips moving. She looked wan as old ivory in the dying firelight, and in the hollows of her immense eyes seemed to dream the mysteries of all ages. "Take a handful of sand," she said to Victoria. "Hold it over thine heart. Now, wish with the whole force of thy soul."

Victoria wished to find Saidee safe, and to be able to help her, if she needed help.

"Put back the sand, sprinkling it over the rest."

The girl, though not superstitious, could not help being interested, even fascinated. It seemed to her that the sand had a magical sparkle.

M'Barka's eyes became introspective, as if she waited for a message, or saw a vision. She was as strange, as remote from modern womanhood as a Cassandra. Presently she started, and began trailing her brown fingers lightly over the sand, pressing them down suddenly now and then, until she had made three long, wavy lines, the lower ones rather like telegraphic dots and dashes.

"Lay the forefinger of thy left hand on any figure in these lines," she commanded. "Now on another—yet again, for the third time. That is all thou hast to do. The rest is for me."

She took from some hiding-place in her breast a little old note-book, bound in dark leather, glossy from constant use. With it came a perfume of sandalwood. Turning the yellow leaves of the book, covered with fine Arab lettering, she read in a murmuring, indistinct voice, that sounded to Victoria like one of those desert voices of which Maïeddine had spoken. Also she measured spaces between the figures the girl had touched, and counted monotonously.

"Thy wish lies a long way from thee," she said at last. "A long way! Thou couldst never reach it of thyself—never, not till the end of the world. I see thee—alone, very helpless. Thou prayest. Allah sends thee a man—a strong man, whose brain and heart and arm are at thy service. Allah is great!"

"Tell her what the man is like, cousin," Maïeddine prompted, eagerly.

"He is dark, and young. He is not of thy country, oh Rose of the West, but trust him, rely upon him, or thou art undone. In thy future, just where thou hast ceased to look for them, I see troubles and disappointments, even dangers. That is the time, above all others, to let thyself be guided by the man Allah has sent to be thy prop. He has ready wit and courage. His love for thee is great. It grows and grows. He tells thee of it; and thou—thou seest between him and thee a barrier, high and fearful as a wall with sharp knives on top. For thine eyes it is impassable. Thine heart is sad; and thy words to him will pierce his soul with despair. But think again. Be true to thyself and to thy star. Speak another word, and throw down that high barrier, as the wall of Jericho was thrown down. Thou canst do it. All will depend on the decision of a moment—thy whole future, the future of the man, and of a woman whose face I cannot see."

M'Barka smoothed away the tracings in the sand.

"What—is there no more?" asked Maïeddine.

"No, it is dark before my eyes now. The light has gone from the sand. I can still tell her a few little things, perhaps. Such things as the luckiest colours to wear, the best days to choose for journeys. But she is different from most girls. I do not think she would care for such hints."

"All colours are lucky. All days are good," said Victoria. "I thank thee for what thou hast told me, Lella M'Barka."

She did not wish to hear more. What she had heard was more than enough. Not that she really believed that M'Barka could see into the future; but because of the "dark man." Any fortune-teller might introduce a dark man into the picture of a fair girl's destiny; but the allusions were so marked that Victoria's vague unrestfulness became distress. She tried to encourage herself by thinking of Maïeddine's dignified attitude, from the beginning of their acquaintance until now. And even now, he had changed only a little. He was too complimentary, that was all; and the difference in his manner might arise from knowing her more intimately. Probably Lella M'Barka, like many elderly women of other and newer civilizations, was over-romantic; and the best thing was to prevent her from putting ridiculous ideas into Maïeddine's head. Such ideas would spoil the rest of the journey for both.

"Remember all I have told thee, when the time comes," M'Barka warned her.

"Yes—oh yes, I will remember."

"Now it is my turn. Read the sand for me," said Maïeddine.

M'Barka made as if she would wrap the sand in its bag. "I can tell thy future better another time. Not now. It would not be wise. Besides, I have done enough. I am tired."

"Look but a little way along the future, then, and say what thou seest. I feel that it will bring good fortune to touch the sand where the hand of Ourïeda has touched it."

Always now, he spoke of Victoria, or to her, as "Rose" (Ourïeda in Arabic); but as M'Barka gave her that name also, the girl could hardly object.

"I tell thee, instead it may bring thee evil."

"For good or evil, I will have the fortune now," Maïeddine insisted.

"Be it upon thy head, oh cousin, not mine. Take thy handful of sand, and make thy wish."

Maïeddine took it from the place Victoria had touched, and his wish was that, as the grains of sand mingled, so their destinies might mingle inseparably, his and hers.

M'Barka traced the three rows of mystic signs, and read her notebook, mumbling. But suddenly she let it drop into her lap, covering the signs with both thin hands.

"What ails thee?" Maïeddine asked, frowning.

"I saw thee stand still and let an opportunity slip by."

"I shall not do that."

"The sand has said it. Shall I stop, or go on?"

"Go on."

"I see another chance to grasp thy wish. This time thou stretchest out thine hand. I see thee, in a great house—the house of one thou knowest, whose name I may not speak. Thou stretchest out thine hand. The chance is given thee——"

"What then?"

"Then—I cannot tell thee, what then. Thou must not ask. My eyes are clouded with sleep. Come Ourïeda, it is late. Let us go to our tent."

"No," said Maïeddine. "Ourïeda may go, but not thou."

Victoria rose quickly and lightly from among the jackal skins and Touareg cushions which Maïeddine had provided for her comfort. She bade him good night, and with all his old calm courtesy he kissed his hand after it had pressed hers. But there was a fire of anger or impatience in his eyes.

Fafann was in the tent, waiting to put her mistress to bed, and to help the Roumia if necessary. The mattresses which had come rolled up on the brown mule's back, had been made into luxurious looking beds, covered with bright-coloured, Arab-woven blankets, beautiful embroidered sheets of linen, and cushions slipped into fine pillow-cases. Folding frames draped with new mosquito nettings had been arranged to protect the sleepers' hands and faces; and there was a folding table on which stood French gilt candlesticks and a glass basin and water-jug, ornamented with gilded flowers; just such a basin and jug as Victoria had seen in the curiosity-shop of Mademoiselle Soubise. There were folded towels, too, of silvery damask.

"What wonderful things we have!" the girl exclaimed. "I don't see how we manage to carry them all. It is like a story of the 'Arabian Nights,' where one has but to rub a lamp, and a powerful djinn brings everything one wants."

"The Lord Maïeddine is the powerful djinn who has brought all thou couldst possibly desire, without giving thee even the trouble to wish for things," said Fafann, showing her white teeth, and glancing sidelong at the Roumia. "These are not all. Many of these things thou hast seen already. Yet there are more." Eagerly she lifted from the ground, which was covered with rugs, a large green earthern jar. "It is full of rosewater to bathe thy face, for the water of the desert here is brackish, and harsh to the skin, because of saltpetre. The Sidi ordered enough rosewater to last till Ghardaia, in the M'Zab country. Then he will get thee more."

"But it is for us both—for Lella M'Barka more than for me," protested Victoria.

Fafann laughed. "My mistress no longer spends time in thinking of her skin. She prays much instead; and the Sidi has given her an amulet which touched the sacred Black Stone at Mecca. To her, that is worth all the rest; and it is worth this great journey, which she takes with so much pain. The rosewater, and the perfumes from Tunis, and the softening creams made in the tent of the Sidi's mother, are all offered to thee."

"No, no," the girl persisted, "I am sure they are meant more for Lella M'Barka than for me. She is his cousin."

"Hast thou never noticed the caravans, when they have passed us in the desert, how it is always the young and beautiful women who rest in the bassourahs, while the old ones trot after the camels?"

"I have noticed that, and it is very cruel."

"Why cruel, oh Roumia? They have had their day. And when a man has but one camel, he puts upon its back his treasure, the joy of his heart. A man must be a man, so say even the women. And the Sidi is a man, as well as a great lord. He is praised by all as a hunter, and for the straightness of his aim with a gun. He rides, thou seest, as if he were one with his horse, and as he gallops in the desert, so would he gallop to battle if need be, for he is brave as the Libyan lion, and strong as the heroes of old legends. Yet there is nothing too small for him to bend his mind upon, if it be for thy pleasure and comfort. Thou shouldst be proud, instead of denying that all the Sidi does is for thee. My mistress would tell thee so, and many women would be dying of envy, daughters of Aghas and even of Bach Aghas. But perhaps, as thou art a Roumia, thou hast different feelings."

"Perhaps," answered Victoria humbly, for she was crushed by Fafann's fierce eloquence. And for a moment her heart was heavy; but she would not let herself feel a presentiment of trouble.

"What harm can happen to me?" she asked. "I haven't been guided so far for nothing. Si Maïeddine is an Arab, and his ways aren't like the ways of men I've known, that's all. My sister's husband was his friend—a great friend, whom he loved. What he does is more for Cassim's sake than mine."

Her cheeks were burning after the long day of sun, and because of her thoughts; yet she was not glad to bathe them with Si Maïeddine's fragrant offering of rosewater, some of which Fafann poured into the glass basin.

Not far away Maïeddine was still sitting by the fire with M'Barka.

"Tell me now," he said. "What didst thou see?"

"Nothing clearly. Another time, cousin. Let me have my mind fresh. I am like a squeezed orange."

"Yet I must know, or I shall not sleep. Thou art hiding something."

"All was vague—confused. I saw as through a torn cloud. There was the great house. Thou wert there, a guest. Thou wert happy, thy desire granted, and then—by Allah, Maïeddine, I could not see what happened; but the voice of the sand was like a storm in my ears, and the knowledge came to me suddenly that thou must not wait too long for thy wish—the wish made with the sand against thine heart."

"Thou couldst not see my wish. Thou art but a woman."

"I saw, because I am a woman, and I have the gift. Thou knowest I have the gift. Do not wait too long, or thou mayest wait for ever."

"What wouldst thou have me do?"

"It is not for me to advise. As thou saidst, I am but a woman. Only—act! That is the message of the sand. And now, unless thou wouldst have my dead body finish the journey in the bassour, take me to my tent."

Maïeddine took her to the tent. And he asked no more questions. But all night he thought of what M'Barka had said, and the message of the sand. It was a dangerous message, yet the counsel was after his own heart.

XXX

In the morning he was still brooding over the message; and as they travelled through the black desert on the way to Ghardaia and the hidden cities of the M'Zab, he fell into long silences. Then, abruptly, he would rouse himself to gaiety and animation, telling old legends or new tales, strange dramas of the desert, very seldom comedies; for there are few comedies in the Sahara, except for the children.

Sometimes he was in danger of speaking out words which said themselves over and over in his head. "If I 'wait too long, I may wait for ever.' Then, by Allah, I will not wait." But he kept his tongue in control, though his brain was hot as if he wore no turban, under the blaze of the sun. "I will leave things as they are while we are in this black Gehenna," he determined. "What is written is written. Yet who has seen the book of the writing? And there is a curse on all this country, till the M'Zab is passed."

After Bou-Saada, he had gradually forgotten, or almost forgotten, his fears. He had been happy in the consciousness of power that came to him from the desert, where he was at home, and Europeans were helpless strangers. But now, M'Barka's warnings had brought the fears back, like flapping ravens. He had planned the little play of the sand-divining, and at first it had pleased him. M'Barka's vision of the dark man who was not of Victoria's country could not have been better; and because he knew that his cousin believed in the sand, he was superstitiously impressed by her prophecy and advice. In the end, he had forced her to go on when she would have stopped, yet he was angry with her for putting doubts into his mind, doubts of his own wisdom and the way to succeed. With a girl of his own people, or indeed with any girl, if he had not loved too much, he would have had no doubts. But he did not know how it was best to treat Victoria. His love for her was so strong, that it was like fear, and in trying to understand her, he changed his mind a dozen times a day. He was not used to this uncertainty, and hated to think that he could be weak. Would she turn from him, if he broke the tacit compact of loyal friendship which had made her trust him as a guide? He could not tell; though an Arab girl would scorn him for keeping it. "Perhaps at heart all women are alike," he thought. "And if, now that I am warned, I should risk waiting, I would be no man." At last, the only question left in his mind was, "When?"

For two days they journeyed through desolation, in a burnt-out world where nothing had colour except the sad violet sky which at evening flamed with terrible sunsets, cruelly beautiful as funeral pyres. The fierce glow set fire to the black rocks which pointed up like dragons' teeth, and turned them to glittering copper; polishing the dead white chalk of the chebka to the dull gleam of dirty silver. Far away there were always purple hills, behind which it seemed that hope and beauty might come to life again; but travelling from morning to night they never appeared any nearer. The evil magic of the black desert, which Maïeddine called accursed because of the M'Zabites, made the beautiful hills recede always, leaving only the ugly brown waves of hardened earth, which were disheartening to climb, painful to descend.

At last, in the midst of black squalor, they came to an oasis like a bright jewel fallen in the trough of swine. It was Berryan, the first town of the M'Zabites, people older than the Arabs, and hated by them with a hatred more bitter than their loathing for Jews.

Maïeddine would not pass through the town, since it could be avoided, because in his eyes the Beni-M'Zab were dogs, and in their eyes he, though heir to an agha, would be as carrion.

Sons of ancient Phœnicians, merchants of Tyre and Carthage, there never had been, never would be, any lust for battle in the hearts of the M'Zabites. Their warfare had been waged by cunning, and through mercenaries. They had fled before Arab warriors, driven from place to place by brave, scornful enemies, and now, safely established in their seven holy cities, protected by vast distances and the barrier of the black desert, they revenged their wrongs with their wits, being rich, and great usurers. Though Mussulmans in these days, the schisms with which they desecrated the true religion were worse in the eyes of Maïeddine than the foolish faith of Christians, who, at least, were not backsliders. He would not even point out to Victoria the strange minaret of the Abadite mosque at Berryan, which tapered like a brown obelisk against the shimmering sky, for to him its very existence was a disgrace.

"Do not speak of it; do not even look at it," he said to her, when she exclaimed at the great Cleopatra Needle. But she did look, having none of his prejudices, and he dared not bid her let down the curtains of her bassour, as he would if she had been a girl of his own blood.

The extraordinary city, whose crowded, queerly-built houses were blocks of gold in the sunlight, seemed beautiful to Victoria, coming in sight of it suddenly after days in the black desert. The other six cities, called holy by the Beni-M'Zab, were far away still. She knew this, because Maïeddine had told her they would not descend into the Wady M'Zab till next day. Berryan and Guerrara were on the upper plateau; and Victoria could hardly bear to pass by, for Berryan was by far the most Eastern-seeming place she had seen. She wondered if, should she ask him as a favour, Maïeddine would rest there that night, instead of camping somewhere farther on, in the hideous desert; for already it was late afternoon. But she would ask nothing of him now, for he was no longer quite the trusty friend she had persuaded herself to think him. One night, since the sand- divining, she had had a fearful dream concerning Maïeddine. Outside her tent she had heard a soft padding sound, and peeping from under the flap, she had seen a splendid, tawny tiger, who looked at her with brilliant topaz eyes which fascinated her so that she could not turn away. But she knew that the animal was Maïeddine; that each night he changed himself into a tiger; and that as a tiger he was more his real self than when by day he appeared as a man.

They filed past Berryan; the meharis, the white stallion, the pack-camel, and the mule, in slow procession, along a rough road which wound close to the green oasis. And from among the palm trees men and women and little children, gorgeous as great tropical birds, in their robes of scarlet, ochre-yellow, and emerald, peered at the little caravan with cynical curiosity. Victoria looked back longingly, for she knew that the way from Berryan to the Wady M'Zab would be grim and toilsome under the burning sun. Hill after hill, they mounted and descended; hills stony yet sandy, always the same dull colour, and so shapeless as to daze the brain with their monotony. But towards evening, when the animals had climbed to the crest of a hill like a dingy wave, suddenly a white obelisk shot up, pale and stiff as a dead man's finger. Tops of tall palms were like the dark plumes on the heads of ten thousand dancing women of the Sahara, and as a steep descent began, there glittered the five hidden cities, like a strange fairyland lost in the desert. The whole Wady M'Zab lay under the eyes of the travellers, as if they looked down over the rim of an immense cup. Here, some who were left of the sons of Tyre and Carthage dwelt safe and snug, crouching in the protection of the valley they had found and reclaimed from the abomination of desolation.

It seemed to Victoria that she looked on one of the great sights of the world: the five cities, gleaming white, and glowing bronze, closely built on their five conical hills, which rose steeply from the flat bottom of the gold-lined cup—Ghardaia, Beni-Isguen, Bou-Noura, Melika, and El-Ateuf. The top of each hill was prolonged to a point by the tapering minaret of one of those Abadite mosques which the girl thought the most Eastern of all things imported from the East. The oasis which gave wealth to the M'Zabites surged round the towns like a green sea at ebb tide, sucked back from a strand of gold; and as the caravan wound down the wonderful road with which the Beni-M'Zab had traced the sheer side of their enchanted cup, the groaning of hundreds of well-chains came plaintively up on the wind.

The well-stones had the obelisk shape of the minarets, in miniature; and Negroes—freed slaves of the rich M'Zabites—running back and forth in pairs, to draw the water, were mere struggling black ants, seen from the cup's rim. The houses of the five towns were like bleached skeletons, and the arches that spanned the dark, narrow streets were their ribs.

Arrived at the bottom of the cup, it was necessary to pass through the longest and only modern street of Ghardaia, the capital of the M'Zab. A wind had sprung up, to lift the sand which sprinkled the hard-trodden ground with thick powder of gold dust, and whirl it westward against the fire of sunset, red as a blowing spray of blood. "It is a sign of trouble when the sand of the desert turns to blood," muttered Fafann to her mistress, quoting a Bedouin proverb.

The men of the M'Zab do not willingly give lodging to strangers, least of all to Arabs; and at Beni-Isguen, holy city and scene of strange mysteries, no stranger may rest for the night. But Maïeddine, respected by the ruling power, as by his own people, had a friend or two at every Bureau Arabe and military station. A French officer stationed at Ghardaia had married a beautiful Arab girl of good family distantly related to the Agha of the Ouled-Serrin, and being at Algiers on official business, his wife away at her father's tent, he had promised to lend his house, a few miles out of the town, to Si Maïeddine. It was a long, low building of toub, the sun-dried sand- blocks of which most houses are made in the ksour, or Sahara villages, but it had been whitewashed, and named the Pearl.

There they slept, in the cool shadow of the oasis, and early next morning went on.

As soon as they had passed out of this hidden valley, where a whole race of men had gathered for refuge and wealth-building, Victoria felt, rather than saw, a change in Maïeddine. She hardly knew how to express it to herself, unless it was that he had become more Arab. His courtesies suggested less the modern polish learned from the French (in which he could excel when he chose) than the almost royal hospitality of some young Bey escorting a foreign princess through his dominions. Always *"très-mâle,"* as Frenchwomen pronounced him admiringly, Si Maïeddine began to seem masculine in an untamed, tigerish way. He was restless, and would not always be contented to ride El Biod, beside the tall, white mehari, but would gallop far ahead, and then race back to rejoin the little caravan, rushing straight at the animals as if he must collide with them, then, at the last instant, when Victoria's heart bounded, reining in his horse, so that El Biod's forefeet—shod Arab-fashion—pawed the air, and the animal sat upon his haunches, muscles straining and rippling under the creamlike skin.

Or, sometimes, Maïeddine would spring from the white stallion's back, letting El Biod go free, while his master marched beside Guelbi, with that panther walk that the older races, untrammelled by the civilization of towns, have kept unspoiled.

The Arab's eyes were more brilliant, never dreamy now, and he looked at Victoria often, with disconcerting steadiness, instead of lowering his eyelids as men of Islam, accustomed to the mystery of the veil, unconsciously do with European women whom they respect, though they do not understand.

So they went on, travelling the immeasurable desert; and Victoria had not asked again, since Maïeddine's refusal, the name of the place to which they were bound. M'Barka seemed brighter, as if she looked forward to something, each day closer at hand; and her courage would have given Victoria confidence, even if the girl had been inclined to forebodings. They were going somewhere, Lella M'Barka knew where, and looked forward joyously to arriving. The girl fancied that their destination was the same, though at first she had not thought so. Words that M'Barka let drop inadvertently now and then, built up this impression in her mind.

The "habitude du Sud," as Maïeddine called it, when occasionally they talked French together, was gradually taking hold of the girl. Sometimes she resented it, fearing that by this time it must have altogether enslaved Saidee, and dreading the insidious fascination for herself; sometimes she found pleasure and peace in it; but in every mood the influence was hard to throw off.

"The desert has taken hold of thee," Maïeddine said one day, when he had watched her in silence for a while, and seen the rapt look in her eyes. "I knew the time would come, sooner or later. It has come now."

"No," Victoria answered. "I do not belong to the desert."

"If not to-day, then to-morrow," he finished, as if he had not heard.

They were going on towards Ouargla. So much he had told her, though he had quickly added, "But we shall not stop there." He was waiting still, though they were out of the black desert and the accursed land of the renegades. He was not afraid of anything or anyone here, in this vastness, where a European did not pass once a year, and few Arabs, only the Spahis, carrying mails from one Bureau Arabe to another, or tired soldiers changing stations. The beautiful country of the golden dunes, with its horizon like a stormy sea, was the place of which he said in his thoughts, "It shall happen there."

On the other side of Ghardaia, even when Victoria had ceased to be actually impatient for her meeting with Saidee, she had longed to know the number of days, that she might count them. But now she had drunk so deep of the colour and the silence that, in spite of herself, she was passing beyond that phase. What were a few days more, after so many years? She wondered how she could have longed to go flying across the desert in Nevill Caird's big motor-car; nevertheless, she never ceased to wish for Stephen Knight. Her thoughts of him and of the desert were inextricably and inexplicably mingled, more than ever since the night when she had danced in the Agha's tent, and Stephen's face had come before her eyes, as if in answer to her call. Constantly she called him now. When there was some fleeting, beautiful effect of light or shadow, she said, "How I wish he were here to see that!" She never named him in her mind. He was "he": that was name enough. Yet it did not occur to her that she was "in love" with Knight. She had never had time to think about falling in love. There had always been Saidee, and dancing; and to Victoria, the desire to make money enough to start out and find her sister, had taken the place which ideas of love and marriage fill in most girls' heads. Therefore she did not know what to make of her feeling for Stephen. But when a question floated into her brain, she answered it simply by explaining that he was different from any other man she had met; and that, though she had known him only a few days, from the first he had seemed more a friend than Si Maïeddine, or any one else whom she knew much better than Stephen.

As they travelled, she had many thoughts which pleased her—thoughts which could have come to her nowhere else except in the desert, and often she talked to herself, because M'Barka could not understand her feelings, and she did not wish to make Maïeddine understand.

"Burning, burning," was the adjective which she repeated oftenest, in an almost awestruck whisper, as her eyes travelled over immense spaces; for she thought that the desert might have dropped out of the sun. The colour of sand and sky was colour on fire, blazing. The whole Sahara throbbed with the unimaginable fire of creative cosmic force, deep, vital orange, needed by the primitive peoples of the earth who had not risen high enough yet to deserve or desire the finer vibrations.

As she leaned out of the bassour, the heat of the sun pressed on her lightly veiled head, like the golden lid of a golden box. She could feel it as an actual weight; and invisible behind it a living power which could crush her in an instant, as the paw of a lion might crush a flower petal.

Africa itself was this savage power, fierce as fire, ever smouldering, sometimes flaming with the revolt of Islam against other creeds; but the heart of the fire was the desert. Only the shady seguias in the oasis towns cooled it, like children's fingers on a madman's forehead; or the sound of a boy's flute in a river bed, playing the music of Pan, changeless, monotonous yet thrilling, as the music of earth and all Nature.

There were tracts in the desert which colour-blind people might have hated; but Victoria grew to think the dreariest stretches beautiful; and even the occasional plagues of flies which irritated M'Barka beyond endurance, only made Victoria laugh.

Sometimes came caravans, in this billowing immensity between the M'Zab and Ouargla—city of Solomon, whither the Queen of Sheba rode on her mehari: caravans blazing red and yellow, which swept like slow lines of flame across the desert, going east towards the sunrise, or west where the sunset spreads over the sky like a purple fan opening, or the tail of a celestial peacock.

What Victoria had once imagined the desert to be of vast emptiness, and what she found it to be of teeming life, was like the difference between a gold-bright autumn leaf seen by the naked eye, and the same leaf swarming under a powerful microscope.

The girl never tired of following with her eyes the vague tracks of caravans that she could see dimly sketched upon the sand, vanishing in the distance, like lines traced on the water by a ship. She would be gazing at an empty horizon when suddenly from over the waves of the dunes would appear a dark fleet; a procession of laden camels like a flotilla of boats in a desolate sea.

They were very effective, as they approached across the desert, these silent, solemn beasts, but Victoria pitied them, because they were made to work till they fell, and left to die in the shifting sand, when no longer useful to their unloving masters.

"My poor dears, this is only one phase," she would say to them as they plodded past, their feet splashing softly down on the sand like big wet sponges, leaving heart-shaped marks behind, which looked like violets as the hollows filled up with shadow. "Wait till your next chance on earth. I'm sure it will make up for everything."

But Maïeddine told her there was no need to be sorry for the sufferings of camels, since all were deserved. Once, he said, they had been men—a haughty tribe who believed themselves better than the rest of the world. They broke off from the true religion, and lest their schism spread, Allah turned the renegades into camels. He compelled them to bear the weight of their sins in the shape of humps, and also to carry on their backs the goods of the Faithful, whose beliefs they had trampled under foot. While keeping their stubbornness of spirit they must kneel to receive their loads, and rise at the word of command. Remembering their past, they never failed to protest with roarings, against these indignities, nor did their faces ever lose the old look of sullen pride. But, in common with the once human storks, they had one consolation. Their sins expiated, they would reincarnate as men; and some other rebellious tribe would take their place as camels.

Five days' journeying from Ghardaia brought the travellers to a desert world full of movement and interest. There were many caravans going northward. Pretty girls smiled at them from swaying red bassourahs, sitting among pots and pans, and bundles of finery. Little children in nests of scarlet rags, on loaded camels, clasped squawking cocks and hens, tied by the leg. Splendid Negroes with bare throats like columns of black marble sang strange, chanting songs as they strode along. White-clad Arabs whose green turbans told that they had been to Mecca, walked beside their young wives' camels. Withered crones in yellow smocks trudged after the procession, driving donkeys weighed down with sheepskins full of oil. Baby camels with waggling, tufted humps followed their mothers. Slim grey sloughis and Kabyle dogs quarrelled with each other, among flocks of black and white goats; and at night, the sky pulsed with the fires of desert encampments, rosy as northern lights.

Just before the walled city of Ouargla, Victoria saw her first mirage, clear as a dream between waking and sleeping. It was a salt lake, in which Guelbi and the other animals appeared to wade knee-deep in azure waves, though there was no water; and the vast, distant oasis hovered so close that the girl almost believed she had only to stretch out her hand and touch the trunks of the crowding palm trees.

M'Barka was tired, and they rested for two days in the strange Ghuâra town, the "City of Roses," founded (according to legend), by Solomon, King of Jerusalem, and built for him by djenoum and angels in a single night. They lived as usual in the house of the Caïd, whose beautiful twin daughters told Victoria many things about the customs of the Ghuâra people, descendants of the ancient Garamantes. How much happier and freer they were than Arab girls, how much purer though gayer was the life at Ouargla, Queen of the Oases, than at any other less enlightened desert city; how marvellous was the moulet-el-rass, the dance cure for headache and diseases of the brain; how wonderful were the women soothsayers; and what a splendid thing it was to see the bridal processions passing through the streets, on the one day of the year when there is marrying and giving in marriage in Ouargla.

The name of the prettier twin was Zorah, and she had black curls which fell straight down over her brilliant eyes, under a scarlet head-dress. "Dost thou love Si Maïeddine?" she asked the Roumia, with a kind of innocent boldness.

"As a friend who has been very kind," Victoria answered.

"Not as a lover, oh Roumia?" Zorah, like all girls of Ouargla, was proud of her knowledge of Arabic.

"No. Not as a lover."

"Is there then one of thine own people whom thou lovest as a lover, Rose of the West?"

"I have no lover, little white moon."

"Si Maïeddine will be thy lover, whether thou desirest him or not."

"Thou mistakest, oh Zorah."

"I do not mistake. If thou dost not yet know I am right, thou wilt know before many days. When thou findest out all that is in his heart for thee, remember our talk to-day, in the court of oranges."

"I will tell thee thou wert wrong in this same court of oranges when I pass this way again without Si Maïeddine."

The Ghuâra girl shook her head, until her curls seemed to ring like bells of jet. "Something whispers to my spirit that thou wilt never again pass this way, oh Roumia; that never again will we talk together in this court of oranges."

XXXI

If it had not been for Zorah and her twin sister Khadijah, Maïeddine would have said to himself at Ouargla, "Now my hour has come." But though his eyes saw not even the shadow of a woman in the Caïd's house, his ears heard the laughter of young girls, in which Victoria's voice mingled; and besides, he knew, as Arabs contrive to know everything which concerns others, that his host had daughters. He was well aware of the freemasonry existing among the wearers of veils, the dwellers behind shut doors; and though Victoria was only a Roumia, the Caïd's daughters would joyfully scheme to help her against a man, if she asked their help.

So he put the hour-hand of his patience a little ahead; and Victoria and he were outwardly on the same terms as before when they left Ouargla, and passed on to the region of the low dunes, shaped like the tents of nomads buried under sand, the region of beautiful jewelled stones of all colours, and the region of the chotts, the desert lakes, like sad, wide-open eyes in a dead face.

As they drew near to the Zaouïa of Temacin, and the great oasis city of Touggourt, the dunes increased in size, surging along the horizon in turbulent golden billows. M'Barka knew that she was close to her old home, the ancient stronghold of her royal ancestors, those sultans who had owned no master under Allah; for though it was many years since she had come this way, she remembered every land-mark which would have meant nothing to a stranger. She was excited, and longed to point out historic spots to Victoria, of whom she had grown fond; but Maïeddine had forbidden her to speak. He had something to say to the girl before telling her that they were approaching another city of the desert. Therefore M'Barka kept her thoughts to herself, not chatting even with Fafann; for though she loved Victoria, she loved Maïeddine better. She had forgiven him for bringing her the long way round, sacrificing her to his wish for the girl's society, because the journey was four-fifths finished, and instead of being worse, her health was better. Besides, whatever Maïeddine wanted was for the Roumia's good, or would be eventually.

When they were only a short march from Touggourt, and could have reached there by dark, Maïeddine nevertheless ordered an early halt. The tents were set up by the Negroes among the dunes, where not even the tall spire of Temacin's mosque was visible. And he led the little caravan somewhat out of the track, where no camels were likely to pass within sight, to a place where there were no groups of black tents in the yellow sand, and where the desert, in all its beauty, appeared lonelier than it was in reality.

By early twilight the camp was made, and the Soudanese were preparing dinner. Never once in all the Sahara journey had there been a sunset of such magical loveliness, it seemed to Maïeddine, and he took it as a good omen.

"If thou wilt walk a little way with me, Ourïeda," he said, "I will show thee something thou hast never seen yet. When my cousin is rested, and it is time for supper, I will bring thee back."

Together they mounted and descended the dunes, until they could no longer see the camp or the friendly smoke of the fire, which rose straight up, a scarf of black gauze, against a sky of green and lilac shot with crimson and gold. It was not the first time that Victoria had strolled away from the tents at sunset with Maïeddine, and she could not refuse, yet this evening she would gladly have stayed with Lella M'Barka.

The sand was curiously crisp under their feet as they walked, and the crystallized surface crackled as if they were stepping on thin, dry toast. By and by they stood still on the summit of a dune, and Maïeddine took from the hood of his burnous a pair of field-glasses of the most modern make.

"Look round thee," he said. "I have had these with me since our start, but I saved them for to-day, to give thee a surprise."

Victoria adjusted the glasses, which were very powerful, and cried out at what she saw. The turmoil of the dunes became a battle of giants. Sand waves as high as the sky rushed suddenly towards her, towering far above her head, as if she were a fly in the midst of a stormy ocean. The monstrous yellow shapes came closing in from all sides, threatening to engulf her. She felt like a butterfly in a cage of angry lions.

"It is terrible!" she exclaimed, letting the glasses fall from her eyes. The cageful of lions sat down, calmed, but now that the butterfly had seen them roused, never could they look the same again.

The effect upon the girl was exactly what Maïeddine had wanted. For once Victoria acted as he expected her to do in given circumstances. "She is only a woman after all," he thought.

"If thou wert alone in this sea of gold, abandoned, to find thine own way, with no guide but the stars, then indeed thou mightst say 'it is terrible,'" he answered. "For these waves roll between thee and the north, whence thou hast come, and still higher between thee and the desired end of thy journey. So high are they, that to go up and down is like climbing and descending mountains, one after another, all day, day after day. And beyond, where thou must soon go if thou art to find thy sister, there are no tracks such as those we have followed thus far. In these shifting sands, not only men and camels, but great caravans, and even whole armies have been lost and swallowed up for ever. For gravestones, they have only the dunes, and no man will know where they lie till the world is rolled up as a scroll in the hand of Allah."

Victoria grew pale.

"Always before thou hast tried to make me love the desert," she said, slowly. "If there were anything ugly to see, thou hast bidden me turn my head the other way, or if I saw something dreadful thou wouldst at once begin to chant a song of happiness, to make me forget. Why dost thou wish to frighten me now?"

"It is not that I mean to give thee pain, Ourïeda." Maïeddine's voice changed to a tone that was gentle and pleading. "It is only that I would have thee see how powerless thou wouldst be alone among the dunes, where for days thou mightst wander, meeting no man. Or if thou hadst any encounter, it might be with a Touareg, masked in blue, with a long knife at his belt, and in his breast a heart colder than steel."

"I see well enough that I would be powerless alone," Victoria repeated. "Dost thou need to tell me that?"

"It may be not," said Maïeddine. "But there is a thing I need to tell thee. My need is very sore. Because I have kept back the words I have burned to speak, my soul is on fire, oh Rose! I love thee. I die for thee. I must have thee for mine!"

He snatched both her hands in his, and crushed them against his lips. Then, carried away by the flower-like touch of her flesh, he let her hands go, and caught her to his heart, folding her in his burnous as if he would hide her even from the eye of the sun in the west. But she threw herself back, and pushed him away, with her palms pressed against his breast. She could feel under her hands a great pounding as of a hammer that would beat down a yielding wall.

"Thou art no true Arab!" she cried at him.

The words struck Maïeddine in a vulnerable place; perhaps the only one.

He had expected her to exclaim, to protest, to struggle, and to beg that he would let her go. But what she said was a sharp, unlooked for stab. Above all things except his manhood, he prided himself on being a true Arab. Involuntarily he loosened his clasp of her waist, and she seized the chance to wrench herself free, panting a little, her eyes dilated. But as she twisted herself out of his arms, he caught her by the wrist. He did not grasp it tightly enough to hurt, yet the grip of his slim brown hand was like a bracelet of iron. She knew that she could not escape from it by measuring her strength against his, or even by surprising him with some quick movement; for she had surprised him once, and he would be on guard not to let it happen again. Now she did not even try to struggle, but stood still, looking up at him steadily. Yet her heart also was like a hammer that beat against a wall; and she thought of the endless dunes in whose turmoil she was swallowed up. If Stephen Knight were here—but he was far away; and Maïeddine, whom she had trusted, was a man who served another God than hers. His thoughts of women were not as Stephen's thoughts.

"Think of thy white angel," she said. "He stands between thee and me."

"Nay, he gives thee to me," Maïeddine answered. "I mean no harm to thee, but only good, as long as we both shall live. My white angel wills that thou shalt be my wife. Thou shalt not say I am no true Arab. I am true to Allah and my own manhood when I tell thee I can wait no longer."

"But thou art not true to me when thou wouldst force me against my will to be thy wife. We have drunk from the same cup. Thou art pledged to loyalty."

"Is it disloyal to love?"

"Thy love is not true love, or thou wouldst think of me before thyself."

"I think of thee before all the world. Thou art my world. I had meant to wait till thou wert in thy sister's arms; but since the night when I saw thee dance, my love grew as a fire grows that feeds upon rezin. If I offend thee, thou alone art to blame. Thou wert too beautiful that night. I have been mad since then. And now thou must give me thy word that thou wilt marry me according to the law of Islam. Afterwards, when we can find a priest of thine own religion, we will stand before him."

"Let my hand go, Si Maïeddine, if thou wishest me to talk further with thee," Victoria said.

He smiled at her and obeyed; for he knew that she could not escape from him, therefore he would humour her a little. In a few more moments he meant to have her in his arms again.

His smile gave the girl no hope. She thought of Zorah and the court of the oranges.

"What wilt thou do if I say I will not be thy wife?" she asked, in a quiet voice; but there was a fluttering in her throat.

A spark lit in his eyes. The moon was rising now, as the sun set, and the two lights, silver and rose, touched his face, giving it an unreal look, as if he were a statue of bronze which had "come alive," Victoria thought, just as she had "come alive" in her statue-dance. He had never been so handsome, but his dark splendour was dreadful to her, for he did not seem like a human man whose heart could be moved to mercy.

For an instant he gave her no answer, but his eyes did not leave hers. "Since thou askest me that question, I would make thee change thy 'no' into 'yes.' But do not force me to be harsh with thee, oh core of my heart, oh soul of my soul! I tell thee fate has spoken. The sand has spoken—sand gathered from among these dunes. It is for that reason in part that I brought thee here."

"The sand-divining!" Victoria exclaimed. "Lella M'Barka told thee——"

"She told me not to wait. And her counsel was the counsel of my own heart. Look, oh Rose, where the moon glitters on the sand—the sand that twined thy life with mine. See how the crystals shape themselves like little hands of Fatma; and they point from thee to me, from me to thee. The desert has brought us together. The desert gives us to one another. The desert will never let us part."

Victoria's eyes followed his pointing gesture. The sand-crystals sparkled in the sunset and moonrise, like myriads of earthbound fireflies. Their bright facets seemed to twinkle at her with cold, fairy eyes, waiting to see what she would do, and she did not know. She did not know at all what she would do.

XXXII

"Dost thou wish me to hate thee, Si Maïeddine?" she asked.

"I do not fear thy hate. When thou belongest to me, I will know how to turn it into love."

"Perhaps if I were a girl of thine own people thou wouldst know, but I see now that thy soul and my soul are far apart. If thou art so wicked, so treacherous, they will never be nearer together."

"The Koran does not teach us to believe that the souls of women are as ours."

"I have read. And if there were no other reason than that, it would be enough to put a high wall between me and a man of thy race."

For the first time Maïeddine felt anger against the girl. But it did not make him love or want her the less.

"Thy sister did not feel that," he said, almost menacingly.

"Then the more do I feel it. Is it wise to use her as an argument?"

"I need no argument," he answered, sullenly. "I have told thee what is in my mind. Give me thy love, and thou canst bend me as thou wilt. Refuse it, and I will break thee. No! do not try to run from me. In an instant I should have thee in my arms. Even if thou couldst reach M'Barka, of what use to grasp her dress and cry to her for help against me? She would not give it. My will is law to her, as it must be to thee if thou wilt not learn wisdom, and how to hold me by a thread of silk, a thread of thy silky hair. No one would listen to thee. Not Fafann, not the men of the Soudan. It is as if we two were alone in the desert. Dost thou understand?"

"Thou hast made me understand. I will not try to run. Thou hast the power to take me, since thou hast forgotten thy bond of honour, and thou art stronger than I. Yet will I not live to be thy wife, Si Maïeddine. Wouldst thou hold a dead girl in thine arms?"

"I would hold thee dead or living. Thou wouldst be living at first; and a moment with thine heart beating against mine would be worth a lifetime—perhaps worth eternity."

"Wouldst thou take me if—if I love another man?"

He caught her by the shoulders, and his hands were hard as steel. "Darest thou to tell me that thou lovest a man?"

"Yes, I dare," she said. "Kill me if thou wilt. Since I have no earthly help against thee, kill my body, and let God take my spirit where thou canst never come. I love another man."

"Tell me his name, that I may find him."

"I will not. Nothing thou canst do will make me tell thee."

"It is that man who was with thee on the boat."

"I said I would not tell thee."

He shook her between his hands, so that the looped-up braids of her hair fell down, as they had fallen when she danced, and the ends loosened into curls. She looked like a pale child, and suddenly a great tenderness for her melted his heart. He had never known that feeling before, and it was very strange to him; for when he had loved, it had been with passion, not with tenderness.

"Little white star," he said, "thou art but a babe, and I will not believe that any man has ever touched thy mouth with his lips. Am I right?"

"Yes, because he does not love me. It is I who love him, that is all," she answered naïvely. "I only knew how I really felt when thou saidst thou wouldst make me love thee, for I was so sure that never, never couldst thou do that. And I shall love the other man all my life, even though I do not see him again."

"Thou shalt never see him again. For a moment, oh Rose, I hated thee, and I saw thy face through a mist red as thy blood and his, which I wished to shed. But thou art so young—so white—so beautiful. Thou hast come so far with me, and thou hast been so sweet. There is a strange pity for thee in my breast, such as I have never known for any living thing. I think it must be that thou hast magic in thine eyes. It is as if thy soul looked out at me through two blue windows, and I could fall down and worship, Allah forgive me! I knew no man had kissed thee. And the man thou sayest thou lovest is but a man in a dream. This is my hour. I must not let my chance slip by, M'Barka told me. Yet promise me but one thing and I will hold thee sacred—I swear on the head of my father."

"What is the one thing?"

"That if thy sister Lella Saïda puts thine hand in mine, thou wilt be my wife."

The girl's face brightened, and the great golden dunes, silvering now in moonlight, looked no longer like terrible waves ready to overwhelm her. She was sure of Saidee, as she was sure of herself.

"That I will promise thee," she said.

He looked at her thoughtfully. "Thou hast great confidence in thy sister."

"Perfect confidence."

"And I——" he did not finish his sentence. "I am glad I did not wait longer," he went on instead. "Thou knowest now that I love thee, that thou hast by thy side a man and not a statue. And I have not let my chance slip by, because I have gained thy promise."

"If Saidee puts my hand in thine."

"It is the same thing."

"Thou dost not know my sister."

"But I know——" Again he broke off abruptly. There were things it were better not to say, even in the presence of one who would never be able to tell of an indiscretion. "It is a truce between us?" he asked.

"Yes."

"Forget, then, that I frightened thee."

"Thou didst not frighten me. I did not know what to do, and I thought I might have to die without seeing Saidee. Yet I was not afraid, I think—I hope—I was not afraid."

"Thou wilt not have to die without seeing thy sister. Now, more than before, I shall be in haste to put thee in her charge. But thou wilt die without seeing again the face of that man whose name, which thou wouldst not speak, shall be as smoke blown before the wind. Never shalt thou see him on earth, and if he and I meet I will kill him."

Victoria shut her eyes, and pressed her hands over them. She felt very desolate, alone with Maïeddine among the dunes. She would not dare to call Stephen now, lest he should hear and come. Nevertheless she could not be wholly unhappy, for it was wonderful to have learned what love was. She loved Stephen Knight.

"Thou wilt let me go back to M'Barka?" she said to Maïeddine.

"I will take thee back," he amended. "Because I have thy promise."

XXXIII

On a flat white roof, which bubbled up here and there in rounded domes, a woman stood looking out over interminable waves of yellow sand, a vast golden silence which had no end on her side of the horizon, east, west, north, or south.

No veil hid her face, but folds of thin woollen stuff beautifully woven, and dyed blue, almost as dark as indigo, fell from her head nearly to her feet, over a loose robe of orange-red, cut low in the neck, with sleeves hiding the elbows. She looked towards the west, shading her eyes with her hand: and the sun near its setting streamed over her face and hair, chiselling her features in marble, brightening her auburn hair to fiery gold, giving her brown eyes the yellow tints of a topaz, or of the amber beads which hung in a long chain, as far down as her knees.

From the white roof many things could be seen besides the immense monotonous dunes along whose ridges orange fire seemed to play unceasingly against the sky.

There was the roof of the Zaouïa mosque, with its low, white domes grouped round the minaret, as somewhere below the youngest boys of the school grouped round the taleb, or teacher. On the roof of the mosque bassourah frames were in the making, splendid bassourahs, which, when finished, would be the property of the great marabout, greatest of all living marabouts, lord of the Zaouïa, lord of the desert and its people, as far as the eye could reach, and farther.

There were other roofs, too, bubbling among the labyrinth of square open courts and long, tunnel-like, covered and uncovered corridors which formed the immense, rambling Zaouïa, or sacred school of Oued Tolga. Things happened on these roofs which would have interested a stranger, for there was spinning of sheep's wool, making of men's burnouses, fashioning of robes for women, and embroidering of saddles; but the woman who looked towards the west with the sun in her eyes was tired of the life on sun-baked roofs and in shadowed courts.

The scent of orange blossoms in her own little high-walled garden came up to her; yet she had forgotten that it was sweet, for she had never loved it. The hum of the students' voices, faintly heard through the open-work of wrought-iron windows, rasped her nerves, for she had heard it too often; and she knew that the mysterious lessons, the lessons which puzzled her, and constantly aroused her curiosity, were never repeated aloud by the classes, as were these everlasting chapters of the Koran.

Men sleeping on benches in the court of the mosque, under arches in the wall, waked and drank water out of bulging goatskins, hanging from huge hooks. Pilgrims washed their feet in the black marble basin of the trickling fountain, for soon it would be time for moghreb, the prayer of the evening.

Far away, eighteen miles distant across the sands, she could see the twenty thousand domes of Oued Tolga, the desert city which had taken its name from the older Zaouïa, and the oued or river which ran between the sacred edifice on its golden hill, and the ugly toub- built village, raised above danger of floods on a foundation of palm trunks.

Far away the domes of the desert city shimmered like white fire in the strange light that hovers over the Sahara before the hour of sunset. Behind those distant, dazzling bubbles of unearthly whiteness, the valley-like oases of the southern desert, El Souf, dimpled the yellow dunes here and there with basins of dark green. Near by, a little to the left of the Zaouïa hill, such an oasis lay, and the woman on the white roof could look across a short stretch of sand, down into its green depths. She could watch the marabout's men repairing the sloping sand-walls with palm trunks, which kept them from caving in, and saved the precious date-palms from being engulfed in a yellow tide. It was the marabout's own private oasis, and brought him in a large income every year. But everything was the marabout's. The woman on the roof was sick to death of his riches, his honours, his importance, for she was the marabout's wife; and in these days she loved him as little as she loved the orange garden he had given her, and all the things that were hers because she was his.

It was very still in the Zaouïa of Oued Tolga. The only sound was the droning of the boys' voices, which came faintly from behind iron window-gratings below, and that monotonous murmur emphasized the silence, as the humming of bees in a hive makes the stillness of a garden in summer more heavy and hot.

No noises came from the courts of the women's quarters, or those of the marabout's guests, and attendants, and servants; not a voice was raised in that more distant part of the Zaouïa where the students lived, and where the poor were lodged and fed for charity's sake. No doubt the village, across the narrow river in its wide bed, was buzzing with life at this time of day; but seldom any sound there was loud enough to break the slumberous silence of the great Zaouïa. And the singing of the men in the near oasis who fought the sand, the groaning of the well-cords woven of palm fibre which raised the buckets of hollowed palm-trunks, was as monotonous as the recitation of the Koran. The woman had heard it so often that she had long ago ceased to hear it at all.

She looked westward, across the river to the ugly village with the dried palm-leaves on its roofs, and far away to the white-domed city, the dimpling oases and the mountainous dunes that towered against a flaming sky; then eastward, towards the two vast desert lakes, or chotts, one of blue water, the other of saltpetre, which looked bluer than water, and had pale edges that met the sand like snow on gold. Above the lake of water suddenly appeared a soaring line of white, spreading and mounting higher, then turning from white to vivid rose. It was the flamingoes rising and flying over the chott, the one daily phenomenon of the desert which the woman on the roof still loved to watch. But her love for the rosy line against the blue was not entirely because of its beauty, though it was startlingly beautiful. It meant something for which she waited each evening with a passionate beating of her heart under the orange-coloured robe and the chain of amber beads. It meant sunset and the coming of a message. But the doves on the green tiled minaret of the Zaouïa mosque had not begun yet to dip and wheel. They would not stir from their repose until the muezzin climbed the steps to call the hour of evening prayer, and until they flew against the sunset the message could not come.

She must wait yet awhile. There was nothing to do till the time of hope for the message. There was never anything else that she cared to do through the long days from sunrise to sunset, unless the message gave her an incentive when it came.

In the river-bed, the women and young girls had not finished their washing, which was to them not so much labour as pleasure, since it gave them their opportunity for an outing and a gossip. In the bed of shining sand lay coloured stones like jewels, and the women knelt on them, beating wet bundles of scarlet and puce with palm branches.

The watcher on the roof knew that they were laughing and chattering together though she could not hear them. She wondered dimly how many years it was since she had laughed, and said to herself that probably she would never laugh again, although she was still young, only twenty-eight. But that was almost old for a woman of the East. Those girls over there, wading knee-deep in the bright water to fill their goatskins and curious white clay jugs, would think her old. But they hardly knew of her existence. She had married the great marabout, therefore she was a marabouta, or woman saint, merely because she was fortunate enough to be his wife, and too highly placed for them to think of as an earthly woman like themselves. What could it matter whether such a radiantly happy being were young or old? And she smiled a little as she imagined those poor creatures picturing her happiness. She passed near them sometimes going to the Moorish baths, but the long blue drapery covered her face then, and she was guarded by veiled negresses and eunuchs. They looked her way reverently, but had never seen her face, perhaps did not know who she was, though no doubt they had all heard and gossiped about the romantic history of the new wife, the beautiful Ouled Naïl, to whom the marabout had condescended because of her far-famed, her marvellous, almost incredible loveliness, which made her a consort worthy of a saint.

The river was a mirror this evening, reflecting the sunset of crimson and gold, and the young crescent moon fought for and devoured, then vomited forth again by strange black cloud-monsters. The old brown palm-trunks, on which the village was built, were repeated in the still water, and seemed to go down and down, as if their roots might reach to the other side of the world.

Over the crumbling doorways of the miserable houses bleached skulls and bones of animals were nailed for luck. The red light of the setting sun stained them as if with blood, and they were more than ever disgusting to the watcher on the white roof. They were the symbols of superstitions the most Eastern and barbaric, ideas which she hated, as she was beginning to hate all Eastern things and people.

The streak of rose which meant a flock of flying flamingoes had faded out of the sky. The birds seemed to have vanished into the sunset, and hardly had they gone when the loud crystalline voice of the muezzin began calling the faithful to prayer. Work stopped for the day. The men and youths of the Zaouïa climbed the worn stairs to the roof of the mosque, where, in their white turbans and burnouses, they prostrated themselves before Allah, going down on their faces as one man. The doves of the minaret—called Imams, because they never leave the mosque or cease to prostrate themselves, flying head downwards—began to wheel and cry plaintively. The moment when the message might come was here at last.

The white roof had a wall, which was low in places, in others very high, so high that no one standing behind it could be seen. This screen of whitewashed toub was arranged to hide persons on the roof from those on the roof of the mosque; but window-like openings had been made in it, filled in with mashrabeyah work of lace-like pattern; an art brought to Africa long ago by the Moors, after perfecting it in Granada. And this roof was not the only one thus screened and latticed. There was another, where watchers could also look down into the court of the fountain, at the carved doors taken from the Romans, and up to the roof of the mosque with all its little domes. From behind those other lace-like windows in the roof- wall, sparkled such eyes as only Ouled Naïl girls can have; but the first watcher hated to think of those eyes and their wonderful fringe of black lashes. It was an insult to her that they should beautify this house, and she ignored their existence, though she had heard her negresses whispering about them.

While the faithful prayed, a few of the wheeling doves flew across from the mosque to the roof where the woman waited for a message. At her feet lay a small covered basket, from which she took a handful of grain. The dove Imams forgot their saintly manners in an unseemly scramble as the white hand scattered the seeds, and while they disputed with one another, complaining mournfully, another bird, flying straight to the roof from a distance, suddenly joined them. It was white, with feet like tiny branches of coral, whereas the doves from the mosque were grey, or burnished purple.

The woman had been pale, but when the bird fluttered down to rest on the open basket of grain, colour rushed to her face, as if she had been struck on each cheek with a rose. None of the doves of the mosque were tame enough to sit on the basket, which was close to her feet, though they sidled round it wistfully; but the white bird let her stroke its back with her fingers as it daintily pecked the yellow grains.

Very cautiously she untied a silk thread fastened to a feather under the bird's wing. As she did so it fluttered both wings as if stretching them in relief, and a tiny folded paper attached to the cord fell into the basket. Instantly the woman laid her hand over it. Then she looked quickly, without moving her head, towards the square opening at a corner of the roof where the stairway came up. No one was there. Nobody could see her from the roof of the mosque, and her roof was higher than any of the others, except that which covered the private rooms of the marabout. But the marabout was away, and no one ever came out on his roof when he was absent.

She opened the folded bit of white paper, which was little more than two inches square, and was covered on one side with writing almost microscopically small. The other side was blank, but the woman had no doubt that the letter was for her. As she read, the carrier-pigeon went on pecking at the seeds in the basket, and the doves of the mosque watched it enviously.

The writing was in French, and no name was at the beginning or the end.

"Be brave, my beautiful one, and dare to do as your heart prompts. Remember, I worship you. Ever since that wonderful day when the wind blew aside your veil for an instant at the door of the Moorish bath, the whole world has been changed for me. I would die a thousand deaths if need be for the joy of rescuing you from your prison. Yet I do not wish to die. I wish to live, to take you far away and make you so happy that you will forget the wretchedness and failure of the past. A new life will begin for both of us, if you will only trust me, and forget the scruples of which you write—false scruples, believe me. As he had a wife living when he married you, and has taken another since, surely you cannot consider that you are bound by the law of God or man? Let me save you from the dragon, as fairy princesses were saved in days of old. If I might speak with you, tell you all the arguments that constantly suggest themselves to my mind, you could not refuse. I have thought of more than one way, but dare not put my ideas on paper, lest some unlucky chance befall our little messenger. Soon I shall have perfected the cypher. Then there will not be the same danger. Perhaps to-morrow night I shall be able to send it. But meanwhile, for the sake of my love, give me a little hope. If you will try to arrange a meeting, to be settled definitely when the cypher is ready, twist three of those glorious threads of gold which you have for hair round the cord when you send the messenger back."

All the rosy colour had died away from the woman's face by the time she had finished reading the letter. She folded it again into a tiny square even smaller than before, and put it into one of the three or four little engraved silver boxes, made to hold texts from the Koran, which hung from her long amber necklace. Her eyes were very wide open, but she seemed to see nothing except some thought printed on her brain like a picture.

On the mosque roof a hundred men of the desert knelt praying in the sunset, their faces turned towards Mecca. Down in the fountain- court, the marabout's lazy tame lion rose from sleep and stretched himself, yawning as the clear voice of the muezzin chanted from the minaret the prayer of evening, "Allah Akbar, Allah il Allah, Mohammed r'soul Allah."

The woman did not know that she heard the prayer, for as her eyes saw a picture, so did her ears listen to a voice which she had heard only once, but desired beyond all things to hear again. To her it was the voice of a saviour-knight; the face she saw was glorious with the strength of manhood, and the light of love. Only to think of the voice and face made her feel that she was coming to life again, after lying dead and forgotten in a tomb for many years of silence.

Yes, she was alive now, for he had waked her from a sleep like death; but she was still in the tomb, and it seemed impossible to escape from it, even with the help of a saviour-knight. If she said "yes" to what he asked, as she was trying to make herself believe she had a moral and legal right to do, they would be found out and killed, that was all.

She was not brave. The lassitude which is a kind of spurious resignation poisons courage, or quenches it as water quenches fire. Although she hated her life, if it could be called life, had no pleasure in it, and had almost forgotten how to hope, still she was afraid of being violently struck down.

Not long ago a woman in the village had tried to leave her husband with a man she loved. The husband found out, and having shot the man before her eyes, stabbed her with many wounds, one for each traitorous kiss, according to the custom of the desert; not one knife-thrust deep enough to kill; but by and by she had died from the shock of horror, and loss of blood. Nobody blamed the husband. He had done the thing which was right and just. And stories like this came often to the ears of the woman on the roof through her negresses, or from the attendants at the Moorish bath.

The man she loved would not be shot like the wretched Bedouin, who was of no importance except to her for whom his life was given; but something would happen. He would be taken ill with a strange disease, of which he would die after dreadful suffering; or at best his career would be ruined; for the greatest of all marabouts was a man of immense influence. Because of his religious vow to wear a mask always like a Touareg, none of the ruling race had ever seen the marabout's features, yet his power was known far and wide—in Morocco; all along the caravan route to Tombouctou; in the capital of the Touaregs; in Algiers; and even in Paris itself.

She reminded herself of these things, and at one moment her heart was like ice in her breast; but at the next, it was like a ball of fire; and pulling out three long bright hairs from her head, she twisted them round the cord which the carrier-pigeon had brought. Before tying it under his wing again, she scattered more yellow seeds for the dove Imams, because she did not want them to fly away until she was ready to let her messenger go. Thus there was the less danger that the carrier-pigeon would be noticed. Only Noura, her negress, knew of him. Noura had smuggled him into the Zaouïa, and she herself had trained him by giving him food that he liked, though his home was at Oued Tolga, the town.

The birds from the mosque had waited for their second supply, for the same programme had been carried out many times before, and they had learned to expect it.

When they finished scrambling for the grain which the white pigeon could afford to scorn, they fluttered back to the minaret, following a leader. But the carrier flew away straight and far, his little body vanishing at last as if swallowed up in the gold of the sunset. For he went west, towards the white domes of Oued Tolga.

XXXIV

Still the woman stood looking after the bird, but the sun had dropped behind the dunes, and she no longer needed to shade her eyes with her hand. There was nothing more to expect till sunset to-morrow, when something might or might not happen. If no message came, then there would be only dullness and stagnation until the day when the Moorish bath was sacredly kept for the great ladies of the marabout's household. There were but two of these, yet they never went to the bath together, nor had they ever met or spoken to one another. They were escorted to the bath by their attendants at different hours of the same day; and later their female servants were allowed to go, for no one but the women of the saintly house might use the baths that day.

The woman on the white roof in the midst of the golden silence gazed towards the west, though she looked for no event of interest; and her eyes fixed themselves mechanically upon a little caravan which moved along the yellow sand like a procession of black insects. She was so accustomed to search the desert since the days, long ago, when she had actually hoped for friends to come and take her away, that she could differentiate objects at greater distances than one less trained to observation. Hardly thinking of the caravan, she made out, nevertheless, that it consisted of two camels, carrying bassourahs, a horse and Arab rider, a brown pack camel, and a loaded mule, driven by two men who walked.

They had evidently come from Oued Tolga, or at least from that direction, therefore it was probable that their destination was the Zaouïa; otherwise, as it was already late, they would have stopped in the city all night. Of course, it was possible that they were on their way to the village, but it was a poor place, inhabited by very poor people, many of them freed Negroes, who worked in the oases and lived mostly upon dates. No caravans ever went out from there, because no man, even the richest, owned more than one camel or donkey; and nobody came to stay, unless some son of the miserable hamlet, who had made a little money elsewhere, and returned to see his relatives. But on the other hand, numerous caravans arrived at the Zaouïa of Oued Tolga, and hundreds of pilgrims from all parts of Islam were entertained as the marabout's guests, or as recipients of charity.

Dimly, as she detached her mind from the message she had sent, the woman began to wonder about this caravan, because of the bassourahs, which meant that there were women among the travellers. There were comparatively few women pilgrims to the Zaouïa, except invalids from the town of Oued Tolga, or some Sahara encampment, who crawled on foot, or rode decrepit donkeys, hoping to be cured of ailments by the magic power of the marabout, the power of the Baraka. The woman who watched had learned by this time not to expect European tourists. She had lived for eight years in the Zaouïa, and not once had she seen from her roof a European, except a French government-official or two, and a few—a very few—French officers. Never had any European women come. Tourists were usually satisfied with Touggourt, three or four days nearer civilisation. Women did not care to undertake an immense and fatiguing journey among the most formidable dunes of the desert, where there was nothing but ascending and descending, day after day; where camels sometimes broke their legs in the deep sand, winding along the fallen side of a mountainous dune, and where a horse often had to sit on his haunches, and slide with his rider down a sand precipice.

She herself had experienced all these difficulties, so long ago now that she had half forgotten how she had hated them, and the fate to which they were leading her. But she did not blame other women for not coming to Oued Tolga.

Occasionally some caïd or agha of the far south would bring his wife who was ill or childless to be blessed by the marabout; and in old days they had been introduced to the marabouta, but it was years now since she had been asked, or even allowed, to entertain strangers. She thought, without any active interest, as she looked at the nodding bassourahs, growing larger and larger, that a chief was coming with his women, and that he would be disappointed to learn that the marabout was away from home. It was rather odd that the stranger had not been told in the city, for every one knew that the great man had gone a fortnight ago to the province of Oran. Several days must pass before he could return, even if, for any reason, he came sooner than he was expected. But it did not matter much to her, if there were to be visitors who would have the pain of waiting. There was plenty of accommodation for guests, and there were many servants whose special duty it was to care for strangers. She would not see the women in the bassourahs, nor hear of them unless some gossip reached her through the talk of the negresses.

Still, as there was nothing else which she wished to do, she continued to watch the caravan.

By and by it passed out of sight, behind the rising ground on which the village huddled, with its crowding brown house-walls that narrowed towards the roofs. The woman almost forgot it, until it appeared again, to the left of the village, where palm logs had been laid in the river bed, making a kind of rough bridge, only covered when the river was in flood. It was certain now that the travellers were coming to the Zaouïa.

The flame of the sunset had died, though clouds purple as pansies flowered in the west. The gold of the dunes paled to silver, and the desert grew sad, as if it mourned for a day that would never live again. Far away, near Oued Tolga, where the white domes of the city and the green domes of the oasis palms all blended together in shadow, fires sprang up in the camps of nomads, like signals of danger.

The woman on the roof shivered. The chill of the coming night cooled her excitement. She was afraid of the future, and the sadness which had fallen upon the desert was cold in her heart. The caravan was not far from the gate of the Zaouïa, but she was tired of watching it. She turned and went down the narrow stairs that led to her rooms, and to the little garden where the fragrance of orange blossoms was too sweet.

XXXV

The caravan stopped in front of the Zaouïa gate. There were great iron doors in a high wall of toub, which was not much darker in colour than the deep gold of the desert sand; and because it was after sunset the doors were closed.

One of the Negroes knocked, and called out something inarticulate and guttural in a loud voice.

Almost at once the gate opened, and a shadowy figure hovered inside. A name was announced, which was instantly shouted to a person unseen, and a great chattering began in the dusk. Men ran out, and one or two kissed the hand of the rider on the white horse. They explained volubly that the lord was away, but the newcomer checked them as soon as he could, saying that he had heard the news in the city. He had with him ladies, one a relative of his own, another who was connected with the great lord himself, and they must be entertained as the lord would wish, were he not absent.

The gates, or doors, of iron were thrown wide open, and the little procession entered a huge open court. On one side was accommodation for many animals, as in a caravanserai, with a narrow roof sheltering thirty or forty stalls; and here the two white meharis were made to kneel, that the women might descend from their bassourahs. There were three, all veiled, but the arms of one were bare and very brown. She moved stiffly, as if cramped by sitting for a long time in one position; nevertheless, she supported her companion, whose bassour she had shared. The two Soudanese Negroes remained in this court with their animals, which the servants of the Zaouïa, began helping them to unload; but the master of the expedition, with the two ladies of his party and Fafann, was now obliged to walk. Several men of the Zaouïa acted as their guides, gesticulating with great respect, but lowering their eyelids, and appearing not to see the women.

They passed through another court, very large, though not so immense as the first, for no animals were kept there. Instead of stalls for camels and horses, there were roughly built rooms for pilgrims of the poorer class, with little, roofless, open-sided kitchens, where they could cook their own food. Beyond was the third court, with lodging for more important persons, and then the travellers were led through a labyrinth of corridors, some roofed with palm branches, others open to the air, and still more covered in with the toub blocks of which the walls were built. Along the sides were crumbling benches of stucco, on which old men lay rolled up in their burnouses; or here and there a door of rotting palm wood hung half open, giving a glimpse into a small, dim court, duskily red with the fire of cooking in an open-air kitchen. From behind these doors came faint sounds of chanting, and spicy smells of burning wood and boiling peppers. It was like passing through a subterranean village; and little dark children, squatting in doorways, or flattening their bodies against palm trunks which supported palm roofs, or flitting ahead of the strangers, in the thick, musky scented twilight, were like shadowy gnomes.

By and by, as the newcomers penetrated farther into the mysterious labyrinth of the vast Zaouïa, the corridors and courts became less ruined in appearance. The walls were whitewashed; the palm-wood doors were roughly carved and painted in bright colours, which could be seen by the flicker of lamps set high in little niches. Each tunnel-like passage had a carved archway at the end, and at last they entered one which was closed in with beautiful doors of wrought iron.

Through the rich network they could see into a court where everything glimmered white in moonlight. They had come to the court of the mosque, which had on one side an entrance to the private house of the marabout, the great Sidi El Hadj Mohammed ben Abd-el-Kader.

"Lella Saïda, oh light of the young moon, if it please thee, thou hast two guests come from very far off," announced an old negress to the woman who had been looking out over the golden silence of the desert.

It was an hour since she had come down from the roof, and having eaten a little bread, with soup, she lay on a divan writing in a small book. Several tall copper lamps with open-work copper shades, jewelled and fringed with coloured glass, gave a soft and beautiful light to the room. It had pure white walls, round which, close to the ceiling, ran a frieze of Arab lettering, red, and black, and gold. The doors and window-blinds and little cupboards were of cedar, so thickly inlaid with mother-o'-pearl, that only dark lines of the wood defined the white patterning of leaves and flowers.

The woman had thrown off the blue drapery that had covered her head, and her auburn hair glittered in the light of the lamp by which she wrote. She looked up, vexed.

"Thou knowest, Noura, that for years I have received no guests," she said, in a dialect of the Soudan, in which most Saharian mistresses of Negro servants learn to talk. "I can see no one. The master would not permit me to do so, even if I wished it, which I do not."

"Pardon, loveliest lady. But this is another matter. A friend of our lord brings these visitors to thee. One is kin of his. She seeks to be healed of a malady, by the power of the Baraka. But the other is a Roumia."

The wife of the great marabout shut the book in which she had been writing, and her mind travelled quickly to the sender of the carrier-pigeon. A European woman, the first who had ever come to the Zaouïa in eight years! It must be that she had a message from him. Somehow he had contrived this visit. She dared ask no more questions.

"I will see these ladies," she said. "Let them come to me here."

"Already the old one is resting in the guest-house," answered the negress. "She has her own servant, and she asks to see thee no earlier than to-morrow, when she has rested, and is able to pay thee her respects. It is the other, the young Roumia, who begs to speak with thee to-night."

The wife of the marabout was more certain than ever that her visitor must come from the sender of the pigeon. She was glad of an excuse to talk with his messenger alone, without waiting.

"Go fetch her," she directed. "And when thou hast brought her to the door I shall no longer need thee, Noura."

Her heart was beating fast. She dreaded some final decision, or the need to make a decision, yet she knew that she would be bitterly disappointed if, after all, the European woman were not what she thought. She shut up the diary in which she wrote each night, and opening one of the wall cupboards near her divan, she put it away on a shelf, where there were many other small volumes, a dozen perhaps. They contained the history of her life during the last nine years, since unhappiness had isolated her, and made it necessary to her peace of mind, almost to her sanity, to have a confidant. She closed the inlaid doors of the cupboard, and locked them with a key which hung from a ribbon inside her dress.

Such a precaution was hardly needed, since the writing was all in English, and she had recorded the events of the last few weeks cautiously and cryptically. Not a soul in the marabout's house could read English, except the marabout himself; and it was seldom he honoured her with a visit. Nevertheless, it had become a habit to lock up the books, and she found a secretive pleasure in it.

She had only time to slip the ribbon back into her breast, and sit down stiffly on the divan, when the door was opened again by Noura.

"O Lella Saïda, I have brought the Roumia," the negress announced.

A slim figure in Arab dress came into the room, unfastening a white veil with fingers that trembled with impatience. The door shut softly. Noura had obeyed instructions.

XXXVI

For ten years Victoria had been waiting for this moment, dreaming of it at night, picturing it by day. Now it had come.

There was Saidee standing before her, found at last. Saidee, well and safe, and lovely as ever, hardly changed in feature, and yet—there was something strange about her, something which stopped the joyous beating of the girl's heart. It was almost as if she had died and come to Heaven, to find that Heaven was not Heaven at all, but a cold place of fear.

She was shocked at the impression, blaming herself. Surely Saidee did not know her yet, that was all; or the surprise was too great. She wished she had sent word by the negress. Though that would have seemed banal, it would have been better than to see the blank look on Saidee's face, a look which froze her into a marble statue. But it was too late now. The only thing left was to make the best of a bad beginning.

"Oh, darling!" Victoria cried. "Have I frightened you? Dearest—my beautiful one, it's your little sister. All these years I've been waiting— waiting to find a way. You knew I would come some day, didn't you?"

Tears poured down her face. She tried to believe they were tears of joy, such as she had often thought to shed at sight of Saidee. She had been sure that she could not keep them back, and that she would not try. They should have been sweet as summer rain, but they burned her eyes and her cheeks as they fell. Saidee was silent. The girl held out her arms, running a step or two, then, faltering, she let her arms fall. They felt heavy and stiff, as if they had been turned to wood. Saidee did not move. There was an expression of dismay, even of fear on her face.

"You don't know me!" Victoria said chokingly. "I've grown up, and I must seem like a different person—but I'm just the same, truly. I've loved you so, always. You'll get used to seeing me changed. You— you don't think I'm somebody else pretending to be Victoria, do you? I can tell you all the things we used to do and say. I haven't forgotten one. Oh, Saidee, dearest, I've come such a long way to find you. Do be glad to see me—do!"

Her voice broke. She put out her hands pleadingly—the childish hands that had seemed pathetically pretty to Stephen Knight.

A look of intense concentration darkened Saidee's eyes. She appeared to question herself, to ask her intelligence what was best to do. Then the tense lines of her face softened. She forced herself to smile, and leaning towards Victoria, clasped the slim white figure in her arms, holding it tightly, in silence. But over the girl's shoulder, her eyes still seemed to search an answer to their question.

When she had had time to control her voice and expression, she spoke, releasing her sister, taking the wistful face between her hands, and gazing at it earnestly. Then she kissed lips and cheeks.

"Victoria!" she murmured. "Victoria! I'm not dreaming you?"

"No, no, darling," the girl answered, more hopefully. "No wonder you're dazed. This—finding you, I mean—has been the object of my life, ever since your letters stopped coming, and I began to feel I'd lost you. That's why I can't realize your being struck dumb with the surprise of it. Somehow, I've always felt you'd be expecting me. Weren't you? Didn't you know I'd come when I could?"

Saidee shook her head, looking with extraordinary, almost feverish, interest at the younger girl, taking in every detail of feature and complexion, all the exquisite outlines of extreme youth, which she had lost.

"No," she said slowly. "I thought I was dead to the world. I didn't think it would be possible for anyone to find me, even you."

"But—you are glad—now I'm here?" Victoria faltered.

"Of course," Saidee answered unhesitatingly. "I'm delighted—enchanted—for my own sake. If I'm frightened, if you think me strange—_farouche_—it's because I'm so surprised, and because—can you believe it?—this is the first time I've spoken English with any human being for nine years—perhaps more. I almost forget—it seems a century. I talk to myself—so as not to forget. And every night I write down what has happened, or rather what I've thought, because things hardly ever do happen here. The words don't come easily. They sound so odd in my own ears. And then—there's another reason why I'm afraid. It's on your account. I'd better tell you. It wouldn't be fair not to tell. I—how are you going to get away again?"

She almost whispered the last words, and spoke them as if she were ashamed. But she watched the girl's face anxiously.

Victoria slipped a protecting arm round her waist. "We are going away together, dearest," she said. "Unless you're too happy and contented. But, my Saidee—you don't look contented."

Saidee flushed faintly. "You mean—I look old—haggard?"

"No—no!" the girl protested. "Not that. You've hardly changed at all, except—oh, I hardly know how to put it in words. It's your expression. You look sad—tired of the things around you."

"I am tired of the things around me," Saidee said. "Often I've felt like a dead body in a grave with no hope of even a resurrection. What were those lines of Christina Rossetti's I used to say over to myself at first, while it still seemed worth while to revolt? Some one was buried, had been buried for years, yet could think and feel, and cry out against the doom of lying 'under this marble stone, forgotten, alone.' Doesn't it sound agonizing—desperate? It just suited me. But now—now——"

"Are things better? Are you happier?" Victoria clasped her sister passionately.

"No. Only I'm past caring so much. If you've come here, Babe, to take me away, it's no use. I may as well tell you now. This is prison. And you must escape, yourself, before the gaoler comes back, or it will be a life-sentence for you, too."

It warmed Victoria's heart that her sister should call her "Babe"—the old pet name which brought the past back so vividly, that her eyes filled again with tears.

"You shall not be kept in prison!" she exclaimed. "It's monstrous—horrible! I was afraid it would be like this. That's why I had to wait and make plenty of money. Dearest, I'm rich. Everything's for you. You taught me to dance, and it's by dancing I've earned such a lot—almost a fortune. So you see, it's yours. I've got enough to bribe Cassim to let you go, if he likes money, and isn't kind to you. Because, if he isn't kind, it must be a sign he doesn't love you, really."

Saidee laughed, a very bitter laugh. "He does like money. And he doesn't like me at all—any more."

"Then—" Victoria's face brightened—"then he will take the ten thousand dollars I've brought, and he'll let you go away with me."

"Ten thousand dollars!" Saidee laughed again. "Do you know who Cassim—as you call him—is?"

The girl looked puzzled. "Who he is?"

"I see you don't know. The secret's been kept from you, somehow, by his friend who brought you here. You'll tell me how you came; but first I'll answer your question. The Cassim ben Halim you knew, has been dead for eight years."

"They told me so in Algiers. But—do you mean—have you married again?"

"I said the Cassim ben Halim you knew, is dead. The Cassim *I* knew, and know now, is alive—and one of the most important men in Africa, though we live like this, buried among the desert dunes, out of the world—or what you'd think the world."

"My world is where you are," Victoria said.

"Dear little Babe! Mine is a terrible world. You must get out of it as soon as you can, or you'll never get out at all."

"Never till I take you with me."

"Don't say that! I must send you away. I *must*—no matter how hard it may be to part from you," Saidee insisted. "You don't know what you're talking about. How should you? I suppose you must have heard *something*. You must anyhow suspect there's a secret?"

"Yes, Si Maïeddine told me that. He said, when I talked of my sister, and how I was trying to find her, that he'd once known Cassim. I had to agree not to ask questions,—and he would never say for certain whether Cassim was dead or not, but he promised sacredly to bring me to the place where my sister lived. His cousin Lella M'Barka Bent Djellab was with us,—very ill and suffering, but brave. We started from Algiers, and he made a mystery even of the way we came, though I found out the names of some places we passed, like El Aghouat and Ghardaia——"

Saidee's eyes widened with a sudden flash. "What, you came here by El Aghouat and Ghardaia?"

"Yes. Isn't that the best way?"

"The best, if the longest is the best. I don't know much about North Africa geographically. They've taken care I shouldn't know! But I— I've lately found out from—a person who's made the journey, that one can get here from Algiers in a week or eight days. Seventeen hours by train to Biskra: Biskra to Touggourt two long days in a diligence, or carriage with plenty of horses; Touggourt to Oued Tolga on camel or horse, or mule, in three or four days going up and down among the great dunes. You must have been weeks travelling."

"We have. I——"

"How very queer! What could Si Maïeddine's reason have been? Rich Arabs love going by train whenever they can. Men who come from far off to see the marabout always do as much of the journey as possible by rail. I hear things about all important pilgrims. Then why did Si Maïeddine bring you by El Aghouat and Ghardaia—especially when his cousin's an invalid? It couldn't have been just because he didn't want you to be seen, because, as you're dressed like an Arab girl no one could guess he was travelling with a European."

"His father lives near El Aghouat," Victoria reminded her sister. And Maïeddine had used this fact as one excuse, when he admitted that they might have taken a shorter road. But in her heart the girl had guessed why the longest way had been chosen. She did not wish to hide from Saidee things which concerned herself, yet Maïeddine's love was his secret, not hers, therefore she had not meant to tell of it, and she was angry with herself for blushing. She blushed more and more deeply, and Saidee understood.

"I see! He's in love with you. That's why he brought you here. How *clever* of him! How like an Arab!"

For a moment Saidee was silent, thinking intently. It could not be possible, Victoria told herself, that the idea pleased her sister. Yet for an instant the white face lighted up, as if Saidee were relieved of heavy anxiety.

She drew Victoria closer, with an arm round her waist. "Tell me about it," she said. "How you met him, and everything."

The girl knew she would have to tell, since her sister had guessed, but there were many other things which it seemed more important to say and hear first. She longed to hear all, all about Saidee's existence, ever since the letters had stopped; why they had stopped; and whether the reason had anything to do with the mystery about Cassim. Saidee seemed willing to wait, apparently, for details of Victoria's life, since she wanted to begin with the time only a few weeks ago, when Maïeddine had come into it. But the girl would not believe that this meant indifference. They must begin somewhere. Why should not Saidee be curious to hear the end part first, and go back gradually? Saidee's silence had been a torturing mystery for years, whereas about her, her simple past, there was no mystery to clear up.

"Yes," she agreed. "But you promised to tell me about yourself and — and — — "

"I know. Oh, you shall hear the whole story. It will seem like a romance to you, I suppose, because you haven't had to live it, day by day, year by year. It's sordid reality to me — oh, *how* sordid! — most of it. But this about Maïeddine changes everything. I must hear what's happened — quickly — because I shall have to make a plan. It's very important — dreadfully important. I'll explain, when you've told me more. But there's time to order something for you to eat and drink, first, if you're tired and hungry. You must be both, poor child — poor, pretty child! You *are* pretty — lovely. No wonder Maïeddine — but what will you have. Which among our horrid Eastern foods do you hate least?"

"I don't hate any of them. But don't make me eat or drink now, please, dearest. I couldn't. By and by. We rested and lunched this side of the city. I don't feel as if I should ever be hungry again. I'm so — — " Victoria stopped. She could not say: "I am so happy," though she ought to have been able to say that. What was she, then, if not happy? "I'm so excited," she finished.

Saidee stroked the girl's hand, softly. On hers she wore no ring, not even a wedding ring, though Cassim had put one on her finger, European fashion, when she was a bride. Victoria remembered it very well, among the other rings he had given during the short engagement. Now all were gone. But on the third finger of the left hand was the unmistakable mark a ring leaves if worn for many years. The thought passed through Victoria's mind that it could not be long since Saidee had ceased to wear her wedding ring.

"I don't want to be cruel, or frighten you, my poor Babe," she said, "but—you've walked into a trap in coming here, and I've got to try and save you. Thank heaven my husband's away, but we've no time to lose. Tell me quickly about Maïeddine. I've heard a good deal of him, from Cassim, in old days; but tell me all that concerns him and you. Don't skip anything, or I can't judge."

Saidee's manner was feverishly emphatic, but she did not look at Victoria. She watched her own hand moving back and forth, restlessly, from the girl's finger-tips, up the slender, bare wrist, and down again.

Victoria told how she had seen Maïeddine on the boat, coming to Algiers; how he had appeared later at the hotel, and offered to help her, hinting, rather than saying, that he had been a friend of Cassim's, and knew where to find Cassim's wife. Then she went on to the story of the journey through the desert, praising Maïeddine, and hesitating only when she came to the evening of his confession and threat. But Saidee questioned her, and she answered.

"It came out all right, you see," she finished at last. "I knew it must, even in those few minutes when I couldn't help feeling a little afraid, because I seemed to be in his power. But of course I wasn't really. God's power was over his, and he felt it. Things always *do* come out right, if you just *know* they will."

Saidee shivered a little, though her hand on Victoria's was hot. "I wish I could think like that," she half whispered. "If I could, I— —"

"What, dearest?"

"I should be brave, that's all. I've lost my spirit—lost faith, too—as I've lost everything else. I used to be quite a good sort of girl; but what can you expect after ten years shut up in a Mussulman harem? It's something in my favour that they never succeeded in 'converting' me, as they almost always do with a European woman when they've shut her up—just by tiring her out. But they only made me sullen and stupid. I don't believe in anything now. You talk about 'God's power.' He's never helped me. I should think 'things came right' more because Maïeddine felt you couldn't get away from him, then and later, and because he didn't want to offend the marabout, than because God troubled to interfere. Besides, things *haven't* come right. If it weren't for Maïeddine, I might smuggle you away somehow, before the marabout arrives. But now, Maïeddine will be watching us like a lynx—or like an Arab. It's the same thing where women are concerned."

"Why should the marabout care what I do?" asked Victoria. "He's nothing to us, is he?—except that I suppose Cassim must have some high position in his Zaouïa."

"A high position! I forgot, you couldn't know—since Maïeddine hid everything from you. An Arab man never trusts a woman to keep a secret, no matter how much in love he may be. He was evidently afraid you'd tell some one the great secret on the way. But now you're here, he won't care what you find out, because he knows perfectly well that you can never get away."

Victoria started, and turned fully round to stare at her sister with wide, bright eyes. "I can and I will get away!" she exclaimed. "With you. Never without you, of course. That's why I came, as I said. To take you away if you are unhappy. Not all the marabouts in Islam can keep you, dearest, because they have no right over you—and this is the twentieth century, not hundreds of years ago, in the dark ages."

"Hundreds of years in the future, it will still be the dark ages in Islam. And this marabout thinks he *has* a right over me."

"But if you know he hasn't?"

"I'm beginning to know it—beginning to feel it, anyhow. To feel that legally and morally I'm free. But law and morals can't break down walls."

"I believe they can. And if Cassim——"

"My poor child, when Cassim ben Halim died—at a very convenient time for himself—Sidi El Hadj Mohammed ben Abd-el-Kadr appeared to claim this maraboutship, left vacant by the third marabout in the line, an old, old man whose death happened a few weeks before Cassim's. This present marabout was his next of kin—or so everybody believes. And that's the way saintships pass on in Islam, just as titles and estates do in other countries. Now do you begin to understand the mystery?"

"Not quite. I——"

"You heard in Algiers that Cassim had died in Constantinople?"

"Yes. The Governor himself said so."

"The Governor believes so. Every one believes—except a wretched hump-backed idiot in Morocco, who sold his inheritance to save himself trouble, because he didn't want to leave his home, or bother to be a marabout. Perhaps he's dead by this time, in one way or another. I shouldn't be surprised. If he is, Maïeddine and Maïeddine's father, and a few other powerful friends of Cassim's, are the only ones left who know the truth, even a part of it. And the great Sidi El Hadj Mohammed himself."

"Oh, Saidee—Cassim is the marabout!"

"Sh! Now you know the secret that's kept me a prisoner in his house long, long after he'd tired of me, and would have got rid of me if he'd dared—and if he hadn't been afraid in his cruel, jealous way, that I might find a little happiness in my own country. And worse still, it's the secret that will keep you a prisoner, too, unless you make up your mind to do the one thing which can possibly help you."

"What thing?" Victoria could not believe that the answer which darted into her mind was the one Saidee really meant to give.

Saidee's lips opened, but with the girl's eyes gazing straight into hers, it was harder to speak than she had thought. Out of them looked a highly sensitive yet brave spirit, so true, so loving and loyal, that disloyalty to it was a crime—even though another love demanded it.

"I—I hate to tell you," she stammered. "Only, what can I do? If Maïeddine hadn't loved you—but if he hadn't, you wouldn't be here. And being here, we—we must just face the facts. The man who calls himself my husband—I can't think of him as being that any more—is like a king in this country. He has even more power than most kings have nowadays. He'll give you to Maïeddine when he comes home, if Maïeddine asks him, as of course he will. Maïeddine wouldn't have given you up, there in the desert, if he hadn't been sure he could bribe the marabout to do exactly what he wanted."

"But why can't I bribe him?" Victoria persisted, hopefully. "If he's truly tired of you, my money——"

"He'd laugh at you for offering it, and say you might keep it for a *dot*. He's too rich to be tempted with money, unless it was far more than you or I have ever seen. From his oasis alone he has an income of thousands and thousands of dollars; and presents—large ones and small ones—come to him from all over North Africa—from France, even. All the Faithful in the desert, for hundreds of miles around, give him their first and best dates of the year, their first-born camels, their first foals, and lambs, and mules, in return for his blessing on their palms and flocks. He has wonderful rugs, and gold plate, and jewels, more than he knows what to do with, though he's very charitable. He's obliged to be, to keep up his reputation and the reputation of the Zaouïa. Everything depends on that—all his ambitions, which he thinks I hardly know. But I do know. And that's why I know that Maïeddine will be able to bribe him. Not with money: with something Cassim wants and values far more than money. You wouldn't understand what I mean unless I explained a good many things, and it's hardly the time for explaining more now. You must just take what I say for granted, until I can tell you everything by and by. But there are enormous interests mixed up with the marabout's ambitions—things which concern all Africa. Is it likely he'll let you and me go free to tell secrets that would ruin him and his hopes for ever?"

"We wouldn't tell."

"Didn't I say that an Arab never trusts a woman? He'd kill us sooner than let us go. And you've learned nothing about Arab men if you think Maïeddine will give you up and see you walk out of his life after all the trouble he's taken to get you tangled up in it. That's why we've got to look facts in the face. You meant to help me, dear, but you can't. You can only make me miserable, because you've spoiled your happiness for my sake. Poor little Babe, you've wandered far, far out of the zone of happiness, and you can never get back. All you can do is to make the best of a bad bargain."

"I asked you to explain that, but you haven't yet."

"You must—promise Maïeddine what he asks, before Cassim comes back from South Oran."

This was the thing Victoria had feared, but could not believe Saidee would propose. She shrank a little, and Saidee saw it. "Don't misunderstand," the elder woman pleaded in the soft voice which pronounced English almost like a foreign language. "I tell you, we can't choose what we *want* to do, you and I. If you wait for Cassim to be here, it will come to the same thing, but it will be fifty times worse, because then you'll have the humiliation of being forced to do what you might seem to do now of your own free will."

"I can't be forced to marry Maïeddine. Nothing could make me do it. He knows that already, unless — —"

"Unless what? Why do you look horrified?"

"There's one thing I forgot to tell you about our talk in the desert. I promised him I would say 'yes' in case something happened — something I thought then couldn't happen."

"But you find now it could?"

"Oh, no — no, I don't believe it could."

"You'd better tell me what it is."

"That you — I said, I would promise to marry him if *you wished* it. He asked me to promise that, and I did, at once."

A slow colour crept over Saidee's face, up to her forehead. "You trusted me," she murmured.

"And I do now — with all my heart. Only you've lived here, out of the world, alone and sad for so long, that you're afraid of things I'm not afraid of."

"I'm afraid because I know what cause there is for fear. But you're right. My life has made me a coward. I can't help it."

"Yes, you can — I've come to help you help it."

"How little you understand! They'll use you against me, me against you. If you knew I were being tortured, and you could save me by marrying Maïeddine, what would you do?"

Victoria's hand trembled in her sister's, which closed on it nervously. "I would marry him that very minute, of course. But such things don't happen."

"They do. That's exactly what will happen, unless you tell Maïeddine you've made up your mind to say 'yes'. You can explain that it's by my advice. He'll understand. But he'll respect you, and won't be furious at your resistance, and want to revenge himself on you in future, as he will if you wait to be forced into consenting."

Victoria sprang up and walked away, covering her face with her hands. Her sister watched her as if fascinated, and felt sick as she saw how the girl shuddered. It was like watching a trapped bird bleeding to death. But she too was in the trap, she reminded herself. Really, there was no way out, except through Maïeddine. She said this over and over in her mind. There was no other way out. It was not that she was cruel or selfish. She was thinking of her sister's good. There was no doubt of that, she told herself: no doubt whatever.

XXXVII

Victoria felt as if all her blood were beating in her brain. She could not think, and dimly she was glad that Saidee did not speak again. She could not have borne more of those hatefully specious arguments.

For a moment she stood still, pressing her hands over her eyes, and against her temples. Then, without turning, she walked almost blindly to a window that opened upon Saidee's garden. The little court was a silver cube of moonlight, so bright that everything white looked alive with a strange, spiritual intelligence. The scent of the orange blossoms was lusciously sweet. She shrank back, remembering the orange-court at the Caïd's house in Ouargla. It was there that Zorah had prophesied: "Never wilt thou come this way again."

"I'm tired, after all," the girl said dully, turning to Saidee, but leaning against the window frame. "I didn't realize it before. The perfume—won't let me think."

"You look dreadfully white!" exclaimed Saidee. "Are you going to faint? Lie down here on this divan. I'll send for something."

"No, no. Don't send. And I won't faint. But I want to think. Can I go out into the air—not where the orange blossoms are?"

"I'll take you on to the roof," Saidee said. "It's my favourite place—looking over the desert."

She put her arm round Victoria, leading her to the stairway, and so to the roof.

"Are you better?" she asked, miserably. "What can I do for you?"

"Let's not speak for a little while, please. I can think now. Soon I shall be well. Don't be anxious about me, darling."

Very gently she slipped away from Saidee's arm that clasped her waist; and the softness of the young voice, which had been sharp with pain, touched the elder woman. She knew that the girl was thinking more of her, Saidee, than of herself.

Victoria leaned on the white parapet, and looked down over the desert, where the sand rippled in silvery lines and waves, like water in moonlight.

"The golden silence!" she thought.

It was silver now, not golden; but she knew that this was the place of her dream. On a white roof like this, she had seen Saidee stand with eyes shaded from the sun in the west; waiting for her, calling for her, or so she had believed. Poor Saidee! Poor, beautiful Saidee; changed in soul, though so little changed in face! Could it be that she had never called in spirit to her sister?

Victoria bowed her head, and tears fell from her eyes upon her cold bare arms, crossed on the white wall.

Saidee did not want her. Saidee was sorry that she had come. Her coming had only made things worse.

"I wish—" the girl was on the point of saying to herself—"I wish I'd never been born." But before the words shaped themselves fully in her mind—terrible words, because she had felt the beauty and sacred meaning of life—the desert spoke to her.

"Saidee does want you," the spirit of the wind and the glimmering sands seemed to say. "If she had not wanted you, do you think you would have been shown this picture, with your sister in it, the picture which brought you half across the world? She called once, long ago, and you heard the call. You were allowed to hear it. Are you so weak as to believe, just because you're hurt and suffering, that such messages between hearts mean nothing? Saidee may not know that she wants you, but she does, and needs you more than ever before. This is your hour of temptation. You thought everything was going to be wonderfully easy, almost too easy, and instead, it is difficult, that's all. But be brave for Saidee and yourself, now and in days to come, for you are here only just in time."

The pure, strong wind blowing over the dunes was a tonic to Victoria's soul, and she breathed it eagerly. Catching at the robe of faith, she held the spirit fast, and it stayed with her.

Suddenly she felt at peace, sure as a child that she would be taught what to do next. There was her star, floating in the blue lake of the sky, like a water lily, where millions of lesser lilies blossomed.

"Dear star," she whispered, "thank you for coming. I needed you just then."

"Are you better?" asked Saidee in a choked voice.

Victoria turned away from sky and desert to the drooping figure of the woman, standing in a pool of shadow, dark as fear and treachery.

"Yes, dearest one, I am well again, and I won't have to worry you any more." The girl gently wound two protecting arms round her sister.

"What have you decided to do?"

Victoria could feel Saidee's heart beating against her own.

"I've decided to pray about deciding, and then to decide. Whatever's best for you, I will do, I promise."

"And for yourself. Don't forget that I'm thinking of you. Don't believe it's *all* cowardice."

"I don't believe anything but good of my Saidee."

"I envy you, because you think you've got Someone to pray to. I've nothing. I'm—alone in the dark."

Victoria made her look up at the moon which flooded the night with a sea of radiance. "There is no dark," she said. "We're together—in the light."

"How hopeful you are!" Saidee murmured. "I've left hope so far behind, I've almost forgotten what it's like."

"Maybe it's always been hovering just over your shoulder, only you forgot to turn and see. It can't be gone, because I feel sure that truth and knowledge and hope are all one."

"I wonder if you'll still feel so when you've married a man of another race—as I have?"

Victoria did not answer. She had to conquer the little cold thrill of superstitious fear which crept through her veins, as Saidee's words reminded her of M'Barka's sand-divining. She had to find courage again from "her star," before she could speak.

"Forgive me, Babe!" said Saidee, stricken by the look in the lifted eyes. "I wish I needn't remind you of anything horrid to-night—your first night with me after all these years. But we have so little time. What else can I do?"

"I shall know by to-morrow what we are to do," Victoria said cheerfully. "Because I shall take counsel of the night."

"You're a very odd girl," the woman reflected aloud. "When you were a tiny thing, you used to have the weirdest thoughts, and do the quaintest things. I was sure you'd grow up to be absolutely different from any other human being. And so you have, I think. Only an extraordinary sort of girl could ever have made her way without help from Potterston, Indiana, to Oued Tolga in North Africa."

"I *had* help—every minute. Saidee—did you think of me sometimes, when you were standing here on this roof?"

"Yes, of course I thought of you often—only not so often lately as at first, because for a long time now I've been numb. I haven't thought much or cared much about anything, or—or any one except——"

"Except——"

"Except—except myself, I'm afraid." Saidee's face was turned away from Victoria's. She looked toward Oued Tolga, the city, whither the carrier-pigeon had flown.

"I wondered," she went on hastily, "what had become of you, and if you were happy, and whether by this time you'd nearly forgotten me. You were such a baby child when I left you!"

"I won't believe you really wondered if I could forget. You, and thoughts of you, have made my whole life. I was just living for the time when I could earn money enough to search for you—and preparing for it, of course, so as to be ready when it came."

Saidee still looked toward Oued Tolga, where the white domes shimmered, far away in the moonlight, like a mirage. Was love a mirage, too?—the love that called for her over there, the love whose voice made the strings of her heart vibrate, though she had thought them broken and silent for ever. Victoria's arms round her felt strong and warm, yet they were a barrier. She was afraid of the barrier, and afraid of the girl's passionate loyalty. She did not deserve it, she knew, and she would be more at ease—she could not say happier, because there was no such word as happiness for her—without it. Somehow she could not bear to talk of Victoria's struggle to come to her rescue. The thought of all the girl had done made her feel unable to live up to it, or be grateful. She did not want to be called upon to live up to any standard. She wanted—if she wanted anything—simply to go on blindly, as fate led. But she felt that near her fate hovered, like the carrier-pigeon; and some terrible force within herself, which frightened her, seemed ready to push away or destroy anything that might come between her and that fate. She knew that she ought to question Victoria about the past years of their separation, one side of her nature was eager to hear the story. But the other side, which had gained strength lately, forced her to dwell upon less intimate things.

"I suppose Mrs. Ray managed to keep most of poor father's money?" she said.

"Mrs. Ray died when I was fourteen, and after that Mr. Potter lost everything in speculation," the girl answered.

"Everything of yours, too?"

"Yes. But it didn't matter, except for the delay. My dancing—*your* dancing really, dearest, because if it hadn't been for you I shouldn't have put my heart into it so—earned me all I needed."

"I said you were extraordinary! But how queer it seems to hear those names again. Mrs. Ray. Mr. Potter. They're like names in a dream. How wretched I used to think myself, with Mrs. Ray in Paris, when she was so jealous and cross! But a thousand times since, I've wished myself back in those days. I was happy, really. I was free. Life was all before me."

"Dearest! But surely you weren't miserable from the very first, with—with Cassim?"

"No-o. I suppose I wasn't. I was in love with him. It seemed very interesting to be the wife of such a man. Even when I found that he meant to make me lead the life of an Arab woman, shut up and veiled, I liked him too well to mind much. He put it in such a romantic way, telling me how he worshipped me, how mad with jealousy he was even to think of other men seeing my face, and falling in love with it. He thought every one must fall in love! All girls like men to be jealous—till they find out how sordid jealousy can be. And I was so young—a child. I felt as if I were living in a wonderful Eastern poem. Cassim used to give me the most gorgeous presents, and our house in Algiers was beautiful. My garden was a dream—and how he made love to me in it! Besides, I was allowed to go out, veiled. It was rather fun being veiled—in those days, I thought so. It made me feel mysterious, as if life were a masquerade ball. And the Arab women Cassim let me know—a very few, wives and sisters of his friends—envied me immensely. I loved that—I was so silly. And they flattered me, asking about my life in Europe. I was like a fairy princess among them, until—one day—a woman told me a thing about Cassim. She told me because she was spiteful and wanted to make me miserable, of course, for I found out afterwards she'd been expressly forbidden to speak, on account of my 'prejudices'—they'd all been forbidden. I wouldn't believe at first,— but it was true—the others couldn't deny it. And to prove what she said, the woman took me to see the boy, who was with his grandmother—an aunt of Maïeddine's, dead now."

"The boy?"

"Oh, I forgot. I haven't explained. The thing she told was, that Cassim had a wife living when he married me."

"Saidee!—how horrible! How horrible!"

"Yes, it was horrible. It broke my heart." Saidee was tingling with excitement now. Her stiff, miserable restraint was gone in the feverish satisfaction of speaking out those things which for years had corroded her mind, like verdigris. She had never been able to talk to anyone in this way, and her only relief had been in putting her thoughts on paper. Some of the books in her locked cupboard she had given to a friend, the writer of to-day's letter, because she had seen him only for a few minutes at a time, and had been able to say very little, on the one occasion when they had spoken a few words to each other. She had wanted him to know what a martyrdom her life had been. Involuntarily she talked to her sister, now, as she would have talked to him, and his face rose clearly before her eyes, more clearly almost than Victoria's, which her own shadow darkened, and screened from the light of the moon as they stood together, clasped in one another's arms.

"Cassim thought it all right, of course," she went on. "A Mussulman may have four wives at a time if he likes—though men of his rank don't, as a rule, take more than one, because they must marry women of high birth, who hate rivals in their own house. But he was too clever to give me a hint of his real opinions in Paris. He knew I wouldn't have looked at him again, if he had—even if he hadn't told me about the wife herself. She had had this boy, and gone out of her mind afterwards, so she wasn't living with Cassim—that was the excuse he made when I taxed him with deceiving me. Her father and mother had taken her back. I don't know surely whether she's living or dead, but I believe she's dead, and her body buried beside the grave supposed to be Cassim's. Anyhow, the boy's living, and he's the one thing on earth Cassim loves better than himself."

"When did you find out about—about all this?" Victoria asked, almost whispering.

"Eight months after we were married I heard about his wife. I think Cassim was true to me, in his way, till that time. But we had an awful scene. I told him I'd never live with him again as his wife, and I never have. After that day, everything was different. No more happiness— not even an Arab woman's idea of happiness. Cassim began to hate me, but with the kind of hate that holds and won't let go. He wouldn't listen when I begged him to set me free. Instead, he wouldn't let me go out at all, or see anyone, or receive or send letters. He punished me by flirting outrageously with a pretty woman, the wife of a French officer. He took pains that I should hear everything, through my servants. But his cruelty was visited on his own head, for soon there came a dreadful scandal. The woman died suddenly of chloral poisoning, after a quarrel with her husband on Cassim's account, and it was thought she'd taken too much of the drug on purpose. The day after his wife's death, the officer shot himself. I think he was a colonel; and every one knew that Cassim was mixed up in the affair. He had to leave the army, and it seemed—he thought so himself—that his career was ruined. He sold his place in Algiers, and took me to a farm-house in the country where we lived for a while, and he was so lonely and miserable he would have been glad to make up, but how could I forgive him? He'd deceived me too horribly—and besides, in my own eyes I wasn't his wife. Surely our marriage wouldn't be considered legal in any country outside Islam, would it? Even you, a child like you, must see that?"

"I suppose so," Victoria answered, sadly. "But——"

"There's no 'but.' I thought so then. I think so a hundred times more now. My life's been a martyrdom. No one could blame me if—but I was telling you about what happened after Algiers. There was a kind of armed truce between us in the country, though we lived only like two acquaintances under the same roof. For months he had nobody else to talk to, so he used to talk with me—quite freely sometimes, about a plan some powerful Arabs, friends of his—Maïeddine and his father among others—were making for him. It sounded like a fairy story, and I used to think he must be going mad. But he wasn't. It was all true about the plot that was being worked. He knew I couldn't betray him, so it was a relief to his mind, in his nervous excitement, to confide in me."

"Was it a plot against the French?"

"Indirectly. That was one reason it appealed to Cassim. He'd been proud of his position in the army, and being turned out, or forced to go—much the same thing—made him hate France and everything French. He'd have given his life for revenge, I'm sure. Probably that's why his friends were so anxious to put him in a place of power, for they were men whose watchword was 'Islam for Islam.' Their hope was—and is—to turn France out of North Africa. You wouldn't believe how many there are who hope and band themselves together for that. These friends of Cassim's persuaded and bribed a wretched cripple—who was next of kin to the last marabout, and ought to have inherited—to let Cassim take his place. Secretly, of course. It was a very elaborate plot—it had to be. Three or four rich, important men were in it, and it would have meant ruin if they'd been found out.

"Cassim would really have come next in succession if it hadn't been for the hunchback, who lived in Morocco, just over the border. If he had any conscience, I suppose that thought soothed it. He told me that the real heir—the cripple—had epileptic fits, and couldn't live long, anyhow. The way they worked their plan out was by Cassim's starting for a pilgrimage to Mecca. I had to go away with him, because he was afraid to leave me. I knew too much. And it was simpler to take me than to put me out of the way."

"Saidee—he would never have murdered you?" Victoria whispered.

"He would if necessary—I'm sure of it. But it was safer not. Besides, I'd often told him I wanted to die, so that was an incentive to keep me alive. I didn't go to Mecca. I left the farm-house with Cassim, and he took me to South Oran, where he is now. I had to stay in the care of a marabouta, a terrible old woman, a bigot and a tyrant, a cousin of Cassim's, on his mother's side, and a sister of the man who invented the whole plot. The idea was that Cassim should seem to be drowned in the Bosphorus, while staying at Constantinople with friends, after his pilgrimage to Mecca. But luckily for him there was a big fire in the hotel where he went to stop for the first night, so he just disappeared, and a lot of trouble was saved. He told me about the adventure, when he came to Oran. The next move was to Morocco. And from Morocco he travelled here, in place of the cripple, when the last marabout died, and the heir was called to his inheritance. That was nearly eight years ago."

"And he's never been found out?"

"No. And he never will be. He's far too clever. Outwardly he's hand in glove with the French. High officials and officers come here to consult with him, because he's known to have immense influence all over the South, and in the West, even in Morocco. He's masked, like a Touareg, and the French believe it's because of a vow he made in Mecca. No one but his most intimate friends, or his own people, have ever seen the face of Sidi Mohammed since he inherited the maraboutship, and came to Oued Tolga. He must hate wearing his mask, for he's as handsome as he ever was, and just as vain. But it's worth the sacrifice. Not only is he a great man, with everything—or nearly everything—he wants in the world, but he looks forward to a glorious revenge against the French, whose interests he pretends to serve."

"How can he revenge himself? What power has he to do that?" the girl asked. She had a strange impression that Saidee had forgotten her, that all this talk of the past, and of the marabout, was for some one else of whom her sister was thinking.

"He has tremendous power," Saidee answered, almost angrily, as if she resented the doubt. "All Islam is at his back. The French humour him, and let him do whatever he likes, no matter how eccentric his ways may be, because he's got them to believe he is trying to help the Government in the wildest part of Algeria, the province of Oran—and with the Touaregs in the farthest South; and that he promotes French interests in Morocco. Really, he's at the head of every religious secret society in North Africa, banded together to turn Christians out of Mussulman countries. The French have no idea how many such secret societies exist, and how rich and powerful they are. Their dear friend, the good, wise, polite marabout assures them that rumours of that sort are nonsense. But some day, when everything's ready — when Morocco and Oran and Algeria and Tunisia will obey the signal, all together, then they'll have a surprise — and Cassim ben Halim will be revenged."

"It sounds like the weavings of a brain in a dream," Victoria said.

"It will be a nightmare-dream, no matter how it ends; — maybe a nightmare of blood, and war, and massacre. Haven't you ever heard, or read, how the Mussulman people expect a saviour, the Moul Saa, as they call him — the Man of the Hour, who will preach a Holy War, and lead it himself, to victory?"

"Yes, I've read that — —"

"Well, Cassim hopes to be the Moul Saa, and deliver Islam by the sword. I suppose you wonder how I know such secrets, or whether I do really know them at all. But I do. Some things Cassim told me himself, because he was bursting with vanity, and simply had to speak. Other things I've seen in writing — he would kill me if he found out. And still other things I've guessed. Why, the boys here in the Zaouïa are being brought up for the 'great work,' as they call it. Not all of them — but the most important ones among the older boys. They have separate classes. Something secret and mysterious is taught them. There are boys from Morocco and Oran, and sons of Touareg chiefs — all those who most hate Christians. No other zaouïa is like this. The place seethes with hidden treachery and sedition. Now you can see where Si Maïeddine's power over Cassim comes in. The Agha, his father, is one of the few who helped make Cassim what he is, but he's a cautious old man, the kind who wants to run with the hare and hunt with the hounds. Si Maïeddine's cautious too, Cassim has said. He approves the doctrines of the secret societies, but he's so ambitious that without a very strong incentive to turn against them, in act he'd be true to the French. Well, now he has the incentive. You."

"I don't understand," said Victoria. Yet even as she spoke, she began to understand.

"He'll offer to give himself, and to influence the Agha and the Agha's people — the Ouled-Sirren — if Cassim will grant his wish. And it's no use saying that Cassim can't force you to marry any man. You told me yourself, a little while ago, that if you saw harm coming to me — —"

"Oh don't—don't speak of that again, Saidee!" the girl cried, sharply. "I've told you—yes—that I'll do anything—anything on earth to save you pain, or more sorrow. But let's hope—let's pray."

"There is no hope. I've forgotten how to pray," Saidee answered, "and God has forgotten me."

XXXVIII

There was no place for a guest in that part of the marabout's house which had been allotted to Saidee. She had her bedroom and reception-room, her roof terrace, and her garden court. On the ground floor her negresses lived, and cooked for their mistress and themselves. She did not wish to have Victoria with her, night and day, and so she had quietly directed Noura to make up a bed in the room which would have been her boudoir, if she had lived in Europe. When the sisters came down from the roof, the bed was ready.

In the old time Victoria had slept with her sister; and her greatest happiness as a child had been the "bed-talks," when Saidee had whispered her secret joys or troubles, and confided in the little girl as if she had been a "grown-up."

Hardly a night had passed since their parting, that Victoria had not thought of those talks, and imagined herself again lying with her head on Saidee's arm, listening to stories of Saidee's life. She had taken it for granted that she would be put in her sister's room, and seeing the bed made up, and her luggage unpacked in the room adjoining, was a blow. She knew that Saidee must have given orders, or these arrangements would not have been made, and again she felt the dreadful sinking of the heart which had crushed her an hour ago. Saidee did not want her. Saidee was sorry she had come, and meant to keep her as far off as possible. But the girl encouraged herself once more. Saidee might think now that she would rather have been left alone. But she was mistaken. By and by she would find out the truth, and know that they needed each other.

"I thought you'd be more comfortable here, than crowded in with me," Saidee explained, blushing faintly.

"Yes, thank you, dear," said Victoria quietly. She did not show her disappointment, and seemed to take the matter for granted, as if she had expected nothing else; but the talk on the roof had brought back something into Saidee's heart which she could not keep out, though she did not wish to admit it there. She was sorry for Victoria, sorry for herself, and more miserable than ever. Her nerves were rasped by an intolerable irritation as she looked at the girl, and felt that her thoughts were being read. She had a hideous feeling, almost an impression, that her face had been lifted off like a mask, and that the workings of her brain were open to her sister's eyes, like the exposed mechanism of a clock.

"Noura has brought some food for you," she went on hastily. "You must eat a little, before you go to bed—to please me."

"I will," Victoria assured her. "You mustn't worry about me at all."

"You'll go to sleep, won't you?—or would you rather talk—while you're eating, perhaps?"

The girl looked at the woman, and saw that her nerves were racked; that she wanted to go, but did not wish her sister to guess.

"You've talked too much already," Victoria said. "The surprise of my coming gave you a shock. Now you must rest and get over it, so you can be strong for to-morrow. Then we'll make up our minds about everything."

"There's only one way to make up our minds," Saidee insisted, dully.

Victoria did not protest. She kissed her sister good-night, and gently refused help from Noura. Then Saidee went away, followed by the negress, who softly closed the door between the two rooms. Her mistress had not told her to do this, but when it was done, she did not say, "Open the door." Saidee was glad that it was shut, because she felt that she could think more freely. She could not bear the idea that her thoughts and life were open to the criticism of those young, blue eyes, which the years since childhood had not clouded. Nevertheless, when Noura had undressed her, and she was alone, she saw Victoria's eyes looking at her sweetly, sadly, with yearning, yet with no reproach. She saw them as clearly as she had seen a man's face, a few hours earlier; and now his was dim, as Victoria's face had been dim when his was clear.

It was dark in the room, except for the moon-rays which streamed through the lacelike open-work of stucco, above the shuttered windows, making jewelled patterns on the wall—pink, green, and golden, according to the different colours of the glass. There was just enough light to reflect these patterns faintly in the mirrors set in the closed door, opposite which Saidee lay in bed; and to her imagination it was as if she could see through the door, into a lighted place beyond. She wondered if Victoria had gone to bed; if she were sleeping, or if she were crying softly—crying her heart out with bitter grief and disappointment she would never confess.

Victoria had always been like that, even as a little girl. If Saidee did anything to hurt her, she made no moan. Sometimes Saidee had teased her on purpose, or tried to make her jealous, just for fun.

As memories came crowding back, the woman buried her face in the pillow, striving with all her might to shut them out. What was the use of making herself wretched? Victoria ought to have come long, long ago, or not at all.

But the blue eyes would look at her, even when her own were shut; and always there was the faint light in the mirror, which seemed to come through the door.

At last Saidee could not longer lie still. She had to get up and open the door, to see what her sister was really doing. Very softly she turned the handle, for she hoped that by this time Victoria was asleep; but as she pulled the door noiselessly towards her, and peeped into the next room, she saw that one of the lamps was burning. Victoria had not yet gone to bed. She was kneeling beside it, saying her prayers, with her back towards the door.

So absorbed was she in praying, and so little noise had Saidee made, that the girl heard nothing. She remained motionless on her knees, not knowing that Saidee was looking at her.

A sharp pain shot through the woman's heart. How many times had she softly opened their bedroom door, coming home late after a dance, to find her little sister praying, a small, childish form in a long white nightgown, with quantities of curly red hair pouring over its shoulders!

Sometimes Victoria had gone to sleep on her knees, and Saidee had waked her up with a kiss.

Just as she had looked then, so she looked now, except that the form in the long, white nightgown was that of a young girl, not a child. But the thick waves of falling hair made it seem childish.

"She is praying for me," Saidee thought; and dared not close the door tightly, lest Victoria should hear. By and by it could be done, when the light was out, and the girl dropped asleep.

Meanwhile, she tiptoed back to her bed, and sat on the edge of it, to wait. At last the thread of light, fine as a red-gold hair, vanished from the door; but as it disappeared a line of moonlight was drawn in silver along the crack. Victoria must have left her windows wide open, or there would not have been light enough to paint this gleaming streak.

Saidee sat on her bed for nearly half an hour, trying to concentrate her thoughts on the present and future, yet unable to keep them from flying back to the past, the long-ago past, which lately had seemed unreal, as if she had dreamed it; the past when she and Victoria had been all the world to each other.

There was no sound in the next room, and when Saidee was weary of her strained position, she crossed the floor on tiptoe again, to shut the door. But she could not resist a temptation to peep in.

It was as she had expected. Victoria had left the inlaid cedar-wood shutters wide open, and through the lattice of old wrought-iron, moonlight streamed. The room was bright with a silvery twilight, like a mysterious dawn; but because the bed-linen and the embroidered silk coverlet were white, the pale radiance focused round the girl, who lay asleep in a halo of moonbeams.

"She looks like an angel," Saidee thought, and with a curious mingling of reluctance and eagerness, moved softly toward the bed, her little velvet slippers from Tunis making no sound on the thick rugs.

Very well the older woman remembered an engaging trick of the child's, a way of sleeping with her cheek in her hand, and her hair spread out like a golden coverlet for the pillow. Just so she was lying now; and in the moonlight her face was a child's face, the face of the dear, little, loving child of ten years ago. Like this Victoria had lain when her sister crept into their bedroom in the Paris flat, the night before the wedding, and Saidee had waked her by crying on her eyelids. Cassim's unhappy wife recalled the clean, sweet, warm smell of the child's hair when she had buried her face in it that last night together. It had smelled like grape-leaves in the hot sun.

"If you don't come back to me, I'll follow you all across the world," the little girl had said. Now, she had kept her promise. Here she was— and the sister to whom she had come, after a thousand sacrifices, was wishing her back again at the other end of the world, was planning to get rid of her.

Suddenly, it was as if the beating of Saidee's heart broke a tight band of ice which had compressed it. A fountain of tears sprang from her eyes. She fell on her knees beside the bed, crying bitterly.

"Childie, childie, comfort me, forgive me!" she sobbed.

Victoria woke instantly. She opened her eyes, and Saidee's wet face was close to hers. The girl said not a word, but wrapped her arms round her sister, drawing the bowed head on to her breast, and then she crooned lovingly over it, with little foolish mumblings, as she used to do in Paris when Mrs. Ray's unkindness had made Saidee cry.

"Can you forgive me?" the woman faltered, between sobs.

"Darling, as if there were anything to forgive!" The clasp of the girl's arms tightened. "Now we're truly together again. How I love you! How happy I am!"

"Don't—I don't deserve it," Saidee stammered. "Poor little Babe! I was cruel to you. And you'd come so far."

"You weren't cruel!" Victoria contradicted her, almost fiercely.

"I was. I was jealous—jealous of you. You're so young and beautiful—just what I was ten years ago, only better and prettier. You're what I can never be again—what I'd give the next ten years to be. Everything's over with me. I'm old—old!"

"You're not to say such things," cried Victoria, horrified. "You weren't jealous. You——"

"I was. I am now. But I want to confess. You must let me confess, if you're to help me."

"Dearest, tell me anything—everything you choose, but nothing you don't choose. And nothing you say can make me love you less—only more."

"There's a great deal to tell," Saidee said, heavily "And I'm tired—sick at heart. But I can't rest now, till I've told you."

"Wouldn't you come into bed?" pleaded Victoria humbly. "Then we could talk, the way we used to talk."

Saidee staggered up from her knees, and the girl almost lifted her on to the bed. Then she covered her with the thyme-scented linen sheet, and the silk coverlet under which she herself lay. For a moment they were quite still, Saidee lying with her head on Victoria's arm. But at last she said, in a whisper, as if her lips were dry: "Did you know I was sorry you'd come?"

"I knew you thought you were sorry," the girl answered. "Yet I hoped that you'd find out you weren't, really. I prayed for you to find out— soon."

"Did you guess why I was sorry?"

"Not—quite."

"I told you I—that it was for your sake."

"Yes."

"Didn't you believe it?"

"I—felt there was something else, beside."

"There was!" Saidee confessed. "You know now—at least you know part. I was jealous. I am still—but I'm ashamed of myself. I'm sick with shame. And I do love you!"

"Of course—of course you do, darling."

"But—there's somebody else I love. A man. And I couldn't bear to think he might see you, because you're so much younger and fresher than I."

"You mean—Cassim?"

"No. Not Cassim."

Silence fell between the two. Victoria did not speak; and suddenly Saidee was angry with her for not speaking.

"If you're shocked, I won't go on," she said. "You can't help me by preaching."

"I'm not shocked," the girl protested. "Only sorry—so sorry. And even if I wanted to preach, I don't know how."

"There's nothing to be shocked about," Saidee said, her tears dry, her voice hard as it had been at first. "I've seen him three times. I've talked with him just once. But we love each other. It's the first and only real love of my life. I was too young to know, when I met Cassim. That was a fascination. I was in love with romance. He carried me off my feet, in spite of myself."

"Then, dearest Saidee, don't let yourself be carried off your feet a second time."

"Why not?" Saidee asked, sharply. "What incentive have I to be true to Cassim?"

"I'm not thinking about Cassim. I'm thinking of you. All one's world goes to pieces so, if one isn't true to oneself."

"*He* says I can't be true to myself if I stay here. He doesn't consider that I'm Cassim's wife. I *thought* myself married, but was I, when he had a wife already? Would any lawyer, or even clergyman, say it was a legal marriage?"

"Perhaps not," Victoria admitted. "But——"

"Just wait, before you go on arguing," Saidee broke in hotly, "until I've told you something you haven't heard yet. Cassim has another wife now—a lawful wife, according to his views, and the views of his people. He's had her for a year. She's a girl of the Ouled Naïl tribe, brought up to be a dancer. But Cassim saw her at Touggourt, where he'd gone on one of his mysterious visits. He doesn't dream that I know the whole history of the affair, but I do, and have known, since a few days after the creature was brought here as his bride. She's as ignorant and silly as a kitten, and only a child in years. She told her 'love story' to one of her negresses, who told Noura—who repeated it to me. Perhaps I oughtn't to have listened, but why not?"

Victoria did not answer. The clouds round Saidee and herself were dark, but she was trying to see the blue beyond, and find the way into it, with her sister.

"She's barely sixteen now, and she's been here a year," Saidee went on. "She hadn't begun to dance yet, when Cassim saw her, and took her away from Touggourt. Being a great saint is very convenient. A marabout can do what he likes, you know. Mussulmans are forbidden to touch alcohol, but if a marabout drinks wine, it turns to milk in his throat. He can fly, if he wants to. He can even make

French cannon useless, and withdraw the bullets from French guns, in case of war, if the spirit of Allah is with him. So by marrying a girl brought up for a dancer, daughter of generations of dancing women, he washes all disgrace from her blood, and makes her a female saint, worthy to live eternally. The beautiful Miluda's a marabouta, if you please, and when her baby is taken out by the negress who nurses it, silly, bigoted people kneel and kiss its clothing."

"She has a baby!" murmured Victoria.

"Yes, only a girl, but better than nothing—and she hopes to be more fortunate next time. She isn't jealous of me, because I've no children, not even a girl, and because for that reason Cassim could repudiate me if he chose. She little knows how desperately I wish he would. She believes—Noura says—that he keeps me here only because I have no people to go to, and he's too kind-hearted to turn me out alone in the world, when my youth's past. You see—she thinks me already old— at twenty-eight! Of course the real reason that Cassim shuts me up and won't let me go, is because he knows I could ruin not only him, but the hopes of his people. Miluda doesn't dream that I'm of so much importance in his eyes. The only thing she's jealous of is the boy, Mohammed, who's at school in the town of Oued Tolga, in charge of an uncle. Cassim guesses how Miluda hates the child, and I believe that's the reason he daren't have him here. He's afraid something might happen, although the excuse he makes is, that he wants his boy to learn French, and know something of French ways. That pleases the Government—and as for the Arabs, no doubt he tells them it's only a trick to keep French eyes shut to what's really going on, and to his secret plans. Now, do you still say I ought to consider myself married to Cassim, and refuse to take any happiness if I can get it?"

"The thing is, what would make you happy?" Victoria said, as if thinking aloud.

"Love, and life. All that women in Europe have, and take for granted," Saidee answered passionately.

"How could it come to you?" the girl asked.

"I would go to it, and find it with the man who's ready to risk his life to save me from this hateful prison, and carry me far away. Now, I've told you everything, exactly as it stands. That's why I was sorry you came, just when I was almost ready to risk the step. I was sure you'd be horrified if you found out, and want to stop me. Besides, if he should see you—but I won't say that again. I know you wouldn't try to take him away from me, even if you tried to take me from him. I don't know why I've told you, instead of keeping the whole thing secret as I made up my mind to do at first. Nothing's changed. I can't save you from Maïeddine, but—there's one difference. I *would* save you if I could. Just at first, I was so anxious for you to be out of the way of my happiness—the chance of it—that the only thing I longed for was that you should be gone."

Victoria choked back a sob that rose in her throat, but Saidee felt, rather than heard it, as she lay with her burning head on the girl's arm.

"I don't feel like that now," she said. "I peeped in and saw you praying—perhaps for me—and you looked just as you used, when you were a little girl. Then, when I came in, and you were asleep, I—I couldn't stand it. I broke down. I love you, dear little Babe. The ice is gone out of my heart. You've melted it. I'm a woman again; but just because I'm a woman, I won't give up my other love to please you or any one. I tell you that, honestly."

Victoria made no reply for a moment, though Saidee waited defiantly, expecting a protest or an argument. Then, at last, the girl said: "Will you tell me something about this man?"

Saidee was surprised to receive encouragement. It was a joy to speak of the subject that occupied all her thoughts, and wonderful to have a confidante.

"He's a captain in the Chasseurs d'Afrique," she said. "But he's not with his regiment. He's an expert in making desert wells, and draining marshes. That's the business which has brought him to the far South, now. He's living at Oued Tolga—the town, I mean; not the Zaouïa. A well had to be sunk in the village, and he was superintending. I watched him from my roof, though it was too far off to see his face. I don't know exactly what made me do it—I suppose it was Fate, for Cassim says we all have our fate hung round our necks—but when I went to the Moorish bath, between here and the village, I let my veil blow away from my face as I passed close to him and his party of workers. No one else saw, except he. It was only for a second or two, but we looked straight into each other's eyes; and there was something in his that seemed to draw my soul out of me. It was as if, in that instant, I told him with a look the whole tragedy of my life. And his soul sprang to mine. There was never anything like it. You can't imagine what I felt, Babe."

"Yes. I—think I can," Victoria whispered, but Saidee hardly heard, so deeply was she absorbed in the one sweet memory of many years.

"It was in the morning," the elder woman went on, "but it was hot, and the sun was fierce as it beat down on the sand. He had been working, and his face was pale from the heat. It had a haggard look under brown sunburn. But when our eyes met, a flush like a girl's rushed up to his forehead. You never saw such a light in human eyes! They were illuminated as if a fire from his heart was lit behind them. I knew he had fallen in love with me—that something would happen: that my life would never be the same again.

"The next time I went to the bath, he was there; and though I held my veil, he looked at me with the same wonderful look, as if he could see through it. I felt that he longed to speak, but of course he could not. It would have meant my ruin.

"In the baths, there's an old woman named Bakta—an attendant. She always comes to me when I go there. She's a great character—knows everything that happens in every house, as if by magic; and loves to talk. But she can keep secrets. She is a match-maker for all the neighbourhood. When there's a young man of Oued Tolga, or of any village round about, who wants a wife, she lets him know which girl who comes to the baths is the youngest and most beautiful. Or if a wife is in love with some one, Bakta contrives to bring letters from him, and smuggle them to the young woman while she's at the Moorish bath. Well, that day she gave me a letter—a beautiful letter.

"I didn't answer it; but next time I passed, I opened my veil and smiled to show that I thanked him. Because he had laid his life at my feet. If there was anything he could do for me, he would do it, without hope of reward, even if it meant death. Then Bakta gave me another letter. I couldn't resist answering, and so it's gone on, until I seem to know this man, Honoré Sabine, better than any one in the world; though we've only spoken together once."

"How did you manage it?" Victoria asked the question mechanically, for she felt that Saidee expected it of her.

"Bakta managed, and Noura helped. He came dressed like an Arab woman, and pretended to be old and lame, so that he could crouch down and use a stick as he walked, to disguise his height. Bakta waited—and we had no more than ten minutes to say everything. Ten hours wouldn't have been enough!—but we were in danger every instant, and he was afraid of what might happen to me, if we were spied upon. He begged me to go with him then, but I dared not. I couldn't decide. Now he writes to me, and he's making a cypher, so that if the letters should be intercepted, no one could read them. Then he hopes to arrange a way of escape if—if I say I'll do what he asks."

"Which, of course, you won't," broke in Victoria. "You couldn't, even though it were only for his sake alone, if you really love him. You'd be too unhappy afterwards, knowing that you'd ruined his career in the army."

"I'm more to him than a thousand careers!" Saidee flung herself away from the girl's arm. "I see now," she went on angrily, "what you were leading up to, when you pretended to sympathize. You were waiting for a chance to try and persuade me that I'm a selfish wretch. I may be selfish, but—it's as much for his happiness as mine. It's just as I thought it would be. You're puritanical. You'd rather see me die, or go mad in this prison, than have me do a thing that's unconventional, according to your schoolgirl ideas."

"I came to take you out of prison," said Victoria.

"And you fell into it yourself!" Saidee retorted quickly. "You broke the spring of the door, and it will be harder than ever to open. But"—her voice changed from reproach to persuasion—"Honoré might save us both. If only you wouldn't try to stop my going with him, you might go too. Then you wouldn't have to marry Maïeddine. There's a chance—just a chance. For heaven's sake do all you can to help, not to hinder. Don't you see, now that you're here, there are a hundred more reasons why I must say 'yes' to Captain Sabine?"

"If I did see that, I'd want to die now, this minute," Victoria answered.

"How cruel you are! How cruel a girl can be to a woman. You pretend that you came to help me, and the one only thing you can do, you refuse to do. You say you want to get me away. I tell you that you can't—and you can't get yourself away. Perhaps Honoré can do what you can't, but you'll try to prevent him."

"If I *could* get you away, would you give him up—until you were free to go to him without spoiling both your lives?"

"What do you mean?" Saidee asked.

"Please answer my question."

Saidee thought for a moment. "Yes. I would do that. But what's the use of talking about it? You! A poor little mouse caught in a trap!"

"A mouse once gnawed a net, and set free a whole lion," said Victoria. "Give me a chance to think, that's all I ask, except— except—that you love me meanwhile. Oh, darling, don't be angry, will you? I can't bear it, if you are."

Saidee laid her head on the girl's arm once more, and they kissed each other.

XXXIX

Maïeddine did not try to see Victoria, or send her any message.

In spite of M'Barka's vision in the sand, and his own superstition, he was sure now that nothing could come between him and his wish. The girl was safe in the marabout's house, to which he had brought her, and it was impossible for her to get away without his help, even if she were willing to go, and leave the sister whom she had come so far to find. Maïeddine knew what he could offer the marabout, and knew that the marabout would willingly pay even a higher price than he meant to ask.

He lived in the guest-house, and had news sometimes from his cousin Lella M'Barka in her distant quarters. She was tired, but not ill, and the two sisters were very kind to her.

So three days passed, and the doves circled and moaned round the minaret of the Zaouïa mosque, and were fed at sunset on the white roof, by hands hidden from all eyes save eyes of birds.

On the third day there was great excitement at Oued Tolga. The marabout, Sidi El Hadj Mohammed ben Abd el Kadr, came home, and was met on the way by many people from the town and the Zaouïa.

His procession was watched by women on many roofs—with reverent interest by some; with joy by one woman who was his wife; with fear and despair by another, who had counted on his absence for a few days longer. And Victoria stood beside her sister, looking out over the golden silence towards the desert city of Oued Tolga, with a pair of modern field-glasses sent to her by Si Maïeddine.

Maïeddine himself went out to meet the marabout, riding El Biod, and conscious of unseen eyes that must be upon him. He was a notable figure among the hundreds which poured out of town, and villages, and Zaouïa, in honour of the great man's return; the noblest of all the desert men in floating white burnouses, who rode or walked, with the sun turning their dark faces to bronze, their eyes to gleaming jewels. But even Maïeddine himself became insignificant as the procession from the Zaouïa was joined by that from the city,—

the glittering line in the midst of which Sidi El Hadj Mohammed sat high on the back of a grey mehari.

From very far off Victoria saw the meeting, looking through the glasses sent by Maïeddine, those which he had given her once before, bidding her see how the distant dunes leaped forward.

Then as she watched, and the procession came nearer, rising and falling among the golden sand-billows, she could plainly make out the majestic form of the marabout. The sun blazed on the silver cross of his saddle, and the spear-heads of the banners which waved around him; but he was dressed with severe simplicity, in a mantle of green silk, with the green turban to which he had earned the right by visiting Mecca. The long white veil of many folds, which can be worn only by a descendant of the Prophet, flowed over the green cloak; and the face below the eyes was hidden completely by a mask of thin black woollen stuff, such as has been named "nun's veiling" in Europe. He was tall, and no longer slender, as Victoria remembered Cassim ben Halim to have been ten years ago; but all the more because of his increasing bulk, was his bearing majestic as he rode on the grey mehari, towering above the crowd. Even the Agha, Si Maïeddine's father, had less dignity than that of this great saint of the southern desert, returning like a king to his people, after carrying through a triumphant mission.

"If only he had been a few days later!" Saidee thought.

And Victoria felt an oppressive sense of the man's power, wrapping round her and her sister like a heavy cloak. But she looked above and beyond him, into the gold, and with all the strength of her spirit she sent out a call to Stephen Knight.

"I love you. Come to me. Save my sister and me. God, send him to us. He said he would come, no matter how far. Now is the time. Let him come."

The silence of the golden sea was broken by cries of welcome to the marabout, praises of Allah and the Prophet who had brought him safely back, shouts of men, and wailing "you-yous" of women, shrill voices of children, and neighing of horses.

Up the side of the Zaouïa hill, lame beggars crawled out of the river bed, each hurrying to pass the others—hideous deformities, legless, noseless, humpbacked, twisted into strange shapes like brown pots rejected by the potter, groaning, whining, eager for the marabout's blessing, a supper, and a few coins. Those who could afford a copper or two were carried through the shallow water on the backs of half-naked, sweating Negroes from the village; but those who had nothing except their faith to support them, hobbled or crept over the stones, wetting their scanty rags; laughed at by black and brown children who feared to follow, because of the djinn who lived in a cave of evil yellow stones, guarding a hidden spring which gushed into the river.

On Miluda's roof there was music, which could be heard from another roof, nearer the minaret where the doves wheeled and moaned; and perhaps the marabout himself could hear it, as he approached the Zaouïa; but though it called him with a song of love and welcome, he did not answer the call at once. First he took Maïeddine into his private reception room, where he received only the guests whom he most delighted to honour.

There, though the ceiling and walls were decorated in Arab fashion, with the words, El Afia el Bakia, "eternal health," inscribed in lettering of gold and red, opposite the door, all the furniture was French, gilded, and covered with brocade of scarlet and gold. The curtains draped over the inlaid cedar-wood shutters of the windows were of the same brocade, and the beautiful old rugs from Turkey and Persia could not soften its crudeness. The larger reception room from which this opened had still more violent decorations, for there the scarlet mingled with vivid blue, and there were curiosities enough to stock a museum—presents sent to the marabout from friends and admirers all over the world. There were first editions of rare books, illuminated missals, dinner services of silver and gold, Dresden and Sèvres, and even Royal Worcester; splendid crystal cases of spoons and jewellery; watches old and new; weapons of many countries, and an astonishing array of clocks, all ticking, and pointing to different hours. But the inner room, which only the intimate friends of Sidi Mohammed ever saw, was littered with no such incongruous collection. On the walls were a few fine pictures by well-known French artists of the most modern school, mostly representing nude women; for though the Prophet forbade the fashioning of graven images, he made no mention of painting. There were comfortable divans, and little tables, on which were displayed boxes of cigars and cigarettes, and egg-shell coffee-cups in filigree gold standards.

In this room, behind shut doors, Maïeddine told his errand, not forgetting to enumerate in detail the great things he could do for the

Cause, if his wish were granted. He did not speak much of Victoria, or his love for her, but he knew that the marabout must reckon her beauty by the price he was prepared to pay; and he gave the saint little time to picture her fascinations. Nor did Sidi Mohammed talk of the girl, or of her relationship to one placed near him; and his face (which he unmasked with a sigh of relief when he and his friend were alone) did not change as he listened, or asked questions about the services Maïeddine would render the Cause. At first he seemed to doubt the possibility of keeping such promises, some of which depended upon the Agha; but Maïeddine's enthusiasm inspired him with increasing confidence. He spoke freely of the great work that was being done by the important societies of which he was the head; of what he had accomplished in Oran, and had still to accomplish; of the arms and ammunition smuggled into the Zaouïa and many other places, from France and Morocco, brought by the "silent camels" in rolls of carpets and boxes of dates. But, he added, this was only a beginning. Years must pass before all was ready, and many more men, working heart and soul, night and day, were needed. If Maïeddine could help, well and good. But would the Agha yield to his influence?

"Not the Agha," Maïeddine answered, "but the Agha's people. They are my people, too, and they look to me as their future head. My father is old. There is nothing I cannot make the Ouled-Sirren do, nowhere I cannot bid them go, if I lead."

"And wilt thou lead in the right way? If I give thee thy desire, wilt thou not forget, when it is already thine?" the marabout asked. "When a man wears a jewel on his finger, it does not always glitter so brightly as when he saw and coveted it first."

"Not always. But in each man's life there is one jewel, supreme above others, to possess which he eats the heart, and which, when it is his, becomes the star of his life, to be worshipped forever. Once he has seen the jewel, the man knows that there is nothing more glorious for him this side heaven; that it is for him the All of joy, though to others, perhaps, it might not seem as bright. And there is nothing he would not do to have and to keep it."

The marabout looked intently at Maïeddine, searching his mind to the depths; and the face of each man was lit by an inner flame, which gave nobility to his expression. Each was passionately sincere in his way, though the way of one was not the way of the other.

In his love Maïeddine was true, according to the light his religion and the unchanging customs of his race had given him. He intended no wrong to Victoria, and as he was sure that his love was an honour for her, he saw no shame in taking her against what she mistakenly believed to be her wish. Her confession of love for another man had shocked him at first, but now he had come to feel that it had been but a stroke of diplomacy on her part, and he valued her more than ever for her subtlety. Though he realized dimly that with years his passion for her might cool, it burned so hotly now that the world was only a frame for the picture of her beauty. And he was sure that never in time to come could he forget the thrill of this great passion, or grudge the price he now offered and meant to pay.

Cassim ben Halim had begun his crusade under the name and banner of the marabout, in the fierce hope of revenge against the power which broke him, and with an entirely selfish wish for personal aggrandizement. But as the years went on, he had converted himself to the fanaticism he professed. Sidi El Hadj Mohammed ben Abd el Kadr had created an ideal and was true to it. Still a selfish sensualist on one side of his nature, there was another side capable of high courage and self-sacrifice for the one cause which now seemed worth a sacrifice. To the triumph of Islam over usurpers he was ready to devote his life, or give his life; but having no mercy upon himself if it came to a question between self and the Cause, he had still less mercy upon others, with one exception; his son. Unconsciously, he put the little boy above all things, all aims, all people. But as for Saidee's sister, the child he remembered, who had been foolish enough and irritating enough to find her way to Oued Tolga, he felt towards her, in listening to the story of her coming, as an ardent student might feel towards a persistent midge which disturbed his studies. If the girl could be used as a pawn in his great game, she had a certain importance, otherwise none—except that her midge-like buzzings must not annoy him, or reach ears at a distance.

Both men were naturally schemers, and loved scheming for its own sake, but never had either pitted his wits against the other with less intention of hiding his real mind. Each was in earnest, utterly sincere, therefore not ignoble; and the bargain was struck between the two with no deliberate villainy on either side. The marabout promised his wife's sister to Maïeddine with as little hesitation as a patriarch of Israel, three thousand years ago, would have promised a lamb for the sacrificial altar. He stipulated only that before the marriage Maïeddine should prove, not his willingness, but his ability to bring his father's people into the field.

314

"Go to the douar," he said, "and talk with the chief men. Then bring back letters from them, or send if thou wilt, and the girl shall be thy wife. I shall indeed be gratified by the connection between thine illustrious family and mine."

Maïeddine had expected this, though he had hoped that his eloquence might persuade the marabout to a more impulsive agreement. "I will do what thou askest," he answered, "though it means delay, and delay is hard to bear. When I passed through the douar, my father's chief caïds were on the point of leaving for Algiers, to do honour to the Governor by showing themselves at the yearly ball. They will have started before I can reach the douar again, by the fastest travelling, for as thou knowest, I should be some days on the way."

"Go then to Algiers, and meet them. That is best, and will be quicker, since journeying alone, thou canst easily arrive at Touggourt in three days from here. In two more, by taking a carriage and relays of horses, thou canst be at Biskra; and after that, there remains but the seventeen hours of train travelling."

"How well thou keepest track of all progress, though things were different when thou wast last in the north," Maïeddine said.

"It is my business to know all that goes on in my own country, north, south, east, and west. When wilt thou start?"

"To-night."

"Thou art indeed in earnest! Thou wilt of course pay thine own respects to the Governor? I will send him a gift by thee, since there is no reason he should not know that we have met. The mission on which thou wert ostensibly travelling brought thee to the south."

"I will take thy gift and messages with pleasure." Maïeddine said. "It was expected that I should return for the ball, and present myself in place of my father, who is too old now for such long journeys; but I intended to make my health an excuse for absence. I should have pleaded a touch of the sun, and a fever caught in the marshes while carrying out the mission. Indeed, it is true that I am subject to fever. However, I will go, since thou desirest. The ball, which was delayed, is now fixed for a week from to-morrow. I will show myself for some moments, and the rest of the night I can devote to a talk with the caïds. I know what the result will be. And a fortnight from to- morrow thou wilt see me here again with the letters."

"I believe thou wilt not fail," the marabout answered. "And neither will I fail thee."

XL

On the night of the Governor's ball, it was four weeks to the day since Stephen Knight and Nevill Caird had inquired for Victoria Ray at the Hotel de la Kasbah, and found her gone.

For rather more than a fortnight, they had searched for her quietly without applying to the police; but when at the end of that time, no letter had come, or news of any kind, the police were called into consultation. Several supposed clues had been followed, and had led to nothing; but Nevill persuaded Stephen to hope something from the ball. If any caïds of the south knew that Roumis had a secret reason for questioning them, they would pretend to know nothing, or give misleading answers; but if they were drawn on to describe their own part of the country, and the facilities for travelling through it, news of those who had lately passed that way might be inadvertently given.

Stephen was no longer in doubt about his feelings for Victoria. He knew that he had loved her ever since the day when she came to Nevill's house, and they talked together in the lily garden. He knew that the one thing worth living for was to find her; but he expected no happiness from seeing her again, rather the contrary. Margot would soon be coming back to England from Canada, and he planned to meet her, and keep all his promises. Only, he must be sure first that Victoria Ray was safe. He had made up his mind by this time that, if necessary, Margot would have to wait for him. He would not leave Algeria until Victoria had been found. It did not matter whether this decision were right or wrong, he would stick to it. Then, he would atone by doing as well as he could by Margot. She should have no cause of complaint against him in the future, so far as his love for Victoria was concerned; but he did not mean to try and kill it. Love for such a girl was too sacred to kill, even though it meant unhappiness for him. Stephen meant to guard it always in his heart, like a lamp to light him over the dark places; and there would be many dark places he knew in a life lived with Margot.

Through many anxious days he looked forward to the Governor's ball, pinning his faith to Nevill's predictions; but when the moment came, his excitement fell like the wind at sunset. It did not seem possible that, after weeks of suspense, he should have news now, or ever. He went with Nevill to the summer palace, feeling dull and depressed. But perhaps the depression was partly the effect of a letter from Margot Lorenzi in Canada, received that morning. She said that she was longing to see him, and "hurrying all she knew," to escape from her friends, and get back to "dear London, and her darling White Knight."

"I'm an ass to expect anything from coming here," he thought, as he saw the entrance gates of the palace park blazing with green lights in a trellis of verdure. The drive and all the paths that wound through the park were bordered with tiny lamps, and Chinese lanterns hung from the trees. There was sure to be a crush, and it seemed absurd to hope that even Nevill's cajoleries could draw serious information from Arab guests in such a scene as this.

The two young men went into the palace, passing through a big veranda where French officers were playing bridge, and on into a charming court, where Turkish coffee was being served. Up from this court a staircase led to the room where the Governor was receiving, and at each turn of the stairs stood a Spahi in full dress uniform, with a long white haïck. Nevill was going on ahead, meaning to introduce Stephen to the Governor before beginning his search for acquaintances among the Arab chiefs who grouped together over the coffee cups. But, turning to speak to Stephen, who had been close behind at starting, he found that somehow they had been swept apart. He stepped aside to wait for his friend, and let the crowd troop past him up the wide staircase. Among the first to go by was an extremely handsome Arab wearing a scarlet cloak heavy with gold embroidery, thrown over a velvet coat so thickly encrusted with gold that its pale-blue colour showed only here and there. He held his turbaned head proudly, and, glancing at Caird as he passed, seemed not to see him, but rather to see through him something more interesting beyond.

Nevill still waited for his friend, but fully two minutes had gone before Stephen appeared. "Did you see that fellow in the red cloak?" he asked. "That was the Arab of the ship."

"Si Maïeddine— —"

"Yes. Did you notice a queer brooch that held his cloak together? A wheel-like thing, set with jewels?"

"No. He hadn't it on. His cloak was hanging open."

"By Jove! You're sure?"

"Certain. I saw the whole breast of his coat."

"That settles it, then. He did recognize me. Hang it, I wish he hadn't."

"I don't know what's in your mind exactly. But I suppose you'll tell me."

"Rather. But no time now. We mustn't lose sight of him if we can help it. I wanted to follow him up, on the instant, but didn't dare, for I hoped he'd think I hadn't spotted him. He can't be sure, anyhow, for I had the presence of mind not to stare. Let's go up now. He was on his way to pay his respects to the Governor, I suppose. He can't have slipped away yet."

"It would seem not," Nevill assented, thoughtfully.

But a few minutes later, it seemed that he had. And Nevill was not surprised, for in the last nine years he had learned never to wonder at the quick-witted diplomacy of Arabs. Si Maïeddine had made short work of his compliments to the Governor, and had passed out of sight by the time that Stephen Knight and Nevill Caird escaped from the line of Europeans and gorgeous Arabs pressing towards their host. It was not certain, however, that he had left the palace. His haste to get on might be only a coincidence, Nevill pointed out. "Frenchified Arabs" like Si Maïeddine, he said, were passionately fond of dancing with European women, and very likely Maïeddine was anxious to secure a waltz with some Frenchwomen of his acquaintance.

The two Englishmen went on as quickly as they could, without seeming to hurry, and looked for Maïeddine in the gaily decorated ball-room where a great number of Europeans and a few Arabs were dancing. Maïeddine would have been easy to find there, for his high-held head in its white turban must have towered above most other heads, even those of the tallest French officers; but he was not to be seen, and Nevill guided Stephen out of the ball-room into a great court decorated with palms and banners, and jewelled with hundreds of coloured lights that turned the fountain into a spouting rainbow.

Pretty women sat talking with officers in uniforms, and watching the dancers as they strolled out arm in arm, to walk slowly round the flower-decked fountain. Behind the chatting Europeans stood many Arab chiefs of different degree, bach aghas, aghas, caïds and adels, looking on silently, or talking together in low voices; and compared with these stately, dark men in their magnificent costumes blazing with jewels and medals, the smartest French officers were reduced to insignificance. There were many handsome men, but Si Maïeddine was not among them.

"We've been told that he's *persona grata* here," Nevill reminded Stephen, "and there are lots of places where he may be in the palace, that we can't get to. He's perhaps hob-nobbing with some pal, having a private confab, and maybe he'll turn up at supper."

"He doesn't look like a man to care about food, I will say that for him," answered Stephen. "He's taken the alarm, and sneaked off without giving me time to track him. I'll bet anything that's the fact. Hiding the brooch is a proof he saw me, I'm afraid. Smart of him! He thought my friend would be somewhere about, and he'd better get rid of damaging evidence."

"You haven't explained the brooch, yet."

"I forgot. It's one *she* wore on the boat—and that day at your house—Miss Ray, I mean. She told me about it; said it had been a present from Ben Halim to her sister, who gave it to her."

"Sure you couldn't mistake it? There's a strong family likeness in Arab jewellery."

"I'm sure. And even if I hadn't been at first, I should be now, from that chap's whisking it off the instant he set eyes on me. His having it proves a lot. As she wore the thing at your house, he must have got it somehow after we saw her. Jove, Nevill, I'd like to choke him!"

"If you did, he couldn't tell what he knows."

"I'm going to find out somehow. Come along, no use wasting time here now, trying to get vague information out of Arab chiefs. We can learn more by seeing where this brute lives, than by catechizing a hundred caïds."

"It's too late for him to get away from Algiers to-night by train, anyhow," said Nevill. "Nothing goes anywhere in particular. And look here, Legs, if he's really onto us, he won't have made himself scarce without leaving some pal he can trust, to see what we're up to."

"There were two men close behind who might have been with him," Stephen remembered aloud.

"Would you recognize them?"

"I—think so. One of the two, anyhow. Very dark, hook-nosed, middle-aged chap, pitted with smallpox."

"Then you may be sure he's chosen the less noticeable one. No good our trying to find Maïeddine himself, if he's left the palace; though I hope, by putting our heads and Roslin's together, that among the three of us we shall pick him up later. But if he's left somebody here to keep an eye on us, our best course is to keep an eye on that somebody. They'll have to communicate."

"You're right," Stephen admitted. "I'm vague about the face, but I'll force myself to recognize it. That's the sort of thing Miss Ray would do. She's got some quaint theory about controlling your subconscious self. Now I'll take a leaf out of her book. By Jove— there's one of the men now. Don't look yet. He doesn't seem to notice us, but who knows? He's standing by the door, under a palm. Let's go back into the ball-room, and see if he follows."

But to "see if he followed" was more easily said than done. The Arab, a melancholy and grizzled but dignified caïd of the south, contrived to lose himself in a crowd of returning dancers, and it was not until later that the friends saw him in the ball-room, talking to a French officer and having not at all the air of one who spied or followed. Whether he remained because they remained was hard to say, for the scene was amusing and many Arabs watched it; but he showed no sign of restlessness, and it began to seem laughable to Nevill that, if he waited for them, they would be forced to wait for him. Eventually they made a pretence of eating supper. The caïd was at the buffet with an Arab acquaintance. The Englishmen lingered so long, that in the end he walked away; yet they were at his beck and call. They must go after him, if he went before them, and it was irritating to see that, when he had taken respectful leave of his host, the sad-faced caïd proceeded quietly out of the palace as if he had nothing to conceal. Perhaps he had nothing or else, suspecting the game, he was forcing the hand of the enemy. Stephen and Nevill had to follow, if they would keep him in sight; and though they walked as far behind as possible, passing out of the brilliantly lighted park, they could not be sure that he did not guess they were after him.

They had walked the short distance from Djenan el Djouad to the Governor's summer palace; and now, outside the gates, the caïd turned to the left, which was their way home also. This was lucky, because, if the man were on the alert, and knew where Nevill lived, he would have no reason to suppose they took this direction on his account.

But he had not gone a quarter of a mile when he stopped, and rang at a gate in a high white wall.

"Djenan el Taleb," mumbled Nevill. "Perhaps Si Maïeddine's visiting there—or else this old beggar is."

"Is it an Arab's house?" Stephen wanted to know.

"Was once—long ago as pirate days. Now a Frenchman owns it— Monsieur de Mora—friend of the Governor's. Always puts up several chiefs at the time of the ball."

The gate opened to let the caïd in and was shut again.

"Hurrah!—just thought of a plan," exclaimed Nevill. "I don't think De Mora can have got home yet from the palace. I saw him having supper. Suppose I dart back, flutter gracefully round him, babble 'tile talk' a bit—he's a tile expert after my own heart—then casually ask what Arabs he's got staying with him. If Maïeddine's in his house it can't be a secret—incidentally I may find out where the fellow comes from and where he's going."

"Good!" said Stephen. "I'll hang about in the shadow of some tree and glue my eye to this gate. Is there any other way out?"

"There is; but not one a visitor would be likely to take, especially if he didn't want to be seen. It opens into a street where a lot of people might be standing to peer into the palace grounds and hear the music. Now run along, Legs, and find a comfortable shadow. I'm off."

He was gone three-quarters of an hour, but nothing happened meanwhile. Nobody went in at the gate, or came out, and the time dragged for Stephen. He thought of a hundred dangers that might be threatening Victoria, and it seemed that Caird would never come. But at last he saw the boyish figure, hurrying along under the light of a street-lamp.

"Couldn't find De Mora at first—then had to work slowly up to the subject," Nevill panted. "But it's all right. Maïeddine *is* stopping with him—leaves to-morrow or day after; supposed to have come from El Aghouat, and to be going back there. But that isn't to say either supposition's true."

"We must find out where he's going—have him watched," said Stephen.

"Yes. Only, the trouble is, if he's on to the game, it's just what he'll expect. But I've been thinking how we may be able to bluff—make him think it was his guilty conscience tricked him to imagine our interest in his movements. You know I'm giving a dinner to-morrow night to a few people?"

"Yes. Lady MacGregor told me."

"Well, a Mademoiselle Vizet, a niece of De Mora's, is coming, so that gave me a chance to mention the dinner to her uncle. Maïeddine can easily hear about it, if he chooses to inquire what's going on at my house. And I said something else to De Mora, for the benefit of the same gentleman. I hope you'll approve."

"Sure to. What was it?"

"That I was sorry my friend, Mr. Knight, had got news which would call him away from Algiers before the dinner. I said you'd be going on board the *Charles Quex* to-morrow when she leaves for Marseilles."

"But Maïeddine can find out——"

"That's just what we want. He can find out that your ticket's taken, if we do take it. He can see you go on board if he likes to watch or send a spy. But he mustn't see you sneaking off again with the Arab porters who carry luggage. If you think anything of the plan, you'll have to stand the price of a berth, and let some luggage you can do without, go to Marseilles. I'll see you off, and stop on board till the last minute. You'll be in your cabin, putting on the clothes I wear sometimes when I want some fun in the old town—striped wool burnous, hood over your head, full white trousers—good 'props,' look a lot the worse for wear—white stockings like my Kabyle servants have; and you can rub a bit of brown grease-paint on your legs where the socks leave off. That's what I do. Scheme sounds complicated; but so is an Arab's brain. You've got to match it. What do you say?"

"I say 'done!'" Stephen answered.

"Thought you would. Some fellows'd think it too sensational; but you can't be too sensational with Arabs, if you want to beat 'em. This ought to put Maïeddine off the scent. If he's watching, and sees you—as he thinks—steam calmly out of Algiers harbour, and if he knows I'm entertaining people at my house, he won't see why he need go on bothering himself with extra precautions."

"Right. But suppose he's off to-morrow morning—or even to-night."

"Then we needn't bother about the boat business. For we shall know if he goes. Either you or I must now look up Roslin. Perhaps it had better be I, because I can run into Djenan el Djouad first, and send my man Saunders to watch De Mora's other gate, and make assurance doubly sure."

"You're a brick, Wings," said Stephen.

XLI

Lady MacGregor had sat up in order to hear the news, and was delighted with Nevill's plan, especially the part which concerned Stephen, and his proposed adventure on the *Charles Quex*. Even to hear about it, made her feel young again, she said. Nothing ever happened to her or to Nevill when they were alone, and they ought to be thankful to Stephen for stirring them up. Not one of the three had more than two hours' sleep that night, but according to her nephew, Lady MacGregor looked sweet sixteen when she appeared at an unusually early hour next morning. "No breakfast in bed for me to-day, or for days to come," said she. "I'll have my hands full every instant getting through what I've got to do, I can tell you. Hamish and Angus are worried about my health, but I say to them they needn't grudge me a new interest in life. It's very good for me."

"Why, what have you got to do?" ventured Nevill, who was ready to go with Stephen and buy a berth on board the *Charles Quex* the moment the office opened.

Lady MacGregor looked at him mysteriously. "Being men, I suppose neither of you *would* guess," she replied. "But you shall both know after Stephen's adventure is over. I hope you'll like the idea. But if you don't I'm sorry to say it won't make any difference."

The so-called "adventure" had less of excitement in it than had been in the planning. It was faithfully carried out according to Nevill's first suggestion, with a few added details, but Stephen felt incredibly foolish, rather like a Guy Fawkes mummer, or a masked and bedizened guest arriving by mistake the night after the ball. So far as he could see, no one was watching. All his trouble seemed to be for nothing, and he felt that he had made a fool of himself, even when it was over, and he had changed into civilized clothing, in a room in the old town, taken by Adolphe Roslin, the detective. It was arranged for Stephen to wait there, until Roslin could give him news of Si Maïeddine's movements, lest the Arab should be subtle enough to suspect a trick, after all.

Toward evening the news came. Maïeddine had taken a ticket for Biskra, and a sleeping berth in the train which would leave at nine o'clock. Nevertheless, Roslin had a man watching Monsieur de

Mora's house, in case the buying of the ticket were a "bluff," or Si Maïeddine should change his plans at the last minute.

Nevill had come in, all excitement, having bought cheap "antique" jewellery in a shop downstairs, by way of an excuse to enter the house. He was with Stephen when Roslin arrived, and they consulted together as to what should be done next.

"Roslin must buy me a ticket for Biskra, of course," said Stephen. "I'll hang about the station in an overcoat with my collar turned up and a cap over my eyes. If Maïeddine gets into the train I'll get in too, at a respectful distance of course, and keep an eye open to see what he does at each stop."

"There's a change of trains, to-morrow morning," remarked Nevill. "There'll be your difficulty, because after you're out of one train you have to wait for the other. Easy to hide in Algiers station, and make a dash for the end of the train when you're sure of your man. But in a little open, road-side halting-place, in broad daylight, you'll have to be sharp if you don't want him to spot you. Naturally he'll keep his eyes as wide open, all along the line, as you will, even though he does think you're on the way to Marseilles."

"If you're working up to a burnous and painted legs for me again, my dear chap, it's no good," Stephen returned with the calmness of desperation. "I've done with that sort of nonsense; but I won't trust myself out of the train till I see the Arab's back. Then I'll make a bolt for it and dodge him, till the new train's run along the platform and he's safely in it."

"Monsieur has confidence in himself as a detective," smiled Roslin.

Knight could have given a sarcastic answer, since the young man from Marseilles had not made much progress with the seemingly simple case put into his hands a month ago. But both he and Nevill had come to think that the case was not simple, and they were lenient with Roslin. "I hope I'm not conceited," Stephen defended himself, "but I do feel that I can at least keep my end up against this nigger, anyhow till the game's played out so far that he can't stop it."

"And till I'm in it with you," Nevill finished. "By the way, that reminds me. Some one else intends to play the game with us, whether we like or not."

"Who?" asked Stephen, surprised and half defiant.

"My aunt. That's the mystery she was hinting at. You know how unnaturally quiet she was while we arranged that you should look after Maïeddine, on your own, till the dinner-party was over, anyhow, and I could get off, on a wire from you—wherever you might be?"

"Yes. She seemed interested."

"And busy. Her 'great work' was getting herself ready to follow you with me, in the car."

"Magnificent!" said Stephen. "And like her. Hurrah for Lady MacGregor!"

"I'm glad you take it that way. I wasn't sure you would, which might have made things awkward for me; because when my aunt wants to do a thing, you know by this time as well as I do, it's as good as done."

"But it's splendid—if she can stand the racket. Of course her idea is, that if we find Miss Ray she oughtn't to come back alone with us, perhaps a long way, from some outlandish hole."

"You've got it. That's her argument. Or rather, her mandate. And I believe she's quite able to stand the racket. Her state of mind is such, that if she looked sixteen in the morning, this afternoon she's gone back to fifteen."

"Wonderful old lady! But she's so fragile—and has nervous headaches——"

"She won't have any in my motor car."

"But Hamish and Angus. Can she get on without them?"

"She intends to have them follow her by train, with luggage. She says she has a 'feeling in her bones' that they'll come in handy, either for cooking or fighting. And by Jove, she may be right. She often is. If you go to Biskra and wire when you get there, I'll start at once—we'll start, I mean. And if Maïeddine goes on anywhere else, and you follow to keep him in sight, I'll probably catch you up with the car, because the railway line ends at Biskra, you know; and beyond, there are only horses or camels."

"Can motors go farther?"

"They can to Touggourt—with 'deeficulty,' as the noble twins would say."

"Maïeddine may take a car."

"Not likely. Though there's just a chance he might get some European friend with a motor to give him a lift. In that case, you'd be rather stuck."

"Motor cars leave tracks," said Stephen.

"Especially in the desert, where they are quite conspicuous," Nevill agreed. "My aunt will be enchanted with your opinion of her and her plan—but not surprised. She thinks you've twice my sense and knowledge of the world."

Nevill usually enjoyed his own dinner-parties, for he was a born host, and knew that guests were happy in his house. That night, however, was an exception. He was absent-minded, and pulled his moustache, and saw beautiful things in the air over people's heads, so often that not only Lady MacGregor but Angus and Hamish glared at him threateningly. He then did his best to atone; nevertheless, for once he was delighted when every one had gone. At last he was able to read for the second time a letter from Roslin, sent in while dinner was in progress. There had been only time for a glance at it, by begging his friends' indulgence for an instant, while he bolted the news that Stephen had followed Maïeddine to Biskra. Now, Nevill and Lady MacGregor both hugely enjoyed the details given by Roslin from the report of an employé; how cleverly Monsieur had kept out of sight, though the Arab had walked up and down the platform, with two friends, looking about keenly. How, when Maïeddine was safely housed in his compartment, his companions looking up to his window for a last word, Monsieur Knight had whisked himself into a second-class compartment at the other end of the train.

Next day, about four o'clock, a telegram was brought to Djenan el Djouad. It came from Biskra, and said: "Arrived here. Not spotted. He went house of French commandant with no attempt at concealment. Am waiting. Will wire again soon as have news. Perhaps better not start till you hear."

An hour and a half later a second blue envelope was put into Nevill's hand.

"He and an officer leave for Touggourt in private carriage three horses relays ordered. Have interviewed livery stable. They start at five will travel all night. I follow."

"Probably some officer was going on military business, and Maïeddine's asked for a lift," Nevill said to Lady MacGregor. "Well, it's too late for us to get away now; but we'll be off as early as you like to-morrow morning."

"If I weren't going, would you start to-day?" his aunt inquired.

"Yes, I suppose so. But — —"

"Then please give orders for the car. I'm ready to leave at five minutes' notice, and I can go on as long as you can. I'm looking forward to the trip."

"But I've often offered to take you to Biskra."

"That's different. Now I've got an incentive."

XLII

Just as he came in sight of the great chott between Biskra and Touggourt, Stephen heard a sound which struck him strangely in the silence of the desert. It was the distant teuf-teuf of a powerful motor car, labouring heavily through deep sand.

Stephen was travelling in a carriage, which he had hired in Biskra, and was keeping as close as he dared to the vehicle in front, shared by Maïeddine and a French officer. But he never let himself come within sight or sound of it. Now, as he began to hear the far-off panting of a motor, he saw nothing ahead but the vast saltpetre lake, which, viewed from the hill his three horses had just climbed, shimmered blue and silver, like a magic sea, reaching to the end of the world. There were white lines like long ruffles of foam on the edges of azure waves, struck still by enchantment while breaking on an unseen shore; and far off, along a mystic horizon, little islands floated on the gleaming flood. Stephen could hardly believe that there was no water, and that his horses could travel the blue depths without wetting their feet.

It was just as he was thinking thus, and wondering if Victoria had passed this way, when the strange sound came to his ears, out of the distance. "Stop," he said in French to his Arab driver. "I think friends of mine will be in that car." He was right. A few minutes later Nevill and Lady MacGregor waved to him, as he stood on the top of a low sand-dune.

Lady MacGregor was more fairylike than ever in a little motoring bonnet made for a young girl, but singularly becoming to her. They had had a glorious journey, she said. She supposed some people would consider that she had endured hardships, but they were not worth speaking of. She had been rather bumped about on the ghastly desert tracks since Biskra, but though she was not quite sure if all her bones were whole, she did not feel in the least tired; and even if she did, the memory of the Gorge of El Kantara would alone be enough to make up for it.

"Anything new?" asked Nevill.

"Nothing," Stephen answered, "except that the driver of the carriage ahead let drop at the last bordj that he'd been hired by the French officer, who was taking Maïeddine with him."

"Just what we thought," Lady MacGregor broke in.

"And the carriage will bring the Frenchman back, later. Maïeddine's going on. But I haven't found out where."

"H'm! I was in hopes we were close to our journey's end at Touggourt," said Nevill. "The car can't get farther, I'm afraid. The big dunes begin there."

"Whatever Maïeddine does, we can follow his example. I mean, I can," Stephen amended.

"So can Nevill. I'm no spoil-sport," snapped the old lady, in her childlike voice. "I know what I can do and what I can't. I draw the line at camels! Angus and Hamish will take care of me, and I'll wait for you at Touggourt. I can amuse myself in the market-place, and looking at the Ouled Naïls, till you find Miss Ray, or——"

"There won't be an 'or,' Lady MacGregor. We must find her. And we must bring her to you," said Stephen.

He had slept in the carriage the night before, a little on the Biskra side of Chegga, because Maïeddine and the French officer had rested at Chegga. Nevill and Lady MacGregor had started from Biskra at five o'clock that morning, having arrived there the evening before. It was now ten, and they could make Touggourt that night. But they wished Maïeddine to reach there first, so they stopped by the chott, and lunched from a smartly fitted picnic-basket Lady MacGregor had brought. Stephen paid his Arab coachman, told him he might go back, and transferred a small suitcase—his only luggage—from the carriage to the car. They gave Maïeddine two hours' grace, and having started on, always slowed up whenever Nevill's field-glasses showed a slowly trotting vehicle on the far horizon. The road, which was hardly a road, far exceeded in roughness the desert track Stephen had wondered at on the way from Msila to Bou-Saada; but Lady MacGregor had the courage, he told her, of a Joan of Arc.

They bumped steadily along, through the heat of the day, protected from the blazing sun by the raised hood, but they were thankful when, after the dinner-halt, darkness began to fall. Talking over ways and means, they decided not to drive into Touggourt, where an automobile would be a conspicuous object since few motors risked springs and tyres by coming so far into the desert. The chauffeur should be sent into the town while the passengers sat in the car a mile away.

Eventually Paul was instructed to demand oil for his small lamps, by way of an excuse for having tramped into town. He was to find out what had become of the two men who must have arrived about an hour before, in a carriage.

While the chauffeur was gone, Lady MacGregor played Patience and insisted on teaching Stephen and Nevill two new games. She said that it would be good discipline for their souls; and so perhaps it was. But Stephen never ceased calculating how long Paul ought to be away. Twenty minutes to walk a mile—or thirty minutes in desert sand; forty minutes to make inquiries; surely it needn't take longer! And thirty minutes back. But an hour and a half dragged on, before there was any sign of the absentee; then at last, Stephen's eye, roving wistfully from the cards, saw a moving spark at about the right height above the ground to be a cigarette.

A few yards away from the car, the spark vanished decorously, and Paul was recognizable, in the light of the inside electric lamp, the only illumination they allowed themselves, lest the stranded car prove attractive to neighbouring nomads.

The French officer was at the hotel for the night; the Arab was dining with him, but instead of resting, would go on with his horse and a Negro servant who, it seemed, had been waiting for several days, since their master had passed through Touggourt on the way to Algiers.

"Then he didn't come from El Aghouat," said Nevill. "Where is he going? Did you find out that?"

"Not for certain. But an Arab servant who talks French, says he believes they're bound for a place called Oued Tolga," Paul replied, delighted with the confidence reposed in him, and with the whole adventure.

"That means three days in the dunes for us!" said Nevill. "Aunt Charlotte, you can practice Patience, in Touggourt."

"I shall invent a new game, and call it Hope," returned Lady MacGregor. "Or if it's a good one, I'll name it Victoria Ray, which is better than Miss Millikens. It will just be done in time to teach that poor child when you bring her back to me."

"Hope wouldn't be a bad name for the game we've all been playing, and have got to go on playing," mumbled Nevill. "We'll give Maïeddine just time to turn his back on Touggourt, before we show our noses there. Then you and I, Legs, will engage horses and a guide."

"You deserve your name, Wings," said Stephen. And he wondered how Josette Soubise could hold out against Caird. He wondered also what she thought of this quest; for her sister Jeanne was in the secret. No doubt she had written Josette more fully than Nevill had, even if he had dared to write at all. And if, as long ago as the visit to Tlemcen, she had been slightly depressed by her friend's interest in another girl, she must by this time see the affair in a more serious light. Stephen was cruel enough to hope that she was unhappy. He had heard women say that no cure for a woman's obstinacy was as sure as jealousy.

When they arrived at the hotel, and ordered all in the same breath, a room for a lady, two horses and a guide, only the first demand could be granted. It would be impossible, said the landlady and her son, to produce horses on the instant. There were some to be had, it was true, but they had come in after a hard day's work, and must have several hours' rest. The gentlemen might get off at dawn, if they wished, but not before.

"After all, it doesn't much matter," Nevill said to Stephen. "Even an Arab must have some sleep. We'll have ours now, and catch up with Maïeddine while he's taking his. Don't worry. Suppose the worst— that he isn't really going to Oued Tolga. We shall get on his track, with an Arab guide to pilot us. There are several stopping places where we can inquire. He'll be seen passing them, even if he goes by."

"But you say Arabs never betray each other to white men."

"This won't be a question of betrayal. Watch and see how ingenuous, as well as ingenious, I'll be in all my inquiries."

"I never heard of Oued Tolga," Stephen said, half to himself.

"Don't confess that to an Arab. It would be like telling a Frenchman you'd never heard of Bordeaux. It's a desert city, bigger than

Touggourt, I believe, and—by Jove, yes, there's a tremendously important Zaouïa of the same name. Great marabout hangs out there—kind of Mussulman pope of the desert. I hope to goodness— —"

"What?" Stephen asked, as Nevill broke off suddenly.

"Oh, nothing to fash yourself about, as the twins would say. Only— it would be awkward if she's there. Harder to get her out. However— time to cross the stile when we come to it."

But Stephen crossed a great many stiles with his mind before that darkest hour before the dawn, when he was called to get ready for the last stage of the journey.

Lady MacGregor was up to see them off, and never had her cap been more elaborate, or her hair been dressed more daintily.

"You'll wire me from the end of the world, won't you?" she asked briskly. "Paul and I (and Hamish and Angus if necessary) will be ready to rush you all three back to civilization the instant you arrive with Miss Ray. Give her my love. Tell her I've brought clothes for her. They mayn't be what she'd choose, but I dare say she won't be sorry to see them. And by the way, if there are telegrams—you know I told the servants to send them on from home—shall I wire them on to Oued Tolga?"

"No. We're tramps, with no address," laughed Nevill. "Anything that comes can wait till we get back."

Stephen could not have told why, for he was not thinking of Margot, but suddenly he was convinced that a telegram from her was on the way, fixing the exact date when she might be expected in England.

XLIII

Since the day when Victoria had called Stephen to her help, always she had expected him. She had great faith, for, in her favourite way, she had "made a picture of him," riding up and down among the dunes, with the "knightly" look on his face which had first drawn her thoughts to him. Always her pictures had materialized sooner or later, since she was a little girl, and had first begun painting them with her mind, on a golden background.

She spent hours on the roof, with Saidee or alone, looking out over the desert, through the field-glasses which Maïeddine had sent to her. Very often Saidee would remain below, for Victoria's prayers were not her prayers, nor were Victoria's wishes her wishes. But invariably the older woman would come up to the roof just before sunset, to feed the doves that lived in the minaret.

At first Victoria had not known that her sister had any special reason for liking to feed the doves, but she was an observant, though not a sophisticated girl; and when she had lived with Saidee for a few days, she saw birds of a different colour among the doves. It was to those birds, she could not help noticing, that Saidee devoted herself. The first that appeared, arrived suddenly, while Victoria looked in another direction. But when the girl saw one alight, she guessed it had come from a distance. It fluttered down heavily on the roof, as if tired, and Saidee hid it from Victoria by spreading out her skirt as she scattered its food.

Then it was easy to understand how Saidee and Captain Sabine had managed to exchange letters; but she could not bear to let her sister know by word or even look that she suspected the secret. If Saidee wished to hide something from her she had a right to hide it. Only — it was very sad.

For days neither of the sisters spoke of the pigeons, though they came often, and the girl could not tell what plans might be in the making, unknown to her. She feared that, if she had not come to Oued Tolga, by this time Saidee would have gone away, or tried to go away, with Captain Sabine; and though, since the night of her arrival, when Saidee had opened her heart, they had been on terms of closest affection, there was a dreadful doubt in Victoria's mind that the confidences were half repented. But when the girl had been rather more than a week in the Zaouïa, Saidee spoke out.

"I suppose you've guessed why I come up on the roof at sunset," she said.

"Yes," Victoria answered.

"I thought so, by your face. Babe, if you'd accused me of anything, or reproached me, I'd have brazened it out with you. But you've never said a word, and your eyes—I don't know what they've been like, unless violets after rain. They made me feel a beast—a thousand times worse than I would if you'd put on an injured air. Last night I dreamed that you died of grief, and I buried you under the sand. But I was sorry, and tore all the sand away with my fingers till I found you again—and you were alive after all. It seemed like an allegory. I'm going to dig you up again, you little loving thing!"

"That means you'll give me back your confidence, doesn't it?" Victoria asked, smiling in a way that would have bewitched a man who loved her.

"Yes; and something else. I'm going to tell you a thing you'll like to hear. I've written to *him* about you—our cypher's ready now—and said that you'd had the most curious effect on me. I'd tried to resist you, but I couldn't, not even to please him—or myself. I told him I'd promised to wait for you to help me; and though I didn't see what you could possibly do, still, your faith was contagious. I said that in spite of myself I felt some vague stirrings of hope now and then. There! does that please you?"

"Oh Saidee, I *am* so happy!" cried the girl, flinging both arms round her sister. "Then I did come at the right time, after all."

"The right time to keep me from happiness in this world, perhaps. That's the way I feel about it sometimes. But I can't be sorry you're here, Babe, as I was at first. You're too sweet—too like the child who used to be my one comfort."

"I could almost die of happiness, when you say that!" Victoria answered, with tears in her voice.

"What a baby you are! I'm sure you haven't much more than I have, to be happy about. Cassim has promised Maïeddine that you shall marry him, whether you say 'yes' or 'no'. And it's horrible when an

Arab girl won't consent to marry the man to whom her people have promised her. I know what they do. She— —"

"Don't tell me about it. I'd hate to hear!" Victoria broke in, and covered her ears with her hands. So Saidee said no more. But in black hours of the night, when the girl could not sleep, dreadful imaginings crept into her mind, and it was almost more than she could do to chase them away by making her "good pictures." "I won't be afraid—I won't, I won't!" she would repeat to herself. "I've called him, and my thoughts are stronger than the carrier pigeons. They fly faster and farther. They travel like the light, so they must have got to him long ago; and he *said* he'd come, no matter when or where. By this time he is on the way."

So she looked for Stephen, searching the desert; and at last, one afternoon long before sunset, she saw a man riding toward the Zaouïa from the direction of the city, far away. She could not see his face, but he seemed to be tall and slim; and his clothes were European.

"Thank God!" she said to herself. For she did not doubt that it was Stephen Knight.

Soon she would call Saidee; but she must have a little time to herself, for silent rejoicing, before she tried to explain. There was no great hurry. He was far off, still.

She kept her eyes to Maïeddine's glasses, and felt it a strange thing that they should have come to her from him. It was almost as if he gave her to Stephen, against his will. She was so happy that she seemed to hear the world singing. "I knew—I knew, through it all!" she told herself, with a sob of joy in her throat. "It had to come right." And she thought that she could hear a voice saying: "It is love that has brought him. He loves you, as much as you love him."

To her mind, especially in this mood, it was not extraordinary that each should love the other after so short an acquaintance. She was even ready to believe of herself that, unconsciously, she had fallen in love with Stephen the first time she met him on the Channel boat. He had interested her. She had remembered his face, and had been sorry to think that she would never see it again. On the ship, going out from Marseilles, she had been so glad when he came on deck that her heart had begun to beat quickly. She had scolded herself at the time, for being silly, and school-girlishly romantic; but now she realized that her soul had known its mate. It could scarcely be real love, she fancied, that was not born in the first moment, when spirit spoke to spirit. And her love could not have drawn a man hundreds of miles across the desert, if it had not met and clasped hands with his love for her.

"Oh, how happy I am!" she thought. "And the glory of it is, that it's *not* strange—only wonderful. The most wonderful thing that ever happened or could happen."

Then she remembered the sand-divining, and how M'Barka had said that "her wish was far from her, but that Allah would send a strong man, young and dark, of another country than her own; a man whose brain, and heart, and arm would be at her service, and in whom she might trust." Victoria recalled these words, and did not try to bring back to her mind what remained of the prophecy.

Almost, she had been foolish enough to be superstitious, and afraid of Maïeddine's influence upon her life, since that night; and of course she had known that it was of Maïeddine M'Barka had thought, whether she sincerely believed in her own predictions or no. Now, it pleased Victoria to feel that, not only had she been foolish, but stupid. She might have been happy in her childish superstition, instead of unhappy, because the description of the man applied to Stephen as well as to Maïeddine.

For the moment, she did not ask herself how Stephen Knight was going to take her and Saidee away from Maïeddine and Cassim, for she was so sure he had not come across miles of desert in vain, that she took the rest for granted in her first joy. She was certain that Saidee's troubles and hers were over, and that by and by, like the prince and princess in the fairy stories, she and Stephen would be married and "live happily ever after." In these magic moments of rapture, while his face and figure grew more clear to her eyes, it seemed to the girl that love and happiness were one, and that all obstacles had fallen down in the path of her lover, like the walls of Jericho that crumbled at the blast of the trumpet.

When she had looked through the glass until she could distinctly see Stephen, and an Arab who rode at a short distance behind him, she called her sister.

Saidee came up to the roof, almost at once, for there was a thrill of excitement in Victoria's voice that roused her curiosity.

She thought of Captain Sabine, and wondered if he were riding toward the Zaouïa. He had come, before his first encounter with her, to pay his respects to the marabout. That was long ago now, yet there might be a reason, connected with her, for a second visit. But the moment she saw Victoria's face, even before she took the glasses the girl held out, she guessed that, though there was news, it was not of Captain Sabine.

"You might have been to heaven and back since I saw you; you're so radiant!" she said.

"I have been to heaven. But I haven't come back. I'm there now," Victoria answered. "Look—and tell me what you see."

Saidee put the glasses to her eyes. "I see a man in European clothes," she said. "I can see that he's young. I should think he's a gentleman, and good looking——"

"Oh, he is!" broke in Victoria, childishly.

"Do you know him?"

"I've been praying and longing for him to find me, and save us. He's an Englishman. His name is Stephen Knight. He promised to come if I called, and I have. Oh, *how* I've called, day and night, night and day!"

"You never told me."

"I waited. Somehow I—couldn't speak of him, even to you."

"I've told *you* everything."

"But I had nothing to tell, really—nothing I could have put into words. And you might only have laughed if I'd said 'There's a man I know in Algiers who hasn't any idea where I am, but I think he'll come here, and take us both away.'"

"Are you engaged to each other?" Saidee asked, curiously, even enviously.

"Oh no! But—but——"

"But what? Do you mean you will be—if you ever get away from this place?"

"I hope so," the girl answered bravely, with a deep blush. "He has never asked me. We haven't known each other long—a very little while, only since the night I left London for Paris. Yet he's the first man I ever cared about, and I think of him all the time. Perhaps he thinks of me in the same way."

"Of course he must, Babe, if he's really come to search for you," Saidee said, looking at her young sister affectionately.

"Thank you a hundred times for saying that, dearest! I do *hope* so!" Victoria exclaimed, hugging the elder woman impulsively, as she used when she was a little child.

But Saidee's joy, caught from her sister's, died down suddenly, like a flame quenched with salt. "What good will it do you—or us—that he is coming?" she asked bitterly. "He can ask for the marabout, and perhaps see him. Any traveller can do that. But he will be no nearer to us, than if we were dead and in our graves. Does Maïeddine know about him?"

"They saw each other on the ship, coming to Algiers—and again just as we landed."

"But has Maïeddine any idea that you care about each other?"

"I had to tell him one day in the desert (the day Si Maïeddine said he loved me, and I promised to consent if *you* put my hand in his) that—that there was a man I loved. But I didn't say who. Perhaps he suspects, though I don't see why he should. I might have meant some one in America."

"You may be pretty sure he suspects. People of the old, old races, like the Arabs, have the most wonderful intuitions. They seem to *know* things without being told. I suppose they've kept nearer nature than more civilized peoples."

"If he does suspect, I can't help it."

"No. Only it's still more sure that your Englishman won't be able to do us any good. Not that he could, anyhow."

"But Si Maïeddine's been very ill since he came back, M'Barka says. Mr. Knight will ask for the marabout."

"Maïeddine will hear of him. Not five Europeans in five years come to Oued Tolga. If only Maïeddine hadn't got back! This man may have been following him, from Algiers. It looks like it, as Maïeddine arrived only yesterday. Now, here's this Englishman! Could he have found out in any way, that you were acquainted with Maïeddine?"

"I don't know, but he might have guessed," said Victoria. "I wonder——"

"What? Have you thought of something?"

"It's just an idea. You know, I told you that on the journey, when Si Maïeddine was being very kind to me—before I knew he cared—I made him a present of the African brooch you gave me in Paris. I hated to take so many favours of him, and give nothing in return; so I thought, as I was on my way to you and would soon see you, I might part with that brooch, which he admired. If Si Maïeddine wore it in Algiers, and Mr. Knight saw——"

"Would he be likely to recognize it, do you think?"

"He noticed it on the boat, and I told him you gave it to me."

"If he would come all the way from Algiers on the strength of a brooch which might have been yours, and you *might* have given to Maïeddine, then he's a man who knows what he wants, and deserves to get it," Saidee said. "If he *could* help us! I should feel rewarded for telling Honoré I wouldn't go with him; because some day I may be free, and then perhaps I shall be glad I waited——"

"You will be glad. Whatever happens, you'll be glad," Victoria insisted.

"Maybe. But now—what are we to do? We can see him, and you can recognize him with the field-glass, but unless he has a glass too, he can't see who you are—he can't see at all, because by the time he rides near enough, the ground dips down so that even our heads will be hidden from him by the wall round the roof. And he'll be hidden from us, too. If he asks for you, he'll be answered only by stares of surprise. Cassim will pretend not to know what he's talking about. And presently he'll have to go away without finding out anything."

"He'll come back," said Victoria, firmly. But her eyes were not as bright with the certainty of happiness as they had been.

"What if he does? Or it may be that he'll try to come back, and an accident will happen to him. I hate to frighten you. But Arabs are jealous—and Maïeddine's a true Arab. He looks upon you almost as his wife now. In a week or two you will be, unless— —"

"Yes. Unless—*unless!*" echoed Victoria. "Don't lose hope, Saidee, for I shan't. Let's think of something to do. He's near enough now, maybe, to notice if we wave our handkerchiefs."

"Many women on roofs in Africa wave to men who will never see their faces. He won't know who waves."

"He will *feel*. Besides, he's searching for me. At this very minute, perhaps, he's thinking of the golden silence I talked about, and looking up to the white roofs."

Instantly they began to wave their handkerchiefs of embroidered silk, such as Arab ladies use. But there came no answering signal. Evidently, if the rider were looking at a white roof, he had chosen one which was not theirs. And soon he would be descending the slope of the Zaouïa hill. After that they would lose sight of each other, more and more surely, the closer he came to the gates.

"If only you had something to throw him!" Saidee sighed. "What a pity you gave the brooch to Maïeddine. He might have recognized that."

"It isn't a pity if he traced me by it," said Victoria. "But wait. I'll think of something."

"He's riding down the dip. In a minute it will be too late," Saidee warned her.

The girl lifted over her head the long string of amber beads she had bought in the curiosity shop of Jeanne Soubise. Wrapping it in her handkerchief, she began to tie the silken ends together.

Stephen was so close to the Zaouïa now that they could no longer see him.

"Throw—throw! He'll be at the gates."

Victoria threw the small but heavy parcel over the wall which hid the dwellers on the roof.

Where it fell, they could not see, and no sound came up from the sand-dune far below. Some beggar or servant of the Zaouïa might have found and snatched the packet, for all that they could tell.

For a time which seemed long, they waited, hoping that something would happen. They did not speak at all. Each heard her own heart beating, and imagined that she could hear the heart of the other.

At last there were steps on the stairs which led from Saidee's rooms to the roof. Noura came up. "O twin stars, forgive me for darkening the brightness of thy sky," she said, "but I have here a letter, given to me to put into the hands of Lella Saïda."

She held out a folded bit of paper, that had no envelope.

Saidee, pale and large-eyed, took it in silence. She read, and then handed the paper to Victoria.

A few lines were scrawled on it in English, in a very foreign handwriting. The language, known to none in this house except the marabout, Maïeddine, Saidee and Victoria, was as safe as a cypher, therefore no envelope had been needed.

"Descend into thy garden immediately, and bring with thee thy sister," the letter said. And it was signed "Thy husband, Mohammed."

"What can it mean?" asked Victoria, giving back the paper to Saidee.

"I don't know. But we shall soon see—for we must obey. If we didn't go down of our own accord, we'd soon be forced to go."

"Perhaps Cassim will let me talk to Mr. Knight," said the girl.

"He is more likely to throw you to his lion, in the court," Saidee answered, with a laugh.

They went down into the garden, and remained there alone. Nothing happened except that, after a while, they heard a noise of pounding. It seemed to come from above, in Saidee's rooms.

Listening intently, her eyes flashed, and a bright colour rushed to her cheeks.

"Now I know why we were told to come into the garden!" she exclaimed, her voice quivering with anger. "They're nailing up the door of my room that leads to the roof!"

"Saidee!" To Victoria the thing seemed too monstrous to believe.

"Cassim threatened to do it once before—a long time ago—but he didn't. Now he has. That's his answer to your Mr. Knight."

"Perhaps you're wrong. How could any one have got into your rooms without our seeing them pass through the garden?"

"I've always thought there was a sliding door at the back of one of my wall cupboards. There generally is one leading into the harem rooms in old houses like this. Thank goodness I've hidden my diaries in a new place lately!"

"Let's go up and make sure," whispered Victoria.

Still the pounding went on.

"They'll have locked us out."

"We can try."

Victoria went ahead, running quickly up the steep, narrow flight of steps that led to the upper rooms which she and Saidee shared. Saidee had been right. The door of the outer room was locked. Standing at the top of the stairs, the pounding sounded much louder than before.

Saidee laughed faintly and bitterly.

"They're determined to make a good job of it," she said.

XLIV

Stephen rode back with his Arab companion, to the desert city where Nevill waited. He had gone to the Zaouïa alone with the guide, because Nevill had thought it well, in case of emergencies, that he should be able to say: "I have a friend in Oued Tolga who knows where I am, and is expecting me." Now he was coming away, thwarted for the moment, but far from hopeless.

It is a four hours' ride among the dunes, between the Zaouïa and the town, for the sand is heavy and the distance is about seventeen miles. The red wine of sunset was drained from the cups of the sand-hollows, and the shadows were cool when Stephen saw the minaret of the town mosque and the crown of an old watch-tower, pointing up like a thumb and finger of a buried hand. Soon after, he passed through the belt of black tents which at all seasons encircles Oued Tolga as a girdle encircles the waist of an Ouled Naïl, and so he rode into the strange city. The houses were crowded together, two with one wall between, like Siamese twins, and they had the pale yellow-brown colour of honeycomb, in the evening light. The roughness of the old, old bricks, made of baked sand, gave an effect of many little cells; so that the honeycomb effect was intensified; and the sand which flowed in small rippling waves round the city, and through streets narrow and broad, was of the same honey-yellow as the houses, except that it glittered with gypsum under the kindling stars. Among the bubbly domes, and low square towers, vague in the dimming light, bunches of palms in hidden gardens nodded over crumbling walls, like dark plumes on the crowns of the dancing- women.

In the market-place was the little hotel, newly built; the only French thing in Oued Tolga, except the military barracks, the Bureau Arabe, and a gurgling artesian well which a French officer had lately completed. But before Stephen could reach the market-place and the hotel, he had to pass through the quarter of the dancing-girls.

It was a narrow street, which had low houses on either side, with a balcony for every mean window. Dark women leaned their elbows on the palm-wood railings, and looked down, smoking cigarettes, and calling across to each other. Other girls sat in lighted doorways below, each with a candle guttering on a steep step of her bare staircase; and in the street walked silent men with black or brown faces, whose white burnouses flowed round their tall figures like blowing clouds. Among them were a few soldiers, whose uniforms glowed red in the twilight, like the cigarette ends pulsing between the painted lips of the Ouled Naïls. All that quarter reeked with the sweet, wicked smell of the East; and in the Moorish café at the far end, the dancing-music had begun to throb and whine, mingling cries of love and death, with the passion of both. But there was no dancing yet, for the audience was not large enough. The brilliant spiders crouched in their webs, awaiting more flies; for caravans were coming in across that desert sea which poured its yellow billows into the narrow street; and in the market-place, camel- drivers only just arrived were cooking their suppers. They would all come a little later into this quarter to drink many cups of coffee, and to spend their money on the dancers.

As Stephen went by on horseback, the girls on the balconies and in the doorways looked at him steadily without smiling, but their eyes sparkled under their golden crowns, or scarlet headkerchiefs and glittering veils. Behind him and his guide, followed a procession of boys and old men, with donkeys loaded with dead palm-branches from the neighbouring oasis, and the dry fronds made a loud swishing sound; but the dancers paid no attention, and appeared to look through the old men and children as if they did not exist.

In the market-place were the tired camels, kneeling down, looking gloomily at their masters busy cooking supper on the sand. Negro sellers of fruit and fly-embroidered lumps of meat, or brilliant-coloured pottery, and cheap, bright stuffs, were rolling up their wares for the night, in red and purple rags or tattered matting. Beggars lingered, hoping for a stray dried date, or a coin before crawling off to secret dens; and two deformed dwarfs in enormous turbans and blue coats, claimed power as marabouts, chanting their own praises and the praises of Allah, in high, cracked voices.

As Stephen rode to the hotel, and stopped in front of the arcade which shaded the ground floor, Nevill and another man sprang up from chairs pushed back against the white house-wall.

"By Jove, Legs, I'm glad to see you!" Nevill exclaimed, heartily, "What news?"

"Nothing very great so far, I'm sorry to say. Much as we expected," Stephen answered. And as he spoke, he glanced at the stranger, as if surprised that Nevill should speak out before him. The man wore the smart uniform of the Chasseurs d'Afrique. He was quite young, not over thirty-four, and had a keen, brave face, as Stephen could see by the crude light of a lamp that was fixed in the wall. But the large grey eyes, somewhat pale in contrast with deep sunburn, were the eyes of a poet rather than those of a born soldier.

"I must introduce you and Captain Sabine to each other," Nevill went on, in French, as Stephen got off his horse and it was led away by the Arab. "He's staying at the hotel. He and I've been talking about the Zaouïa and—the marabout. The upshot of our conversation will astonish you. I feel sure, when you hear it, you will think we can talk freely about our business to Captain Sabine."

Stephen said something polite and vague. He was interested, of course, but would have preferred to tell his adventure to Nevill alone.

"Monsieur Caird and I made acquaintance, and have been chatting all the afternoon," volunteered Sabine. "To begin with, we find we have many friends in common, in Algiers. Also he knows relations of mine, who have spoken of me to him, so it is almost as if we had known each other longer. He tells me that you and he are searching for a young lady who has disappeared. That you have followed here a man who must know where she is; that in the city, you lost track of the man but heard he had gone on to the Zaouïa; that this made you hope the young lady was there with her sister, whose husband might perhaps have some position under the marabout."

"I told him these things, because I thought, as Captain Sabine's been sinking an artesian well near the Zaouïa, he might have seen Miss Ray, if she were there. No such luck. He hasn't seen her; however, he's given me a piece of information which makes it just about as sure she *is* there, as if he had. You shall have it from him. But first let me ask you one question. Did you get any news of her?"

"No. I heard nothing."

"Does that mean you saw — —"

"No. I'll tell you later. But anyhow, I went into the Zaouïa, almost certain she was there, and that she'd seen me coming. That was a good start, because of course I'd had very little to go on. There was only a vague hope. I asked for the marabout, and they made me send a visiting-card—quaint in the desert. Then they kept me moving about a while, and insisted on showing me the mosque. At last they took me to a hideous reception room, with a lot of good and vile things in it, mixed up together. The marabout came in, wearing the black mask we'd heard about—a fellow with a splendid bearing, and fine eyes that looked at me very hard over the mask. They were never off my face. We complimented each other in French. Then I said I was looking for a Miss Ray, an American girl who had disappeared from Algiers, and had been traced to the Zaouïa, where I had reason to believe she was staying with a relative from her own country, a lady married to some member of his staff. I couldn't give him the best reason I had for being sure she *was* there, as you'll see when I tell you what it was. But he said gravely that no European lady was married to any one in the Zaouïa; that no American or any other foreign person, male or female, was there. In the guest-house were one or two Arab ladies, he admitted, who had come to be cured of maladies by virtue of his power; but no one else. His denial showed me that he was in the plot to hide Miss Ray. That was one thing I wanted to know; so I saw that the best thing for her, would be for me to pretend to be satisfied. If it hadn't been for what happened before I got to the Zaouïa gates, I should almost have been taken in by him, perhaps, he had such an air of noble, impeccable sincerity. But just as I dipped down into a kind of hollow, on the Zaouïa side of the river, something was thrown from somewhere. Unluckily I couldn't be sure where. I'd been looking up at the roofs behind the walls, but I must have had my eyes on the wrong one, if this thing fell from a roof, as I believe it did. It was a little bundle, done up in a handkerchief, and I saw it only as it touched the ground, about a dozen yards in front. Then I hurried on, you may be sure, hoping it was meant for me, to grab the thing before any one else could appear and lay hands on it."

"Well?"

"Luckily I'd outridden the guide. I made him think afterward that I'd jumped off my horse to pick up the whip, which I dropped for a blind, in case of spying eyes. Tied up in the silk handkerchief—an Arab-looking handkerchief—was a string of amber beads. Do you remember the beads Miss Ray bought of Miss Soubise, and wore to your house?"

"I remember she had a handsome string of old prayer-beads."

"Is this the one?" Stephen took the handkerchief and its contents from his pocket, and Nevill examined the large, round lumps of gleaming amber, which were somewhat irregular in shape. Captain Sabine looked on with interest.

"I can't be sure," Nevill said reluctantly.

"Well, I can," Stephen answered with confidence. "She showed it to me, in your garden. I remember a fly in the biggest bead, which was clear, with a brown spot, and a clouded bead on either side of it. I had the necklace in my hand. Besides, even if I weren't as certain as I am, who would throw a string of amber beads at my feet, if it weren't some one trying to attract my attention, in the only way possible? It was as much as to say, 'I know you've come looking for me. If you're told I'm not here, it's false.' I was a good long way from the gates; but much nearer to a lot of white roofs grouped behind the high wall of the Zaouïa, than I would have been in riding on, closer to the gates. Unfortunately there are high parapets to screen any one standing on the roofs. And anyhow, by the time the beads were thrown, I was too low down in the hollow to see even a waved hand or handkerchief. Still, with that necklace in my pocket, I knew pretty well what I was about, in talking with the marabout."

"You thought you did," said Nevill. "But you'd have known a lot more if only you could have made Captain Sabine's acquaintance before you started."

Stephen looked questioningly at the Frenchman.

"Perhaps it would be better to speak in English," suggested Sabine. "I have not much, but I get on. And the kitchen windows are not far away. Our good landlord and his wife do not cook with their ears. I was telling your friend that the marabout himself has a European wife—who is said to be a great beauty. These things get out. I have heard that she has red hair and skin as white as cream. That is also the description which Mr. Caird gave me of the young lady seeking a sister. It makes one put two and two together, does it not?"

"By Jove!" exclaimed Stephen. He and Nevill looked at each other, but Nevill raised his eyebrows slightly. He had not thought it best, at present, to give the mystery of Cassim ben Halim, as he now deciphered it, into a French officer's keeping. It was a secret in which France would be deeply, perhaps inconveniently, interested. A little later, the interference of the French might be welcome, but it would be just as well not to bring it in prematurely, or separately from their own personal interests. "I wish to heaven," Stephen went on, "I'd known this when I was talking to the fellow! And yet—I'm not sure it would have made much difference. We were deadly polite to each other, but I hinted in a veiled way that, if he were concealing any secret from me, the French authorities might have something to say to him. I was obsequious about the great power of Islam in general, and his in particular, but I suggested that France was the upper dog just now. Maybe his guilty conscience made him think I knew more than I did. I hope he expects to have the whole power of France down on him, as well as the United States, which I waved over his head, Miss Ray being an American. Of course I remembered your advice, Nevill, and was tactful—for her sake, for fear anything should be visited on her. I didn't say I thought he was hiding her in the Zaouïa. I put it as if I wanted his help in finding her. But naturally he expects me back again; and we must make our plans to storm the fortress and reduce it to subjection. There isn't an hour to waste, either, since this necklace, and Captain Sabine's knowledge, have proved to us that she's there. Too bad we didn't know it earlier, as we might have done something decisive in the beginning. But now we do know, with Captain Sabine's good will and introduction we may get the military element here to lend a hand in the negotiations. A European girl can't be shut up with impunity, I should think, even in this part of the world. And the marabout has every reason not to get in the bad books of the French."

"He is in their very best books at present," said Sabine. "He is thought much of. The peace of the southern desert is largely in his hands. My country would not be easily persuaded to offend him. It might be said in his defence that he is not compelled to tell strangers if he has a European wife, and her sister arrives to pay her a visit. Arab ideas are peculiar; and we have to respect them."

"I think my friend and I must talk the whole matter over," said Stephen, "and then, perhaps, we can make up our minds to a plan of action we couldn't have taken if it weren't for what you've told us— about the marabout and his European wife."

"I am glad if I have helped," Sabine answered. "And"—rather wistfully—"I should like to help further."

XLV

"Oh Lella Saïda, there is a message, of which I hardly dare to speak," whispered Noura to her mistress, when she brought supper for the two sisters, the night when the way to the roof had been closed up.

"Tell me what it is, and do not be foolish," Saidee said sharply. Her nerves were keyed to the breaking point, and she had no patience left. It was almost a pleasure to visit her misery upon some one else. She hated everybody and everything, because all hope was gone now. The door to the roof was nailed shut; and she and Victoria were buried alive.

"But one sends the message who must not be named; and it is not even for thee, lady. It is for the Little Rose, thy sister."

"If thou dost not speak out instantly, I will strike thee!" Saidee exclaimed, on the verge of hysterical tears.

"And if I speak, still thou wilt strike! Be this upon thine own head, my mistress. The Ouled Naïl has dared send her woman, saying that if the Little Rose will visit her house after supper, it will be for the good of all concerned, since she has a thing to tell of great importance. At first I would have refused even to take the message, but her woman, Hadda, is my cousin, and she feared to go back without some answer. The Ouled Naïl is a demon when in a temper, and she would thrust pins into Hadda's arms and thighs."

Saidee blushed with anger, disgustful words tingling on her tongue; but she remained silent, her lips parted.

"Of course I won't go," said Victoria, shocked. The very existence of Miluda was to her a dreadful mystery upon which she could not bear to let her mind dwell.

"I'm not sure," Saidee murmured. "Let me think. This means something very curious, I can't think what. But I should like to know. It can't make things worse for us if you accept her invitation. It may make them better. Will you go and see what the creature wants?"

"Oh, Saidee, how can I?"

"Because I ask it," Saidee answered, the girl's opposition deciding her doubts. "She can't eat you."

"It isn't that I'm afraid— —"

"I know! It's because of your loyalty to me. But if I send you, Babe, you needn't mind. It will be for my sake."

"Hadda is waiting for an answer," Noura hinted.

"My sister will go. Is the woman ready to take her?"

"I will find out, lady."

In a moment the negress came back. "Hadda will lead the Little Rose to her mistress. She is glad that it is to be now, and not later."

"Be very careful what you say, and forget nothing that *she* says," was Saidee's last advice. And it sounded very Eastern to Victoria.

She hated her errand, but undertook it without further protest, since it was for Saidee's sake.

Hadda was old and ugly. She and Noura had been born in the quarter of the freed Negroes, in the village across the river, and knew nothing of any world beyond; yet all the wiliness and wisdom of female things, since Eve—woman, cat and snake—glittered under their slanting eyelids.

Victoria had not been out of her sister's rooms and garden, except to visit M'Barka in the women's guest-house, since the night when Maïeddine brought her to the Zaouïa; and when she had time to think of her bodily needs, she realized that she longed desperately for exercise. Physically it was a relief to walk even the short distance between Saidee's house and Miluda's; but her cheeks tingled with some emotion she could hardly understand when she saw that the Ouled Naïl's garden-court was larger and more beautiful than Saidee's.

Miluda, however, was not waiting for her in the garden. The girl was escorted upstairs, perhaps to show her how much more important was the favourite wife of the marabout than a mere Roumia, an unmarried maiden.

A meal had been cleared away, in a room larger and better furnished than Saidee's and on the floor stood a large copper incense-burner, a thin blue smoke filtering through the perforations, clouding the atmosphere and loading it with heavy perfume. Behind the mist Victoria saw a divan, spread with trailing folds of purple velvet, stamped with gold; and something lay curled up on a huge tiger-skin, flung over pillows.

As the blue incense wreaths floated aside the curled thing on the tiger skin moved, and the light from a copper lamp like Saidee's, streamed through huge coloured lumps of glass, into a pair of brilliant eyes. A delicate brown hand, ringed on each finger, waved away the smoke of a cigarette it held, and Victoria saw a small face, which was like the face of a perfectly beautiful doll. Never had she imagined anything so utterly pagan; yet the creature was childlike, even innocent in its expression, as a baby tigress might be innocent.

Having sat up, the little heathen goddess squatted in her shrine, only bestirring herself to show the Roumia how beautiful she was, and what wonderful jewellery she had. She thought, that without doubt, the girl would run back jealously to the sister (whom Miluda despised) to pour out floods of description. She herself had heard much of Lella Saïda, and supposed that unfortunate woman had as eagerly collected information about her; but it was especially piquant that further details of enviable magnificence should be carried back by the forlorn wife's sister.

The Ouled Naïl tinkled at the slightest movement, even with the heaving of her bosom, as she breathed, making music with many necklaces, and long earrings that clinked against them. Dozens of old silver cases, tubes, and little jewelled boxes containing holy relics; hairs of Mohammed's beard; a bit of web spun by the sacred spider which saved his life; moles' feet blessed by marabouts, and texts from the Koran; all these hung over Miluda's breast, on chains of turquoise and amber beads. They rattled metallically, and her bracelets and anklets tinkled. Some luscious perfume hung about her, intoxicatingly sweet. A thick, braided clump of hair was looped on each side of the small face painted white as ivory, and her eyes, under lashes half an inch long, were bright and unhuman as those of an untamed gazelle.

"Wilt thou sit down?" she asked, waving the hand with the cigarette towards a French chair, upholstered in red brocade. "The Sidi gave me that seat because I asked for it. He gives me all I ask for."

"I will stand," answered Victoria.

"Oh, it is true, then, thou speakest Arab! I had heard so. I have heard much of thee and of thy youth and beauty. I see that my women did not lie. But perhaps thou art not as young as I am, though I have been a wife for a year, and have borne a beautiful babe. I am not yet sixteen."

Victoria did not answer, and the Ouled Naïl gazed at her unwinkingly, as a child gazes.

"Thou hast travelled much, even more than the marabout himself, hast thou not?" she inquired, graciously. "I have heard that thou hast been to England. Are there many Arab villages there, and is it true that the King was deposed when the Sultan, the head of our faith, lost his throne?"

"There are no Arab villages, and the King still reigns," said Victoria. "But I think thou didst not send for me to ask these questions?"

"Thou art right. Yet there is no harm in asking them. I sent for thee, for three reasons. One is, that I wished to see thee, to know if indeed thou wert as beautiful as I; another is, that I had a thing to give thee, and before I tell thee my third reason, thou shalt have the gift."

She fumbled in the tawny folds of the tiger-skin on which she lay, and presently held out a bracelet, made of flexible squares of gold, like scales, jewelled with different stones.

"It is thy wedding present from me," she said. "I wish to give it, because it is not long since I myself was married, and because we are both young. Besides, Si Maïeddine is a good friend of the marabout. I have heard that he is brave and handsome, all that a young girl can most desire in a husband."

"I am not going to marry Si Maïeddine," said Victoria. "I thank thee; but thou must keep thy gift for his bride when he finds one."

"He has found her in thee. The marriage will be a week from to-morrow, if Allah wills, and he will take thee away to his home. The marabout himself has told me this, though he does not know that I have sent for thee, and that thou art with me now."

"Allah does not will," said the girl.

"Perhaps not, since thy bridegroom-to-be lies ill with marsh fever, so Hadda has told me. He came back from Algiers with the sickness heavy upon him, caught in the saltpetre marshes that stretch between Biskra and Touggourt. I know those marshes, for I was in Biskra with my mother when she danced there; but she was careful, and we did not lie at night in the dangerous regions where the great mosquitoes are. Men are never careful, though they do not like to be ill, and thy bridegroom is fretting. But he will be better in a few days if he takes the draughts which the marabout has blessed for him; and if the wedding is not in a week, it will be a few days later. It is in Allah's hands."

"I tell thee, it will be never," Victoria persisted. "And I believe thou but sayest these things to torture me."

"Dost thou not love Si Maïeddine?" Miluda asked innocently.

"Not at all."

"Then it must be that thou lovest some other man. Dost thou, Roumia?"

"Thou hast no right to ask such questions."

"Be not angry, Roumia, for we are coming now to the great reason why I sent for thee. It is to help thee. I wish to know whether there is a man of thine own people thou preferest to Si Maïeddine."

"Why shouldst thou wish to help me? Thou hast never seen me till now."

"I will speak the truth with thee," said Miluda, "because thy face pleases me, though I prefer my own. Thine is pure and good, like the face of the white angel that is ever at our right hand; and even if I should speak falsely, I think thou wouldst not be deceived. Before I saw thee, I did not care whether thou wert happy or sad. It was nothing to me; but I saw a way of getting thee and thy sister out of my husband's house, and for a long time I have wished thy sister gone. Not that I am jealous of her. I have not seen her face, but I know she is already old, and if she were not friendless in our land, the Sidi would have put her away at the time of my marriage to him, since long ago he has ceased to care whether she lives or dies. But his heart is great, and he has kept her under his roof for kindness' sake, though she has given him no child, and is no longer a wife to him. I alone fill his life."

She paused, hoping perhaps that Victoria would answer; but the girl was silent, biting her lip, her eyes cast down. So Miluda talked on, more quietly.

"There is a wise woman in the city, who brings me perfumes and silks which have come to Oued Tolga by caravan from Tunis. She has told me that thy sister has ill-wished me, and that I shall never have a boy—a real child—while Lella Saïda breathes the same air with me. That is the reason I want her to be gone. I will not help thee to go, unless thou takest her with thee."

"I will never, never leave this place unless we go together," Victoria answered, deeply interested and excited now.

"That is well. And if she loves thee also, she would not go alone; so my wish is to do what I can for both."

"What canst thou do?" the girl asked.

"I will tell thee. But first there is something to make clear. I was on my roof to-day, when a young Roumi rode up to the Zaouïa on the road from Oued Tolga. He looked towards the roofs, and I wondered. From mine, I cannot see much of thy sister's roof, but I watched, and I saw an arm outstretched, to throw a packet. Then I said to myself that he had come for thee. And later I was sure, because my women told me that while he talked with the marabout, the door which leads to thy sister's roof was nailed up hastily, by command of the master. Some order must have gone from him, unknown to the Roumi, while the two men were together. I could coax nothing of the story from the Sidi when he came to me, but he was vexed, and his brows drew together over eyes which for the first time did not seem to look at me with pleasure."

"Thou hast guessed aright," Victoria admitted, thankful that Miluda's suspicions concerned her affairs only, and not Saidee's. "The man who came here was my friend. I care for him more than for any one in the world, except my sister; and if I cannot marry him, I will die rather than marry Si Maïeddine or any other."

"Then, unless I help thee, thou wilt have to die, for nothing which thou alone, or thy sister can do, will open the gates for thee to go out, except as Si Maïeddine's wife."

"Then help me," said Victoria, boldly, "and thou wilt be rid of us both forever."

"It is with our wits we must work, not with our hands," replied the Ouled Naïl. "The power of the marabout is great. He has many men to serve him, and the gates are strong, while women are very, very weak. Yet I have seen into the master's heart, and I can give thee a key which will unlock the gates. Only it had better be done soon, for when Si Maïeddine is well, he will fight for thee; and if thou goest forth free, he will follow, and take thee in the dunes."

Victoria shivered, for the picture was vivid before her eyes, as Miluda painted it. "Give me the key," she said in a low voice.

"The key of the master's heart is his son," the other answered, in a tone that kept down anger and humiliation. "Even me he would sacrifice to his boy. I know it well, and I hate the child. I pray for one of my own, for because the Sidi loves me, and did not love the boy's mother, he would care ten thousand times more for a child of mine. The wise woman says so, and I believe it. When thy sister is gone, I shall have a boy, and nothing left to wish for on earth. Send a message to thy lover, saying that the marabout's only son is at school in Oued Tolga, the city. Tell him to steal the child and hide it, making a bargain with the marabout that he shall have it safely back, if he will let thee and thy sister go; otherwise he shall never see it again."

"That would be a cruel thing to do, and my sister could not consent," said Victoria, "even if we were able to send a message."

"Hadda would send the message. A friend from the village is coming to see her, and the master has no suspicion of me at present, as he has of thee. We could send a letter, and Hadda would manage everything. But there is not much time, for now while my husband is with Si Maïeddine, treating him for his fever, is our only chance, to- night. We have perhaps an hour in which to decide and arrange everything. After that, his coming may be announced to me. And no harm would happen to the child. The master would suffer in his mind for a short time, till he decided to make terms, that is all. As for me, have no fear of my betraying thee. Thou needst but revenge thyself by letting the master know how I plotted for the stealing of his boy, for him to put me out of his heart and house forever. Then I should have to kill myself with a knife, or with poison; and I am young and happy, and do not desire to die yet. Go now, and tell thy sister what I have said. Let her answer for thee, for she knows this land and the people of it, and she is wiser than thou."

Without another word or look at the beautiful pagan face, Victoria went out of the room, and found Hadda waiting to hurry her away.

XLVI

It was after one o'clock when Stephen and Nevill bade each other good night, after a stroll out of the town into the desert. They had built up plans and torn them down again, and no satisfactory decision had been reached, for both feared that, if they attempted to threaten the marabout with their knowledge of his past, he would defy them to do their worst. Without Saidee and Victoria, they could bring forward no definite and visible proof that the great marabout, Sidi El Hadj Mohammed Abd el Kadr, and the disgraced Captain Cassim ben Halim were one. And the supreme difficulty was to produce Saidee and Victoria as witnesses. It was not even certain, if the marabout were threatened and thought himself in danger, that he might not cause the sisters to disappear. That thought prevented the two men from coming easily to any decision. Sabine had not told them that he knew Saidee, or that he had actually heard of the girl's arrival in the Zaouïa. He longed to tell and join with them in their quest; but it would have seemed a disloyalty to the woman he loved. It needed a still greater incentive to make him speak out; while as for the Englishmen, though they would gladly have taken his advice, they hesitated to give away the secret of Saidee Ray's husband to a representative of Ben Halim's stern judge, France.

Various plans for action had been discussed, yet Stephen and Nevill both felt that all were subject to modification. Each had the hope that the silent hours would bring inspiration, and so they parted at last. But Stephen had not been in his room ten minutes when there came a gentle tap at his door. He thought that it must be Nevill, returning to announce the birth of a new idea; but in the dark corridor stood a shadowy Arab, he who did most of the work in the hotel outside the kitchen.

"A person has come with a letter for Monsieur," the man mumbled in bad French, his voice so sleepy as to be almost inarticulate. "He would not give it to me, the foolish one. He insists on putting it into the hand of Monsieur. No doubt it is a pourboire he wants. He has followed me to the head of the stairs, and he has no French."

"Where does he come from?" asked Stephen.

"He will not say. But he is a Negro whom I have never seen in the city."

"Call him," Stephen said. And in a moment a thin young Negro, dusted all over with sand, came into the square of light made by the open door. His legs were bare, and over his body he appeared to have no other garment but a ragged, striped gandourah. In a purple-black hand he held a folded piece of paper, and Stephen's heart jumped at sight of his own name written in a clear handwriting. It was not unlike Victoria's but it was not hers.

"The man says he cannot take a letter back," explained the Arab servant. "But if Monsieur will choose a word to answer, he will repeat it over and over until he has it by heart. Then he will pass it on in the same way."

Stephen was reading his letter and scarcely heard. It was Victoria's sister who wrote. She signed herself at the bottom of the bit of paper — a leaf torn from a copy book — "Saidee Ray," as though she had never been married. She had evidently written in great haste, but the thing she proposed was clearly set forth, as if in desperation. Victoria did not approve, she said, and hoped some other plan might be found; but in Saidee's opinion there was no other plan which offered any real chance of success. In their situation, they could not afford to stick at trifles, and neither could Mr. Knight, if he wished to save Victoria from being married against her will to an Arab. There was no time to lose if anything were to be done; and if Mr. Knight were willing to take the way suggested, would he say the word "yes," very distinctly, to the messenger, as it would not be safe to try and smuggle a letter into the Zaouïa.

It was a strange, even a detestable plot, which Saidee suggested; yet when Stephen had turned it over in his mind for a moment he said the word "yes" with the utmost distinctness. The sand-covered Negro imitated him several times, and having achieved success, was given more money than he had ever seen in his life. He would not tell the Arab, who escorted him downstairs again, whence he had come, but it was a long distance and he had walked. He must return on foot, and if he were to be back by early morning, he ought to get off at once. Stephen made no effort to keep him, though he would have liked Saidee's messenger to be seen by Caird.

Nevill had not begun to undress, when Stephen knocked at his door. He was about to begin one of his occasional letters to Josette, with his writing materials arranged abjectly round one tallow candle, on a washhand stand.

"That beast of a Cassim! He's going to try and marry the poor child off to his friend Maïeddine!" Nevill growled, reading the letter. "Stick at trifles indeed! I should think not. This is Providential—just when we couldn't quite make up our minds what to do next."

"You're not complimentary to Providence," said Stephen. "Seems to me a horrid sort of thing to do, though I'm not prepared to say I won't do it. *She* doesn't approve, her sister says, you see——"

"Who knows the man better, his wife or the girl?"

"That goes without saying. Well, I'm swallowing my scruples as fast as I can get them down, though they're a lump in my throat. However, we wouldn't hurt the little chap, and if the father adores him, as she says, we'd have Ben Halim pretty well under our thumbs, to squeeze him as we chose. Knowing his secret as we do, he wouldn't dare apply to the French for help, for fear we'd give him away. We must make it clear that we well know who he is, and that if he squeals, the fat's in the fire!"

"That's the right spirit. We'll make him shake in his boots for fear we give not only the secret, but the boy, over to the tender mercies of the authorities. For it's perfectly true that if the Government knew what a trick had been played on them, they'd oust the false marabout in favour of the rightful man, whoever he may be, clap the usurper into prison, and make the child a kind of—er—ward in chancery, or whatever the equivalent is in France. Oh, I can tell you, my boy, this idea is the inspiration of a genius! The man will see we're making no idle threat, that we can't carry out. He'll have to hand over the ladies, or he'll spend some of his best years in prison, and never see his beloved boy again."

"First we've got to catch our hare. But there Sabine could help us, if we called him in."

"Yes. And we couldn't do better than have him with us, I think, Legs, now we've come to this turn in the road."

"I agree so far. Still, let's keep Ben Halim's secret to ourselves. We must have it to play with. I believe Sabine's a man to trust; but he's a French officer; and a plot of that sort he might feel it his duty to make known."

"All right. We'll keep back that part of the business. It isn't necessary to give it away. But otherwise Sabine's the man for us. He's a romantic sort of chap, not unlike me in that; it's what appealed to me in him the minute we began to draw each other out. He'll snap at an adventure to help a pretty girl even though he's never seen her; and he knows the marabout's boy and the guardian-uncle. He was talking to me about them this afternoon. Let's go and rout him out. I bet he'll have a plan to propose."

"Rather cheek, to rouse him up in the middle of the night. We might wait till morning, since I don't see that we can do anything useful before."

"He only got in from seeing some friend in barracks, about one. He doesn't look like a sleepy-head. Besides, if I'm not mistaken, I smell his cigarettes. He's probably lying on his bed, reading a novel."

But Sabine was reading something to him far more interesting than any novel written by the greatest genius of all ages; a collection of Saidee's letters, which he invariably read through, from first to last, every night before even trying to sleep.

The chance to be in the game of rescue was new life to him. He grudged Saidee's handwriting to another man, even though he felt that, somehow, she had hoped that he would see it, and that he would work with the others. He laughed at the idea that the adventure would be more dangerous for him as a French officer, if anything leaked out, than for two travelling Englishmen.

"I would give my soul to be in this!" he exclaimed, before he knew what he was saying, or what meaning might be read into his words. But both faces spoke surprise. He was abashed, yet eager. The impulse of his excitement led him on, and he began stammering out the story he had not meant to tell.

"I can't say the things you ought to know, without the things that no one ought to know," he explained in his halting English, plunging back now and then inadvertently into fluent French. "It is wrong not to confess that all the time I know that young lady is there—in the Zaouïa. But there is a reason I feel it not right to confess. Now it will be different because of this letter that has come. You must hear all and you can judge me."

So the story was poured out: the romance of that wonderful day when, while he worked at the desert well in the hot sun, a lady went by, with her servants, to the Moorish baths. How her veil had fallen aside, and he had seen her face—oh, but the face of a houri, an angel.

Yet so sad—tragedy in the beautiful eyes. In all his life he had not seen such beauty or felt his heart so stirred. Through an attendant at the baths he had found out that the lovely lady was the wife of the marabout, a Roumia, said not to be happy. From that moment he would have sacrificed his hopes of heaven to set her free. He had written—he had laid his life at her feet. She had answered. He had written again. Then the sister had arrived. He had been told in a letter of her coming. At first he had thought it impossible to confide a secret concerning another—that other a woman—even to her sister's friends. But now there was no other way. They must all work together. Some day he hoped that the dear prisoner would be free to give herself to him as his wife. Till then, she was sacred, even in his thoughts. Even her sister could find no fault with his love. And would the new friends shake his hand wishing him joy in future.

So all three shook hands with great heartiness; and perhaps Sabine would have become still more expansive had he not been brought up to credit Englishmen stolid fellows at best with a favourite motto: "Deeds, not words."

As Sabine told his story, Stephen's brain had been busily weaving. He did not like the thing they had to do, but if it must be done, the only hope lay in doing it well and thoroughly. Sabine's acquaintance with the boy and his guardian would be a great help.

"I've been thinking how we can best carry out this business," he said, when the pact of friendship had been sealed by clasp of hands. "We can't afford to have any row or scandal. It must somehow be managed without noise, for the sake of—the ladies, most of all, and next, for the sake of Captain Sabine. As a Frenchman and an officer, it would certainly be a lot worse for him than for us, if we landed him in any mess with the authorities."

"I care nothing for myself." Sabine broke in, hotly.

"All the more reason for us to keep our heads cool if we can, and look after you. We must get the boy to go away of his own accord."

"That is more easy to propose than to do," said Sabine, with a shrug of the shoulders.

"Well, an idea has come into my head. There may be something in it— if you can help us work it. We couldn't do it without you. Do you know the child and his uncle so well that it wouldn't seem queer to invite them to the hotel for a meal—say luncheon to-morrow, or rather to-day—for it's morning now?"

"Yes, I could do that. And they would come. It would be an amusement for them. Life is dull here," Sabine eagerly replied.

"Good. Does the child speak French?"

"A little. He is learning in the school."

"That's lucky, for I don't know a dozen words of Arab, and even my friend Caird can't be eloquent in it. Wings, do you think you could work up the boy to a wild desire for a tour in a motor-car?"

"I would bet on myself to do that. I could make him a motor fiend, between the *hors d'œuvres* and fruit."

"Our great stumbling block, then, is the uncle. I suppose he's a sort of watch-dog, who couldn't be persuaded to leave the boy alone a minute?"

"I am not sure of that," said Sabine. "It is true he is a watch-dog; but I could throw him a bone I think would tempt him to desert his post—if he had no suspicion of a trap. What you want, I begin to see, is to get him out of the way, so that Monsieur Caird could induce the little Mohammed to go away willingly?"

"Yes."

"*Eh bien!* It is as good as done. I see the way. Hassan ben Saad, the respectable uncle, has a secret weakness which I have found out. He has lost his head for the prettiest and youngest dancer in the quarter of the Ouled Naïls. She is a great favourite, Nedjma, and she will not look at him. He is too old and dry. Besides, he has no money except what the marabout gives him as guardian to the boy at school. Hassan sends Nedjma such presents as he can afford, and she laughs at them with the other girls, though she keeps them, of course. To please me, she will write a letter to Ben Saad, telling him that if he comes to her at once, without waiting a moment, he may find her heart soft for him. This letter shall be brought to our table, at the hotel, while Hassan finishes his *déjeuner* with us. He will make a thousand apologies and tell a thousand lies, saying it is a call of business. Probably he will pretend that it concerns the marabout, of whom he boasts always as his relative. Then he will go, in a great hurry, leaving the child, because we will kindly invite him to do so;

and he will promise to return soon for his nephew. But Nedjma will be so sweet that he will not return soon. He will be a long time away — hours. He will forget the boy, and everything but his hope that at last Nedjma will love him. Does that plan of mine fit in with yours, Monsieur?"

"Perfectly," said Knight. "What do you think, Wings?"

"As you do. You're both geniuses. And I'll try to keep my end up by fascinating the child. He shall be mine, body and soul, by the end of lunch. When he finds that we're leaving Oued Tolga, instantly, and that he must be sent ignominiously home, he shall be ready to howl with grief. Then I'll ask him suddenly, how he'd like to go on a little trip, just far enough to meet my motor-car, and have a ride in it. He'll say yes, like a shot, if he's a normal boy. And if the uncle's away, it will be nobody's business even if they see the marabout's son having a ride behind me on my horse, as he might with his own father. Trust me to lure the imp on with us afterward, step by step, in a dream of happiness. I was always a born lurer—except when I wanted a thing or person for myself."

"You say, lure him on with 'us'" Stephen cut in. "But it will have to be you alone. I must stay at this end of the line, and when the time comes, give the marabout our ultimatum. The delay will be almost intolerable, but of course the only thing is to lie low until you're so far on the way to Touggourt with the child, that a rescue scheme would be no good. Touggourt's a bit on the outskirts of the marabout's zone of influence, let's hope. Besides, he wouldn't dare attack you there, in the shadow of the French barracks. It's his business to help keep peace in the desert, and knowing what we know of his past, I think with the child out of his reach he'll be pretty well at our mercy."

"When Hassan ben Saad finds the boy gone, he will be very sick," said Sabine. "But I shall be polite and sympathetic, and will give him good advice. He is in deadly awe of the marabout, and I will say that, if the child's father hears what has happened, there will be no forgiveness— nothing but ruin. Waiting is the game to play, I will counsel Hassan. I shall remind him that, being Friday, no questions will be asked at school till Monday, and I shall raise his hopes that little Mohammed will be back soon after that, if not before. At worst, I will say, he can pretend the child is shut up in the house with a cough. I shall assure him that Monsieur Caird is a man of honour and great riches; that no harm can come to little Mohammed in his care. I will explain how the boy pleaded to go, and make Hassan happy with the expectation that in a few days Monsieur Caird is coming back to fetch his friend; that certainly Mohammed will be with him, safe and sound; and that, if he would not lose his position, he must say nothing of what has happened to any one who might tell the marabout."

"Do you think you can persuade him to keep a still tongue in his head till it suits us to have him speak, or write a letter for me to take?" asked Stephen.

"I am sure of it. Hassan is a coward, and you have but to look him in the face to see he has no self-reliance. He must lean on some one else. He shall lean on me. And Nedjma shall console him, so that time will pass, and he shall hardly know how it is going. He will speak when we want him to speak or write, not before."

The three men talked on in Stephen's room till dawn, deciding details which cropped up for instant settlement. At last it was arranged — taking the success of their plan for granted — that Stephen should wait a day and a half after the departure of Nevill's little caravan. By that time, it should have got half-way to Touggourt; but there was one bordj where it would come in touch with the telegraph. Stephen would then start for the Zaouïa, for an interview with the marabout, who, no doubt, was already wondering why he did not follow up his first attempt by a second. He would hire or buy in the city a racing camel fitted with a bassour large enough for two, and this he would take with him to the Zaouïa, ready to bring away both sisters. No allusion to Saidee would be made in words. The "ultimatum" would concern Victoria only, as the elder sister was wife to the marabout, and no outsider could assume to have jurisdiction over her. But as it was certain that Victoria would not stir without Saidee, a demand for one was equivalent to a demand for the other.

This part of the plan was to be subject to modification, in case Stephen saw Victoria, and she proposed any course of action concerning her sister. As for Sabine, having helped to make the plot he was to hold himself ready at Oued Tolga, the city, for Stephen's return from the Zaouïa. And the rest was on the knees of the gods.

XLVII

For the second time Stephen entered by the great gates of the Zaouïa. The lounging Negro, who had let him in before, stared at the grey mehari with the red-curtained bassour, whose imposing height dwarfed the Roumi's horse. No doubt the man wondered why it was there, since only women or invalids travelled in a bassour;—and his eyes dwelt with interest on the two Arabs from the town of Oued Tolga. Perhaps he thought that they would satisfy his curiosity, when the visitor had gone inside. But Stephen thought differently. The Arabs would tell nothing, because they knew nothing which could explain the mystery.

The Negro had no French, and either did not understand or pretended not to understand the Roumi's request to see the marabout. This looked ominous, because Stephen had been let in without difficulty the first time; and the Negro seemed intelligent enough to be stupid in accordance with instructions. Great insistance, however, and the production of documents (ordinary letters, but effective to impress the uneducated intelligence) persuaded the big gate-keeper to send for an interpreter.

Stephen waited with outward patience, though a loud voice seemed crying in his ears, "What will happen next? What will the end be—success, or a sudden fluke that will mean failure?" He barred his mind against misgivings, but he had hoped for some sign of life when he rode in sight of the white roofs; and there had been no sign.

For many minutes he waited; and then came an old man who had showed him to the marabout's reception room on his first visit. Stephen was glad to see this person, because he could speak a little French, and because he had a mild air, as if he might easily be browbeaten.

"I must see Sidi Mohammed on important business," Stephen said.

The old man was greatly grieved, but Sidi Mohammed was indisposed and not able to speak with any one. Would Monsieur care to visit the mosque again, and would he drink coffee?

So this was the game! Stephen was not surprised. His face flushed and his jaw squared. He would not drink coffee, and he would not give himself the pleasure of seeing the mosque; but would trouble the interpreter with a message to the marabout; and would await an answer. Then Stephen wrote on one of his visiting cards, in English. "I have important news of your son, which you would regret not hearing. And it can be told to no one but yourself."

In less than ten minutes the messenger came back. The marabout, though not well, would receive Monsieur. Stephen was led through the remembered labyrinth of covered passages, dim and cool, though outside the desert sand flamed under the afternoon sun; and as he walked he was aware of softly padding footsteps behind him. Once, he turned his head quickly, and saw that he was followed by a group of three tall Negroes. They looked away when they met his eyes, as if they were on his heels by accident; but he guessed that they had been told to watch him, and took the caution as a compliment. Yet he realized that he ran some risk in coming to this place on such an errand as his. Already the marabout looked upon him as an enemy, no doubt; and it was not impossible that news of the boy's disappearance had by this time reached the Zaouïa, in spite of his guardian's selfish cowardice. If so, and if the father connected the kidnapping of his son with to-day's visitor, he might let his desire for revenge overcome prudence. To prove his power by murdering an Englishman, his guest, would do the desert potentate more harm than good in the end; yet men of mighty passions do not always stop to think of consequences, and Stephen was not blind to his own danger. If the marabout lost his temper, not a man in the Zaouïa but would be ready to obey a word or gesture, and short work might be made of Victoria Ray's only champion. However, Stephen counted a good deal on Ben Halim's caution, and on the fact that his presence in the Zaouïa was known outside. He meant to acquaint his host with that fact as a preface to their conversation.

"The marabout will come presently," the mild interpreter announced, when he had brought Stephen once more to the reception room adjoining the mosque. So saying, he bowed himself away, and shut the door; but Stephen opened it almost instantly, to look out. It was as he expected. The tall Negroes stood lazily on guard. They scarcely showed surprise at being caught, yet their fixed stare was somewhat strained.

"I wonder if there's to be a signal?" thought Stephen.

It was very still in the reception-room of Sidi Mohammed. The young man sat down opposite the door of that inner room from which the marabout had come to greet him the other day, but he did not turn his back fully upon the door behind which were the watchers. Minutes passed on. Nothing happened, and there was no sound. Stephen grew impatient. He knew, from what he had heard of the great Zaouïa, that manifold and strenuous lives were being lived all around him in this enormous hive, which was university, hospice, mosque, and walled village in one. Yet there was no hum of men talking, of women chatting over their work, or children laughing at play. The silence was so profound that it was emphasized to his ears by the droning of a fly in one of the high, iron-barred windows; and in spite of himself he started when it was suddenly and ferociously broken by a melancholy roar like the thunderous yawn of a bored lion. But still the marabout did not appear. Evidently he intended to show the persistent Roumi that he was not to be intimidated or browbeaten, or else he did not really mean to come at all.

The thought that perhaps, while he waited, he had been quietly made a prisoner, brought Stephen to his feet. He was on the point of trying the inner door, when it opened, and the masked marabout stood looking at him, with keen eyes which the black veil seemed to darken and make sinister.

Without speaking, the Arab closed, but did not latch, the door behind him; and standing still he spoke in the deep voice that was slightly muffled by the thin band of woollen stuff over the lower part of his face.

"Thou hast sent me an urgent summons to hear tidings of my son," he said in his correct, measured French. "What canst thou know, which I do not know already?"

"I began to think you were not very desirous to hear my news," replied Stephen, "as I have been compelled to wait so long that my friends in Oued Tolga will be wondering what detains me in the Zaouïa, or whether any accident has befallen me."

"As thou wert doubtless informed, I am not well, and was not prepared to receive guests. I have made an exception in thy favour, because of the message thou sent. Pray, do not keep me in suspense, if harm has come to my son." Sidi Mohammed did not invite his guest to sit down.

"No harm has come to the boy," Stephen reassured him. "He is in good hands."

"In charge of his uncle, whom I have appointed his guardian," the marabout broke in.

"He doesn't know anything yet," Stephen said to himself, quickly. Then, aloud: "At present, he is not in charge of his uncle, but is with a friend of mine. He will be sent back safe and well to Oued Tolga, when you have discovered the whereabouts of Miss Ray—the young lady of whom you knew nothing the other day—and when you have produced her. I know now, with absolute certainty, that she is here in the Zaouïa. When she leaves it, with me and the escort I have brought, to join her friends, you will see your son again, but not before; and never unless Miss Ray is given up."

The marabout's dark hands clenched themselves, and he took a step forward, but stopped and stood still, tall and rigid, within arm's-length of the Englishman.

"Thou darest to come here and threaten me!" he said. "Thou art a fool. If thou and thy friends have stolen my child, all will be punished, not by me, but by the power which is set above me to rule this land—France."

"We have no fear of such punishment, or any other," Stephen answered. "We have 'dared' to take the boy; and I have dared, as you say, to come here and threaten, but not idly. We have not only your son, but your secret, in our possession; and if Miss Ray is not allowed to go, or if anything happens to me, you will never see your boy again, because France herself will come between you and him. You will be sent to prison as a fraudulent pretender, and the boy will become a ward of the nation. He will no longer have a father."

The dark eyes blazed above the mask, though still the marabout did not move. "Thou art a liar and a madman," he said. "I do not understand thy ravings, for they have no meaning."

"They will have a fatal meaning for Cassim ben Halim if they reach the ears of the French authorities, who believe him dead," said Stephen, quietly. "Ben Halim was only a disgraced officer, not a criminal, until he conspired against the Government, and stole a great position which belonged to another man. Since then, prison doors are open for him if his plottings are found out."

Unwittingly Stephen chose words which were as daggers in the breast of the Arab. Although made without knowledge of the secret work to which the marabout had vowed himself and all that was his, the young man's threat sounded like a hint so terrible in its meaning that Ben Halim's heart turned suddenly to water. He saw himself exposed, defeated, hand and foot in the enemy's power. How this Roumi had wormed out the hidden truth he could not conceive; but he realized on the instant that the situation was desperate, and his brain seemed to him to become a delicate and intricate piece of mechanism, moving with oiled wheels. All the genius of a great soldier and a great diplomat were needed at one and the same time, and if he could not call such inspiration to his aid he was lost. He had been tempted for one volcanic second to stab Stephen with the dagger which he always carried under his burnous and embroidered vest, but a lightning-flash of reason bade him hold his hand. There were other ways—there must be other ways. Fortunately Maïeddine had not been told of the Roumi's presence in the Zaouïa, and need not learn anything concerning him or his proposals until the time came when a friend could be of use and not a hindrance. Even in this moment, when he saw before his eyes a fiery picture of ruin, Ben Halim realized that Maïeddine's passion for Victoria Ray might be utilized by and by, for the second time.

Not once did the dark eyes falter or turn from the enemy's, and Stephen could not help admiring the Arab's splendid self-control. It was impossible to feel contempt for Ben Halim, even for Ben Halim trapped. Stephen had talked with an air of cool indifference, his hands in his pockets, but in one pocket was a revolver, and he kept his fingers on it as the marabout stood facing him silently after the ultimatum.

"I have listened to the end," the Arab said at last, "because I wished to hear what strange folly thou hadst got in thy brain. But now, when thou hast finished apparently, I cannot make head or tail of thy accusations. Of a man named Cassim ben Halim I may have heard, but he is dead. Thou canst hardly believe in truth that he and I are one; but even if thou dost believe it, I care little, for if thou wert unwise enough to go with such a story to my masters and friends the French, they could bring a hundred proofs that thy tale was false, and they would laugh thee to scorn. I have no fear of anything thou canst do against me; but if it is true that thou and thy friend have stolen my son, rather than harm should come to him who is my all on earth, I may be weak enough to treat with thee."

"I have brought proof that the boy is gone," returned Stephen. For the moment, he tacitly accepted the attitude which the marabout chose to take up. "Let the fellow save his face by pretending to yield entirely for the boy's sake," he said to himself. "What can it matter so long as he does yield?"

In the pocket with the revolver was a letter which Sabine had induced Hassan ben Saad to write, and now Stephen produced it. The writing was in Arabic, of course; but Sabine, who knew the language well, had translated every word for him before he started from Oued Tolga. Stephen knew, therefore, that the boy's uncle, without confessing how he had strayed from duty, admitted that, "by an incredible misfortune," the young Mohammed had been enticed away from him. He feared, Hassan ben Saad added, to make a disturbance, as an influential friend—Captain Sabine—advised him to inform the marabout of what had happened before taking public action which the child's father might disapprove.

The Arab frowned as he read on, not wholly because of his anger with the boy's guardian, though that burned in his heart, hot as a new-kindled fire, and could be extinguished only by revenge.

"This Captain Sabine," he said slowly, "I know slightly. He called upon me at a time when he made a well in the neighbourhood. Was it he who put into thine head these ridiculous notions concerning a dead man? I warn thee to answer truly if thou wouldst gain anything from me."

"My countrymen don't, as a rule, transact business by telling diplomatic lies," said Stephen smiling, as he felt that he could now afford to smile. "Captain Sabine did not put the notion into my head."

"Hast thou spoken of it to him?"

Stephen shrugged his shoulders slightly. "I do not see that I'm called upon to answer that question. All I will say is, you need have no fear of Captain Sabine or of any one else, once Miss Ray is safely out of this place."

The marabout turned this answer over quickly in his mind. He knew that, if Sabine or any Frenchman suspected his identity and his plans for the future, he was irretrievably lost. No private consideration would induce a French officer to spare him, if aware that he hoped eventually to overthrow the rule of France in North Africa. This being the case (and believing that Knight had learned of the plot), he reflected that Sabine could not have been taken into the secret, otherwise the Englishman dare not make promises. He saw too, that it would have been impolitic for Knight to take Sabine into his confidence. A Frenchman in the secret would have ruined this *coup d'état*; and, beginning to respect Stephen as an enemy, he decided that he was too clever to be in real partnership with the officer. Ben Halim's growing conviction was that his wife, Saidee, had told Victoria all she knew and all she suspected, and that the girl had somehow contrived to smuggle a letter out of the Zaouïa to her English lover.

The distrust and dislike he had long felt for Saidee suddenly burst into a flame of hatred. He longed to crush under his foot the face he had once loved, to grind out its beauty with a spurred heel. And he hated the girl, too, though he could not punish her as he could punish Saidee, for he must have Maïeddine's help presently, and Maïeddine would insist that she should be protected, whatever might happen to others. But he was beginning to see light ahead, if he might take it for granted that his secret was suspected by no more than four persons— Saidee, Victoria, and the two Englishmen who were acting for the girl.

"I see by this letter from my brother-in-law that it is even as thou sayest; thou and thy friend together have committed the cruel wrong of which thou boastest," Ben Halim said at last. "A father robbed of his one son is as a stag pinned to earth with a spear through his heart. He is in the hands of the hunter, his courage ebbing with his life-blood. Had this thing been done when thou wert here before, I should have been powerless to pay the tribute, for the lady over whom thou claimst a right was not within my gates. Now, I admit, she has come. If she wish to go with thee, she is free to do so. But I will send with her men of my own, to travel by her side, and refuse to surrender her until my child is given into their hands."

"That is easy to arrange," Stephen agreed. "I will telegraph to my friend, who is by this time—as you can see by your letter—two days' journey away or more. He will return with your son, and an escort, but only a certain distance. I will meet him at some place appointed, and we will hand the boy over to your men."

"It will be better that the exchange should be made here," said the marabout.

"I can see why it might be so from your point of view, but that view is not ours. You have too much power here, and frankly, I don't trust you. You'll admit that I'd be a fool if I did! The meeting must be at some distance from your Zaouïa."

The marabout raised his eyebrows superciliously. They said—"So thou art afraid!" But Stephen was not to be taunted into an imprudence where Victoria's safety was at stake.

"Those are our terms," he repeated.

"Very well, I accept," said the Arab. "Thou mayest send a message to the lady, inviting her to leave my house with thee; and I assure thee, that in any case I would have no wish to keep her, other than the desire of hospitality. Thou canst take her at once, if she will go; and passing through the city, with her and my men, thou canst send thy telegram. Appoint as a meeting place the Bordj of Toudja, one day's march from the town of Oued Tolga. When my men have the child in their keeping, thou wilt be free to go in peace with the girl and thy friend."

"I should be glad if thou wouldst send for her, and let me talk with her here," Stephen suggested.

"No, that cannot be," the marabout answered decidedly. "When she is out of my house, I wash my hands of her; but while she is under my roof it would be shameful that she should speak, even in my presence, with a strange man."

Stephen was ready to concede a point, if he could get his wish in another way. "Give me paper, then, and I will write to the lady," he said. "There will be an answer, and it must be brought to me quickly, for already I have stopped longer than I expected, and Captain Sabine, who knows I have come to call upon you and fetch a friend, may be anxious."

He spoke his last words with a certain emphasis, knowing that Ben Halim would understand the scarcely veiled threat.

The marabout went into the next room, and got some French writing paper. Stephen wrote a hasty note, begging Victoria to leave the Zaouïa under his care. He would take her, he said, to Lady MacGregor, who had come to Touggourt on purpose to be at hand if wanted. He wrote in English, but because he was sure that Ben Halim knew the language, he said nothing to Victoria about her sister. Only he mentioned, as if carelessly, that he had brought a good camel with a comfortable bassour large enough for two.

When the letter was in an envelope, addressed to Miss Ray, the marabout took it from Stephen and handed it to somebody outside the door, no doubt one of the three watchers. There were mumbled instructions in Arabic, and ten minutes later an answer came back. Stephen could have shouted for joy at sight of Victoria's handwriting. There were only a few lines, in pencil, but he knew that he would keep them always, with her first letter.

"Oh, how glad I am that you're here!" she wrote. "By and by I hope to thank you—but of course I can't come without my sister. She is wretched, and wants to leave the man who seems to her no longer a husband, but she thinks he will not want to let her go. Tell him that it must be both of us, or neither. Or if you feel it would be better, give him this to read, and ask him to send an answer."

Stephen guessed why the girl had written in French. She had fancied that the marabout would not choose to admit his knowledge of English, and he admired the quickness of her wit in a sudden emergency.

As he handed the letter to the Arab, Stephen would have given a great deal to see the face under the black mask. He could read nothing of the man's mind through the downcast eyelids, with their long black fringe of close-set lashes. And he knew that Ben Halim must have finished the short letter at least sixty seconds before he chose to look up from the paper.

"It is best," the marabout said slowly, "that the two sisters go together. A man of Islam has the right to repudiate a woman who gives him no children, but I have been merciful. Now an opportunity has come to rid myself of a burden, without turning adrift one who is helpless and friendless. For my son's sake I have granted thy request; for my own sake I grant the girl's request: but both, only on one condition—that thou swearest in the name of thy God, and upon the head of thy father, never to breathe with thy lips, or put with thy hand upon paper, the malicious story about me, at which thou hast to-day hinted; that thou enforce upon the two sisters the same silence, which, before going, they must promise me to guard for ever. Though there is no foundation for the wicked fabrication, and no persons of intelligence who know me would believe it, even if I had no proof, still for a man who holds a place of spiritual eminence, evil gossip is a disgrace."

"I promise for myself, for my friend, and for both the ladies, silence on that subject, so long as we may live. I swear before my God, and on the head of my dead father, that I will keep my word, if you keep yours to me," said Stephen, who knew only half the secret. Yet he was astonished at gaining his point so easily. He had expected more trouble. Nevertheless, he did not see how the marabout could manage to play him false, if he wanted to get his boy and hide the truth about himself.

"I am content," said the Arab. "And thou shouldst be content, since thou hast driven a successful bargain, and it is as if the contract between us were signed in my heart's blood. Now, I will leave thee. When the ladies are ready, thou shalt be called by one of the men who will be of their escort. It is not necessary that thou and I meet again, since we have, I hope, finished our business together, once and for ever."

"Why is it that he lets me go, without even trying to make me swear never to tell what I know?" Saidee asked Victoria, while all in haste and in confusion they put together a few things for the long journey. Saidee packed the little volumes of her diary, with trembling fingers, and looked a frightened question at her sister.

"I'm thankful that he doesn't ask us," Victoria answered, "for we couldn't promise not to tell, unless he would vow never to do the dreadful things you say he plans—lead a great rising, and massacre the French. Even to escape, one couldn't make a promise which might cost thousands of lives."

"We could perhaps evade a promise, yet seem to do what he asked," said Saidee, who had learned subtle ways in a school of subtlety. "I'm terrified that he *doesn't* ask. Why isn't he afraid to let us go, without any assurances?"

"He knows that because you've been his wife, we wouldn't betray him unless we were forced to, in order to prevent massacres," Victoria tried to reassure her sister. "And perhaps for the sake of getting his boy back, he's willing to renounce all his horrible plans."

"Perhaps—since he worships the child," Saidee half agreed. "Yet—it doesn't seem like Cassim to be so easily cowed, and to give up the whole ambition of his life, with scarcely a struggle, even for his child."

"You said, when you told me how you had written to Mr. Knight, that Cassim would be forced to yield, if they took the boy, and so the end would justify the means."

"Yes. It was a great card to play. But—but I expected him to make me take a solemn oath never to tell what I know."

"Don't let's think of it," said Victoria. "Let's just be thankful that we're going, and get ready as quickly as we can, lest he should change his mind at the last moment."

"Or lest Maïeddine should find out," Saidee added. "But, if Cassim really means us to go, he won't let Maïeddine find out. He will thank Allah and the Prophet for sending the fever that keeps Maïeddine in his bedroom."

"Poor Maïeddine!" Victoria half whispered. In her heart lurked kindness for the man who had so desperately loved her, even though love had driven him to the verge of treachery. "I hope he'll forget all about me and be happy," she said. And then, because she was happy herself, and the future seemed bright, she forgot Maïeddine, and thought only of another.

XLVIII

"That must be the bordj of Toudja, at last," Victoria said, looking out between the curtains of her bassour. "Aren't you thankful, Saidee? You'll feel happier and freer, when Cassim's men have gone back to the Zaouïa, and our ransom has been paid by the return of the little boy. That volume of your life will be closed for ever and ever, and you can begin the next."

Saidee was silent. She did not want to think that the volume was closed for ever, because in it there was one chapter which, unless it could be added to the new volume, would leave the rest of the book without interest for her. Half involuntarily she touched the basket which Honoré Sabine had given her when they parted in the desert city of Oued Tolga early that morning. In the basket were two carrier pigeons. She had promised to send one from the Bordj of Toudja, and another at the end of the next day's journey. After that she would be within reach of the telegraph. Her reason told her it was well that Sabine was not with her now, yet she wished for him, and could not be glad of his absence. Perhaps she would never see him again. Who could tell? It would have been unwise for Sabine, as an officer and as a man, to leave his duty to travel with her: she could see that, yet she was secretly angry with Victoria, because Victoria, happy herself, seemed to have little sympathy with her sister's hopes. The girl did not like to talk about Sabine, or discuss any connection he might possibly have with Saidee's future; and because Victoria was silent on that subject, Saidee revenged herself by being reticent on others. Victoria guessed the reason, and her heart yearned over Saidee; but this was something of which they could not talk. Some day, perhaps, Saidee would understand, and they would be drawn together again more closely than before.

"There's Toudja," Stephen said, as the girl looked out again from the bassour. Whenever he saw her face, framed thus by the dark red curtains, his heart beat, as if her beauty were new to him, seen that instant for the first time. This was the flood-tide of his life, now when they travelled through the desert together, he and she, and she depended upon his help and protection. For to-day, and the few more days until the desert journey should come to an end at Biskra, the tide would be at flood: then it would ebb, never to rise again, because at Algiers they must part, she to go her way, he to go his;

and his way would lead him to Margot Lorenzi. After Algiers there would be no more happiness for him, and he did not hope for it; but, right or wrong, he was living passionately in every moment now.

Victoria smiled down from the high bassour at the dark, sunburnt face of the rider. How different it was from the dark face of another rider who had looked up at her, between her curtains, when she had passed that way before! There was only one point of resemblance between the two: the light of love in the eyes. Victoria could not help recognizing that likeness. She could not help being sure that Stephen loved her, and the thought made her feel safe, as well as happy. There had been a sense of danger in the knowledge of Maïeddine's love.

"The tower in the bordj is ruined," she said, looking across the waving sea of dunes to a tall black object like the crooked finger of a giant pointing up out of the gold into the blue. "It wasn't so when I passed before."

"No," Stephen answered, welcoming any excuse for talk with her. "But it was when we came from Touggourt. Sabine told me there'd been a tremendous storm in the south just before we left Algiers, and the heliograph tower at Toudja was struck by lightning. They'll build it up again soon, for all these heliograph stations are supposed to be kept in order, in case of any revolt; for the first thing a rebellious tribe does is to cut the telegraph wires. If that happened, the only way of communication would be by heliograph; and Sabine says that from Touggourt to Tombouctou this chain of towers has been arranged always on elevations, so that signals can be seen across great stretches of desert; and inside the walls of a bordj whenever possible, for defence. But the South is so contented and peaceful now, I don't suppose the Government will get out of breath in its hurry to restore the damage here."

At the sound of Sabine's name Saidee had instantly roused to attention, and as Stephen spoke calmly of the peace and content in the South, she smiled. Then suddenly her face grew eager.

"Did the marabout appoint Toudja as the place to make the exchange, or was it you?" she asked, over Victoria's shoulder.

"The marabout," said Stephen. "I fell in with the idea because I'd already made objections to several, and I could see none to Toudja. It's a day's journey farther north than the Zaouïa, and I remembered the bordj being kept by two Frenchmen, who would be of use if——"

He checked himself, not wishing to hint that it might be necessary to guard against treason. "If we had to stop for the night," he amended, "no doubt the bordj would be better kept than some others. And we shall have to stop, you know, because my friend, Caird, can't arrive from Touggourt with the boy till late, at best."

"Did—the marabout seem bent on making this bordj the rendezvous?" Saidee asked.

Stephen's eyes met hers in a quick, involuntary glance, then turned to the ruined tower. He saw it against the northern sky as they came from the south, and, blackened by the lightning, it accentuated the desolation of the dunes. In itself, it looked sinister as a broken gibbet. "If the marabout had a strong preference for the place, he didn't betray it," was the only answer he could make. "Have you a special reason for asking?"

"No," Saidee echoed. "No special reason."

But Stephen and Victoria both guessed what was in her mind. As they looked at the tower all three thought of the Arabs who formed their caravan. There were six, sent out from the Zaouïa to take back the little Mohammed. They belonged body and soul to the marabout. At the town of Oued Tolga, Stephen had added a third to his escort of two; but though they were good guides, brave, upstanding fellows, he knew they would turn from him if there were any question between Roumis and men of their own religion. If an accident had happened to the child on the way back from Touggourt, or if any other difficulty arose, in which their interest clashed with his, he would have nine Arabs against him. He and Caird, with the two Highlanders, if they came, would be alone, no matter how large might be Nevill's Arab escort. Stephen hardly knew why these thoughts pressed upon him suddenly, with new insistence, as he saw the tower rise dark against the sky, jagged as if it had been hacked with a huge, dull knife. He had known from the first what risks they ran. Nevill and he and Sabine had talked them all over, and decided that, on the whole, there was no great danger of treachery from the marabout, who stood to lose too much, to gain too little, by breaking faith. As for Maïeddine, he was ill with fever, so the sisters said, and Saidee and Victoria believed that he had been kept in ignorance of the marabout's bargain. Altogether, circumstances seemed to have combined in their favour. Ben Halim's wife was naturally suspicious and fearful, after her long martyrdom, but there was no new reason for uneasiness. Only, Stephen reminded himself, he must not neglect the slightest wavering of the weather-vane. And in every shadow he must look for a sign.

They had not made a hurried march from the desert city, for Stephen and Sabine had calculated the hour at which Nevill might have received the summons, and the time he would take on the return journey. It was possible, Lady MacGregor being what she was, that she might have rewired the telegram to a certain bordj, the only telegraph station between Touggourt and Oued Tolga. If she had done this, and the message had caught Nevill, many hours would be saved. Instead of getting to the bordj about midnight, tired out with a long, quick march, he might be expected before dark. Even so, Stephen would be well ahead, for, as the caravan came to the gate of the bordj, it was only six o'clock, blazing afternoon still, and hot as midday, with the fierce, golden heat of the desert towards the end of May.

The big iron gates were wide open, and nothing stirred in the quadrangle inside; but as Stephen rode in, one of the Frenchmen he remembered slouched out of a room where the wooden shutters of the window were closed for coolness. His face was red, and he yawned as he came forward, rubbing his eyes as if he had been asleep. But he welcomed Stephen politely, and seeing that a good profit might be expected from so large a party, he roused himself to look pleased.

"I must have a room for two ladies," said Stephen, "and I am expecting a friend with a small caravan, to arrive from the north. However, six of my Arabs will go back when he comes. You must do the best you can for us, but nothing is of any importance compared to the ladies' comfort."

"Certainly, I will do my best," the keeper of the bordj assured him. "But as you see, our accommodation is humble. It is strained when we have four or five officers for the night, and though I and my brother have been in this God-forsaken place—worse luck!—for nine years, we have never yet had to put up ladies. Unfortunately, too, my brother is away, gone to Touggourt to buy stores, and I have only one Arab to help me. Still, though I have forgotten many useful things in this banishment, I have not forgotten how to cook, as more than one French officer could tell you."

"One has told me," said Stephen. "Captain Sabine, of the Chasseurs d'Afrique."

"Ah, ce beau sabreur! He stopped with me on his way to Oued Tolga, for the well-making. If he has recommended me, I shall be on my mettle, Monsieur."

The heavy face brightened; but there were bags under the bloodshot eyes, and the man's breath reeked of alcohol. Stephen was sorry the brother was away. He had been the more alert and prepossessing of the two.

As they talked, the quadrangle of the bordj—which was but an inferior caravanserai—had waked to animation. The landlord's one Arab servant had appeared, like a rat out of a hole, to help the new arrivals with their horses and camels. The caravans had filed in, and the marabout's men and Stephen's guides had dismounted.

None of these had seen the place since the visitation of the storm, and one or two from the Zaouïa had perhaps never been so far north before, yet they looked at the broken tower with grave interest rather than curiosity. Stephen wondered whether they had been primed with knowledge before starting, or if their lack of emotion were but Arab stoicism.

As usual in a caravanserai or large bordj, all round the square courtyard were series of rooms: a few along one wall for the accommodation of French officers and rich Arabs, furnished with elementary European comforts; opposite, a dining-room and kitchen; to the left, the quarters of the two landlords and their servants; along the fourth wall, on either side of the great iron gate, sheds for animals, untidily littered with straw and refuse, infested with flies. Further disorder was added by the débris from the broken heliograph-tower which had been only partially cleared away since the storm. Other towers there were, also; three of them, all very low and squat, jutting out from each corner of the high, flat-topped wall, and loopholed as usual, so that men stationed inside could defend against an escalade. These small towers were intact, though the roof of one was covered with rubbish from the ruined shell rising above; and looking up at this, Stephen saw that much had fallen away since he passed with Nevill, going to Oued Tolga. One entire wall had been sliced off, leaving the inside of the tower, with the upper chamber, visible from below. It was like looking into a half-dissected body, and the effect was depressing.

"If we should be raided by Arabs now," said the landlord, laughing, as he saw Stephen glance at the tower, "we should have to pray for help: there would be no other means of getting it."

"You don't seem to worry much," replied Stephen.

"No, for the Arabs in these parts are sheep nowadays," said the Frenchman. "Like sheep, they might follow a leader; but where is the leader? It is different among the Touaregs, where I spent some time before I came here. They are warriors by nature, but even they are quiet of late."

"Do you ever see any here?" Stephen asked.

"A few occasionally, going to Touggourt, but seldom. They are formidable-looking fellows, in their indigo-coloured masks, which stain their skin blue, but they are tractable enough if one does not offend them."

There was only one room which could be made passably habitable for Saidee and Victoria, and they went into it, out of the hot sun, as soon as it could be prepared. The little luggage they had brought went with them, and the basket containing the two carrier pigeons. Saidee fed the birds, and scribbled a few words on a scrap of paper, to tell Sabine that they had arrived safely at Toudja. On second thoughts, she added a postscript, while Victoria unpacked what they needed for the night. "*He* chose the rendezvous," Saidee wrote. "I suppose I'm too superstitious, but I can't help wondering if his choice had anything to do with the ruined tower? Don't be anxious, though. You will probably receive another line to-morrow night, to say that we've reached the next stage, and all's well."

"I suppose you think I'm doing wrong to write to him?" she said to Victoria, as she took one of the pigeons out of its basket.

"No," the girl answered. "Why shouldn't you write to say you're safe? He's your friend, and you're going far away."

Saidee almost wished that Victoria had scolded her. Without speaking again, she began to fasten her letter under the bird's wing, but gave a little cry, for there was blood on her fingers. "Oh, he's hurt himself somehow!" she exclaimed. "He won't be able to fly, I'm afraid. What shall I do? I must send the other one. And yet—if I do, there'll be nothing for to-morrow."

"Won't you wait until after Mr. Caird has come, and you can tell about the little boy?" Victoria suggested.

"He mayn't arrive till very late, and—I promised Captain Sabine that he should hear to-night."

"But think how quickly a pigeon flies! Surely it can go in less than half the time we would take, riding up and down among the dunes."

"Oh, much less than half! Captain Sabine said that from the bordj of Toudja the pigeon would come to him in an hour and a half, or two at most."

"Then wait a little longer. Somehow I feel you'll be glad if you do."

Saidee looked quickly at the girl. "You make me superstitious," she said.

"Why?"

"With your 'feelings' about things. They're almost always right. I'm afraid of them. I shouldn't dare send the pigeon now, for fear——"

"For fear of what?"

"I hardly know. I told you that you made me superstitious."

Stephen stood between the open gates of the bordj, looking north, whence Nevill should come. The desert was empty, a great, waving stretch of gold, but a caravan might be engulfed among the dunes. Any moment horses or camels might come in sight; and he was not anxious about Nevill or the boy. It was impossible that they could have been cut off by an attacking party from the Zaouïa. Captain Sabine and he, Stephen, had kept too keen a watch for that to happen, for the Zaouïa lay south of Oued Tolga the city.

Others besides himself were searching the sea of sand. One of his own guides was standing outside the gates, talking with two of the marabout's men, and looking into the distance. But rather oddly, it seemed to him, their faces were turned southward, until the guide said something to the others. Then, slowly, they faced towards the north. Stephen remembered how he had told himself to neglect no sign. Had he just seen a sign?

For some moments he did not look at the Arabs. Then, glancing quickly at the group, he saw that the head man sent by the marabout was talking emphatically to the guide from Oued Tolga, the city. Again, their eyes flashed to the Roumi, before he had time to turn away, and without hesitation the head man from the Zaouïa came a few steps towards him. "Sidi, we see horses," he said, in broken French. "The caravan thou dost expect is there," and he pointed.

Stephen had very good eyesight, but he saw nothing, and said so.

"We Arabs are used to looking across great distances," the man answered. "Keep thy gaze steadily upon the spot where I point, and presently thou wilt see."

It was as he prophesied. Out of a blot of shadow among the tawny dunes crawled some dark specks, which might have been particles of the shadow itself. They moved, and gradually increased in size. By and by Stephen could count seven separate specks. It must be Nevill and the boy, and Stephen wondered if he had added two more Arabs to the pair who had gone back with him from Oued Tolga, towards Touggourt.

"Hurrah for Lady MacGregor!" the watcher said under his breath. "She wired on my telegram, and caught him before he'd passed the last station. I might have known she would, the glorious old darling!" He hurried inside the bordj to knock at the ladies' door, and tell the news. "They're in sight!" he cried. "Would you like to come outside the gate and look?"

Instantly the door opened, and the sisters appeared. Victoria looked flushed and happy, but Saidee was pale, almost haggard in comparison with the younger girl. Both were in Arab dress still, having nothing else, even if they had wished to change; and as she came out, Saidee mechanically drew the long blue folds of her veil closely over her face. Custom had made this a habit which it would be hard to break.

All three went out together, and the Arabs, standing in a group, turned at the sound of their voices. Again they had been looking southward. Stephen looked also, but the dazzle of the declining sun was in his eyes.

"Don't seem to notice anything," said Saidee in a low voice.

"What is there to notice?" he asked in the same tone.

"A big caravan coming from the south. Can't you see it?"

"No. I see nothing."

"You haven't stared at the desert for eight years, as I have. There must be eighteen or twenty men."

"Do you think they're from the Zaouïa?" asked Victoria.

"Who can tell? We can't know till they're very close, and then——"

"Nevill Caird will get here first," Stephen said, half to himself. "You can see five horses and two camels plainly now. They're travelling fast."

"Those Arabs have seen the others," Saidee murmured. "But they don't want us to know they're thinking about them."

"Even if men are coming from the Zaouïa," said Stephen, "it may easily be that they've only been sent as an extra escort for the boy, owing to his father's anxiety."

"Yes, it may be only that," Saidee admitted. "Still, I'm glad——" She did not finish her sentence. But she was thinking about the carrier pigeon, and Victoria's advice.

All three looked northward, watching the seven figures on horseback, in the far distance; but now and then, when they could hope to do so without being noticed by the Arabs, they stole a hasty glance in the other direction. "The caravan has stopped," Saidee declared at last. "In the shadow of a big dune."

"I see, now," said Stephen.

"And I," added Victoria.

"Perhaps after all, it's just an ordinary caravan," Saidee said more hopefully. "Many nomads come north at this time of year. They may be making their camp now. Anyway, its certain they haven't moved for some time."

And still they had not moved, when Nevill Caird was close enough to the bordj for a shout of greeting to be heard.

"There are two of the strangest-looking creatures with him!" cried Saidee. "What can they be—on camels!"

"Why," exclaimed Victoria, "it's those men in kilts, who waited on the table at Mr. Caird's house!"

"Hurrah for Lady MacGregor again!" laughed Stephen. "It's the twins, Angus and Hamish." He pulled off his panama hat and waved it, shouting to his friend in joy. "We're a regiment!" he exclaimed gaily.

XLIX

The boy Mohammed was proud and very happy. He had not been in a motor-car, for he had not got to Touggourt; but it was glorious to have travelled far north, almost out of the dunes, and not only to have seen giant women in short skirts with bare legs, but not to be afraid of them, as the grown-up Arabs were. The giant women were Hamish and Angus, and it was a great thing to know them, and to be able to explain them to his father's men from the Zaouïa.

He was a handsome little fellow, with a face no darker than old ivory, and heavily lashed, expressive eyes, like those which looked over the marabout's mask. His dress was that of a miniature man; a white silk burnous, embroidered with gold, over a pale blue vest, stitched in many colours; a splendid red cloak, whose embroidery of stiff gold stood out like a bas-relief; a turban and chechia of thin white muslin; and red-legged boots finer than those of the Spahis. Though he was but eleven years old, and had travelled hard for days, he sat his horse with a princely air, worthy the son of a desert potentate; and like a prince he received the homage of the marabout's men who rushed to him with guttural cries, kissing the toes of his boots, in their short stirrups, and fighting for an end of his cloak to touch with their lips. He did not know that he had been "kidnapped." His impression was that he had deigned to favour a rather agreeable Roumi with his company. Now he was returning to his own people, and would bid his Roumi friend good-bye with the cordiality of one gentleman to another, though with a certain royal condescension fitted to the difference in their positions.

Nevill was in wild spirits, though pale with heat and fatigue. He had nothing to say of himself, but much of his aunt and of the boy Mohammed. "Ripping little chap," he exclaimed, when Saidee had gone indoors. "You never saw such pluck. He'd die sooner than admit he was tired. I shall be quite sorry to part from him. He was jolly good company, a sort of living book of Arab history. And what do you say to our surprise,—the twins? My aunt sent them off at the same time with the telegram, but of course they put in an appearance much later. They caught me up this morning, riding like devils on racing camels, with one guide. No horses could be got big enough for them. They've frightened every Arab they've met—but they're used to that and vain of it. They've got rifles—and bagpipes too, for all I know. They're capable of them."

"I can't tell you how glad I am to see you, Wings," said Stephen, "and only a little less glad to see those big fellows with their brave faces." Then he mentioned to Nevill the apparition of that mysterious caravan which had appeared, and vanished. Also he described the behaviour of the Zaouïa men when they had looked south, instead of north.

"Oh, that's all right, I'll bet," exclaimed Nevill, exuberant with the joy of success, and in the hope of coolness, food and rest. "Might have been any old caravan, on its own business—nothing to do with us. That's the most likely thing. But if the marabout's mixed up with it, I should say it's only because he couldn't bear to stop at home and wait in suspense, and I don't blame him, now I've made acquaintance with the kid. He'd be too proud to parade his anxiety under our noses, but would lurk in the distance, out of our sight, he probably flatters himself, to welcome his son, and take him back to Oued Tolga. Not unnatural—and in spite of all, I can't help being a little sorry for the man. We've humiliated and got the better of him, because we happen to have his secret. It's a bit like draining a chap's blood, and then challenging him to fight. He's got all he can expect now, in receiving the child back and if I can judge him by myself, he'll be so happy, that he'll be only too thankful to see our backs for the last time."

"He might feel safer to stick a knife in them."

"Oh, lord, I'm too hot to worry!" laughed Nevill. "Let's bid the boy Godspeed, or the Mussulman equivalent, which is a lot more elaborate, and then turn our thoughts to a bath of sorts and a dinner of sorts. I think Providence has been good to us so far, and we can afford to trust It. I'm sure Miss Ray would agree with me there." And Nevill glanced with kind blue eyes toward the shut door behind which Victoria had disappeared with her sister.

When at last the little Mohammed had been despatched with great ceremony of politeness, as well as a present of Stephen's gold watch, the two Englishmen watched him fade out of sight with his cavalcade of men from the Zaouïa, and saw that nothing moved in the southern distance.

"All's right with the world, and now for a wash and food!" cried Nevill, turning in with a sigh of relief at the gate of the bordj. "But

389

oh, by the way—Hamish has got a letter for you—or is it Angus? Anyhow, it's from my fairy aunt, which I would envy you, if she hadn't sent me on something better—a post-card from Tlemcen. My tyrant goddess thinks letters likely to give undue encouragement, but once in a while she sheds the light of a post-card on me. Small favours thankfully received—from that source!"

Inside the courtyard, the Highlanders were watching the three Arabs who had travelled with them and their master, attending to the horses and camels. These newcomers were being shown the ropes by the one servant of the bordj, Stephen's men helping with grave good-nature. They all seemed very friendly together, as is the way of Arabs, unless they inhabit rival districts.

Hamish had the letter, and gave it to Stephen, who retired a few steps to read it, and Nevill, seeing that the twins left all work to the Arabs, ordered them to put his luggage into the musty-smelling room which he was to share with Stephen, and to get him some kind of bath, if it were only a tin pan.

Stephen did not listen to these directions, nor did he hear or see anything that went on in the courtyard, for the next ten minutes. There was, indeed, a short and characteristic letter from Lady MacGregor, but it was only to say that she had finished and named the new game of Patience for Victoria Ray, and that, after all, she enclosed him a telegram, forwarded from Algiers to Touggourt. "I know Nevill told me that everything could wait till you got back," she explained, "but as I am sending the twins, they might as well take this. It may be of importance; and I'm afraid by the time you get it, the news will be several days old already."

He guessed, before he looked, whence the telegram came; and he dreaded to make sure. For an instant, he was tempted to put the folded bit of paper in his pocket, unread until Touggourt, or even Biskra. "Why shouldn't I keep these few days unspoiled by thoughts of what's to come, since they're the only happy days I shall ever have?" he asked himself. But it would be weak to put off the evil moment, and he would not yield. He opened the telegram.

"Sailing on Virginian. Hope you can meet me Liverpool May 22nd. Love and longing. Margot."

To-day was the 25th.

When he looked up, the courtyard was empty, and quiet, save for the quacking of two or three forlorn ducks. Nevill had gone inside, and the Highlanders were waiting upon him, no doubt—for Nevill liked a good deal of waiting upon. The Arabs had left the animals peacefully feeding, and had disappeared into the kitchen, or perhaps to have a last look at the vanishing escort of the marabout's sacred son.

Stephen was suddenly conscious of fatigue, and a depression as of great weariness. He envied Nevill, whose boyish laugh he heard. The girl Nevill loved had refused to marry him, but she smiled when she saw him, and sent him post-cards when he was absent. There was hope for Nevill. For him there was none; although—and it was as if a fierce hand seized and wrenched his heart—sometimes it had seemed, in the last few hours, that in Victoria Ray's smile for him there was the same lovely, mysterious light which made the eyes of Josette Soubise wonderful when she looked at Nevill. If it were not for Margot—but there was no use thinking of that. He could not ask Margot to set him free, after all that had passed, and even if he should ask, she would refuse. Shuddering disgustfully, the thought of a new family scandal shot through his mind: a breach-of-promise case begun by Margot against him, if he tried to escape. It was the sort of thing she would do, he could not help recognizing. Another *cause célèbre*, more vulgar than the fight for his brother's title! How Victoria would turn in shocked revulsion from the hero of such a coarse tragi-comedy. But he would never be that hero. He would keep his word and stick to Margot. When he should come to the desert telegraph station between Toudja and Touggourt, he would wire to the Carlton, where she thought of returning, and explain as well as he could that, not expecting her quite yet, he had stayed on in Africa, but would see her as soon as possible.

"Better hurry up and get ready for dinner!" shouted Nevill, through a crack of their bedroom door. "I warn you, I'm starving!"

By this time the Highlanders were out in the courtyard again—two gigantic figures, grotesque and even fearful in the eyes of Arabs; but there were no Arabs to stare at them now. All had gone about their business in one direction or other.

Stephen said nothing to his friend about the enclosure in Lady MacGregor's letter, mentioning merely the new game of cards named in honour of Miss Ray, at which they both laughed. And it seemed rather odd to Stephen just then, to hear himself laugh.

The quick-falling twilight had now given sudden coolness and peace to the desert. The flies had ceased their persecutions. The whole air was blue as the light seen through a pale star-sapphire, for the western sky was veiled with a film of cloud floating up out of the sunset like the smoke of its fire, and there was no glow of red.

As the two friends made themselves ready for dinner, and talked of such adventures as each had just passed through, they heard the voice of the landlord, impatiently calling, "Abdallah! Abdallah!"

There was no reply, and again he roared the name of his servant, from the kitchen and from the courtyard, into which he rushed with a huge ladle in his hand; then from farther off, outside the gate, which remained wide open. Still there came no answer; and presently Stephen, looking from his bedroom, saw the Frenchman, hot and red-faced, slowly crossing the courtyard, mumbling to himself.

Nevill had not quite finished his toilet, for he had a kind of boyish vanity, and wished to show how well and smart he could look after the long, tiresome journey. But Stephen was ready, and he stepped out, closing the door behind him.

"Can't you find your servant?" he asked the keeper of the bordj.

"No," said the man, adding some epithets singularly unflattering to the absent one and his ancestors. "He has vanished as if his father, the devil, had dragged him down to hell."

"Where are the others?" inquired Stephen. "My men and my friend's men? Are they still standing outside the gates, watching the boy and his caravan?"

"I saw them nowhere," returned the Frenchman. "It is bad enough to keep one Arab in order. I do not run after others. Would that the whole nation might die like flies in a frost! I hate them. What am I to do for my dinner, and ladies in the bordj for the first time? It is just my luck. I cannot leave the kitchen, and that brute Abdallah has not laid the table! When I catch him I will wring his neck as if he were a hen."

He trotted back to the kitchen, swearing, and an instant later he was visible through the open door, drinking something out of a bottle.

Stephen went to the door of the third and last guest-room of the bordj. It was larger than the others, and had no furniture except a number of thick blue and red rugs spread one on top of the other, on the floor. This was the place where those who paid least were accommodated, eight or ten at a time if necessary; and it was expected that Hamish and Angus would have to share the room with the Arab guides of both parties.

Stephen looked in at the twins, as they scornfully inspected their quarters.

"Where are the Arabs?" he asked, as he had asked the landlord.

"We dinna ken whaur they've ta'en theirsel's," replied Angus. "All we ken is, we wull not lie in the hoose wi' 'em. Her leddyship wadna expect it, whateffer. We prefair t' sleep in th' open."

Stephen retired from the argument, and mounted a steep, rough stairway, close to the gate, which led to the flat top of the wall, and had formerly been connected by a platform with the ruined heliograph tower. The wall was perhaps two feet thick, and though the top was rough and somewhat broken, it was easy to walk upon it. Once it had been defended by a row of nails and bits of glass, but most of these were gone. It was an ancient bordj, and many years of peace had passed since it was built in the old days of raids and razzias.

Stephen looked out over the desert, through the blue veil of twilight, but could see no sign of life anywhere. Then, coming down, he mounted into each squat tower in turn, and peered out, so that he might spy in all directions, but there was nothing to spy save the shadowy dunes, more than ever like waves of the sea, in this violet light. He was not reassured, however, by the appearance of a vast peace and emptiness. Behind those billowing dunes that surged away toward the horizon, north, south, east, and west, there was hiding-place for an army.

As he came down from the last of the four towers, his friend sauntered out from his bedroom. "I hope the missing Abdallah's turned up, and dinner's ready," said Nevill gaily.

Then Stephen told him what had happened, and Nevill's cheerful face settled into gravity.

"Looks as if they'd got a tip from the marabout's men," he said slowly.

"It can be nothing else," Stephen agreed.

"I blame myself for calling the twins inside to help me," said Nevill. "If I'd left them to moon about the courtyard, they'd have seen those sneaks creeping away, and reported."

"They wouldn't have thought it strange that the Arabs stood outside, watching the boy go. You're not to blame, because you didn't see the sly look in my fellows' faces. I had the sign, and neglected it, in spite of my resolutions. But after all, if we're in for trouble, I don't know that it isn't as well those cowards have taken French leave. If they'd stayed, we'd only have had an enemy inside the gates, as well as out. And that reminds me, we must have the gates shut at once. Thank heaven we brought those French army rifles and plenty of cartridges from Algiers, when we didn't know what we might be in for. Now we *do* know; and all are likely to come handy. Also our revolvers."

"Thank heaven and my aunt for the twins, too," said Nevill. "They might be better servants, but I'll bet on them as fighters. And perhaps you noticed the rifles her 'leddyship' provided them with at Touggourt?"

"I saw the muzzles glitter as they rode along on camel-back," Stephen answered. "I was glad even then, but now — —" He did not need to finish the sentence. "We'd better have a word with our host," he said.

To reach the dining-room, where the landlord was busy, furiously clattering dishes, they had to pass the door of the room occupied by the sisters. It was half open, and as they went by, Victoria came out.

"Please tell me things," she said. "I'm sure you're anxious. When we heard the landlord call his servant and nobody answered, Saidee was afraid there was something wrong. You know, from the first she thought that her—that Cassim didn't mean to keep his word. Have the Arabs all gone?"

Nevill was silent, to let Stephen take the responsibility. He was not sure whether or no his friend meant to try and hide their anxiety from the women. But Stephen answered frankly. "Yes, they've gone. It may be that nothing will happen, but we're going to shut the gates at once, and make every possible preparation."

"In case of an attack?"

"Yes. But we have a good place for defence here. It would be something to worry about if we were out in the open desert."

"There are five men, counting your Highlanders," said Victoria, turning to Nevill. "I think they are brave, and I know well already what you both are." Her eyes flashed to Stephen's with a beautiful look, all for him. "And Saidee and I aren't cowards. Our greatest grief is that we've brought you into this danger. It's for our sakes. If it weren't for us, you'd be safe and happy in Algiers."

Both men laughed. "We'd rather be here, thank you," said Stephen. "If you're not frightened, that's all we want. We're as safe as in a fort, and shall enjoy the adventure, if we have any."

"It's like you to say that," Victoria answered. "But there's no use pretending, is there? Cassim will bring a good many men, and Si Maïeddine will be with them, I think. They couldn't afford to try, and fail. If they come, they'll have to—make thorough work."

"Yet, on the other hand, they wouldn't want to take too many into their secret," Stephen tried to reassure her.

"Well, we may soon know," she said. "But what I came out to say, is this. My sister has two carrier pigeons with her. One has hurt its wing and is no use. But the other is well, and—he comes from Oued Tolga. Not the Zaouïa, but the city. We've been thinking, she and I, since the Arab servant didn't answer, that it would be a good thing to send a letter to—to Captain Sabine, telling him we expected an attack."

"It would be rather a sell if he got the message, and acted on it—and then nothing happened after all," suggested Nevill.

"I think we'll send the message," said Stephen. "It would be different if we were all men here, but——"

Victoria turned, and ran back to the open door.

"The pigeon shall go in five minutes," she called over her shoulder.

Stephen and Nevill went to the dining-room.

The landlord was there, drunk, talking to himself. He had broken a dish, and was kicking the fragments under the table. He laughed at first when the two Englishmen tried to impress upon him the gravity of the situation; at last, however, they made him understand that this was no joke, but deadly earnest. They helped him close and bar the heavy iron gates; and as they looked about for material with which to build up a barrier if necessary, they saw the sisters come to the door. Saidee had a pigeon in her hands, and opening them suddenly, she let it go. It rose, fluttered, circling in the air, and flew southward. Victoria ran up the dilapidated stairway by the gate, to see it go, but already the tiny form was muffled from sight in the blue folds of the twilight.

"In less than two hours it will be at Oued Tolga," the girl cried, coming down the steep steps.

At that instant, far away, there was the dry bark of a gun.

They looked at each other, and said nothing, but the same doubt was in the minds of all.

It might be that the message would never reach Oued Tolga.

Then another thought flashed into Stephen's brain. He asked himself whether it would be possible to climb up into the broken tower. If he could reach the top, he might be able to call for help if they should be hard-pressed; for some years before he had, more for amusement than anything else, taken a commission in a volunteer battalion and among many other things which he considered more or less useless, had learned signalling. He had not entirely forgotten the accomplishment, and it might serve him very well now, only—and he looked up critically at the jagged wall—it would be difficult to get into that upper chamber, a shell of which remained. In any case, he would not think of so extreme a measure, until he was sure that, if he gave an alarm, it would not be a false one.

"Let's have dinner," said Nevill. "If we have fighting to do, I vote we start with ammunition in our stomachs as well as in our pockets."

Saidee had gone part way up the steps, and was looking over the wall.

"I see something dark, that moves," she said. "It's far away, but I am sure. My eyes haven't been trained in the desert for nothing. It's a caravan—quite a big caravan, and it's coming this way. That's where the shot came from. If they killed the pigeon, or winged it, we're all lost. It would only be childish to hope. We must look our fate in the face. The men will be killed, and I, too. Victoria will be saved, but I think she'd rather die with the rest of us, for Maïeddine will take her."

"It's never childish to hope, it seems to me," said Nevill. "This little fort of ours isn't to be conquered in an hour, or many hours, I assure you."

"And we have no intention of letting you be killed, or Miss Ray carried off, or of dying ourselves, at the hands of a few Arabs," Knight added. "Have confidence."

"In our star," Victoria half whispered, looking at Stephen. They both remembered, and their eyes spoke, in a language they had never used before.

In England, Margot Lorenzi was wondering why Stephen Knight had not come to meet her, and angrily making up her mind that she would find out the reason.

L

Somehow, they all contrived to take a little food, three watching from the wall-towers while the others ate; and Saidee prepared strong, delicious coffee, such as had never been tasted in the bordj of Toudja.

When they had dined after a fashion, each making a five-minute meal, there was still time to arrange the defence, for the attacking party—if such it were—could not reach the bordj in less than an hour, marching as fast as horses and camels could travel among the dunes.

The landlord was drunk. There was no disguising that, but though he was past planning, he was not past fighting. He had a French army rifle and bayonet. Each of the five men had a revolver, and there was another in the bordj, belonging to the absent brother. This Saidee asked for, and it was given her. There were plenty of cartridges for each weapon, enough at all events to last out a hot fight of several hours. After that—but it was best not to send thoughts too far ahead.

The Frenchman had served long ago in the Chasseurs d'Afrique, and had risen, he said, to the rank of sergeant; but the fumes of absinthe clouded his brain, and he could only swagger and boast of old exploits as a soldier, crying from time to time "Vive l'entente cordiale," and assuring the Englishmen that they could trust him to the death. It was Stephen who, by virtue of his amateur soldiering experience, had to take the lead. He posted the Highlanders in opposite watch-towers, placing Nevill in one which commanded the two rear walls of the bordj. The next step was the building of bonfires, one at each corner of the roof, so that when the time for fighting came, the defenders might confound the enemy by lighting the surrounding desert, making a surprise impossible. Old barrels were broken up, therefore, and saturated with oil. The spiked double gates of iron, though apparently strong, Stephen judged incapable of holding out long against battering rams, but he knew heavy baulks of wood to be rare in the desert, far from the palms of the oases. What he feared most was gunpowder; and though he was ignorant of the marabout's secret ambitions and warlike preparations, he thought it not improbable that a store of gunpowder might be kept in the Zaouïa. True, the French Government forbade Arabs to have more than a small supply in their possession; but the marabout was greatly trusted, and was perhaps allowed to deal out a certain amount of the coveted treasure for "powder play" on religious fête days. To prevent the bordj falling into the hands of the Arabs if the gate were blown down, Stephen and his small force built up at the further corner of the yard, in front of the dining-room door, a barrier of mangers, barrels, wooden troughs, iron bedsteads and mattresses from the guest-rooms. Also they reinforced the gates against pressure from the outside, using the shafts of an old cart to make struts, which they secured against the side walls or frame of the gateway. These formed buttresses of considerable strength; and the landlord, instead of grumbling at the damage which might be done to his bordj, and the danger which threatened himself, was maudlin with delight at the prospect of killing a few detested Arabs.

"I don't know what your quarrel's about, unless it's the ladies," he said, breathing vengeance and absinthe, "but whatever it is, I'll make it mine, whether you compensate me or not. Depend upon me, *mon capitaine*. Depend on an old soldier."

But Stephen dared not depend upon him to man one of the watch-towers. Eye and hand were too unsteady to do good service in picking off escaladers. The ex-soldier was brave enough for any feat, however, and was delighted when the Englishman suggested, rather than gave orders, that his should be the duty of lighting the bonfires. That done, he was to take his stand in the courtyard, and shoot any man who escaped the rifles in the wall-towers.

It was agreed among all five men that the gate was to be held as long as possible; that if it fell, a second stand should be made behind the crescent-shaped barricade outside the dining-room door; that, should this defence fall also, all must retreat into the dining-room, where the two sisters must remain throughout the attack; and this would be the last stand.

Everything being settled, and the watch-towers well supplied with food for the rifles, Stephen went to call Saidee and Victoria, who were in their almost dismantled room. The bedstead, washstand, chairs and table had ceased to be furniture, and had become part of the barricade.

"Let me carry your things into the dining-room now," he said. "And your bed covering. We can make up a sort of couch there, for you may as well be comfortable if you can. And you know, it's on the cards that all our fuss is in vain. Nothing whatever may happen."

They obeyed, without objection; but Saidee's look as she laid a pair of Arab blankets over Stephen's arm, told how little rest she expected. She gathered up a few things of her own, however, to take from the bedroom to the dining-room, and as she walked ahead, Stephen asked Victoria if, in the handbag she had brought from the Zaouïa there was a mirror.

"Yes," she answered. "There's quite a good-sized one, which I used to have on my dressing-table in the theatre. How far away that time seems now!"

"Will you lend the mirror to me—or do you value it too much to risk having it smashed?"

"Of course I'll lend it. But——" she looked up at him anxiously, in the blue star-dusk. "What are you going to do?"

"Nothing particular, unless we've reason to believe that an attack will be made; that is, if a lot of Arabs come near the bordj. In that case, I want to try and get up into the tower, and do some signalling—for fear the shot we heard hit your sister's messenger. I used to be rather a nailer at that sort of thing, when I played at soldiering a few years ago."

"But no one could climb the tower now!" the girl exclaimed.

"I don't know. I almost flatter myself that I could. I've done the Dent Blanche twice, and a Welsh mountain or two. To be sure, I must be my own guide now, but I think I can bring it off all right. I've been searching about for a mirror and reflector, in case I try the experiment; for the heliographing apparatus was spoilt in the general wreckage of things by the storm. I've got a reflector off a lamp in the kitchen, but couldn't find a looking-glass anywhere, and I saw there was only a broken bit in your room. My one hope was in you."

As he said this, he felt that the words meant a great deal more than he wished her to understand.

"I hate being afraid of things," said Victoria. "But I am afraid to have you go up in the tower. It's only a shell, that looks as if it might blow down in another storm. It could fall with you, even if you got up safely to the signalling place. And besides, if Cassim's men were near, they might see you and shoot. Oh, I don't think I could bear to have you go!"

"You care—a little—what becomes of me?" Stephen had stammered before he had time to forbid himself the question.

"I care a great deal—what becomes of you."

"Thank you for telling me that," he said, warmly. "I—" but he knew he must not go on. "I shan't be in danger," he finished. "I'll be up and back before any one gets near enough to see what I'm at, and pot at me."

As he spoke, the sound of a strange, wild singing came to them, with the desert wind that blew from the south.

"That's a Touareg song," exclaimed Saidee, turning. "It isn't Arab. I've heard Touaregs sing it, coming to the Zaouïa."

"Madame is right," said the landlord. "I, too, have heard Touaregs sing it, in their own country, and also when they have passed here, in small bands. Perhaps we have deceived ourselves. Perhaps we are not to enjoy the pleasure of a fight. I feared it was too good to be true."

"I can see a caravan," cried Nevill, from his cell in a wall-tower. "There seem to be a lot of men."

"Would they come like that, if they wanted to fight?" asked the girl. "Wouldn't they spread out, and hope to surprise us?"

"They'll either try to rush the gate, or else they'll pretend to be a peaceful caravan," said Stephen.

"I see! Get the landlord to let their leaders in, and then .... That's why they sing the Touareg song, perhaps, to put us off our guard."

"Into the dining-room, both of you, and have courage! Whatever happens, don't come out. Will you give me the mirror?"

"Must you go?"

"Yes. Be quick, please."

On the threshold of the dining-room Victoria opened her bag, and gave him a mirror framed in silver. It had been a present from an enthusiastic millionairess in New York, who admired her dancing. That seemed very odd now. The girl's hand trembled as for an instant it touched Stephen's. He pressed her fingers, and was gone.

"Babe, I think this will be the last night of my life," said Saidee, standing behind the girl, in the doorway, and pressing against her. "Cassim will kill me, when he kills the men, because I know his secret and because he hates me. If I could only have had a little happiness! I don't want to die. I'm afraid. And it's horrible to be killed."

"I love being alive, but I want to know what happens next," said Victoria. "Sometimes I want it so much, that I almost long to die. And probably one feels brave when the minute comes. One always does, when the great things arrive. Besides, we're sure it must be glorious as soon as we're out of our bodies. Don't you know, when you're going to jump into a cold bath, you shiver and hesitate a little, though you know perfectly well it will be splendid in an instant. Thinking of death's rather like that."

"You haven't got to think of it for yourself to-night. Maïeddine will——"

"No," the girl broke in. "I won't go with Maïeddine."

"If they take this place—as they must, if they've brought many men, you'll have to go, unless——"

"Yes; 'unless.' That's what I mean. But don't ask me any more. I—I can't think of ourselves now."

"You're thinking of some one you love better than you do me."

"Oh, no, not better. Only——" Victoria's voice broke. The two clung to each other. Saidee could feel how the girl's heart was beating, and how the sobs rose in her throat, and were choked back.

Victoria watched the tower, that looked like a jagged black tear in the star-strewn blue fabric of the sky. And she listened. It seemed as if her very soul were listening.

The wild Touareg chant was louder now, but she hardly heard it, because her ears strained for some sound which the singing might cover: the sound of rubble crumbling under a foot that climbed and sought a holding-place.

From far away came the barking of Kabyle dogs, in distant camps of nomads. In stalls of the bordj, where the animals rested, a horse stamped now and then, or a camel grunted. Each slightest noise made Victoria start and tremble. She could be brave for herself, but it was harder to be brave for one she loved, in great danger.

"They'll be here in ten minutes," shouted Nevill. "Legs, where are you?"

There was no answer; but Victoria thought she heard the patter of falling sand. At least, the ruin stood firm so far. By this time Stephen might have nearly reached the top. He had told her not to leave the dining-room, and she had not meant to disobey; but she had made no promise, and she could bear her suspense no longer. Where she stood, she could not see into the shell of the broken tower. She must see!

Running out, she darted across the courtyard, pausing near the Frenchman, Pierre Rostafel, who wandered unsteadily up and down the quadrangle, his torch of alfa grass ready in his hand. He did not know that one of the Englishmen was trying to climb the tower, and would not for an instant have believed that any human being could reach the upper chamber, if suddenly a light had not flashed out, at the top, seventy feet above his head.

Dazed already with absinthe, fantastic ideas beat stupidly upon his brain, like bats that blunder against a lamp and extinguish it with foolish, flapping wings. He thought that somehow the enemy must have stolen a march upon the defenders: that the hated Arabs had got into the tower, from a ladder raised outside the wall, and that soon they would be pouring down in a swarm. Before he knew what he was doing, he had stumbled up the stairs on to the flat wall by the gate. Scrambling along with his torch, he got on to the bordj roof, and lit bonfire after bonfire, though Victoria called on him to stop, crying that it was too soon—that the men outside would shoot and kill him who would save them all.

The sweet silence of the starry evening was crashed upon with lights and jarring sounds.

Stephen, who had climbed the tower with a lantern and a kitchen lamp-reflector slung in a table-cover, on his back, had just got his makeshift apparatus in order, and standing on a narrow shelf of floor which overhung a well-like abyss, had begun his signalling to the northward.

Too late he realized that, for all the need of haste, he ought to have waited long enough to warn the drunken Frenchman what he meant to do. If he had, this contretemps would not have happened. His telegraphic flashes, long and short, must have told the enemy what was going on in the tower, but they could not have seen him standing there, exposed like a target to their fire, if Rostafel had not lit the bonfires.

Suddenly a chorus of yells broke out, strange yells that sprang from savage hearts; and one sidewise glance down showed Stephen the desert illuminated with red fire. He went on with his work, not stopping to count the men on horses and camels who rode fast towards the bordj, though not yet at the foot of that swelling sand hill on which it stood. But a picture—of uplifted dark faces and pointing rifles—was stamped upon his brain in that one swift look, clear as an impression of a seal in hot wax. He had even time to see that those faces were half enveloped in masks such as he had noticed in photographs of Touaregs, yet he was sure that the twenty or thirty men were not Touaregs. When close to the bordj all flung themselves from their animals, which were led away, while the riders took cover by throwing themselves flat on the sand. Then they began shooting, but he looked no more. He was determined to keep on signalling till he got an answer or was shot dead.

There were others, however, who looked and saw the faces, and the rifles aimed at the broken tower. The bonfires which showed the figure in the ruined heliographing-room, to the enemy, also showed the enemy to the watchers in the wall-towers, on opposite sides of the gates.

The Highlanders open fire. Their skill as marksmen, gained in the glens and mountains of Sutherlandshire, was equally effective on different game, in the desert of the Sahara. One shot brought a white mehari to its knees. Another caused a masked man in a striped gandourah to wring his hand and squeal.

The whole order of things was changed by the sudden flashes from the height of the dark ruin, and the lighting of the bonfires on the bordj roof.

Two of the masked men riding on a little in advance of the other twenty had planned, as Stephen guessed, to demand admittance to the bordj, declaring themselves leaders of a Touareg caravan on its way to Touggourt. If they could have induced an unsuspecting landlord to open the gates, so much the better for them. If not, a parley would have given the band time to act upon instructions already understood. But Cassim ben Halim, an old soldier, and Maïeddine, whose soul was in this venture, were not the men to meet an emergency unprepared. They had calculated on a check, and were ready for surprises.

It was Maïeddine's camel that went down, shot in the neck. He had been keeping El Biod in reserve, when the splendid stallion might be needed for two to ride away in haste—his master and a woman. As the mehari fell, Maïeddine escaped from the saddle and alighted on his feet, his blue Touareg veil disarranged by the shock. His face uncovered, he bounded up the slope with the bullets of Angus and Hamish pattering around him in the sand.

"She's bewitched, whateffer!" the twins mumbled, each in his watch-tower, as the tall figure sailed on like a war-cloud, untouched. And they wished for silver bullets, to break the charm woven round the "fanatic" by a wicked spirit.

Over Maïeddine's head his leader was shooting at Stephen in the tower, while Hamish returned his fire, leaving the running man to Angus. But suddenly Angus wheeled after a shot, to yell through the tower door into the courtyard. "Oot o' the way, wimmen! He's putten gunpowder to the gate if I canna stop him." Then, he wheeled into place, and was entranced to see that the next bullet found its billet under the Arab's turban. In the orange light of the bonfires, Angus could see a spout of crimson gush down the bronze forehead and over the glittering eyes. But the wounded Arab did not fall back an inch or drop a burden which he carried carefully. Now he was sheltering behind the high, jutting gate-post. In another minute it would be too late to save the gate.

But Angus did not think of Victoria. Nor did Victoria stop to think of herself. Something seemed to say in her heart, "Maïeddine won't let them blow up the gate, if it means your death, and so, maybe, you can save them all."

This was not a thought, since she had no time for thought. It was but a murmur in her brain, as she ran up the steep stairway close to the gate, and climbed on to the wall.

Maïeddine, streaming with blood, was sheltering in the narrow angle of the gate-post where the firing from the towers struck the wall instead of his body. He had suspended a cylinder of gunpowder against the gate, and, his hands full of powder to sprinkle a trail, he was ready to make a dash for life when a voice cried his name.

Victoria stood on the high white wall of the bordj, just above the gate, on the side where he had hung the gunpowder. A few seconds more— his soul sickened at the thought. He forgot his own danger, in thinking of hers, and how he might have destroyed her, blotting out the light of his own life.

"Maïeddine!" she called, before she knew who had been ready to lay the fuse, and that, instead of crying to a man in the distance, she spoke to one at her feet. He stared up at her through a haze of blood. In the red light of the fire, she was more beautiful even than when she had danced in his father's tent, and he had told himself that if need be he would throw away the world for her. She recognized him as she looked down, and started back with an impulse to escape, he seemed so near and so formidable. But she feared that, if the gate were blown up, the ruined tower might be shaken down by the explosion. She must stay, and save the gate, until Stephen had reached the ground.

"Thou!" exclaimed Maïeddine. "Come to me, heart of my life, thou who art mine forever, and thy friends shall be spared, I promise thee."

"I am not thine, nor ever can be," Victoria answered him. "Go thou, or thou wilt be shot with many bullets. They fire at thee and I cannot stop them. I do not wish to see thee die."

"Thou knowest that while thou art on the wall I cannot do what I came to do," Maïeddine said. "If they kill me here, my death will be on thy head, for I will not go without thee. Yet if thou hidest from me, I will blow up the gate."

Victoria did not answer, but looked at the ruined tower. One of its walls and part of another stood firm, and she could not see Stephen in the heliographing-chamber at the top. But through a crack between the adobe bricks she caught a gleam of light, which moved. It was Stephen's lantern, she knew. He was still there. Farther down, the crack widened. On his way back, he would see her, if she were still on the wall above the gate. She wished that he need not learn she was there, lest he lose his nerve in making that terrible descent. But every one else knew that she was trying to save the gate, and that while she remained, the fuse would not be lighted. Saidee, who had come out from the dining-room into the courtyard, could see her on the wall, and Rostafel was babbling that she was "une petite lionne, une merveille de courage et de finesse." The Highlanders knew, too, and were doing their best to rid her of Maïeddine, but, perhaps because of the superstition which made them doubt the power of their bullets against a charmed life, they could not kill him, though his cloak was pierced, and his face burned by a bullet which had grazed his cheek. Suddenly, however, to the girl's surprise and joy, Maïeddine turned and ran like a deer toward the firing line of the Arabs. Then, as the bullets of Hamish and Angus spattered round him, he wheeled again abruptly and came back towards the bordj as if borne on by a whirlwind. With a run, he threw himself towards the gate, and leaping up caught at the spikes for handhold. He grasped them firmly, though his fingers bled, got a knee on the wall, and freeing a hand snatched at Victoria's dress.

LI

Saidee, down in the courtyard, shrieked as she saw her sister's danger. "Fire!—wound him—make him fall!" she screamed to Rostafel. But to fire would be at risk of the girl's life, and the Frenchman danced about aimlessly, yelling to the men in the watch- towers.

In the tower, Stephen heard a woman's cry and thought the voice was Victoria's. His work was done. He had signalled for help, and, though this apparatus was a battered stable lantern, a kitchen-lamp reflector, and a hand-mirror, he had got an answer. Away to the north, a man whom perhaps he would never see, had flashed him back a message. He could not understand all, for it is easier to send than to receive signals; but there was something about soldiers at Bordj Azzouz, changing garrison, and Stephen believed that they meant marching to the rescue. Now, his left arm wounded, his head cut, and eyes half blinded with a rain of rubble brought down by an Arab bullet, he had made part of the descent when Saidee screamed her high-pitched scream of terror.

He was still far above the remnant of stairway, broken off thirty feet above ground level. But, knowing that the descent would be more difficult than the climb, he had torn into strips the stout tablecloth which had wrapped his heliographing apparatus. Knotting the lengths together, he had fastened one end round a horn of shattered adobe, and tied the other in a slip-noose under his arms. Now, he was thankful for this precaution. Instead of picking his way, from foothold to foothold, at the sound of the cry he lowered himself rapidly, like a man who goes down a well on the chain of a bucket, and dropped on a pile of bricks which blocked the corkscrew steps. In a second he was free of the stretched rope, and, half running, half falling down the rubbish-blocked stairway, he found himself, giddy and panting, at the bottom. A rush took him across the courtyard to the gate; snatching Rostafel's rifle and springing up the wall stairway, a bullet from Maïeddine's revolver struck him in the shoulder. For the space of a heart-beat his brain was in confusion. He knew that the Arab had a knee on the wall, and that he had pulled Victoria to him by her dress, which was smeared with blood. But he did not know whether the blood was the girl's or Maïeddine's, and the doubt, and her danger, and the rage of his wound drove him mad. It was not a sane man who crashed down Rostafel's rifle on Maïeddine's head, and laughed as he struck. The Arab dropped over the wall and fell on the ground outside the gate, like a dead man, his body rolling a little way down the slope. There it lay still, in a crumpled heap, but the marabout and two of his men made a dash to the rescue, dragging the limp form out of rifle range. It was a heroic act, and the Highlanders admired it while they fired at the heroes. One fell, to rise no more, and already two masked corpses had fallen from the wall into the courtyard, daring climbers shot by Rostafel as they tried to drop. Sickened by the sight of blood, dazed by shots and the sharp "ping" of bullets, frenzied with horror at the sight of Victoria struggling in the grasp of Maïeddine, Saidee sank down unconscious as Stephen beat the Arab off the wall.

"Darling, precious one, for God's sake say you're not hurt!" he stammered, as he caught Victoria in his arms, holding her against his heart, as he carried her down. He was still a madman, mad with fear for her, and love for her—love made terrible by the dread of loss. It was new life to hold her so, to know that she was safe, to bow his forehead on her hair. There was no Margot or any other woman in existence. Only this girl and he, created for each other, alone in the world.

Victoria clung to him thankfully, sure of his love already, and glad of his words.

"No, my dearest, I'm not hurt," she answered. "But you—you are wounded!"

"I don't know. If I am, I don't feel it," said Stephen. "Nothing matters except you."

"I saw him shoot you. I—I thought you were killed. Put me down. I want to look at you."

She struggled in his arms, as they reached the foot of the stairs, and gently he put her down. But her nerves had suffered more than she knew. Strength failed her, and she reached out to him for help. Then he put his arm round her again, supporting her against his wounded shoulder. So they looked at each other, in the light of the bonfires, their hearts in their eyes.

"There's blood in your hair and on your face," she said. "Oh, and on your coat. Maïeddine shot you."

"It's nothing," he said. "I feel no pain. Nothing but rapture that you're safe. I thought the blood on your dress might be— —"

"It was his, not mine. His hands were bleeding. Oh, poor Maïeddine—I can't help pitying him. What if he is killed?"

"Don't think of him. If he's dead, I killed him, not you, and I don't repent. I'd do it again. He deserved to die."

"He tried to kill you!"

"I don't mean for that reason. But come, darling. You must go into the house, I have to take my turn in the fighting now— —"

"You've done more than any one else!" she cried, proudly.

"No, it was little enough. And there's the wall to defend. I—but look, your sister's fainting."

"My Saidee! And I didn't see her lying there!" The girl fell on her knees beside the white bundle on the ground. "Oh, help me get her into the house."

"I'll carry her."

But Victoria would help him. Together they lifted Saidee, and Stephen carried her across the courtyard, making a détour to avoid passing the two dead Arabs. But Victoria saw, and, shuddering, was speechless.

"This time you'll promise to stay indoors!" Stephen said, when he had laid Saidee on the pile of blankets in a corner of the room.

"Yes—yes—I promise!"

The girl gave him both hands. He kissed them, and then, without turning, went out and shut the door. It was only at this moment that he remembered Margot, remembered her with anguish, because of the echo of Victoria's voice in his ears as she named him her "dearest."

As Stephen came from behind the barricade which screened the dining-room from the courtyard, he found Rostafel shooting right and left at men who tried to climb the rear wall, having been missed by Nevill's fire. Rostafel had recovered the rifle snatched by Stephen in his stampede to the stairway, and, sobered by the fight, was making good use of it. Stephen had now armed himself with his own, left for safety behind the barrier while he signalled in the tower; and together the two men had hot work in the quadrangle. Here and there an escalader escaped the fire from the watch-towers, and hung half over the wall, but dropped alive into the courtyard, only to be bayoneted by the Frenchman. The signalling-tower gave little shelter against the enemy, as most of the outer wall had fallen above the height of twenty feet from the ground; but, as without it only three sides of the quadrangle could be fully defended, once again Stephen scrambled up the choked and broken stairway. Screening himself as best he could behind a jagged ledge of adobe, he fired through a crack at three or four Arabs who made a human ladder for a comrade to mount the wall. The man at the top fell. The next mounted, to be shot by Nevill from a watch-tower. The bullet pierced the fellow's leg, which was what Nevill wished, for he, who hated to rob even an insect of its life, aimed now invariably at arms or legs, never at any vital part. "All we want," he thought half guiltily, "is to disable the poor brutes. They must obey the marabout. We've no spite against 'em!"

But every one knew that it was a question of moments only before some Arab, quicker or luckier than the rest, would succeed in firing the trail of gunpowder already laid. The gate would be blown up. Then would follow a rush of the enemy and the second stand of the defenders behind the barricade. Last of all, the retreat to the dining-room.

Among the first precautions Stephen had taken was that of locking the doors of all rooms except the dining-room, and pulling out the keys, so that, when the enemy got into the quadrangle, they would find themselves forced to stay in the open, or take shelter in the watch-towers vacated by the defenders. From the doorways of these, they could not do much harm to the men behind the barricade. But there was one thing they might do, against which Stephen had not guarded. The idea flashed into his head now, too late. There were the stalls where the animals were tied. The Arabs could use the beasts for a living barricade, firing over their backs. Stephen grudged this advantage, and was puzzling his brain how to prevent the enemy from taking it, when a great light blazed into the sky, followed by the roar of an explosion.

The tower shook, and Stephen was thrown off his feet. For half a second he was dazed, but came to himself in the act of tumbling down stairs, still grasping his rifle.

A huge hole yawned where the gate had stood. The iron had shrivelled and curled like so much cardboard, and the gap was filled with circling wreaths of smoke and a crowd of Arabs. Mad with fear, the camels and horses tethered in the stables of the bordj broke their halters and plunged wildly about the courtyard, looming like strange monsters in the red light and belching smoke. As if to serve the defenders, they galloped toward the gate, cannoning against each other in the struggle to escape, and thus checked the first rush of the enemy. Nearly all were shot down by the Arabs, but a few moments were gained for the Europeans. Firing as he ran, Stephen made a dash for the barricade, where he found Rostafel, and as the enemy swarmed into the quadrangle, pouring over dead and dying camels, the two Highlanders burst with yells like the slogans of their fighting ancestors, out from the watch-towers nearest the gateway.

The sudden apparition of these gigantic twin figures, bare-legged, dressed in kilts, appalled the Arabs. Some, who had got farthest into the courtyard, were taken in the rear by Angus and Hamish; and as the Highlanders laid about them with clubbed rifles, the superstitious Easterners wavered. Imagining themselves assailed by giant women with the strength of devils, they fell back dismayed, and for some wild seconds the twins were masters of the quadrangle. They broke heads with crushing blows, and smashed ribs with trampling feet, yelling their fearsome yells which seemed the cries of death and war. But it was the triumph of a moment only, and then the Arabs—save those who would fight no more—rallied round their leader, a tall, stout man with a majestic presence. Once he had got his men in hand—thirteen or fourteen he had left—the open courtyard was too hot a place even for the Highland men. They retreated, shoulder to shoulder, towards the barricade, and soon were firing viciously from behind its shelter. If they lived through this night, never again, it would seem, could they be satisfied with the daily round of preparing an old lady's bath, and pressing upon her dishes which she did not want. And yet—their mistress was an exceptional old lady.

Now, all the towers were vacant, except the one defended by Nevill, and it had been agreed from the first that he was to stick to his post until time for the last stand. The reason of this was that the door of his tower was screened by the barricade, and the two rear walls of the bordj (meeting in a triangle at this corner) must be defended while the barricade was held. These walls unguarded, the enemy could climb them from outside and fire down on the backs of the Europeans, behind the barrier. Those who attempted to climb from the courtyard (the gate-stairway being destroyed by the explosion) must face the fire of the defenders, who could also see and protect themselves against any one mounting the wall to pass over the scattered débris of the ruined signal-tower. Thus every contingency was provided for, as well as might be by five men, against three times their number; and the Europeans meant to make a stubborn fight before that last resort—the dining-room. Nevertheless, it occurred to Stephen that perhaps, after all, he need not greatly repent the confession of love he had made to Victoria. He had had no right to speak, but if there were to be no future for either in this world, fate need not grudge him an hour's happiness. And he was conscious of a sudden lightness of spirit, as of an exile nearing home.

The Arabs, sheltering behind the camels and horses they had shot, fired continuously in the hope of destroying a weak part of the barricade or killing some one behind it. Gradually they formed of the dead animals a barricade of their own, and now that the bonfires were dying it was difficult for the Europeans to touch the enemy behind cover. Consulting together, however, and calculating how many dead each might put to his credit, the defenders agreed that they must have killed or disabled more than a dozen. The marabout, whose figure in one flashing glimpse Stephen fancied he recognized, was still apparently unhurt. It was he who seemed to be conducting operations, but of Si Maïeddine nothing had been seen since his unconscious or dead body was dragged down the slope by his friends. Precisely how many Arabs remained to fight, the Europeans were not sure, but they believed that over a dozen were left, counting the leader.

By and by the dying fires flickered out, leaving only a dull red glow on the roofs. The pale light of the stars seemed dim after the blaze which had lit the quadrangle, and in the semi-darkness, when each side watched the other as a cat spies at a rat-hole, the siege grew wearisome. Yet the Europeans felt that each moment's respite meant sixty seconds of new hope for them. Ammunition was running low, and soon they must fall back upon the small supply kept by Rostafel, which had already been placed in the dining-room; but matters were not quite desperate, since each minute brought the soldiers from Bordj Azzouz nearer, even if the carrier pigeon had failed.

"Why do they not blow us up?" asked the Frenchman, sober now, and extremely pessimistic. "They could do it. Or is it the women they are after?"

Stephen was not inclined to be confidential. "No doubt they have their own reasons," he answered. "What they are, can't matter to us."

"It matters that they are concocting some plan, and that we do not know what it is," said Rostafel.

"To get on to the roof over our heads is what they'd like best, no doubt," said Stephen. "But my friend in the tower here is saving us from that at the back, and they can't do much in front of our noses."

"I am not sure they cannot. They will think of something," grumbled the landlord. "We are in a bad situation. I do not believe any of us will see to-morrow. I only hope my brother will have the spirit to revenge me. But even that is not my luck."

He was right. The Arabs had thought of something—"a something" which they must have prepared before their start. Suddenly, behind the mound of dead animals arose a fitful light, and while the Europeans wondered at its meaning, a shower of burning projectiles flew through the air at the barricade. All four fired a volley in answer, hoping to wing the throwers, but the Arab scheme was a success. Tins of blazing pitch were rolling about the courtyard, close to the barrier, but before falling they had struck the piled mattresses and furniture, splashing fire and trickles of flame poured over the old bedticking, and upholstered chairs from the dining-room. At the same instant Nevill called from the door of his tower: "More cartridges, quick! I'm all out, and there are two chaps trying to shin up the wall. Maïeddine's not dead. He's there, directing 'em."

Stephen gave Nevill his own rifle, just reloaded. "Fetch the cartridges stored in the dining-room," he said to Rostafel, "while we beat the fire out with our coats." But there was no need for the Frenchman to leave his post. "Here are the cartridges," said Victoria's voice, surprising them. She had been at the door, which she held ajar, and behind this screen had heard and seen all that passed. As Stephen took the box of cartridges, she caught up the large pail of water which early in the evening had been placed in the dining-room in case of need. "Take this and put out the fire," she cried to Hamish, who snatched the bucket without a word, and dashed its contents over the barricade.

Then she went back to Saidee, who sat on the blankets in a far corner, shivering with cold, though the night was hot, and the room, with its barred wooden shutters, close almost beyond bearing. They

414

had kept but one tallow candle lighted, that Victoria might more safely peep out from time to time, to see how the fight was going.

"What if our men are all killed," Saidee whispered, as the girl stole back to her, "and nobody's left to defend us? Cassim and Maïeddine will open the door, over their dead bodies, and then — then — —"

"You have a revolver," said Victoria, almost angrily. "Not for them, I don't mean that. Only — they mustn't take us. But I'm not afraid. Our men are brave, and splendid. They have no thought of giving up. And if Captain Sabine got our message, he'll be here by dawn."

"Don't forget the shot we heard."

"No. But the pigeon isn't our only hope. The signals!"

"Who knows if an answer came?"

"I know, because I know Stephen. He wouldn't have come down alive unless he'd got an answer."

Saidee said no more, and they sat together in silence, Victoria holding her sister's icy hand in hers, which was scarcely warmer, though it tingled with the throbbing of many tiny pulses. So they listened to the firing outside, until suddenly it sounded different to Victoria's ears. She straightened herself with a start, listening even more intensely.

"What's the matter? What do you hear?" Saidee stammered, dry-lipped.

"I'm not sure. But — I think they've used up all the cartridges I took them. And there are no more."

"But they're firing still."

"With their revolvers."

"God help us, then! It can't last long," the older woman whispered, and covered her face with her hands.

Victoria did not stop for words of comfort. She jumped up from the couch of blankets and ran to the door, which Stephen had shut. It must be kept wide open, now, in case the defenders were obliged to rush in for the last stand. She pressed close to it, convulsively grasping the handle with her cold fingers.

Then the end came soon, for the enemy had not been slow to detect the difference between rifle and revolver shots. They knew, even before Victoria guessed, exactly what had happened. It was the event they had been awaiting. With a rush, the dozen men dashed over the mound of carcasses and charged the burning barricade.

"Quick, Wings," shouted Stephen, defending the way his friend must take. The distance was short from the door of the watch-tower to the door of the dining-room, but it was just too long for safety. As Nevill ran across, an Arab close to the barricade shot him in the side, and he would have fallen if Stephen had not caught him round the waist, and flung him to Hamish, who carried him to shelter.

A second more, and they were all in the dining-room. Stephen and Angus had barred the heavy door, and already Hamish and Rostafel were firing through the two round ventilating holes in the window shutters. There were two more such holes in the door, and Stephen took one, Angus the other. But the enemy had already sheltered on the other side of the barricade, which would now serve them as well as it had served the Europeans. The water dashed on to the flames had not extinguished all, but the wet mattresses and furniture burned slowly, and the Arabs began beating out the fire with their gandourahs.

Again there was a deadlock. For the moment neither side could harm the other: but there was little doubt in the minds of the besieged as to the next move of the besiegers. The Arabs were at last free to climb the wall, beyond reach of the loopholes in door or window, and could make a hole in the roof of the dining-room. It would take them some time, but they could do it, and meanwhile the seven prisoners were almost as helpless as trapped rats.

Of the five men, not one was unwounded, and Stephen began to fear that Nevill was badly hurt. He could not breathe without pain, and though he tried to laugh, he was deadly pale in the wan candlelight. "Don't mind me. I'm all right," he said when Victoria and Saidee began tearing up their Arab veils for bandages. "Not worth the bother!" But the sisters would not listen, and Victoria told him with pretended cheerfulness what a good nurse she was; how she had learned "first aid" at the school at Potterston, and taken a prize for efficiency.

In spite of his protest, Nevill was made to lie down on the blankets in the corner, while the two sisters played doctor; and as the firing of the Arabs slackened, Stephen left the twins to guard door and window, while he and Rostafel built a screen to serve when the breaking of the roof should begin. The only furniture left in the dining-room consisted of one large table (which Stephen had not added to the barricade because he had thought of this contingency) and in addition a rough unpainted cupboard, fastened to the wall. They tore off the doors of this cupboard, and with them and the table made a kind of penthouse to protect the corner where Nevill lay.

"Now," said Stephen, "if they dig a hole in the roof they'll find — —"

"Flag o' truce, sir," announced Hamish at the door. And Stephen remembered that for three minutes at least there had been no firing. As he worked at the screen, he had hardly noticed the silence.

He hurried to join Hamish at the door, and, peeping out, saw a tall man, with a bloodstained bandage wrapped round his head, advancing from the other side of the barricade, with a white handkerchief hanging from the barrel of his rifle. It was Maïeddine, and somehow Stephen was glad that the Arab's death did not lie at his door. His anger had cooled, now, and he wondered at the murderous rage which had passed.

As Maïeddine came forward, fearlessly, he limped in spite of an effort to hide the fact that he was almost disabled.

"I have to say that, if the ladies are given up to us, no harm shall come to them or to the others," he announced in French, in a clear, loud voice. "We will take the women with us, and leave the men to go their own way. We will even provide them with animals in place of those we have killed, that they may ride to the north."

"Do not believe him!" cried Saidee. "Traitors once, they'll be traitors again. If Victoria and I should consent to go with them, to save all your lives, they wouldn't spare you really. As soon as we were in their hands, they'd burn the house or blow it up."

"There can be no question of our allowing you to go, in any case," said Stephen. "Our answer is," he replied to Maïeddine, "that the ladies prefer to remain with us, and we expect to be able to protect them."

"Then all will die together, except one, who is my promised wife," returned the Arab. "Tell that one that by coming with me she can save her sister, whom she once seemed to love more than herself, more than all the world. If she stays, not only will her eyes behold the death of the men who failed to guard her, but the death of her sister. One who has a right to decide the lady's fate, has decided that she must die in punishment of her obstinacy, unless she gives herself up."

"Tell Si Maïeddine that before he or the marabout can come near us, we shall be dead," Victoria said, in a low voice. "I know Saidee and I can trust you," she went on, "to shoot us both straight through the heart rather than they should take us. That's what you wish, too, isn't it, Saidee?"

"Yes—yes, if I have courage or heart enough to wish anything," her sister faltered.

But Stephen could not or would not give that message to Maïeddine. "Go," he said, the fire of his old rage flaming again. "Go, you Arab dog!"

Forgetting the flag of truce in his fury at the insult, Maïeddine lifted his rifle and fired; then, remembering that he had sinned against a code of honour he respected, he stood still, waiting for an answering shot, as if he and his rival were engaged in a strange duel. But Stephen did not shoot, and with a quick word forbade the others to fire. Then Maïeddine moved away slowly and was lost to sight behind the barricade.

As he disappeared, a candle which Victoria had placed near Nevill's couch on the floor, flickered and dropped its wick in a pool of grease. There was only one other left, and the lamp had been forgotten in the kitchen: but already the early dawn was drinking the starlight. It was three o'clock, and soon it would be day.

For some minutes there was no more firing. Stillness had fallen in the quadrangle. There was no sound except the faint moaning of some wounded animal that lived and suffered. Then came a pounding on the roof, not in one, but in two or three places. It was as if men worked furiously, with pickaxes; and somehow Stephen was sure that Maïeddine, despite his wounds, was among them. He would wish to be the first to see Victoria's face, to save her from death, perhaps, and keep her for himself. Still, Stephen was glad he had not killed the Arab, and he felt, though they said nothing of it to each other, that Victoria, too, was glad.

They must have help soon now, if it were to come in time. The knocking on the roof was loud.

"How long before they can break through?" Victoria asked, leaving Nevill to come to Stephen, who guarded the door.

"Well, there are several layers of thick adobe," he said, cheerfully.

"Will it be ten minutes?"

"Oh, more than that. Much more than that," Stephen assured her.

"Please tell me what you truly think. I have a reason for asking. Will it be half an hour?"

"At least that," he said, with a tone of grave sincerity which she no longer doubted.

"Half an hour. And then — —"

"Even then we can keep you safe for a little while, behind the screen. And help may come."

"Have you given up hope, in your heart?"

"No. One doesn't give up hope."

"I feel the same. I never give up hope. And yet — we may have to die, all of us, and for myself, I'm not afraid, only very solemn, for death must be wonderful. But for you — to have you give your life for ours — —"

"I would give it joyfully, a hundred times for you."

"I know. And I for you. That's one thing I wanted to tell you, in case — we never have a chance to speak to each other again. That, and just this beside: one reason I'm not afraid, is because I'm with you. If I die, or live, I shall be with you. And whichever it's to be, I shall find it sweet. One will be the same as the other, really, for death's only a new life."

"And I have something to tell you," Stephen said. "I worship you, and to have known you, has made it worth while to have existed, though I haven't always been happy. Why, just this moment alone is worth all the rest of my life. So come what may, I have lived."

The pounding on the roof grew louder. The sound of the picks with which the men worked could be heard more clearly. They were rapidly getting through those layers of adobe, of whose thickness Stephen had spoken.

"It won't be half an hour now," Victoria murmured, looking up.

"No. Promise me you'll go to your sister and Nevill Caird behind the screen, when I tell you."

"I promise, if— —"

The pounding ceased. In the courtyard there was a certain confusion—the sound of running feet, and murmur of excited voices, though eyes that looked through the holes in the door and window could not see past the barricade.

Then, suddenly, the pounding began again, more furiously than ever. It was as if demons had taken the place of men.

"It is Maïeddine, I'm sure!" cried Victoria. "I seem to know what is in his mind. Something has made him desperate."

"There's a chance for us," said Stephen. "What I believe has happened, is this. They must have stationed a sentinel or two outside the bordj in case of surprise. The raised voices we heard, and the stopping of the work on the roof for a minute, may have meant that a sentinel ran in with news—good news for us, bad news for the Arabs."

"But—would they have begun to work again, if soldiers were coming?"

"Yes, if help were so far off that the Arabs might hope to reach us before it came, and get away in time. Ben Halim's one hope is to make an end of—some of us. It was well enough to disguise the whole band as Touaregs, in case they were seen by nomads, or the landlord here should escape, and tell of the attack. But he'd risk anything to silence us men, and— —"

"He cares nothing for Saidee's life or mine. It's only Maïeddine who cares," the girl broke in. "I suppose they've horses and meharis waiting for them outside the bordj?"

"Yes. Probably they're being got ready now. The animals have had a night's rest."

As he spoke, the first bit of ceiling fell in, rough plaster dropping with a patter like rain on the hard clay floor.

Saidee cried out faintly in her corner, where Nevill had fallen into semi-unconsciousness behind the screen. Rostafel grumbled a "sapriste!" under his breath, but the Highlanders were silent.

Down poured more plaster, and put out the last candle. Though a faint dawn-light stole through the holes in door and window, the room was dim, almost dark, and with the smell of gunpowder mingled the stench of hot tallow.

"Go now, dearest, to your sister," Stephen said to the girl, in a low voice that was for her alone.

"You will come?"

"Yes. Soon. But the door and window must be guarded. We can't have them breaking in two ways at once."

"Give me your hand," she said.

He took one of hers, instead, but she raised his to her lips and kissed it. Then she went back to her sister, and the two clung together in silence, listening to the patter of broken adobe on the floor. At first it was but as a heavy shower of rain; then it increased in violence like the rattle of hail. They could hear men speaking on the roof, and a gleam of daylight silvered a crack, as Stephen looked up, a finger on the trigger of his revolver.

"Five minutes more," were the words which repeated themselves in his mind, like the ticking of a watch. "Four minutes. Three. Can I keep my promise to her, when the time comes!"

A shout broke the question short, like a snapped thread.

He remembered the voice of the marabout, and knew that the sisters must recognize it also.

"What does he say?" Stephen called across the room to Victoria, speaking loudly to be heard over voices which answered the summons, whatever it might be.

"He's ordering Maïeddine to come down from the roof. He says five seconds' delay and it will be too late—they'll both be ruined. I can't hear what Maïeddine answers. But he goes on working still—he won't obey."

"Fool—traitor! For thy sentimental folly wilt thou sacrifice thy people's future and ruin my son and me?" Cassim shouted, as the girl stood still to listen. "Thou canst never have her now. Stay, and thou canst do naught but kill thyself. Come, and we may all be saved. I command thee, in the name of Allah and His Prophet, that thou obey me."

The pounding stopped. There was a rushing, sliding sound on the roof. Then all was quiet above and in the courtyard.

Saidee broke into hysterical sobbing, crying that they were rescued, that Honoré Sabine was on his way to save them. And Victoria thought that Stephen would come to her, but he did not. They were to live, not to die, and the barrier that had been broken down was raised again.

"What if it's only a trap?" Saidee asked, as Stephen opened the door. "What if they're behind the barricade, watching?"

"Listen! Don't you hear shots?" Victoria cried.

"Yes. There are shots—far away," Stephen answered. "That settles it. There's no ambush. Either Sabine or the soldiers marching from Azzouz are after them. They didn't go an instant too soon to save their skins."

"And ours," murmured Nevill, roused from his stupor. "Queer, how natural it seems that we should be all right after all." Then his mind wandered a little, leading him back to a feverish dream. "Ask Sabine, when he comes—if he's got a letter for me—from Josette."

Stephen opened the door, and let in the fresh air and morning light, but the sight in the quadrangle was too ugly for the eyes of women. "Don't come out!" he called sharply over his shoulder as he turned past the barricade, with Rostafel at his back.

The courtyard was hideous as a slaughter-house. Only the sky of rose and gold reminded him of the world's beauty and the glory of morning, after that dark nightmare which wrapped his spirit like the choking folds of a black snake.

Outside the broken gate, in the desert, there were more traces of the night's work; blood-stains in the sand, and in a shadowy hollow here and there a huddled form which seemed a denser shadow. But it would not move when other shadows crept away before the sun.

Far in the distance, as Stephen strained his eyes through the brightening dawn, he saw flying figures of men on camels and horses; and sounds of shooting came faintly to his ears. At last it ceased altogether. Some of the figures had vanished. Others halted. Then it seemed to Stephen that these last were coming back, towards the bordj. They were riding fast, and all together, as if under discipline. Soldiers, certainly: but were they from the north or south? Stephen could not tell; but as his eyes searched the horizon, the doubt was solved. Another party of men were riding southward, toward Toudja, from the north.

"It's Sabine who has chased the Arabs. The others are just too late," he thought. And he saw that the rescuers from Oued Tolga must reach the bordj half an hour in advance of the men from Azzouz.

He was anxious to know what news Sabine had, and the eagerness he felt to hear details soothed the pain and shame which weighed upon his heart.

"How am I to explain—to beg her forgiveness?" was the question that asked itself in his mind; but he had no answer to give. Only this he could see: after last night, he was hers, if she would take him. But he believed that she would send him away, that she would despise him when she had heard the whole story of his entanglement. She would say that he belonged to the other woman, not to her. And though he was sure she would not reproach him, he thought there were some words, some looks which, if she could not forget, it would be hard for even her sweet nature to forgive.

He went back to the dining-room with the news of what he had seen. And as there was no longer any need of protection for the women, the Highlanders came out with him and Rostafel. All four stood at the gate of the bordj as the party of twelve soldiers rode up, on tired horses; but Stephen was in advance, and it was he who answered Sabine's first breathless question.

"She's safe. They're both safe, thank God. So are we all, except poor Caird, who's damaged a good deal worse than any of us. But not dangerously, I hope."

"I brought our surgeon," said Sabine, eagerly. "He wanted to be in this with me. I had to ask for the command, because you know I'm on special duty at Tolga. But I had no trouble with Major Duprez when I told him how friends of mine were attacked by Arab robbers, and how I had got the message."

"So that's what you told him?"

"Yes. I didn't want a scandal in the Zaouïa, for *her* sake. Nobody knows that the marabout is for anything in this business. But, of course, if you've killed him — -"

"We haven't. He's got clear away. Unless your men have nabbed him and his friend Maïeddine."

"Not we. I'm not sure I cared to—unless we could kill him. But we did honestly try—to do both. There were six we chased — — "

"Only six. Then we must have polished off more than we thought."

"We can find out later how many. But the last six didn't get off without a scratch, I assure you. They must have had a sentinel watching. We saw no one, but as we were hoping to surprise the bordj these six men, who looked from a distance like Touaregs, rushed out, mounted horses and camels and dashed away, striking westward."

"They dared not go north. I'd been signalling — — "

"From the broken tower?"

"Yes. As you came, you must have sighted the men from Azzouz. But tell me the rest."

"There's little to tell, and I want your news more than you can want mine. The Arabs' animals were fresh, and ours tired, for I'd given them no rest. The brutes had a good start of us and made the best of it, but at first I thought we were gaining. We got within gunshot, and fired after them. Two at least were hit. We came on traces of fresh blood afterward, but the birds themselves were flown. In any case, it was to bring help I came, not to make captures. Do you think *she* would like me to see her now?"

"Come with me and try, before the other rescue party arrives. I'm glad the surgeon's with you. I'm worried about Caird, and we're all a bit dilapidated. How we're to get him and the ladies away from this place, I don't know. Our animals are dead or dying."

"You will probably find that the enemy has been generous in spite of himself and left you some—all that couldn't be taken away. Strange how those men looked like Touaregs! You are sure of what they really were?"

"Sure. But since no one else knows, why should the secret leak out? Better for the ladies if the Touareg disguise should hide the truth, as it was meant to do."

"Why not indeed? Since we weren't lucky enough to rid his wife— and the world of the marabout."

"Then we're agreed: unless something happens to change our minds, we were attacked by Touaregs."

Sabine smiled grimly. "Duprez bet," he answered, "that I should find they were not Arabs, but Touaregs. He will enjoy saying 'I told you so.'"

That night, and for many nights to come, there was wailing in the Zaouïa. The marabout had gone out to meet his son, who had been away from school on a pilgrimage, and returning at dark, to avoid the great heat of the day, had been bitten by a viper. Thus, at least, pronounced the learned Arab physician. It was of the viper bite he died, so it was said, and no one outside the Zaouïa knew of the great man's death until days afterwards, when he was already buried. Even in the Zaouïa it was not known by many that he had gone away or returned from a journey, or that he lay ill. In spite of this secrecy and mystery, however, there was no gossip, but only wild wailing, of mourners who refused to be comforted. And if certain persons, to the number of twenty or more, were missing from their places in the Zaouïa, nothing was said, after Si Maïeddine had talked with the holy men of the mosque. If these missing ones were away, and even if they should never come back, it was because they were needed to carry out the marabout's wishes, at a vast distance. But now, the dearest wishes of Sidi Mohammed would never be fulfilled. That poignant knowledge was a knife in every man's heart; for men of ripe age or wisdom in the Zaouïa knew what these wishes were, and how some day they were to have come true through blood and fire.

All were sad, though no tongue spoke of any other reason for sadness, except the inestimable loss of the Saint. And sadder than the saddest was Si Maïeddine, who seemed to have lost his youth.

LII

It is a long cry from the bordj of Toudja among the dunes of the southern desert, to Algiers, yet Nevill begged that he might be taken home. "You know why," he said to Stephen, and his eyes explained, if Stephen needed explanations. Nevill thought there might be some chance of seeing Josette in Algiers, if he were dying. But the army surgeon from Oued Tolga pronounced it unsafe to take him so far.

Yet away from Toudja he must go, since it was impossible to care for him properly there, and the bullet which had wounded him was still in his side.

Fortunately the enemy had left plenty of camels. They had untethered all, hoping that the animals might wander away, too far to be caught by the Europeans, but more than were needed remained in the neighbourhood of Toudja, and Rostafel took possession of half a dozen good meharis, which would help recoup him for his losses in the bordj. Not one animal had any mark upon it which could identify the attackers, and saddles and accoutrements were of Touareg make. The dead men, too, were impossible to identify, and it was not likely that much trouble would be taken in prosecuting inquiries. Among those whose duty it is to govern Algeria, there is a proverb which, for various good reasons, has come to be much esteemed: "Let sleeping dogs lie."

Not a man of the five who defended the bordj but had at least one wound to show for his night's work. Always, however, it is those who attack, in a short siege, who suffer most; and the Europeans were not proud of the many corpses they had to their credit. There was some patching for the surgeon to do for all, but Nevill's was the only serious case. The French doctor, De Vigne, did not try to hide the truth from the wounded man's friend; there was danger. The best thing would have been to get Nevill to Algiers, but since that was impossible, he must travel in a bassour, by easy stages, to Touggourt. Instead of two days' journey they must make it three, or more if necessary, and he—De Vigne—would go with them to put his patient into the hands of the army surgeon at Touggourt.

They had only the one bassour; that in which Saidee and Victoria had come to Toudja from Oued Tolga, but Nevill was delirious more often than not, and had no idea that a sacrifice was being made for him. Blankets, and two of the mattresses least damaged by fire in the barricade, were fastened on to camels for the ladies, after the fashion in use for Bedouin women of the poorest class, or Ouled Naïls who have not yet made their fortune as dancers; and so the journey began again.

There was never a time during the three days it lasted, for Stephen to confess to Victoria. Possibly she did not wish him to take advantage of a situation created as if by accident at Toudja. Or perhaps she thought, now that the common danger which had drawn them together, was over, it would be best to wait until anxiety for Nevill had passed, before talking of their own affairs.

At Azzouz, where they passed a night full of suffering for Nevill, they had news of the marabout's death. It came by telegraph to the operator, just before the party was ready to start on; yet Saidee was sure that Sabine had caused it to be sent just at that time. He had been obliged to march back with his men—the penalty of commanding the force for which he had asked; but a letter would surely come to Touggourt, and Saidee could imagine all that it would say. She had no regrets for Ben Halim, and said frankly to Victoria that it was difficult not to be indecently glad of her freedom. At last she had waked up from a black dream of horror, and now that it was over, it hardly seemed real. "I shall forget," she said. "I shall put my whole soul to forgetting everything that's happened to me in the last ten years, and every one I've known in the south— except one. But to have met him and to have him love me, I'd live it all over again—all."

She kept Victoria with her continually, and in the physical weakness and nervous excitement which followed the strain she had gone through, she seemed to have forgotten her interest in Victoria's affairs. She did not know that her sister and Stephen had talked of love, for at Toudja after the fight began she had thought of nothing but the danger they shared.

Altogether, everything combined to delay explanations between Stephen and Victoria. He tried to regret this, yet could not be as sorry as he was repentant. It was not quite heaven, but it was almost paradise to have her near him, though they had a chance for only a few words occasionally, within earshot of Saidee, or De Vigne, or the twins, who watched over Nevill like two well-trained nurses. She loved him, since a word from her meant more than vows from other women. Nothing had happened yet to disturb her love, so these few days belonged to Stephen. He could not feel that he had stolen them. At Touggourt he would find a time and place to speak, and then it would be over forever. But one joy he had, which never could have come to him, if it had not been for the peril at Toudja. They knew each other's hearts. Nothing could change that. One day, no doubt, she would learn to care for some other man, but perhaps never quite in the same way she had cared for him, because Stephen was sure that this was her first love. And though she might be happy in another love — he tried to hope it, but did not succeed sincerely — he would always have it to remember, until the day of his death, that once she had loved him.

As far out from Touggourt as Temacin, Lady MacGregor came to meet them, in a ramshackle carriage, filled with rugs and pillows in case Nevill wished to change. But he was not in a state to wish for anything, and De Vigne decided for him. He was to go on in the bassour, to the villa which had been let to Lady MacGregor by an officer of the garrison. It was there the little Mohammed was to have been kept and guarded by the Highlanders, if the great scheme had not been suddenly changed in some of its details. Now, the child had inherited his father's high place. Already the news had reached the marabout of Temacin, and flashed on to Touggourt. But no one suspected that the viper which had bitten the Saint had taken the form of a French bullet. Perhaps, had all been known to the Government, it would have seemed poetical justice that the arch plotter had met his death thus. But his plots had died with him; and if Islam mourned because the Moul Saa they hoped for had been snatched from them, they mourned in secret. For above other sects and nations, Islam knows how to be silent.

When they were settled in the villa near the oasis (Saidee and Victoria too, for they needed no urging to wait till it was known whether Nevill Caird would live or die) Lady MacGregor said with her usual briskness to Stephen: "Of course I've telegraphed to that *creature.*"

Stephen looked at her blankly.

"That hard-hearted little beast, Josette Soubise," the fairy aunt explained.

Stephen could hardly help laughing, though he had seldom felt less merry. But that the tiny Lady MacGregor should refer to tall Josette, who was nearly twice her height, as a "little beast," struck him as somewhat funny. Besides, her toy-terrier snappishness was comic.

"I've nothing *against* the girl," Lady MacGregor felt it right to go on, "except that she's an idiot to bite off her nose to spite her own face — and Nevill's too. I don't approve of her at all as a wife for him, you must understand. Nevill could marry a *princess*, and she's nothing but a little school-teacher with a dimple or two, whose mother and father were less than *nobody*. Still, as Nevill wants her, she might have the grace to show appreciation of the honour, by not spoiling his life. He's never been the same since he went and fell in love with her, and she refused him."

"You've telegraphed to Tlemcen that Nevill is ill?" Stephen ventured.

"I've telegraphed to the creature that she'd better come here at once, if she wants to see him alive," replied Lady MacGregor. "I suppose she loves him in her French-Algerian way, and she must have saved up enough money for the fare. Anyhow, if Nevill doesn't live, I happen to know he's left her nearly everything, except what the poor boy imagines I ought to have. That's pouring coals of fire on her head!"

"Don't think of his not living!" exclaimed Stephen.

"Honestly I believe he won't live unless that idiot of a girl comes and purrs and promises to marry him, deathbed or no deathbed."

Again Stephen smiled faintly. "You're a matchmaker, Lady MacGregor," he said. "You are one of the most subtle persons I ever saw."

The old lady took this as a compliment. "I haven't lived among Arabs, goodness knows how many years, for nothing," she retorted. "I telegraphed for her about five minutes after you wired from Azzouz. In fact, my telegram went back by the boy who brought yours."

"She may be here day after to-morrow, if she started at once," Stephen reflected aloud.

"She did, and she will," said Lady MacGregor, drily.

"You've heard?"

"The day I wired."

"You have quite a nice way of breaking things to people, you dear little ladyship," said Stephen. And for some reason which he could not in the least understand, this speech caused Nevill's aunt to break into tears.

That evening, the two surgeons extracted the bullet from Nevill's side. Afterwards, he was extremely weak, and took as little interest as possible in things, until Stephen was allowed to speak to him for a moment.

Most men, if told that they had just sixty seconds to spend at the bedside of a dear friend, would have been at a loss what to say in a space of time so small yet valuable. But Stephen knew what he wished to say, and said it, as soon as Nevill let him speak; but Nevill began first.

"Maybe—going to—deserve name of Wings," he muttered. "Shouldn't wonder. Don't care much."

"Is there any one thing in this world you want above everything else?" asked Stephen.

"Yes. Sight of—Josette. One thing I—can't have."

"Yes, you can," said Stephen quietly. "She's coming. She started the minute she heard you were ill, and she'll be in Touggourt day after to-morrow."

"You're not—pulling my leg?"

"To do that would be very injurious. But I thought good news would be better than medicine."

"Thank you, Legs. You're a great doctor," was all that Nevill answered. But his temperature began to go down within the hour.

"He'll get the girl, of course," remarked Lady MacGregor, when Stephen told her. "That is, if he lives."

"He will live, with this hope to buoy him up," said Stephen. "And she can't hold out against him for a minute when she sees him as he is. Indeed, I rather fancy she's been in a mood to change her mind this last month."

"Why this last month?"

"Oh, I think she misunderstood Nevill's interest in Miss Ray, and that helped her to understand herself. When she finds out that it's for her he still cares, not some one else, she'll do anything he asks." Afterwards it proved that he was right.

The day after the arrival at Touggourt, the house in its garden near the oasis was very quiet. The Arab servants, whom Lady MacGregor had taken with the place, moved silently, and for Nevill's sake voices were lowered. There was a brooding stillness of summer heat over the one little patch of flowery peace and perfumed shade in the midst of the fierce golden desert. Yet to the five members of the oddly assembled family it was as if the atmosphere tingled with electricity. There was a curious, even oppressive sense of suspense, of waiting for something to happen.

They did not speak of this feeling, yet they could see it in each other's eyes, if they dare to look.

It was with them as with people who wait to hear a clock begin striking an hour which will bring news of some great change in their lives, for good or evil.

The tension increased as the day went on; still, no one had said to another, "What is there so strange about to-day? Do you feel it? Is it only our imagination—a reaction after strain, or is it that a presentiment of something to happen hangs over us?"

Stephen had not yet had any talk with Victoria. They had seen each other alone for scarcely more than a moment since the night at Toudja; but now that Nevill was better, and the surgeons said that if all went well, danger was past, it seemed to Stephen that the hour had come.

After they had lunched in the dim, cool dining-room, and Lady MacGregor had proposed a siesta for all sensible people, Stephen stopped the girl on her way upstairs as she followed her sister.

"May I talk to you for a little while this afternoon?" he asked.

Voice and eyes were wistful, and Victoria wondered why, because she was so happy that she felt as if life had been set to music. She had hoped that he would be happy too, when Nevill's danger was over, and he had time to think of himself—perhaps, too, of her.

"Yes," she said, "let's talk in the garden, when it's cooler. I love being in gardens, don't you? Everything that happens seems more beautiful."

Stephen remembered how lovely he had thought her in the lily garden at Algiers. He was almost glad that they were not to have this talk there; for the memory of it was too perfect to mar with sadness.

"I'm going to put Saidee to sleep," she went on. "You may laugh, but truly I can. When I was a little girl, she used to like me to stroke her hair if her head ached, and she would always fall asleep. And once she's asleep I shan't dare move, or she'll wake up. She has such happy dreams now, and they're sure to come true. Shall I come to you about half-past five?"

"I'll be waiting," said Stephen.

It was the usual garden of a villa in the neighbourhood of a desert town, but Stephen had never seen one like it, except that of the Caïd, in Bou-Saada. There were the rounded paths of hard sand, the colour of pinkish gold in the dappling shadows of date palms and magnolias, and there were rills of running water that whispered and gurgled as they bathed the dark roots of the trees. No grass grew in the garden, and the flowers were not planted in beds or borders. Plants and trees sprang out of the sand, and such flowers as there were—roses, and pomegranate blossoms, hibiscus, and passion flowers—climbed, and rambled, and pushed, and hung in heavy drapery, as best they could without attention or guidance. But one of the principal paths led to a kind of arbour, or temple, where long ago palms had been planted in a ring, and had formed a high green dome, through which, even at noon, the light filtered as if through a dome of emerald. Underneath, the pavement of gold was hard and smooth, and in the centre whispered a tiny fountain ornamented with old Algerian tiles. It trickled rather than played, but its delicate music was soothing and sweet as a murmured lullaby; and from the shaded seat beside it there was a glimpse between tree trunks of the burning desert gold.

On this wooden seat by the fountain Stephen waited for Victoria, and saw her coming to him, along the straight path that led to the round point. She wore a white dress which Lady MacGregor had brought her, and as she walked, the embroidery of light and shadow made it look like lace of a lovely pattern. She stopped on the way, and, gathering a red rose with a long stem, slipped it into her belt. It looked like a spot of blood over her heart, as if a sword had been driven in and drawn out. Stephen could not bear to see it there. It was like a symbol of the wound that he was waiting to inflict.

She came to him smiling, looking very young, like a child who expects happiness.

"Have I kept you waiting long?" she asked. Her blue eyes, with the shadow of the trees darkening them, had a wonderful colour, almost purple. A desperate longing to take her in his arms swept over Stephen like a wave. He drew in his breath sharply and shut his teeth. He could not answer. Hardly knowing what he did, he held out his hands, and very quietly and sweetly she laid hers in them.

"Don't trust me—don't be kind to me," he said, crushing her hands for an instant, then putting them away.

She looked up in surprise, as he stood by the fountain, very tall and pale, and suddenly rather grim, it seemed to her, his expression out of tune with the peace of the garden and the mood in which she had come.

"What is the matter?" she asked, simply.

"Everything. I hardly know how to begin to tell you. Yet I must. Perhaps you'll think I shouldn't have waited till now. But there's been no chance—at least, I——"

"No, there's been no chance for us to talk, or even to think very much about ourselves," Victoria tried to reassure him. "Begin just as you like. Whatever you say, whatever you have to tell, I won't misunderstand."

"First of all, then," Stephen said, "you know I love you. Only you don't know how much. I couldn't tell you that, any more than I could tell how much water there is in the ocean. I didn't know myself that it was possible to love like this, and such a love might turn the world into heaven. But because I am what I am, and because I've done what I have done, it's making mine hell. Wait—you said you wouldn't misunderstand! The man who loves you ought to offer some sort of spiritual gold and diamonds, but I've got only a life half spoiled to offer you, if you'll take it. And before I can even ask you to take it, I'll have to explain how it's spoiled."

Victoria did not speak, but still looked at him with that look of an expectant, anxious child, which made him long to snatch her up and turn his back forever on the world where there was a Margot Lorenzi, and gossiping people, and newspapers.

But he had to go on. "There's a woman," he said, "who—perhaps she cares for me—I don't know. Anyhow, she'd suffered through our family. I felt sorry for her. I—I suppose I admired her. She's handsome—or people think so. I can hardly tell how it came about, but I—asked her to marry me, and she said yes. That was—late last winter—or the beginning of spring. Then she had to go to Canada, where she'd been brought up—her father died in England, a few months ago, and her mother, when she was a child; but she had friends she wanted to see, before—before she married. So she went, and I came to Algiers, to visit Nevill. Good heavens, how banal it sounds! How—how different from the way I feel! There aren't words—I don't see how to make you understand, without being a cad. But I must tell you that I didn't love her, even at first. It was a wish— a foolish, mistaken wish, I see now—and I saw long ago, the moment it was too late—to make up for things. She was unhappy, and—no, I give it up! I can't explain. But it doesn't change things between us— you and me. I'm yours, body and soul. If you can forgive me for—for trying to make you care, when I had no right—if, after knowing the truth, you'll take me as I am, I——"

"Do you mean, you'd break off your engagement?"

Perhaps it was partly the effect of the green shadows, but the girl looked very pale. Except for her eyes and hair, and the red rose that was like a wound over her heart, there was no colour about her.

"Yes, I would. And I believe it would be right to break it," Stephen said, forcefully. "It's abominable to marry some one you don't love, and a crime if you love some one else."

"But you must have cared for her once," said Victoria.

"Oh, cared! I cared in a way, as a man cares for a pretty woman who's had very hard luck. You see—her father made a fight for a title that's in our family, and claimed the right to it. He lost his case, and his money was spent. Then he killed himself, and his daughter was left alone, without a penny and hardly any friends——"

"Poor, poor girl! I don't wonder you were sorry for her—so sorry that you thought your pity was love. You couldn't throw her over now, you know in your heart you couldn't. It would be cruel."

"I thought I couldn't, till I met you," Stephen answered frankly. "Since then, I've thought—no, I haven't exactly thought. I've only felt. That night at Toudja, I knew it would be worse than death to have to keep my word to her. I wouldn't have been sorry if they'd killed me then, after you said—that is, after I had the memory of a moment or two of happiness to take to the next world."

"Ah, that's because I let you see I loved you," Victoria explained softly, and a little shyly. "I told you I wouldn't misunderstand, and I don't. Just for a minute I was hurt—my heart felt sick, because I couldn't bear to think—to think less highly of you. But it was only for a minute. Then I began to understand—so well! And I think you are even better than I thought before—more generous, and chivalrous. You were sorry for *her* in those days of her trouble, and then you were engaged, and you meant to marry her and make her happy. But at Toudja I showed you what was in my heart—even now I'm not ashamed that I did, because I knew you cared for me."

"I worshipped you, only less than I do now," Stephen broke in. "Every day I love you more—and will to the end of my life. You can't send me away. You can't send me to another woman."

"I can, for my sake and yours both, because if I kept you, feeling that I was wronging some one, neither of us could be happy. But I want you to know I understand that you have *me* to be sorry for now, as well as her, and that you're torn between us both, hardly seeing which way honour lies. I'm sure you would have kept true to her, if you hadn't hated to make me unhappy. And instead of needing to forgive you, I will ask you to forgive me, for making things harder."

"You've given me the only real happiness I've ever known since I was a boy," Stephen said.

"If that's true—and it must be, since you say it—neither of us is to be pitied. I shall be happy always because you loved me enough to be made happy by my love. And you must be happy because you've done right, and made me love you more. I don't think there'll be any harm in our not trying to forget, do you?"

"I could as easily forget to breathe."

"So could I. Ever since the first night I met you, you have seemed different to me from any other man I ever knew, except an ideal man who used to live in the back of my mind. Soon, that man and you grew to be one. You wouldn't have me separate you from him, would you?"

"If you mean that you'll separate me from your ideal unless I marry Margot Lorenzi, then divide me from that cold perfection forever. I'm not cold, and I'm far from perfect. But I can't feel it a decent thing for a man to marry one woman, promising to love and cherish her, if his whole being belongs to another. Even you can't——"

"I used to believe it wrong to marry a person one didn't love," Victoria broke in, quickly. "But it's so different when one talks of an imaginary case. This poor girl loves you?"

"I suppose she thinks she does."

"She's poor?"

"Yes."

"And she depends upon you."

"Of course she counts on me. I always expected to keep my word."

"And now you'd break it—for me! Oh, no, I couldn't let you do it. Were you—does she expect to be married soon?"

Stephen's face grew red, as if it had been struck. "Yes," he answered, in a low voice.

"Would you mind—telling me how soon?"

"As soon as she gets back from Canada."

Victoria's bosom rose and fell quickly.

"Oh!—and when——"

"At once. Almost at once."

"She's coming back immediately?"

"Yes. I—I'm afraid she's in England now."

"How dreadful! Poor girl, hoping to see you—to have you meet her, maybe, and—you're here. You're planning to break her heart. It breaks mine to think of it. I *couldn't* have you fail."

"For God's sake don't send me away from you. I can't go. I won't."

"Yes, if I beg you to go. And I do. You must stand by this poor girl, alone in the world except for you. I see from what you tell me, that she needs you and appeals to your chivalry by lacking everything except what comes from you. It can't be wrong to protect her, after giving your promise, even though you mayn't love her in the way you once thought you did: but it *would* be wrong to abandon her now — — "

A rustling in the long path made Stephen turn. Some one was coming. It was Margot Lorenzi.

He could not believe that it was really she, and stared stupidly, thinking the figure he saw an optical illusion.

She had on a grey travelling dress, and a grey hat trimmed with black ribbon, which, Stephen noted idly, was powdered with dust. Her black hair was dusty, too, and her face slightly flushed with heat, nevertheless she was beautiful, with the luscious beauty of those women who make a strong physical appeal to men.

Behind her was an Arab servant, whom she had passed in her eagerness. He looked somewhat troubled, but seeing Stephen he threw up his hands in apology, throwing off all responsibility. Then he turned and went back towards the house.

Margot, too, had seen Stephen. Her eyes flashed from him to the figure of the girl, which she saw in profile. She did not speak, but walked faster; and Victoria, realizing that their talk was to be interrupted by somebody, looked round, expecting Lady MacGregor or Saidee.

"It is Miss Lorenzi," Stephen said, in a low voice. "I don't know how — or why—she has come here. But for your sake—it will be better if you go now, at once, and let me talk to her."

There was another path by which Victoria could reach the house. She might have gone, thinking that Stephen knew best, and that she had no more right than wish to stay, but the tall young woman in grey began to walk very fast, when she saw that the girl with Stephen was going.

"Be kind enough to stop where you are, Miss Ray. I know you must be Miss Ray," Margot called out in a loud, sharp voice. She spoke as if Victoria were an inferior, whom she had a right to command.

Surprised and hurt by the tone, the girl hesitated, looking from the newcomer to Stephen.

At first glance and at a little distance, she had thought the young woman perfectly beautiful, perhaps the most beautiful creature she had ever seen—even more glorious than Saidee. But when Miss Lorenzi came nearer, undisguisedly angry and excited, the best part of her beauty was gone, wiped away, as a face in a picture may be smeared before the paint is dry. Her features were faultless, her hair and eyes magnificent. Her dress was pretty, and exquisitely made, if too elaborate for desert travelling; her figure charming, though some day it would be too stout; yet in spite of all she looked common and cruel. The thought that Stephen Knight had doomed himself to marry this woman made Victoria shiver, as if she had heard him condemned to imprisonment for life.

She had thought before seeing Miss Lorenzi that she understood the situation, and how it had come about. She had said to Stephen, "I understand." Now, it seemed to her that she had boasted in a silly, childish way. She had not understood. She had not begun to understand.

Suddenly the girl felt very old and experienced, and miserably wise in the ways of the world. It was as if in some other incarnation she had known women like this, and their influence over men: how, if they tried, they could beguile chivalrous men into being sorry for them, and doing almost anything which they wished to be done.

A little while ago Victoria had been thinking and speaking of Margot Lorenzi as "poor girl," and urging Stephen to be true to her for his own sake as well as hers. But now, in a moment, everything had changed. A strange flash of soul-lightning had shown her the real Margot, unworthy of Stephen at her best, crushing to his individuality and aspirations at her worst. Victoria did not know what to think, what to do. In place of the sad and lonely girl she had pictured, here stood a woman already selfish and heartless, who might become cruel and terrible. No one had ever looked at Victoria Ray as Miss Lorenzi was looking now, not even Miluda, the Ouled

Naïl, who had stared her out of countenance, curiously and maliciously at the same time.

"I have heard a great deal about Miss Ray in Algiers," Margot went on. "And I think—you will *both* understand why I made this long, tiresome journey to Touggourt."

"There is no reason why Miss Ray should understand," said Stephen quickly. "It can't concern her in the least. On your own account it would have been better if you had waited for me in London. But it's too late to think of that now. I will go with you into the house."

"No," Margot answered. "Not yet. And you're not to put on such a tone with me—as if I'd done something wrong. I haven't! We're engaged, and I have a perfect right to come here, and find out what you've been doing while I was at the other side of the world. You promised to meet me at Liverpool—and instead, you were here—with *her*. You never even sent me word. Yet you're surprised that I came on to Algiers. Of course, when I was *there*, I heard everything—or what I didn't hear, I guessed. You hadn't bothered to hide your tracks. I don't suppose you so much as thought of me—poor me, who went to Canada for your sake really. Yes! I'll tell you why I went now. I was afraid if I didn't go, a man who was in love with me there—he's in love with me now and always will be, for that matter!—would come and kill you. He used to threaten that he'd shoot any one I might marry, if I dared throw him over; and he's the kind who keeps his word. So I didn't want to throw him over. I went myself, and stayed in his mother's house, and argued and pleaded with him, till he'd promised to be good and let me be happy. So you see—the journey was for you—to save you. I didn't want to see him again for myself, though *his* is real love. You're cold as ice. I don't believe you know what love is. But all the same I can't be jilted by you—for another woman. I won't have it, Stephen—after all I've gone through. If you try to break your solemn word to me, I'll sue you. There'll be another case that will drag your name before the public again, and not only yours——"

"Be still, Margot," said Stephen.

She grew deadly pale. "I will not be still," she panted. "I *will* have justice. No one shall take you away from me."

"No one wishes to take me away," Stephen flung at her hotly. "Miss Ray has just refused me. You've spared me the trouble of taking her advice——"

"What was it?" Margot looked suddenly anxious, and at the same time self-assertive.

"That I should go at once to England—and to you."

Victoria took a step forward, then paused, pale and trembling. "Oh, Stephen!" she cried. "I take back that advice. I—I've changed my mind. You can't—you can't do it. You would be so miserable that she'd be wretched, too. I see now, it's not right to urge people to do things, especially when—one only *thinks* one understands. She doesn't love you really. I feel almost sure she cares more for some one else, if—if it were not for things you have, which she wants. If you're rich, as I suppose you must be, don't make this sacrifice, which would crush your soul, but give her half of all you have in the world, so that she can be happy in her own way, and set you free gladly."

As Victoria said these things, she remembered M'Barka, and the prophecy of the sand; a sudden decision to be made in an instant, which would change her whole life.

"I'll gladly give Miss Lorenzi more than half my money," said Stephen. "I should be happy to think she had it. But even if you begged me to marry her, Victoria, I would not now. It's gone beyond that. Her ways and mine must be separate forever."

Margot's face grew eager, and her eyes flamed.

"What I want and insist on," she said, "is that I must have my rights. After all I've hoped for and expected, I *won't* be thrown over, and go back to the old, dull life of turning and twisting every shilling. If you'll settle thirty thousand pounds on me, you are free, so far as I care. I wouldn't marry a man who hated me, when there's one who adores me as if I were a saint—and I like him better than ever I did you—a lot better. I realize that more than I did before."

The suggestion of Margot Lorenzi as a saint might have made a looker-on smile, but Victoria and Stephen passed it by, scarcely hearing.

"If I give you thirty thousand pounds, it will leave me a poor man," he said.

"Oh, *do* give her the money and be a poor man," Victoria implored. "I shall be so happy if we are poor—a thousand times happier than she could be with millions."

Stephen caught the hand that half unconsciously the girl held out to him, and pressed it hard. "If you will go back to your hotel now," he said to Margot, in a quiet voice, "I will call on you there almost at once, and we can settle our business affairs. I promise that you shall be satisfied."

Margot looked at them both for a few seconds, without speaking. "I'll go, and send a telegram to Montreal which will make somebody there happier than any other man in Canada," she answered. "And I'll expect you in an hour."

When she had gone, they forgot her.

"Do you really mean, when you say we—*we* shall be happy poor, that you'll marry me in spite of all?" Stephen asked.

"Oh, yes, if you want me still," Victoria said.

"Does a man want Heaven!" He took her in his arms and held her close, closer than he had held her the night at Toudja, when he had thought that death might soon part them. "You've brought me up out of the depths."

"Not I," the girl said. "Your star."

"Your star. You gave me half yours."

"Now I give it to you all," she told him. "And all myself, too. Oh, isn't it wonderful to be so happy—in the light of our star—and to know that the others we love will be happy, too—my Saidee, and your Mr. Caird——"

"Yes," Stephen answered. "But just at this moment I can't think much about any one except ourselves, not even your sister and my best friend. You fill the universe for me."

"It's filled with love—and it *is* love," said Victoria. "The music is sweeter for us, though, because we know it's sweet for others. I *couldn't* let her spoil your life, Stephen."

"My life!" he echoed. "I didn't know what life was or might be till this moment. Now I know."